Copyright © 2023 by H F Cunningham

All rights reserved. No part of this book may be reproduced or used in any manner without written permission of the copyright owner except for the for the use of quotations in a book review. For more information, address:
holly.f.cunningham@gmail.com

FIRST EDITION
www.hfcunningham.com

Content Warning: Violence, gore, strong language and implied sex

Disclaimer: a section of this book alludes to chest binding. This can cause injury if done incorrectly. Please research thoroughly before attempting.

Cover Design and Map Design by Jessica Cameron www.jcamerondesign.com
Editing by EB Editorial Services

The Remnants of Blood Series

Remnants of Blood

Remnants of Power

REMNANTS
OF
POWER

H.F. Cunningham

Thank you to all the readers that encouraged me
to keep going.

THE FIVE KINGDOMS
STONESTEAD
CASCAIRN
TARK
WOODREN
RILL
ARMODAN
SHEY RIVER
DUNOAK
THE BROCHLANDS
TAYFORT
FALCON'S REST
GORMBRAE
RAVENSMORE
N
W
E
S

Chapter One

A Shite Way to Die

"What a shite way to die," Tannin muttered to herself.

After days of sprinkling muggy rain, the sun was finally shining and making the canvas ceiling of her tent glow. It was also making it hot. Too damn hot. Tannin kicked off her blankets sluggishly and then regretted it immediately as a wave of feverish shivers shot down her spine. She groaned as fresh pain radiated from the stab wound in her shoulder. She knew it was infected. That much was obvious. It had started getting bad a few days after she had been so rudely ejected from the city to begin her banishment, and it had gotten steadily worse until she'd torn the whole damn thing open again – but that was hardly her fault. The wound was swollen and angry and leaked foul excretions that had made her companions distinctly queasy when they'd unwrapped the bandages.

Dana had cut up one of Adair's tunics to bind it again, but it hardly mattered at this point. Tannin knew she was dying. She tried to spit out the bitterwart leaf she'd been chewing to numb the pain but only succeeded in dribbling the green mush down her chin. Her good hand scrabbled for another one. She'd already taken more than the healer had recommended. It was fogging her mind and making everything slow and sparkly, but she didn't care.

If I'm dying anyway, I'm sure as hell not doing it sober.

Sommer would be ecstatic at the news she had managed to kill her after all.

Tannin's questing fingers found the parchment twist containing the leaves and accidentally flicked it further away. She cursed blearily and listened to the muted sounds of Dana and Adair arguing. Her wargish rescuers-turned-travelling-companions argued often, but one thing they agreed on was that they'd camped in this clearing for too long already. With Armodian scouts, the Gormbraen army menacing the Brochlands' countryside, not to mention glory hunters scouring the forests looking to mount the Beast of Armodan's head on their walls, they never stayed in one place more than two nights even though Tannin was in no state to travel.

Their slow pace had brought even more bad luck recently. The last people in the world Tannin ever wanted to see again had caught up to them.

Adair had informed her of an unusual pair following their trail since very early on. Tannin had known instantly who it was. She had been caught between anger and longing at the thought of seeing her ex-best friend, Flint, and ex...whatever-Ava-was, but their reunion had quickly turned sour.

6 hours earlier

"What the hell are you doin' here?"

"Tannin!" Ava's face lit up in a smile, and her whole body seemed to sag with relief. "I am so glad we found you!"

Tannin snorted. "You didn't find me. Adair's been trackin' you for days. I'm only here to tell you to go the fuck home."

"What?" Ava's smile dropped.

Tannin narrowed her eyes at Flint. "You can piss off too. What are you two doin' out here?"

"We came to find you. They told me you'd been hurt." Ava looked utterly crestfallen, and for a moment, Tannin was tempted to feel sorry for her, but the hollow rawness in her heart hadn't healed. She hadn't remotely forgotten nor forgiven the fact that Ava had abandoned her in the city gaol to await her execution. The princess had made her priorities painfully clear.

"Aye, just a wee bit," Tannin said sarcastically. She gestured to the walking staff she was using to prop up her aching body and the arm that was still held securely in a sling. "Just a mild stabbing and semi-dismemberment."

"Are you alright?" Flint tried to steady her when her movements made her wobble. She snarled at him, making him recoil.

"You've changed your tune. What happened to me bein' a horrible monster, huh? Thought I was dead to you?"

"I didn't mean it like that! I—"

"Aye, you did. Let me guess, you heard what happened and realised there's worse monsters than me?" Tannin said flatly. It was true. She had gone from the fearsome Beast of Armodan to being pathetically skewered by her cousin in front of half the city. There were definitely worse monsters than her out there.

"Both of you, go home. Neither of you are my friends, and you're only here because of your guilty fuckin' conscience. Well, guess what? That's not my problem. Go home."

"Go home?!" Ava's voice pitched a little higher. "Tannin, I gave up everything to come find you!"

"No one asked you to," Tannin retorted. "This fixes nothing."

"I am trying to help you!" Ava cried, gesturing wildly back in the direction they had come from. Back towards Armodan. "To mitigate some of the mess you made!"

"The mess I made?!" Tannin's jaw dropped in outrage. "Don't you dare put this all on me!"

"Why not? Look at us now!" The princess was on the edge of hysteria. "Grow up, Tannin, and take some responsibility."

"Watch your mouth," Tannin warned.

Rage fizzed in her belly. She was going to do something stupid, she knew it, but pain and anger were drowning out common sense. And if ever there was a face in need of punching, it was Ava's.

"You were in that cell because you killed that man – Clach or whatever his name was. You did that! No one else! That rampage you went on? Again, all you. You killed so many people, Tannin! At some point, you have to own up to the fact that a lot of this is *your fault*. Not to mention—!"

That's it.

Tannin launched herself at Ava, claws extending from her fingertips, and muscles bunching up under her skin. Her injured joint was wrenched apart under the strain, and she choked out a scream. Skin and stitches tore, and she collapsed to the ground with a yell as blood blossomed through her bandages and soaked her tunic. Her muscles rippled and contracted and grew and shrank as she fought with her own panic to control her warg side. Voices swam around her, scared and angry, while she panted and pressed her face to the dirt. Hands tore at her bandages and she glanced at the wound. It pulsed and oozed and flesh wriggled and...and then...darkness.

When surfaced back into consciousness, Tannin found herself back to her now familiar tent. She wasn't sure if she really would have beaten Ava to a pulp or not, but she hadn't had the opportunity to find out.

"Hey." Flint had heard her lamenting groans, and he ducked inside from where he'd been sitting at the opening. "How you feeling?"

His usually cheerful face was pinched with worry, and as he leaned over her, his blonde hair fanned out around his head like a halo.

Tannin closed her eyes and turned her face away. "Leave me alone, Flint."

The tent flap rustled again.

"Gods, you look ghastly." Ava knelt beside her and placed the back of her hand on Tannin's sweat-beaded forehead and then froze as she noticed the chewed-up leaves crusting her chin.

"What are these?" she demanded, picking up the discarded package of bitterwart leaves. "Tannin, how many of these did you take?!"

"Go away," Tannin grunted through gritted teeth.

"How *many*?"

"Leave me alone."

"This is not the time," Ava said sternly, pulling back the rest of the blankets that had been piled on top of Tannin. "You can be dramatic later, but right now, this is serious. These are bitterwart. How many did you take?"

Tannin glared at her through bleary eyes. "Dunno. Not you." She muttered again. "Or you." She glared at Flint too.

"Listen to me," Ava said firmly, "you will die if I don't clear up this infection. And now thanks to your stupidity, I can't sedate you while I do it."

"Why do you care," Tannin mumbled. "Left me to die... before."

Ava visibly flinched. "I'm making it up to you by being here, aren't I?"

"Not even a wee bit."

A muscle twitched in Ava's jaw. "I'm healing you whether you like it or not. That's the end of it." She pulled aside Tannin's sweat-soaked shirt and cut through the makeshift bandages. Ava examined the mess underneath with increasing dismay.

"Don't...fuckin' touch me." Tannin's eyes rolled back with the effort of talking.

"Don't be a baby." She turned and said something to Flint in a voice low enough that Tannin couldn't make out the words as she once again tried and failed to wriggle away from Ava's touch.

"How... bad is it?" Tannin gasped.

Ava bit her lip. "It was already infected, but now..."

"Oh, for fuck's sake just spit it out!"

The look on Ava's face was enough of an answer.

"We'll clean up this mess first and then do a purge," Ava stated, mostly to herself.

She then whispered something to Flint that to Tannin sounded warped and distorted, but he looked at her in alarm. Particles of dust floated behind his head like tiny diamonds.

"It needs to be done," Ava said firmly. "Tell Dana as well and then help me bring her outside. I need all the light I can get."

Together, Flint and Ava hauled the blanket Tannin was laying on out into the daylight while she groaned her complaints. Tannin squinted in the bright light. Ava was speaking to Dana somewhere off to the side. They both sounded stressed. Whatever Ava wanted to do, she had to get Dana's approval first. There was no question who was in charge.

It was bizarre seeing them together. Ava somehow still managed to be straight-backed and demanding, even though, as a wargish warrior, Dana could have squashed her like a bug if she'd wanted to. She stood half a head taller than the princess and was considerably broader in the shoulders. When she looked over at Tannin sprawled on her blanket, her sharp features were indecipherable, but she nodded once.

Seemingly decided, Ava knelt by Tannin's side again and sponged at her wound with a warm cloth.

"Stop...hurts," Tannin ground out. The last leaf she'd chewed had well and truly kicked in, and her tongue didn't want to form words properly.

Ava ignored her and continued cleaning the area, stony-faced and determined.

"Okay, Flint," she said sitting up. "It's time."

Flint swallowed hard and nodded. He looked like he was going to be sick as he disappeared from Tannin's view.

He returned a moment later holding a sharp knife at arm's length. Its blade was red-hot and glowing. Tannin's eyes went wide.

"No," she whimpered.

Ava shushed her.

"There's no other way. I have to cut away the infected flesh, and a sedative will react with the bitterwart. I'm sorry, Tannin, but you're going to feel every second of it, so bite down on this." Ava held a stick with a scrap of cloth wound around it up to Tannin's mouth.

"Nuh-uh." She tried to turn away.

"Trust me, you will want something to bite down on," she said, jamming it between Tannin's teeth. "Don't spit that out and try not to move. Flint, can you help me hold her?"

Flint handed Ava the knife, then carefully straddled Tannin's legs and took hold of her hands. Tannin whined as his weight pressed down on the wound to her thigh. It wasn't nearly as gruesome an injury as her shoulder but having Flint's weight on it hurt like hell. Ignoring Tannin's muffled noises of protest, Ava lifted the red-hot blade to her skin.

"I'll try and make this quick," she whispered.

"'uck 'oo, Awa," was all that Tannin managed in response as she squeezed her eyes shut.

Pain seared through the fog of the bitterwart as cleanly as the glowing knife cut into her, and she was jolted horribly into a heightened state of awareness. Sweat glistened on Ava's forehead as it scrunched up in concentration, and Tannin's ears rang with the sound of her own pained howls. Flint struggled to keep her still and winced as she squeezed the life out of his hands. The stench of burning flesh made her gag.

"Can't you keep her quieter?" Dana hissed as she brought another knife fresh from the fire. "Half the forest will hear her."

Tannin's throat was already so raw from screaming that she thought she couldn't anymore. She quickly found out that wasn't the case as Ava dug into her flesh with a freshly heated blade. Dana cursed and disappeared from view.

"Deep breaths," Ava said smoothing Tannin's hair back after setting her tools aside. "That's that part over with...lie back...shhh...that's it. This will sting a little." Something glittered in her hand, but Tannin was too slow to react before she tipped the little vial of clear liquid into the gaping gash on her shoulder.

It didn't just sting. It scorched. Tannin screeched through the cloth and wood, feeling it splinter between her teeth, but it was over in a second and she blinked her watery eyes.

As soon as she was done, Ava tugged the stick from Tannin's mouth so that she didn't choke as she coughed out sobs.

"What the fuck," Tannin gasped finally, "was that?"

"Belacine. It's to clear out the infection and stop it returning," Ava stated grimly. "It's rare and expensive, so do not do anything stupid again because that was all I had."

She sighed and rubbed her eyes with the back of her wrist.

"You still need stitches, so keep lying still."

The needle tugged and pulled as Ava threaded Tannin's skin back together, but by comparison, she barely even registered the sting of it and was half dozing by the time Ava finished tying a fresh bandage in place.

"Now to get the bitterwart poison out of you. Gods, you do not make this easy, do you?"

"Poison?" Tannin muttered drowsily.

"Yes. Poison. You utter, utter fool. These leaves take your pain, but at a very steep cost. Where did you even get this?"

Ava took another vial from her kit. Tannin flinched.

"Oh, calm down. This one won't hurt," she said uncorking it. "But it won't be pleasant."

"Can't I rest?" Tannin was beyond exhausted.

"No," Ava said sternly. "You need that out of body sooner rather than later. Who knows what damage it's already done."

"The healer gave me them."

"Did they indeed?" Ava supported the back of her head and lifted the vial to her lips.

"What's this gonna do?" Tannin narrowed her eyes at the little glass bottle.

"It's going to help the poison...exit."

"Oh joy."

Tannin vomited more than she thought possible over the next few hours, not to mention the other ways the poison had left her body.

She was shivering, soaked in sweat and lying in puddles of putrid mess without the strength to move away.

"I think... it's over," Tannin said weakly.

Ava had stayed close but politely kept her back turned. Humiliation washed over her in waves as Tannin thought about how the princess had probably heard every moment of her misery.

"Alright, now you need rest and – oh gods." Ava had turned around and was staring at her in dismay. Her nose wrinkled. "And a bath. Immediately. Oh gods."

"My banishment specifically included stayin' away from you. You're gonna get me killed," Tannin said for what felt like the thousandth time.

She was already mortified that Ava had not only seen her post-purge but also had to help clean her up too. Well, as clean as she could get from being doused in copious buckets of cold river water and mercilessly scrubbed with a hard bar of soap that had been in her banishment care package from Armodan. She was still shivering even though she was lying next to the fire, bundled up with blankets. She had never wanted a cup of tea more in her life.

"I just saved your life."

"I didn't ask you to. Go home, princess."

Funnily enough, Tannin's desire to claw holes in Ava was what led to her being allowed to stay with them. No one had been particularly happy about it apart from Flint. He'd somehow taken a shine to the princess, even after everything that had happened. The point became moot when no one else had a clue how to sew up Tannin's wound except for Ava, and no one else even wanted to so much as look at the gruesome mess of ripped up flesh. However, her presence hadn't been accepted without conditions.

While Tannin had been unconscious, Dana and Adair had presented the other two with their terms.

"An oath of service?" Tannin exclaimed. "Are you insane?"

"Your companions should have no problem swearing an oath to you, and as a future ruler, you should start already with ensuring fealties," Dana said with a shrug.

She said it nonchalantly, but the way she looked at the two new additions to their party was distinctly hawk-like. She had wanted to move on immediately after Tannin had made so much noise, but Ava had argued that she wasn't up to it. Dana had then disappeared for several hours and come back bloody, citing she had found a solution to them being overheard. Adair was still absent.

"Oh gods," Tannin groaned. "There is so much wrong with what you just said, but I'm too tired right now. Remind me tomorrow that I wanna argue about this."

"They've both already taken the oath," Dana said dismissively. She didn't even look up from her task of re-braiding her long, black hair.

"What does that even mean?"

"It means I'm trying to earn your forgiveness," Ava said.

"Ha. Fat chance of that happenin'," Tannin snorted. "Although havin' an indentured princess does kinda amuse me."

"I'm not some sort of thrall," Ava snapped. "All it means is that I will continue to act as healer for you and provide counsel if you are to continue down this path of leadership."

"I think I'd rather you fucked off."

"Well, tough. It's decided." Ava sniffed. "Especially since someone gave you bitterwart. They expected you to die, and you would have if not for me. The cost of it taking away the pain is that it stops you healing. If someone is beyond saving, and all you can do is ease their passing, then you give them bitterwart. You might know them as mercy leaves."

Tannin groaned. She'd been chewing on mercy leaves?!

Gods be fuckin' damned. No wonder I feel like shit.

Ava grimaced. "That's also why there are scouts trailing you. I suspected something like this when I heard them talking at the castle. They're not out here to hunt you down, Tannin. They're out here to recover your body."

Dana cleared her throat lightly and muttered, "Not anymore."

Tannin's exhausted mind was too tired to muster up any fear at the thought of how close she'd come, yet again, to being murdered. She let out a low, bitter chuckle.

"So much for being able to leave Armodan freely," she said and gave Ava a dark look. "Your father is a fuckin' bastard."

"He probably felt he had no choice—" Ava started but Tannin cut her off with a growl.

She let her head loll onto her good shoulder and stared into the flames of the campfire even though it made her eyes itch.

"Like father like daughter."

Chapter Two

A Sluggish Start

Tannin

Tannin made a disgusted noise as she picked a fat, oozing slug off her shoe. She was so over camping and the creepy crawlies that seemed to appear out of nowhere and get into everything. The first few times they had moved on, Tannin had to be carried on a jostling, makeshift stretcher made from their tent canvases, but the dangers of staying put too long outweighed the risk of travelling. By now, she could walk and they'd made a little more headway, although the warg siblings lamented their slow pace.

Tannin rubbed her eyes. She'd slept like shit again and could feel a bad mood hovering over her like a storm cloud. Inside the tent behind her, Ava snored in her sleep. She'd snored most of the morning, even when Tannin kicked her.

As begrudgingly as she admitted it, Ava had done a good job with her injuries, and she could more or less function. If Ava hadn't found her, Tannin knew she would have died. Ava was reining in her smugness, but it was still there. Tannin hated it. Hated her. Hated that she could just waltz back into her life and try and smooth over what she'd done with a few clever tricks. Well, Tannin wasn't going to forgive that easily, and she damn well wasn't going to let Ava forget it either.

There were...complicated feelings where Ava was concerned that she'd rather not deal with, and it was only made worse by the fact they had to sleep next to each other. The tents they slept in were nothing fancy. Just a sheet of water-proofed canvas, wooden pegs and thin cords that somehow held it all together. She'd tried every negotiating tactic she knew to try and get out of sharing a tent with the princess, but with Adair and Flint sharing one and Dana solidly refusing to give up hers, there was little choice. Ava knew that Tannin needed her, and it made her insufferable. Worse than that – she kept trying to talk. Like really talk. About what happened in Armodan. Tannin did not want to talk about it, and she refused to accept Ava's apologies.

Maybe if they did talk it out, it would be better than this horrible stalemate they were in, but Tannin was bitter about the whole thing, and Ava lording it over her while she was at her weakest wasn't doing anything to improve her attitude.

"What're you scowling at?" Flint asked as he emerged, tousle-haired, from his tent. His long limbs unfolded as he yawned and stretched out his cramped muscles. It must be a tight fit in the boys' tent, Tannin thought. Flint was long and lanky, and Adair was even taller, and quite frankly, built like a house.

"Nothin'. Everythin'."

"The usual then."

"How come you managed to just up and leave Armodan so easily?" The question had been bothering her. She remembered how she had once planned to run away to escape the debts her grandfather had left her with after he died, but she'd have thought Flint was more firmly entrenched in Skirter life to cut his losses so quickly.

"Oh, you know," he said, idly flipping a stick in his hands. "I live my life on the edge. The Armodan scene was getting stale, and you know what they say – fluidity is the way to profit."

Tannin gave him a blank look until he sighed and came to sit with her.

"Look, after your fight with the other warg, your name was out there and it's no secret that we're friends. I had a couple of close calls, and a brick got thrown through my window with a note to give you up or else. It was a relief when Ava showed up and said you'd gone. It was the only reason I'd stayed so long. I wasn't gonna leave when I had no idea what had happened to you."

"Eve?" Tannin asked immediately. If people knew she and Flint were friends, then it wasn't a huge leap to think they would know where she worked. Eve, technically her manager at the bakery but much more a friend, would be squarely in the firing line.

"She's fine. Her, Graeme and the bairn got out of the city ages ago. His parents have a place in the countryside but, Tan...Fletcher's was burnt to the ground.

Tannin frowned. Fletcher's bakery was a Skirts institution. It couldn't be gone. It just couldn't.

Tannin was about to reply when she was interrupted by a shriek from inside her tent. Ava came barrelling out, wild-eyed and holding a slug at arm's length.

"Did you put a slug on me while I was sleeping?!" she demanded, brandishing the slug at Tannin.

"No," Tannin replied innocently.

Ava glared and scoured her face for any trace of a lie. When she didn't find one, she threw the poor slug aside and stomped off in the direction of the river to wash the slime from her clothes.

Tannin chuckled and poked at the fire she was trying to get going. Flint leaned forward, chin on his hand, and gave her a hard look. She glanced at him slyly out of the corner of her eye.

"Tannin," he said sternly.

"Yes?" She gave him her most angelic face.

"How many slugs?"

She grinned evilly just as another shriek came from the river.

"TANNIN!"

She doubled over cackling as Ava stormed back.

"They were squashed in my hair!" Ava yelled, throwing half a slug at Tannin's face.

That made Tannin laugh more, and Ava just stalked off muttering, "You're disgusting."

Tannin was still chuckling a few minutes later. Flint shook his head.

"Oh, come on, that was funny."

"Slugs? Really?"

"I'm workin' with limited materials here."

"She's trying her best."

"She left me in a dungeon."

Flint winced.

"Uh-huh. So don't you be givin' her any damn sympathy. She doesn't deserve it."

"But does she deserve slugs on her face?"

"Absolutely."

"Well, we still have to live together for now, and she's the one patching you up. For the sake of the peace, go apologise." He brandished the stick at her, and she made a face but resignedly ducked back under the canvas. Like hell was she going to apologise, but he'd have a go at her if she didn't at least make a show of it.

"Hey, princess."

"Go away," Ava sniffed.

Tannin blanched. Ava was crying.

"Whatever you're going to say, save it, Tannin. I know exactly what you're doing. If you think I'm going to break and go home due to a little hardship, then you are sorely mistaken."

"I didn't—"

"You'll have to do better than pathetic practical jokes if you want rid of me." Ava set her jaw defiantly, even if her brilliantly blue eyes were still moist.

"I can definitely do better."

"How much longer are you going to continue to torture me?"

"Oh, I don't know." Tannin tapped her chin thoughtfully. "If you take the number of days you left me in that cell, multiplied by the number of times you lied to me, plus how much I hate your stupid face...hmmm, *forever.*"

"I'll remember that the next time I'm saving your life."

"I don't need you to save me," Tannin retorted.

"Because you have your warg friends now? Who didn't even realise you were dying? How well do you even know them?"

"Better than I apparently ever knew you."

Ava opened her mouth angrily to respond and then closed it again, folding her arms across her chest. "Are you done? Care to leave me alone now?"

Tannin flipped her off and stormed out of the tent.

"Ten out of ten apology," Flint said, giving her a sarcastic thumbs up.

She flipped him off too.

How much do I know about Dana and Adair?

Dammit, Ava had gotten into her head. It had been years since her and Dana had been friends, and Dana had been through rigorous wargish training since then while Tannin was living the small life in the Skirts of Armodan. Although Adair was the elder of the two siblings, Dana was most certainly the one in charge. He had chosen to take the route of scout and ranger, more of a silently following instructions kind of warg, whereas Dana had risen up in the ranks of the Golden to become captain of her own unit. Dana had been a rule follower but always a fierce friend no matter what. How much of her childhood friend was still in there?

Gah! I hate it when she's right.

"Hey Dana!" Tannin limped over to where Dana was sharpening a sword. "I've got questions."

"Hm?" Dana didn't look up, sliding a whetstone over the blade with an expert hand. A hundred tiny scars on her fingers told of varied experience with sharp blades.

"Tell me again what happened in Stonestead. How come Sommer is in charge and why exactly did you save me?"

Dana frowned. "I already told you all of this. After the riots the night you left, people were disillusioned with the council, and there was a big movement to reinstate a monarchy. Led by Sommer's parents because they had the old blood claim to it. Your aunt and uncle, I suppose. They're technically ruling Stonestead right now while Sommer is out conquering kingdoms. They don't really have her...ambition, let's call it. They're placeholders until she takes the throne."

Dana sighed and put her sword aside. "We saved you because your claim is just as strong as hers. The same reasons she wants you dead. No one else has a hope of challenging her. As long as you're alive, you're a threat to the legitimacy of her rule. With you gone, there is really no alternative to Sommer if they want to reinstate the old-blood monarchy."

"Do you regret savin' me now that you've seen how much of a non-warg I am?"

"I won't lie to you."

"Ouch, that's a yes."

"This is going to be a lot more work than we expected. It's going to set our timeline back quite a bit until you're an actual contender."

"I don't want to take the throne," Tannin said earnestly. "I really don't."

"Your blood claim puts you in danger whether you want to accept it or not," Adair said flatly as he stomped over to retrieve the sword Dana had been sharpening and slid in into the sheath on his hip. "Sommer wants you dead."

"She didn't kill me, though. She could have so easily, but she wanted to know where the vials are."

The vials. The only reason she was alive. Her grandfather had stolen the serum that could turn warg-blood Remnants into full-blooded Fair Folk era wargs the night they had both run from Stonestead. And she didn't have a damn clue what he'd done with them.

Adair and Dana exchanged a loaded look.

"I don't know, by the way, in case you were thinkin' of asking again. I barely remember anythin'." The same serum that had made her the warg she was had been responsible for that. She had been given the third and final dose in a moment of panic instead of at the correct time, and thanks to a subsequent bout of blood poisoning, she had more or less lost her mind. A fact her grandfather had then used to keep her in the dark about who and what she was.

"My grandad didn't *want* me to remember anythin' about any of this."

"That presents its own...unique problems."

"You can't make more wargs, can you?" Ava had wandered over while they were talking. Flint, not wanting to be left out, wasn't far behind.

"Wait, not at all?" Tannin asked. "What about if two wargs..."

She made a lewd hand gesture, which earned her horrified looks in varying degrees.

"No," Dana said stiffly. "As far as we know, full wargs cannot reproduce. None have been able to."

"Huh." Tannin said. "Like not at all?...Huh."

"That's why Sommer needs the vials so badly. We're a dying race."

"We were never supposed to exist in the first place," Tannin pointed out. "And if they start up with the Academy again, loads of warg-blood children will die with the first dose just like before." She shook her head. "Even if I did know where they were, I think I'd leave them hidden. That was horrific what they did. So many dead and for what? So we can resurrect a dead race of monsters?"

"We are not monsters," Adair said firmly. "Wargs are an ancient and noble race."

"Well said. Would you rather Sommer got a hold of them?" Dana scoffed. "We can discuss the finer points of it when we join the others. We can keep the vials safe from her. First things first. We get somewhere safe and defendable and meet up with the rest of our group."

Dana and Adair were not the only turncoats to Sommer's budding reign of terror.

"Can we trust them?"

"You shouldn't trust anyone," Dana said seriously. "But we've made our choice, and we won't abandon you if that's what you're worried about."

"Were you at Tark?" Tannin asked, changing the subject. Tark had been the first city to fall to Sommer and the wargs and announced to the world that they existed.

"Yes." The intense look Dana gave her made her stumble over her words.

"What was...I mean, what was it like? What happened?"

"It was short and bloody, for the most part. They weren't expecting us, and we could take out smaller towns in the night before they even realised what was happening. The longer part came when we took Tark itself. Sommer's plan worked better than we expected it to though, and they were overflowing with refugees by the time we started raiding their supply lines. They couldn't hope to last. They gave in quite easily when we presented terms that meant survival for the majority. We installed some of our best in positions of power, and now, the city and the whole kingdom of Cascairn is mostly functional under wargish rule." Dana smiled at Tannin's confusion. "We didn't massacre everyone like some of the bards are singing about. Dead cities are of no use to us."

There were so many other important things she needed to know, but the next question that spilled out of Tannin's mouth was, "Why are you never naked?"

"What?" Dana asked bemused.

"I mean after you Change into your warg-shape. How come your clothes don't get all ripped? I've seen both of you do it, and Sommer did it too back in Armodan." Tannin asked accusingly. "Whenever I do it..."

She trailed off as Dana and Adair snickered.

"Well. You—" Adair started to explain but his sister interrupted.

"No, let's see if she can work it out," Dana said crossing her arms, clearly amused.

"I have a theory," Ava ventured cautiously.

The wargs seemed content enough to let her join the conversation, and Adair motioned for her to continue. "Let's hear it."

"Well, I...I had a look at one of your tunics," she said quickly to Dana.

"You were in my tent?"

"Well, yes, I had a theory..."

"You," Dana repeated, low and threateningly, "were in my tent."

"I..." Ava faltered, seemingly realising what she had just admitted to and to whom. "I didn't think you would mind. It's a tent, and we're mostly sharing everything...I didn't realise..."

"My tent," Dana growled, "is my tent. My property is my property. Touch my things again and you will regret it, little princess."

Ava paled.

"Forget it, she didn't break anythin'," Tannin interjected before Ava said something stupid and Dana actually did decide to punish her for her snooping. "Do you know what it is or not?"

"Ooh, Tannin's actually stopping a fight. Someone take a note of the day. This should be made a national holiday," crooned Flint, joining in.

"Shut up." Tannin rolled her eyes and looked back at Ava. "Well?"

She took a deep breath. "Wargs shed. Don't they?"

"Clever girl," Dana said, still with a hint of violence in her tone while Adair nodded in what almost looked like approval.

"You mean to tell me your clothes are made of...you?" Tannin crinkled her nose.

"Don't make a face. It's exactly the same as wearing wool," Adair said and then cocked his head. "You haven't even had your first shed, have you? Just a wee baby warg."

Dana grinned.

"It's the most logical solution if you think about it," Ava said happily, clearly very glad she hadn't just made a fool of herself. "Warg fur will assume the form that you do."

"So, if I wore one of your tunics..." Tannin mused.

"Yes. But that's kind of...I guess the best way to describe it would be extremely...intimate. Wargs do not share clothing," Dana said seriously. "And you." She jabbed a finger at Ava. "I haven't forgotten you went through my things."

"I have more questions."

"So do I," Flint said, walking slowly around Adair, eyeing him critically. "You make your own clothes, and this is what you went with?"

Adair's clothing was shapeless and grey.

They all wore some sort of brownish, grey coloured rags to blend into the forest and not stand out amongst the countryside peasantry. The fine travelling clothes Tannin had been gifted by the same healer who had poisoned her were crumpled at the bottom of her pack somewhere. The clothing she now wore had been swiped from various washing lines as they made their way past, same as the others, and Tannin took great joy in the fact that Ava looked terrible in it. Anything that made Ava miserable gave her a kind of sadistic delight.

"It's not about style."

"Clearly," Tannin said, catching Flint's eye with a smirk. "You should ask Ava for style tips. She still wears fancy princess things under her clothes."

"That is none of your business! That is for…support." Ava gaped.

"And lace is an important part of that?"

Ava went scarlet and stuttered something between a denial and an attempt at nonchalance.

"I was thinking about that actually," Flint said tapping his chin.

"You were thinkin' about Ava's underthings?"

Ava gave an indignant squawk.

"Indirectly," Flint assured her. "I was thinking about disguises."

"There's no need for disguises where we're going," Dana interrupted. "As long as we make it there in one piece."

"Where are we goin' again?"

"Dunoak. We have friends there. The rest of my unit is already there awaiting orders."

Flint made a face. "Dunoak is a shitehole."

"It's the perfect place to lay low," Dana countered sternly.

"And speaking of, I want to make good headway, so grab your gear," Adair added and shooed them back to their tents to break camp.

Chapter Three

Candlelit Confessions

Ava

Ava didn't think her feet had ever hurt this much, or that she'd ever been this physically exhausted in her life, but that didn't stop her brain from keeping her awake with cruel, unanswered questions. She was adamant that her father would never have authorised tricking Tannin into taking bitterwart. He could be a strict man, ruthless occasionally, but never one for such underhanded tactics. That left the mysterious healer as the only link to whoever had tried to poison Tannin.

In the daylight hours, Ava had to save her breath, scrambling to keep up as they traipsed across never-ending fields and forests. She was almost a little glad that, due to Tannin's injuries, they had to take very regular breaks and her own lack of fitness was not so evident.

When night fell, however, Tannin indulged her in her fishing for answers on the condition that she would then "shut the hell up" for the rest of the night afterwards. Ava felt a twinge of guilt for grilling her so much, especially as she still looked so pale and haggard. Her patient had been recovering steadily though, and when Ava thought back on how much worse she had looked when her and Flint had first caught up to the wargs, she felt a glow of pride.

"Are you sure there was no one else?" Ava asked exasperatedly.

Again, Tannin recounted everything she could remember from her time in the castle healer, but since she'd spent most of the time either barely hanging onto consciousness or completely asleep, it was precious little.

"The only person I remember ever even touchin' me was that one healer." Tannin screwed up her face in concentration. "I don't even remember her name."

Encouraged by the fact that Tannin was actually talking to her and not just to swear at her, Ava kept pressing.

"What did she look like then?"

"I dunno. A bit older? Grey hair but not like old old. Average height, average kinda face? I don't know, Ava. I had other priorities than the healer. Did I mention I'd been stabbed? And I was chained to the bed? And I thought I was gonna get executed...again?"

Despite the growing bitterness in Tannin's tone and the tautness of her jaw, Ava decided to push a little more.

"Did she give you the bitterwart?"

"Aye. If you want to know more, you should go home and ask her yourself."

"Nice try."

Ava had then spent the next hour muttering to herself. She had a few theories – each as likely as the next. Either her father or someone else high up in Armodan had ordered Tannin's poisoning, the healer worked for the Triquetra and they weren't done trying to eliminate her, or even the healer simply took her own initiative to take out the Beast of Armodan. Thousands in the city would be happy to see the Beast dead.

The healer...Could it be?

Ava chewed her lip. She couldn't help but think of her old nursemaid, Mo. Silver-haired, mild-faced...druid-blood. She would know exactly what bitterwart would do to Tannin. But what motive would she have? Why would she even be working as a healer? If she was still in the castle, why hadn't Ava seen or heard from her in years? Did she not care about her anymore? She had practically raised her. Had that just been a job? An excuse to get close? Ava shook herself.

The Triquetra is still the most likely explanation.

They had sent assassins after Tannin before, and they had almost succeeded. The secret society's whole design was about eliminating powerful Remnants from the shadows. Ava had dedicated the last several years looking into their activities, researching them, trying to recruit Remnants into stopping them.

And it was all for nothing in the end.

Ava shook herself. That kind of thinking was not helpful. Even if she was now living in a forest with no resources and nothing to show for all her work except a grouchy warg patient who hated her, it couldn't have been for nothing. Attilo couldn't have given his life for nothing.

The night drew on, Ava scribbled away in a notebook, her quill scratching on the parchment.

"Argh! Will you stop that?"

"Hm?" Ava looked up in surprise to find Tannin glaring at her.

"That noise!"

"I'm not making noise."

"You are! With your quill!"

"Am I?"

"Aye! And if you don't stop it and let me sleep, I'm gonna find an interesting place to shove it!"

Ava rolled her eyes.

Always so dramatic.

Tannin was bluffing, of course, but Ava didn't want to have to sew her up yet again if she tore her stiches. Reluctantly, she stowed her quill and ink safely back into her pack. It had originally been Attilo's. He had insisted on having "grab bags" hidden strategically around the castle, their abandoned crypt hideout and other places in case anything went wrong – in case the Triquetra realised she was onto them. She never thought she'd have to use one.

Thoughts of her old friend threatened to overwhelm her to the point she was almost glad of the distraction when Tannin's eyes snapped open and she seized Ava's arm.

"Ow, what? I put the quill away!"

"The cat!" Tannin exclaimed.

"The cat?"

"Attilo had a cat!" Tannin dug her fingers into Ava's arm in earnest. "It'll still be in his house. Ava, it'll starve!"

Ava pried herself from Tannin's grip, frowning in annoyance.

Does she really think so little of me? ...Of course, she does.

Ava had tried everything to apologise about what happened in Armodan. About how she had seemingly abandoned Tannin to her death. She knew there was nothing she could say to take back what she had done, what she had said, but she could try. She could keep Tannin alive.

"It would have starved already." She continued over Tannin's anguished gasp, "And do you really think I would let that happen?"

"You knew about the cat?"

"Of course, I did." She clicked her tongue. "He tried to keep it a secret at first, but the abundance of hairs on his kilt gave it away rather quickly."

When she'd inquired about it, Attilo had insisted that it was a temporary thing and he was just feeding it until it moved on. The hairs had continued to season his clothing for months.

"So...the cat is okay?"

"The cat is okay, Tannin. I had it taken to the castle kitchens. It's living the high life, chasing mice and drinking cream from a little silver saucer." Ava sighed. "It was the least I could do...It was my fault."

It's all my fault.

Tannin had rolled onto her back and had her eyes closed. Ava thought she was going to pretend she hadn't heard her, like she quite often did.

"It wasn't your fault." Her voice was quiet but earnest.

"He still died because of me. Because I didn't see what Erlan was planning in time."

Ava pressed her lips together. If she kept talking, she was going to say too much. If she kept thinking about it, she would fall apart. She refused to play that day over in her head again, and instead, rummaged briefly in her pack until she found what she was looking for. It took her a few tries to strike the match properly to light the simple, wax candle.

When Ava straightened again, Tannin was watching her, the flame of the candle reflected in her dark eyes, but she didn't speak. Ava murmured the words she had been saying every night since that day. She held a small leather pouch that she wore around her neck tight in her hands as she watched the candle's flame flicker.

Ava blew out the candle and watched the last wisps of smoke disappear. She tucked the pouch back down the front of her dress when she saw Tannin looking at it curiously. She wasn't ready to share that just yet.

Tannin turned her head to look up at the canvas ceiling and sighed heavily.

"Give me one."

"What?"

"A candle. Give me one."

A please wouldn't go amiss.

Ava slid her rolled-up cloak behind Tannin's head to help her sit up a little and relit her own candle as well as offering one to Tannin. Her fingers shook a little as she took it.

She misses him almost as much as I do.

They watched the tiny flames flicker and dance in silence until Tannin uttered her own prayer. An echo of Ava's own words.

"I'm sorry."

Chapter Four

Sulking

Tannin

Tannin was sulking again.

She was tired, sore, and well and truly pissed off as she wandered around the woodlands, occasionally smacking at shrubbery with her staff. The trees and plants had become scragglier as they had come further and further East, but the terrain was no less wild, and she still struggled to walk more than a mile without needing to stop. She couldn't even carry her pack properly and needed to have it tied on carefully to avoid it pressing on her bad shoulder. The dull, aching throb in her leg as she walked was a constant reminder that she was useless.

Although they moved painfully slowly, both siblings refused to Change into their warg form and let her ride as they had done the first day. No matter how much she asked. Apparently, transformation was not to be used for frivolous activities and only to be called upon in times of great need – like when they needed that first head start to get Tannin as far away from the city as possible. *Sacred this and blessed that.* Tannin had rolled her eyes so much that she thought they might roll out of her head but had to concede to walking nonetheless. It wasn't like she could risk trying to perform a Change herself anyway. She was still barely held together, plus Changing took a lot of energy and they hardly had enough food as it was. Adair and Dana constantly grumbled about their slow progress.

Her mood today, however, was because, again, she'd been left behind while Flint went off into one of the villages to get supplies. The five of them had only a few crowns between them, and Flint was naturally the light-fingered choice to make the trip to rustle up some coin or food. Tannin would have gladly gone too. When they were younger, her and Flint had made a game out of picking pockets, the winner being whoever pinched the most interesting things. Now though, she was a liability. Flint, the

traitor, had sided with Adair and Dana when they said it was too
risky for Tannin to go.

Too risky.

Tannin snorted as she beheaded a stocky wildflower with a
vicious swipe of her staff. They'd let Ava go with Flint into the
village this time. That was what had really pissed her off. She knew
in the back of her mind that they were probably right, and that if
anything did go wrong, she wasn't fit enough to run to safety, but
to let the princess go? There was a ton of risk there! Someone could
recognise her, or the damn eejit could give herself away.

Adair and Dana were treating Tannin like a child, and she
was thoroughly sick of it. She was supposed to be back at their
makeshift campsite right now, listening to all kinds of lore from
back home about how bloody fantastic it was to be a warg. She
didn't feel fantastic. She felt weak and useless, and she couldn't
stomach their company.

Tannin scowled up at the tree she'd chosen to rest against.
Some kind of vine was coiling around the ancient trunk, digging
into the bark and pock-marking the brown with fresh green leaves.
Beautiful in its own way, but a parasite nonetheless, choking the
life out of the old tree. She shoved herself back upright to resume
her stomping. Stomping helped a little. Crushing tiny flowers
beneath her boots gave her a pathetically fleeting feeling of power.

Being so reliant on Ava put Tannin in a perpetually bad
mood, and even Flint's light-hearted joking around couldn't pierce
the black cloud she was under. She smacked an evil looking
mushroom with her staff, and it exploded satisfyingly in a cloud of
yellowish spores.

Tannin thought about the haunted look that had lingered
on the princess' face for a split second when she'd spoken of Attilo
before she regained control, and it slipped behind her façade. Ava
was going to put the blame on herself whatever Tannin said, so she
didn't even try to convince her otherwise. She didn't tell her that
she replayed that day over and over in her head too. If she hadn't
been so rash and charged in. If she hadn't stumbled. If she'd taken
the brunt of the explosion and not him. She was as much to blame,
if not more, than Ava was.

Lost in her thoughts, Tannin had wandered further from the
campsite than she usually dared to go. A soft braying sound drew
her onwards until she found a weather-beaten fence and the small
herd of sheep grazing behind it.

She paused, leaning on a post to watch the sheep chew
languidly on piles of hay strewn around their pen. They seemed to
have been recently bathed and brushed and some wore ribbons or
bells around their necks. She hastily looked around to check she

was alone and then clicked her tongue to try and get them to come close enough that she could pet them.

"You're wastin' your time there." A voice sailed over the pen and Tannin jumped. She looked up to see a young woman straightened up from where she'd been hidden from view behind one of the sheep. "They're only interested in what they can eat."

She had yellow and blue ribbons in her hands and was deftly weaving them around a ring made of twigs. A matching set of ribbons adorned her light brown hair as it curled gently to her waist.

Pretty.

Tannin eyed her warily but stooped to rip up some grass anyway, baa-ing back at the sheep when they crooned at her curiously. She could forget herself for a while here. The sheep seemed to have absolutely no idea that she was a vicious predator — either that or they did, and they didn't care. Looking at their strangely slit-pupiled eyes, Tannin thought it was probably the former. There was absolutely nothing going on behind those eyes as they nibbled at the strands of grass that she held out for them. What a lovely life. To eat grass all day and not give a damn about anything.

"Passin' through or stayin' a while?" The girl had sauntered around to stand next to her.

Tannin knew that people, any people, were dangerous right now. She was supposed to be in hiding. On the run. But she was also so starved for friendly conversation that wasn't tinged with guilt or responsibility that she didn't move away.

Tannin shrugged. "Maybe a day or two."

"We dinnae get new faces here often." The girl looked her up and down in a way that made Tannin's eyebrow quirk up in response.

Oh?

The possibility of more than just friendly conversation gave her butterflies. Gods knew she certainly had a ton of stress to relieve.

"Like what you see?" she quipped.

"Could say that." The girl grinned impishly and Tannin's pulse quickened.

"Why're the sheep all fancy?" she asked, tearing her gaze away from the girl.

"Village festival." The girl leaned with one elbow on the fence. "It's tomorrow night – down the hill there. You should come by."

"Maybe I will."

"Maybe I'll see you there?"

"Maybe you will."

Wooooow, I am so smooth.

Tannin cursed herself in her head.

"I should go."

The girl shook her head in amusement. "Come by tomorrow. I'll make it fun," she said in a low voice as she passed, brushing against Tannin as she did in a way that gave her tingles. "Promise."

Dana and Adair would say no immediately if she asked about the village fair, no doubt about it. But, then again, who were they to give her permission to do anything? They were helping her, yes, but not exactly for free. They expected a hell of a lot in return. To take up the mantle of heir against Sommer. Fight her, eventually. Lead the wargs. Tannin felt truly sick at the thought of it. They said they would take it step by step and let her take her time, but she wasn't that stupid. She could see their end goal for her. And she did not want it. But at the same time, she needed them if she had any hope of surviving. But that didn't mean she had to do everything they said. That didn't mean she couldn't go to one wee festival.

Tannin mulled it over in her head, and by the time she was back at the camp, she was feeling distinctly mutinous.

Chapter Five

Just Borrowing

Strolling around the local market and trawling through small shops and crafting workshops was fascinating. The trip to the village had raised her spirits. She had always been curious about how people lived outside of Armodan. Whenever her family had travelled to their summer residence in Highholde, she would always gaze out of the carriage windows and wish she could disappear into anonymity for a while in one of the quaint little residences. The smell of livestock had always reminded her that it was just a fantasy and that the people there lived hard lives, dependent entirely on the land, and without any of the luxuries she was accustomed to. It was nice to pretend for a while, though.

Ava was so caught up in the hustle and bustle and had almost managed to put her worries out of her mind when she saw Flint slipping something under his shirt. Ava was jolted back to reality.

"Do you have to steal?" she whispered as soon as they left the shop. "These people have so little."

"Ah yes, I'll just pay for things with my massive overflowing coin purse," he countered with a smile. "I'm only taking what we need, don't worry about it."

They spent most of the day gathering supplies under the guise of exploring the village, with Flint doing all of the actual gathering. Well, almost all of it.

Ava had found it in an apothecary attached to the tiniest healery she'd ever seen. The leather-bound book gave off the most druidic aura she had ever felt. Her Senses all but took control. The frayed pages seemed to whisper to her of the magic they contained. The pull was irrefusable, and the book had been stuffed into her bag before she could even formulate all of the reasons not to take it.

As soon as she'd done it, a hand shot out from behind her to clamp around her upper arm, and her heart stuttered in fear. In the city, a thief risked a flogging, or depending on what they stole, losing a hand. In the countryside, though, where no formal guards could be found, who knew what the penalty would be.

Her knees weakened in relief when she looked up to see that it was Flint who had caught her.

"That was the most unsubtle thing I've ever seen. What were you thinking?" he muttered as he all but dragged her from the healer. "Leave the artistry to me, alright?"

"Wait, I'll give it back—"

"And admit you took it and get us both arrested? You'll do no such thing!"

"I don't know what came over me...Flint, let me go put it back. I can't do this to these people."

"It's a book." Flint rolled his eyes. "Honestly, live a little, princess. Sort of confused as to why you stole a book of all things anyway."

"It's one of a kind!" she lamented. "I can tell it's druidic, and I've encountered so few true records and..."

What is there to say? I wanted it and I took it. Oh gods, a few weeks away from home and I become a petty criminal. How pitiful.

On the walk back to their campsite, Ava was burning up with guilt and regret, but when she opened the first page as they arrived back at their campsite, the scent of old book washed away her regrets instantly. Again, the pull of druidic knowledge spoke to her. This book belonged with a druid-blood. With her.

"Where is everybody?"

"Tannin's in there," Ava said to Flint, jutting her chin towards their shared tent. She could always Sense when Tannin was close by. It was one of her particular traits that had come with being a druid-blood Remnant. She had been the same with Attilo and her brother Florian. The three people she'd been closest too. That she'd cared about the most.

"Hey grump," Flint said, poking his head in through the tent flap. "Come on out. Got you a present."

Ava could see Tannin out of the corner of her eye, glowering at the name, as she gracelessly exited the tent. Her fair hair fell over her face. Ava had offered to pin it for her, but Tannin had stoutly refused and all but shoved Ava out of the way. Ava had winced when she worked out why that had made Tannin so angry. The last time Ava had done Tannin's hair had been the last day they had been...together. And, also, the day Tannin had been arrested.

"What did you get?" Tannin asked.

Flint bent over his pack which was almost full to bursting.

"Neeps!" he said triumphantly dumping a few of the lumpy, dirt-covered vegetables onto the ground.

"And?"

"More neeps." Flint winked and tipped a few more out.

"Did you actually get anythin' useful though?"

Ava rolled her eyes at Tannin's petulant tone. She had spoken to Flint while they were in town, and he had promised to try and reason with Tannin. Yes, she had her reasons for being so angry, but it was getting very tiring trying to tiptoe around her.

"I got what I could."

"Meaning no. Dinner is going to be shite since you didn't get any salt...again."

Tannin had taken on the job of camp cook, and Ava had to admit, she wasn't half bad – when they had ingredients, that was.

"Salt is surprisingly hard to steal."

"Buy some then."

"With what money?"

"Sell somethin'."

"What?"

"I don't know. Supplies are your area of expertise."

"And moping about them is yours," Ava said, her irritation getting the better of her. Tannin glared at her.

"We got this today as well." Ava held up the green, leatherbound book.

"A book," Tannin said incredulously. "You got a book. We're bloody half-starving and you want a bedtime story?"

"Tannin." Ava closed her eyes and took a deep breath. "This is a medical book. On healing. I'm not lugging around a heavy book for the fun of it. I'm doing it so I can fix you, you ungrateful—"

"Tread fuckin' carefully, princess," Tannin warned. "I'm in no mood to hear how ungrateful and selfish I am. I'm well aware of that, thank you very much."

"You know something? I—"

"Let's not?" Flint stepped between them, holding his hands up placatingly. "Let's just get the food on and everyone calm down a bit."

Ava perched herself on an old stump and flicked through the first few pages of her new book. The language was old and complicated, but the text was most certainly of druidic origin. She had only managed to read a little when Adair returned alone with a brace of rabbits strung over his shoulder.

"Where's Dana?" Flint asked, pausing in his attempt to juggle the veg in a spirited attempt to lighten the mood.

"Scouting," Adair replied dropping the rabbits next to Tannin where she sat at the fire. "Still remember how to skin these, novice?"

Amusement dripped from his statement, and Ava saw the tension in Tannin's posture as she stabbed viciously at the fledgling fire that had finally accepted a spark.

"Aye," she replied acidly. "But not one-handed."

"Show one of the others how to do it then. They can start pulling their weight." Adair had never been shy about his distaste for the "dead weight" of the group, as he sometimes put it. Ava didn't think that was particularly fair. From the way she saw it, Adair didn't do anything that Dana couldn't do, whereas she and Flint at least brought other skills to the group.

"What was that about?" Flint asked as Adair left to go wash up in the nearby stream.

"Nothin'," Tannin muttered.

"Tan."

She sighed and put down her stick. Ava could see just enough of her face to see a pained expression flash across her features.

"When I was wee, I really liked the rabbits the hunters used to bring in. We kept them alive when we could so that they'd be fresh. I kept wanting to keep them as pets."

Ava had long suspected that where Tannin grew up in the far north was far harsher than she let on. She could tell Tannin wanted to end the story there, but Flint prodded her in the ribs until she continued.

"I got caught tryin' to steal one." Tannin's gaze was set firmly on the fire. "My punishment was kitchen duty, and I had to skin every single rabbit that came in that season. We had communal kitchens so...it was a lot of rabbits."

"How old were you?" Ava couldn't stop herself from asking. Tannin's carefully blank face twisted into a snarl at the pity in her voice.

"Was I talkin' to you?" Tannin snapped and then said in a quieter voice, "Eight maybe? I'm not sure. Anyway, it doesn't matter. I stopped tryin' to keep them as pets. One of you, I don't care who, grab a knife and do what I say."

"I'll do it," Ava offered, and Flint shot her a grateful look and blew a kiss.

Tannin talked Ava through the skinning, and she managed it with only mildly desecrating the carcasses. She had some knife skills from slicing up various roots and plants for her balms and ointments, but this was in no way comparable. By the time the skins were set aside, Ava was feeling distinctly queasy.

Dana returned, longbow slung over her back, as Ava was cutting the rabbit into roastable chunks. The warg also smirked as she walked past. Ava was sure the warg siblings had been laughing about the rabbit story while they had been out hunting. It disturbed her to think that, to them, it was an amusing anecdote. Every time she got the slightest bit comfortable with the wargs, they did something to remind her that she shouldn't be.

"What is that?" Dana asked sharply and Ava looked over to see what she was talking about.

The wargish warrior was standing over the book Ava had left on the tree stump, poking it with the tip of her dagger.

"The village had a healer so I...borrowed it. It has some interesting theories that I was thinking of using on Tannin's wounds."

"You just want to prod and poke at me like I'm some kind of experiment," Tannin said with distaste.

"You do realise this is to help you?"

"It'll get better with time. You don't have to get all occult about it, just give me a tiny bit of bitterwart leaf and it'll be fine." Tannin held out her hand.

On her worst days, when Tannin was really struggling, Ava reluctantly let her take tiny fragments of the confiscated leaves. Powdered and mixed with water, they helped dull the pain. However, Ava rationed them strictly. They were highly addictive and likely the reason that Tannin wasn't healing as a warg should have according to Dana and Adair's mutterings.

"No. It's poisonous."

"I need a wee bit."

"No. You don't." Ava stood firm. It hurt her to see Tannin in pain, but it was a far better option than letting the fool poison herself again for the sake of a little relief.

"Give me my damn leaves, Ava!"

"You already had enough."

"Give it to me!"

"Don't whine."

"I'll find where you've hidden them," Tannin warned.

"They're not hidden. They're in my pocket and you're not getting any more today."

"Give me it!" Tannin lunged for her, but Ava stepped away neatly, just like Attilo had taught her in those days spent learning how to defend herself.

"Come and get it." Ava stuck her chin out in challenge. Provoking her opponent was not something Attilo had encouraged but with Tannin, she couldn't help it.

Plus, as much as she was recovering, Tannin still limped and everything she did was clumsy with her limited movement. She was in no state to fight Ava for the leaves and she knew it. Ava gave a grim smile of satisfaction. Even Tannin wouldn't be foolish enough to —

Oh no.

Ava's eyes widened momentarily as Tannin's tackle took her down.

"Where are they?" Tannin demanded as she sat on top of her, pawing at Ava's pockets. Surprise had let her get the upper hand, but Ava could see pain written across her face as the motion pulled at her wound. Any more strain and the fine threads holding it together would snap.

Ava slapped at her hands. "Get off me! You're not getting them."

"Says you!"

"Okaaaay." An arm looped around Tannin's waist and pulled her off Ava, who gratefully sucked in a lungful of air. Tannin might have been small, but that didn't mean she was weightless. "That's enough of that."

Ava nodded her thanks to Flint as she got back to her feet followed by a meaningful look. He winced but nodded.

"I'll talk to her."

"Talk to me about what?" Tannin demanded, pulling at the restraining arm Flint had kept around her.

"Those leaves are dangerous and you can't be trusted with them. You're only going to hurt yourself. You'll thank me later," Ava said primly, dusting herself off.

Tannin looked like she was about to respond something violently rude when Dana's stern voice interrupted her.

"Tannin. Ava."

Tannin rolled her eyes, but Ava's stomach churned. The memory of the look Dana had given her after she revealed she'd been snooping in her belongings was one Ava was not likely to forget. She firmly believed that if Tannin didn't still need her, Dana would have gutted her on the spot. She wouldn't make the mistake of angering her needlessly again.

The warg clicked her tongue disapprovingly.

"That is no way—"

"No way for a mighty warg to behave, yeah, yeah. Tell it to someone who gives a shit."

Flint quickly stepped between them as Dana's eyes narrowed. Ava pinched the bridge of her nose. Tannin really needed to pay more attention to whom she was speaking

"Can I borrow you for a minute? Fabulous," Flint said taking Tannin by the arm. Ava watched them until they disappeared behind the trees.

Finally. At least there is one person she'll listen to.

Chapter Six

Baaaaa'd Decisions

Tannin

"Can you stop being a prick for ten minutes?" Flint snapped as soon as they were far enough from the camp. The light bubbling of a nearby stream helped mask their voices from even wargish ears.

"Excuse me?"

Tannin was startled. Flint rarely snapped.

"You have been nothing but an arse this whole time. I get that you're hurting and this is a lot, but dammit, we're all trying." He whispered harshly.

"You have no idea what this is like for me."

"Am I not in the same damn forest?"

Tannin stared at him incredulously. "Okay, first off, I am horribly injured and you're not. Second, I'm still wrapping my head around all this warg stuff, and thirdly and most importantly, there is a psycho out there who wants to kill me, and these two eejits want me to go up against her for a throne I don't fuckin' want!"

Tannin's voice cracked a little, "I don't want to do this, Flint. Any of it. I want to go home."

Home.

She was instantly filled with the thought of being curled up in her little room in Mrs O'Baird's lodging house. Which had burned to the ground and Mrs O'Baird's shattered body along with it. Tannin squirmed as guilt stabbed straight through her insides.

"Home's gone." Flint let her thud her head against his chest and wrapped his arms about her as she sniffled. "But you've still got me, right? And your beastie pals. And Ava – I know you don't like her. You don't need to say it, but it's true. She'll do anything for you." He rubbed her back. "So cut it out, alright?"

"I can't sleep," she mumbled into his shirt.

"Nightmares?"

"Mhm."

"Me too, mate." Flint sighed. "It'll be better once we get to Dunoak. I dunno 'bout you, but I tend to sleep better when I'm not sleeping on literal dirt."

It had been strange to hear him upset. Out of all of them, he had seemed to be taking to the nomad life the best. Tannin had suspected it was just because Flint was probably the most easy-going person she'd ever met, but now she wondered if he was just better at hiding things.

Tannin managed a small smile and wiped her eyes. "You mentioned a present for me?"

Flint rolled his eyes, "Come on then."

Tannin stretched as they wandered back into the camp.

"Alright, what have I got." He tossed a small box onto the ground beside the pile of turnips. "Tinderbox...some cheese, apples."

Tannin tapped her foot, miming impatience.

"Aaaaand Tannin's present!" He tossed her a brown package tied with string, which she tried and failed to catch.

"One-armed here, arsehole."

"Oh right, yeah." Flint grinned sheepishly.

She knelt down next to the fallen package and cut open the string with her knife. The earthy, florally scent that poured from within filled her with instant comfort.

"Tea!"

After they had eaten that night, Tannin listened in amusement while Flint peppered the wargs about other monsters that might be lurking in the forest. If she was truly honest, she wanted to know too and had been too afraid to ask.

"Vampires?" Flint asked brandishing a tree branch like a sword.

"No."

"Ghosts?"

"Wraiths would be the most similar, but no, you won't find any here."

"Ohhh, what about dragons?"

Adair sighed heavily. "No."

Tannin had been quiet after her talk with Flint. She had realised she was being horrible, relished in it in fact, but the talking to he had given her had been an unpleasant wake-up call. She felt like a scolded child. She sat by the fire, lost in thought, clutching her precious cup of tea in both hands before turning in early.

Tannin waited until Ava's breathing became slow and even to grab her boots and slide noiselessly out of the tent. She grinned at Flint as he poked his head out of the tent he shared with Adair. The other reason she had been so quiet all evening was so that no one would suspect her planned evening of shenanigans. It had only taken the mere suggestion of a little fun to tempt Flint into joining her. Plus, she felt like she owed him a night of fun.

Tannin shot Flint a look out of the corner of her eye. He seemed back to his old self. grinning like a madman, but then again, the opportunity for mischief always had that effect on him.

Adrenaline buzzed through her veins as they scurried between the trees. There was something thrilling about having to sneak away, even if it was just for a shitty village get-together that was most likely not worth the effort. Adair was away, so they didn't have to worry about waking him. The flap to Dana's tent was closed, and as they crept away from the campsite nothing stirred from within. They were just out of sight of the tents when the snap of a twig had her skidding to a stop and whirling around.

"Oh, for fuck's sake!" she groaned in a whisper.

"What do you think you're doing?" Ava panted. She'd clearly had to sprint to catch up with them, and she clutched her side like she had a stitch.

"Tannin, you know you can't go running off. It's not safe. Sommer could have spies not to mention soldiers and bounty hunters from Armodan. Even the villagers themselves could be dangerous."

"I know, alright? I know, but it'll be fine. Nothin's gonna happen and I need this. I need one night to be normal. I'm losing my mind with all this. Please just let me have one night."

"I can't just let you risk yourself like this. I have to tell Dana and Adair." Ava shook her head ruefully. "It's for your own good."

She turned to walk back the way she came but was jerked to a halt as Tannin caught her wrist.

"You are not gonna bloody clipe on us," Tannin hissed.

"Let go," Ava said firmly. "You're being foolish."

Flint and Tannin exchanged a loaded glance. She frowned. He shrugged.

"What?" Ava demanded, still trying to shake off Tannin's hold on her. "Let go of me."

"Guess you're comin' too then," Tannin said, annoyed. She gave Ava a little tug. "Come on."

"What? No. Tannin, no. I'm not going anywhere. You are coming back to the tent." She dug her heels in, but Tannin's strength far outweighed hers and she was towed along regardless. "I swear I'll scream for Dana."

"Don't you dare. I will make your life hell if you ruin this," Tannin warned her.

"You are a hazard to yourself," Ava grunted, trying to twist away. "As your healer, I—"

"Oh, loosen up, princess." Flint winked at her. "You might actually have fun."

"You shouldn't be encouraging her. You know this is a foolish risk," Ava protested.

"I also know that I don't wanna stay in that camp a moment longer either. Life without a wee bit of risk isn't worth living. If it seems sketchy, we'll leave, alright? Straight away. We'll stay one hour, tops. Promise."

Ava continued to berate them the entire walk to the village and then through a few short streets to what would probably have been called the main square. Tannin wouldn't have called it anything. It was just a slightly larger area between some of the low cottages with a twisty old tree in the middle, decked out in coloured ribbons. A bonfire crackled happily off to one side.

They joined the jumble of village folk in the small crowd that snaked up to where a pyramid of barrels stood waiting to be cracked open. Brass taps were hammered into the barrels by mallet-toting, muscle-bound men that Tannin assumed were the brewers. A cheer ripped through the crowd as foamy beer sloshed out to fill huge tankards. Tannin bounced on the balls of her feet as the babble of voices and first few notes from a fiddle filled the air. A couple of villagers whooped and linked arms, heading for the empty parts of the square to start the dancing. As she watched, Tannin saw a familiar face on the edge of the crowd. The girl she'd met the day before gave her an almost shy wave.

"Get me a drink. I'll be right back." Tannin patted Flint's shoulder as she passed him. He frowned.

"Don't even say it. I said, I'll be right back." Tannin pointed a warning finger at Ava, who had opened her mouth to protest.

She wound her way through the throng to where the girl stood leaning on the side of a house, seemingly waiting for her.

"Hey sheep-girl." Tannin grinned.

"Sheep-girl?"

"Well, you never told me your name."

"Do you need to know my name?" The girl's chin tilted in playful defiance as she stepped closer. Her cheeks were a little flushed.

"I mean, I'd like to."

"You haven't told me anythin' about yourself either," the girl countered.

Tannin laughed. "I'm just not that interestin'."

"I think you're very interestin'."

"Is that so?" Tannin arched an eyebrow.

"That is so." Her voice had become so low it was almost a purr. "And I think I'm right in thinkin' I've caught your interest too."

"Possibly."

"D'you want to go somewhere…quieter?" she murmured.

That's a bad idea.

Tannin bit her lip and was about to decline when the girl slipped her hand in hers and tugged gently. "What's the matter? You shy?"

"No," Tannin replied hoarsely. She let the girl lead her away from the square. Her hand was warm and a little clammy as she guided her away from the bustling square. They could still hear the beat of the drums and the faint tune of the music, but apart from that, the rest of the village was still.

Tannin followed her between two of the cottages and then bumped into the girl when she stopped abruptly and turned to face her.

"Where—?"

The girl cut off her question with a kiss. A gentle kiss that quickly hardened when Tannin reciprocated. The girl slid her hands around her waist. She pressed forward so that Tannin backed into the shadows of the cottage.

Tannin gasped as the girl suddenly pushed her so hard that her back slammed against the stone wall.

"Oof, that's a little rougher than I—Oh." She froze at the touch of cold steel at her throat.

"Right, don't do anythin' stupid and this don't have to go bad." The girl wiped her mouth with the back of her hand and shrugged apologetically. "You're cute, lass, but I need the money."

"You're robbin' me?" Tannin demanded. "Then why the fuck did you kiss me?!"

"Perks of the job." The girl winked. "Coin, now!"

Tannin continued to be momentarily outraged, but then she threw back her head and laughed.

Of all the things that could go wrong, I did not think of this.

"It ain't personal like. We've had a rough year." The girl seemed unnerved by how unbothered Tannin was to have a blade at her throat.

Tannin laughed again. It was a slightly hysterical sound, and the girl responded with increased pressure on the knife.

"I haven't got all night," she snapped. "Where's your coin?"

One night. That's all I bloody wanted and I can't even have that.

Tannin stopped laughing. "I don't have any, wouldn't give you it if I did, you're not as intimidating as you think you are," she said, counting on her fingers. "And you've just ruined my night, so back the fuck off."

"Big talk from the lass at the wrong end of the dagger," the girl retorted, pressing down on the blade hard enough that anyone else's skin would've broken. "You can either gimme what I want, or I'll take it from your dead body."

"HEY!"

Tannin groaned as Flint and Ava skidded into view.

The girl yanked Tannin forward to wrap her arm around her and hold the knife to her throat from behind. Tannin squirmed as the girl's breathing tickled her neck.

"Walk away!" she yelled at Flint and then ducked her head to murmur into Tannin's ear. "Don't move."

"Tan, are you—?"

Flint didn't get to finish asking her if she was okay. Tannin had had enough. She grabbed the arm that held the knife, easily drawing it away from her skin. The girl gasped and tried to rip her arm out of Tannin's hold.

There was a crack and a moment's silence before the girl gave a startled cry. The knife fell with a clatter as the girl staggered against the wall, cradling her broken arm in disbelief.

Fuckshitdammit.

Tannin straightened her tunic and looked around beseechingly to see Ava and Flint still watching her open-mouthed.

"I didn't mean that." Tannin looked desperately between the girl, Ava and Flint, who were looking at her in horror. "I swear I didn't!"

The girl started wailing.

"I didn't!" she said in reply to their shocked faces. "Besides, she started it."

"Let's go. Now," Flint said urgently and then to Tannin in a lower voice, "What is wrong with you?"

"What?"

"You were spoiling for a fight, weren't you?"

"A fight wasn't actually what I was after," Tannin replied blithely.

Flint glanced at the girl, who stared back with eyes like saucers. He gestured with a jut of his chin back towards the village square. "Get lost."

She didn't need to be told twice and scrambled off without a backward glance.

"You didn't need to hurt her," he said quietly not meeting Tannin's eyes.

"She was trying to mug me!"

"Aye, but—Oh no."

Dana's face was nothing short of murderous as she stalked into the alley where they stood.

"What," Dana growled, "do you three think you are doing?"

"Uh..."

Adair appeared from the other end of the alley. "There you are."

"Look, we were just gonna stay a wee bit, then come back," Tannin said in an attempt at reason, but Adair simply growled.

"You are coming back to the camp right now!"

He reached for her and she shook him off angrily.

"Get off, I'm not a child, Adair."

"Do you know how irresponsible it is to go off on your own?! And into the villages, no less."

"I'm sure you're about to tell me," she muttered, turning to walk past him.

"Don't walk away from me!"

"Walking away," she sang over her shoulder.

"This is the worst mission you've ever set us on," he hissed at his sister.

"Why don't you take my place?" Tannin snorted. "Go fight Sommer yourself if I'm so terrible? Then you can be rid of me."

"I would if it would make a difference, but unfortunately, it's a matter of blood, so we're stuck with a you," he snarled. "So, stop being a petulant child!"

"Make me."

Tannin kicked at a loose stone in the road as she strode away from Adair. She had expected him to either storm off or have another loud rant, but he followed her silently. She braced herself for another argument as he stalked around in front of her, making her skid to a stop.

"I told you, I'm not—HEY!"

Adair grabbed her around the middle and unceremoniously slung her over his shoulder.

"PUT ME DOWN!" Tannin screeched in outrage, twisting and trying to kick, but Adair had a firm grip across the back of her legs and her fist thudding on his back didn't seem to bother him in the slightest.

Tannin hated being picked up. One of the worst things about being on the smaller side was that people seemed determined to just scoop her up. Flint had done it once and only once. The swift knee to the groin he'd received was enough to discourage him from ever doing it again.

"Stop squirming or I'll drag you back by your ankles," Adair said simply, readjusting his grip like she weighed nothing.

"You wouldn't."

"Try me."

"UUUUGH!"

With the villagers at the celebrations, the streets they walked through were deserted and silent apart from Tannin cursing every step of the way.

"This is kidnapping," Tannin snarled.

"Stop being dramatic," Dana scolded from somewhere to her left. "It's babysitting."

Tannin squirmed and wriggled until she was thoroughly exhausted and flopped limply with her head in her hands. She hoped her elbows were digging in.

"Hey, Tan. How's it hanging?"

Twisting, she saw Flint failing to hide his laughter behind his hand. "This isn't funny!"

"It's a wee bit funny."

"It is not! You've made your point, Adair. Put me down," she said wearily, trying to shift a little so that his muscular shoulder wasn't pressing into her stomach quite so much.

"So you can run off again? Get yourself killed?"

"I didn't do anythin' wrong!"

"You can't keep avoiding your responsibilities."

"And you can't manhandle me just 'cause I take a wee bit time off!"

"This is war. There is no time off."

"Oh, put me down, you pretentious sack of shit!" She twisted to slap the back of his head, and he responded with an equally hard slap across the back of her thigh.

"OW!"

Adair's long strides meant they were mercifully back in the campsite sooner than she'd expected. He finally lifted her off his shoulder to dump her in the dirt beside their unlit campfire.

"Don't you ever do that again!" she snapped, scrambling to her feet and shoving him hard. "I am not a thing that you can just pick up and carry about!"

"I wouldn't have to if you had a shred of common sense," he retorted.

She tried to push him again, but he side-stepped and then swept her feet out from under her so that she landed back on the ground in a heap.

"You do not have the skills to be out on your own yet. Accept that." He towered over her. "You are a weak and vulnerable target, and that makes you a liability until you are trained. So until you are, stay put. It's hard enough to keep you alive without you actively seeking out trouble."

She swore at him viciously and rubbed her backside where she'd hit the ground as he walked off to his own tent, unbothered. As she brushed dirt off her breeches, she saw Ava out of the corner of her eye, a self-satisfied smile playing around the corners of her mouth.

"If you say 'I told you so', I'm gonna make you eat the slugs this time."

Ava's eyebrow arched. "I wasn't going to say a word."

"Mhm, sure," Tannin said sourly as she marched passed her.

"Where are you going?" Dana asked sharply as Tannin headed in the direction of the trees.

"Oh, do I need your permission to relieve myself now too?"

"Be quick about it."

"I'll take my damn time, thank you very much."

Tannin stomped away from the camp.

As much as she just wanted away from the other wargs, she did actually need to relieve herself too. She made her way into the thick undergrowth to find a private enough space to do her business. She had just settled into a squat when the sound of someone clearing their throat made her head snap up.

Standing just beyond her patch of bushes, back turned and arms crossed, was Ava.

"Ava? What the fuck? I'm...indisposed. Go away!"

"I know, and ideally, I'd have this conversation more civilly, but you won't talk to me. Now you can't run away."

Tannin's mouth flapped open and shut a few times. There were some things in life that should just be off limits.

"You're a terrible person," she said flatly. "Go on then. What's the lecture?"

"It's not a lecture."

"It feels like it's going to be a lecture."

"It's not—" Ava took a deep breath. "You need to be more careful."

"Aha! I knew it."

"No, I mean it. You might not take this seriously, but if anyone finds out who you are and where you are, it could get back to Sommer or they could sell you out to any one of the hundreds of bounty hunters and sellswords that are looking for you. So many people want you dead, Tannin, and you're not taking it seriously."

"We haven't seen any signs of anyone other than country folk, and you said all this already before we went to the village, *so why are you disturbin' me right now*?"

"I'm just saying. We're only safe here because we're anonymous. Don't throw it all away for some..."

"For some what exactly?"

"You know what I mean. I know why you went off with that girl. I'm not oblivious."

"Is that what this is really about? Because I kissed that girl?" Tannin demanded.

"Don't be ridiculous. I—wait what? You kissed her?"

The tinge of hurt in Ava's voice was so satisfying.

"None of your business," Tannin said a little smugly.

"It is when it could bring an army down on my head. You're not the only one worth a price here."

Tannin scoffed. "They'd just take you home and get your weight in gold from your father. Oh, how terrible."

"I'd be in a lot of trouble back home, actually."

"That's mostly your own fault and we can argue about it later. Now will you kindly piss off, so I can finish up in peace?"

"I also wanted to talk about...about us. About what happened."

"Right now?!" Tannin shifted uncomfortably. Her muscles were already burning from holding her squatted position for so long.

Tannin groaned. Ava wasn't going to leave without saying her piece.

"Make it quick."

"I'm sorry."

"That's it?"

"That's all I can say."

"You know I can't forgive you."

"I can't forgive myself," Ava admitted in a small voice. "I don't think I ever will."

The heavy silence that followed was only broken by the shuffling of leaves as Tannin adjusted her position slightly.

"Ava?" Tannin said softly.

"Yes?"

"I still *really* have to go."

Chapter Seven

Civilisation at Last

Ava

"There." Adair pointed to a ridge in the distance. "Dunoak."

"It's still so far," Ava said disheartened, staring at the distant smudge and then quickly clamped her mouth shut. She hadn't meant to speak aloud, but she had been so hoping for the end to be near.

"Nonsense. If we keep the pace up, we'll be there by dusk."

The speed he set was gruelling, and when they finally arrived at the wooden walls of the city, all Ava wanted to do was curl up somewhere warm and sleep. She had never in her life travelled so far from home and on *foot*. Once upon a time, this would have been an unthinkable circumstance to find herself in.

The ground underfoot was trampled and slick. Ava wrinkled her nose as it splattered onto the hem of her dress. Beside her, Tannin cursed as she slipped in the mud. Flint caught her at the last second, almost slipping himself, and they clung to each other as they found their balance on the slippery surface. Ava managed to pick more stable places to plant her boots and managed with only slightly more dignity.

Guards bearing half-rusted spears stood at the gateway into the city and let them pass without comment, although Ava swore she spotted a conspiratorial nod between Dana and one of them. Tannin caught her eye. She'd seen it too.

Well, she did say we had friends here. Guards can be useful.

Ava had heard of Dunoak before, of course, from one of her many tutors but only in passing. It wasn't a useful trade hub, and the entire kingdom of Woodren mostly kept to itself anyway. Her education had been focused more on the valuable resources of Rill and Cascairn and the tumultuous relations with Gormbrae. Flint had filled them in on some Dunoak details on the way.

"It's a shithole," he said and as they passed through the gates, and as she got her first glimpse of the city, she found that she agreed with the sentiment. Even calling it a city was a generous description for the odd assortment of ramshackle dwellings and small shops that sprawled in the mud. The further east they had travelled, the wetter and boggier the ground had become, and it seemed civilisation itself was no exception. They squelched their way through muck-coated streets, skirting around grubby stalls and even grubbier children.

"Told ya," Flint muttered, slapping away a small hand that was trying to creep into his pocket. "Fucking shithole. And I'm saying that as a proud Skirter."

"Charming," Ava said, wrinkling her nose again as they passed a drunk urinating on the side of a building.

Adair and Dana seemed to know their way around and swept through the streets with ease and purpose until they reached a non-descript door in the middle of a blank wall. Adair made directly for it and yanked it open.

Warmth poured from inside along with the scent of pipe smoke, sweat and stale beer. A tavern. Possibly the grimiest establishment Ava had ever been in, but at least it had walls, a roof and a promise to let her rest her feet. She gratefully followed her companions inside.

"Ugh, thank the gods," Tannin groaned as she crumpled onto one of the long benches and let her heavy pack thud onto the sawdust covered floor. Ava followed suit, suppressing a moan of her own as she finally took her weight off her aching legs. A handful of patrons occupied other benches and lopsided round tables, but no one gave the newcomers a second glance. From the outside, they looked like exhausted travellers, and with bandit raids happening more and more frequently on the isolated villages since the threat of war between the Brochlands and Gormbrae, Dunoak probably saw more than its fair share of new faces.

"Here, get yourselves a hot dinner." Dana shook some coins out of her pouch and handed them to Tannin before pointing a warning finger at each of them. "Nothing stronger than ale. No spirits."

"Killjoy," Flint muttered under his breath.

"Where are you two goin'?" Tannin asked as the siblings turned to leave again.

"We've got things to do. Stay here until I come get you."

Ava was not particularly sorry to see the back of the wargs for a little while. Dana especially unnerved her, and she was glad to have a chance to relax in relative comfort.

Flint took charge of ordering for them. Ava shook her head as he gave the barmaid a charming smile. Even tired and travel-worn, he just couldn't help himself it seemed. Tannin had always said he was a shameless flirt, and it appeared that she hadn't exaggerated.

Soon, three overflowing tankards were set on their table followed by three, lumpy, misshapen pies. Flint fell on his immediately, taking a huge bite and dribbling gravy down his chin.

"What kind of meat is this?" Ava asked, peeling back the pastry and poking at the greyish contents suspiciously. She had sampled unusual delicacies from all across the Five Kingdoms, and in rare instances, from across the sea too but nothing ever quite prepared her for what the peasantry were willing to accept as edible.

Tannin and Flint exchanged glances.

"Yes," said Tannin simply as she gave a shrug and bit into her own lukewarm pie.

Ava took a small, cautious bite and immediately made a face. It was slimy and salty and awful.

"Just bloody eat it. It's not *that* bad."

"You're a terrible liar, Tannin. That is disgusting." Ava sniffed, pushing her plate away. "Also, don't talk with your mouth full. You're spraying that muck everywhere."

No amount of coaxing could convince Ava to eat the filling, but after a little wheedling and the fact that she was unbearably hungry, she at least ate the pastry from the top. Flint and Tannin arm-wrestled for the rest of it.

"You're a cheat," Flint grumbled, rubbing his sore shin where Tannin had kicked him under the table.

"You only said I couldn't warg out. No other rules were specified." Tannin grinned at him through a mouthful of her winnings. "Since I'm so generous though, here, you can have a bite...hey, I said a bite!"

"I don't know how you can eat that," Ava said wrinkling her nose.

"Because I'm hungry and it's food."

Peasant.

Ava noticed Flint had stopped chewing and wasn't paying attention to them. Instead, his eye was focused on a wavy-haired young man across the room.

"Is something wrong?" she asked, concernedly. Following his gaze, she saw the youth slip something subtly into his jacket.

"Not especially," Flint replied, not shifting his gaze.

The man's head snapped up and locked gazes with Flint. Panic flashed across the stranger's narrow features for a split second before it was replaced by an easy smile as Flint winked at him.

"So," the young man said as he sidled up to their table and rested an elbow on it. It was far too relaxed a gesture for the tension in his shoulders and the tightness around his mouth. His green eyes scanned each of them shrewdly. "How 'bout a drink for me new very good friend?"

Flint smiled broadly. "I'd say that's the start of a budding friendship. And one for the ladies too."

The young man considered it, his tongue darting out to moisten his lips before spreading his hands wide. "I'm a gentleman. Can never say no to pretty girls, now can I?"

"What's going on?" Ava whispered as their new friend waved down the barmaid.

"We're making friends. Weren't you listening?" Flint drained the last of his ale. "And I'm getting us free drinks, so shut your mouth."

"And watch your wallet," he muttered under his breath as an afterthought.

"To new friends then." The stranger toasted when the drinks arrived. It was the cheapest spirit available, but Tannin clearly wasn't about to complain as she snatched one of the glasses and threw it back. She had missed their whole conversation, too preoccupied with her food, but had perked up at the mention of free drinks.

Ava took her own tiny glass and sipped at it. It burned horrendously like she had tried to swallow hot ash and she spluttered it all over the table.

Oh gods. How is this supposed to be pleasurable?

Ava instinctively cast around for a napkin to wipe her mouth, but of course, there were none. She settled for her sleeve and then suppressed a smile.

Oh, if mother could see me right now.

Her attention flicked back to their new acquaintance.

"My name's Flint. That's Tannin. Ava." Flint held out his hand after polishing off his own spirit, and the youth shook it.

"Eoghan." He nodded to the door where a larger, broader version of himself had just walked in. "And that's me brother, Collum. Maybe you've heard of us?"

"Why? You famous?" Tannin raised an eyebrow.

"The stage calls us." Eoghan winked.

"Oh, so you're bards as well as pickpockets," Flint said slyly and Eoghan's face darkened.

"Musicians. And let's have less of that now, seein' that we're friends and all."

Collum frowned slightly as he saw his brother sitting with strangers, but his features quickly found the same easy smile.

"So," he said as a way of greeting as he squeezed onto the bench, "what we drinking?"

Eoghan and Collum turned out to be welcome company, and for the first time in weeks, the tension started to leak out of Ava's neck and shoulders as they laughed and joked and coaxed Collum into buying another round. Ava quickly discovered that the burning liquid was even worse if she tried to sip it slowly.

The brothers had been in town for a while, initially just planning on staying a few nights before heading further south, but they'd found that Dunoak had surprisingly good pickings for those with clever fingers. Ava twitched every time they so casually mentioned it. All it would take would be someone overhearing, and they would be in trouble too.

We could be discovered. We could be arrested. The wargs could get involved...Someone could get hurt.

"So, what about you three? What's your business here then?" Eoghan asked lightly.

Ava and Flint both looked at Tannin. Hers was the biggest secret to hide after all.

"No fuckin' clue, mate," she said taking a large swig. "Just ended up here."

He laughed and clicked his glass against hers. "Here's to that!"

The door swung open with a thunk and Flint made a face instantly. Ava didn't really have to turn around to guess who it was. She quickly hid her glass under the table and nudged Tannin to do the same, but Adair hardly gave them a second glance and headed straight to the bar. He spoke with the barmaid in hushed tones and passed her a small pouch.

He stopped at their table on his way out.

"You three are staying here tonight," he said without so much has a hello. "The room is paid for as well as breakfast. Do not leave this tavern, understood?"

Without even waiting for an answer, he stomped out.

"He's a charmer," Eoghan muttered, flicking his hair from his eyes.

"You've no idea," Tannin replied, sticking her tongue out at the closing door. "But I guess we're stayin'. Whose round is it?"

As it turned out, none of them had enough coin for another round, and if she was honest, Ava wasn't disappointed to be calling it a night. She didn't think she could choke down any more of that cheap spirit even if it had warmed her to her bones.

The room Adair had secured for them had barely enough space in it to hold a narrow bed and a leaky bucket of water for washing. Tannin collapsed onto the bed immediately and it creaked alarmingly. Ava perched on the end of the bed and peered at the greyish sheets. She really didn't want to think about the last time they had been washed. She rubbed the back of her neck and sighed in defeat. It was one night. She could do one night.

Even as she steeled herself, Ava couldn't help but think longingly of her soft, fluffy pillows in her own bed back home. Scented with rosewater and plumped up by her ladies' maid so that she could sink into dreamless sleep. Looking now at the thin, filthy mattress she was to sleep on, Ava's resolve wavered.

"Oh, I suppose I'm taking the floor then," Flint said with an exaggerated pout. "You cruel, cruel women."

"Here." Tannin flung the only pillow at him. "Compensation."

By this point, the three of them were too tired to talk much, and although the sun was still glinting through the rags that hung over the window, they unanimously decided it was bedtime.

The bed was a tight fit.

"Never thought there would be a day when having a bed to myself would be a luxury," Ava sighed as she tried to get comfortable. "Move your elbow."

"My elbow was there first."

"Move. It."

"Fine."

Tannin rolled over to face the wall, taking her offending elbow with her.

Hours later, sleep was somehow still evading her as Ava stared at the back of Tannin's head. There was a time, not so long ago, when Tannin wanted to share a bed with her. Ava had wanted it too. But that was the past. That time was gone. Sharing a bed now was just an uncomfortable necessity. It didn't matter that as Tannin had drifted off and her muscles relaxed, she had sunk back against Ava. It didn't matter that she was warm and soft and that the curve of her body fit perfectly against Ava's own.

Ava exhaled slowly.

This had better just be for one night.

Chapter Eight

Egg-spect the Un-egg-spected

Tannin

Regaining consciousness the next morning was like trying to wade through mud. Sleep kept pulling her back under even as Tannin managed to crack one eye open. She was unbelievably warm and comfortable, and she was very much about to snuggle back into the soft pillow when it moved under her head.

Oh shit.

She wasn't laying with her head on the pillow at all. She was laying with her head tucked under Ava's chin, and the movement she felt was the slow rise and fall of her breathing. Ava had one arm around her, the other rested on her waist. Their legs were hopelessly entangled.

Shit shit shit.

She couldn't think of a way she could ease away without waking the sleeping princess and having to deal with the embarrassment of their intimacy. She should have let Flint take the bed.

Damn it, why does she have to feel so good?

Ava must have felt her waken because she stirred and her eyelids fluttered.

"Hm?"

Tannin took the opportunity of her bleariness and wriggled out of her embrace and rolled over to face the wall as fast as she could. Her heart rattled in her chest like dice in a cup. Half of her wanted to get as far away as possible and deny that this ever happened. The other half very much still wanted to cuddle.

She stayed in bed for at least another hour. It felt too early to rise, but she couldn't fall back asleep. Beside her, Ava was rigidly still. Tannin could tell she wasn't asleep either. Had she lain awake last night as Tannin cuddled in? Had she held her all night as she slept? Tannin didn't like any of the possible answers to those questions and tried as best she could to put it out of her mind. She had bigger things to worry about than inconvenient feelings.

When they did get up, neither of them said a word and Flint cheerfully filled the silence with a detailed explanation of a bizarre dream he had had and running commentary on his rumbling belly as they headed downstairs.

The tavern looked much worse for wear with daylight trickling in through the tiny windows. The floor hadn't been swept, and beer-soaked hay stuck to their shoes. Adair had paid in advance for their breakfast, so when a dead-eyed, older woman brought it to the table in the now much quieter tavern, she genuinely snarled when it was clear she wasn't going to get a copper for her troubles.

"What a lovely place," Flint muttered, stuffing a spoonful of scrambled eggs into his mouth. "Mmm! Decent breakfast though."

"Might even say it was..." Tannin said slyly, "...egg-cellent."

Ava groaned.

"Egg-ceptional." Flint grinned.

"Oh, not you too!"

"Egg-straordinary," Tannin continued.

"Egg-squisite."

"Really crackin'."

"Will you two stop!" Ava said, exasperated.

They were quiet for a moment until Tannin caught Flint's eye across the table.

"Egg."

Ava glared at her as Flint chortled into his tea.

"Are you quite finished?"

Tannin shrugged and then winced. The bed had somehow been worse for her shoulder than sleeping in the tent had been.

"You need to let me take a look at that," Ava said.

"It's fine." Tannin massaged it gingerly. "Just slept awkwardly."

In your arms.

From Ava's expression, Tannin knew she had had the same thought and cringed.

"What are we doin' here? And I don't mean here as in this tavern," Flint continued, oblivious to the fact that they were having a moment. "I mean in Dunoak."

"Dana said they had friends here. Dunno if that means we're stayin' or not. They don't tell me any more than they tell you."

"Does it bother either of you that we're just blindly following them?" Ava asked.

"Do you have a different plan? No? Then shut up and finish your breakfast."

They were about halfway through their meal when the door burst open and a dazed-looking man stumbled in.

"Wargs!" he declared loudly to no one in particular.

The three of them exchanged alarmed looks.

"Wargs?" Flint prompted, leaning back in his chair in an effort to look relaxed.

"So much for laying low," Tannin muttered.

"They've..." The man blinked hard. "They've taken the city."

"In one night?" Ava said at the same time as Flint said, "Taken the city?" and Tannin said, "What the fuck?"

The man collapsed against the bar, seized an unattended glass and downed the contents. "The laird is dead, some of the nobles too. And half the guards."

"This shithole has nobles?" Flint muttered.

Although it was barely nine in the morning, the few occupants of the tavern chipped in to buy the man another few drinks to loosen his tongue about what had actually happened. He kept repeating "we couldn't do nothing" until he finally choked down the last gulp and gave into their prodding for more information.

"I seen it. I seen it all," he said finally. "I light the lanterns, see? So, I was out last night. I seen them close the gates and thought it weren't none o' my business, but then...but then..."

He shook his head despairingly. "There's nothing we can do. They've been here all along. Hiding in plain sight. Even the whole city can't do anything against a hundred wargs."

They had struck in the dead of night. Silently and strategically, they'd barred the gates, taken the armoury and had the laird and his family executed in the town square all before anyone knew what was happening. The nobles were dragged from their beds either to pledge an oath to Dana or to lose their heads. Most of them chose the oath. The wargs had worked so quickly that no alarm had been raised until sunlight glittered off the blood-splattered main square, and by then, it was too late to do anything.

The man's voice crumbled and broke and he had to be given another drink to continue.

Apparently, some of the guards had tried to take up arms, but the "crazy warg bitch" as the man kept calling her, had slashed them to pieces, and their bodies were hung up on display as a warning.

"The rest o' the guards seemed tae know," the man mumbled into his empty glass. "They didnae help. Just stood by an' watched. Said to go back to our homes, and we'd get information in due time. What does in due time mean, anyway?"

He was starting to slur his words.

As soon as the man had said some of the guards were killed, the bartender had gone white as a sheet and fled the tavern without a backward glance, so Flint hopped behind the empty bar and sloshed out tankards for the few people who remained.

There was some hushed discussion as to whether they should go out and see for themselves, but when the other option was to sit in what seemed like safety with an unattended bar, no one left. The tavern sat in such a tense, sombre silence that when the door banged open, Tannin wasn't the only one who spilled her drink.

"Adair!" she exclaimed, "What the hell is goin' on?"

He glowered around the room before answering.

"Wargs have taken Dunoak," he said flatly. "Come on, you three. We're going."

He turned to stomp out before they had left their seats. Flint hastily gulped down the rest of his ale.

"Where are we going?" Ava pressed as they stumbled out into the street.

Tannin shaded her eyes and squinted. The morning sunlight was unsettling after the smoky gloom of the tavern. From the story the man had spun, she had been expecting dark clouds and the clap of thunder as the background for the apparent massacre and not a pleasantly sunny day.

"The keep," Adair answered gruffly.

"Are there really a hundred wargs here?"

The man had been very much slurring when he'd given the estimate.

Adair huffed. "I wish."

"How many?"

"Ten. Plus about fifty warg-blood Remnants. Give or take. The time for talking is later. Now is time for walking."

They passed what must have been the main square the man had spoken of. The mud under their feet was wet with a steady stream of blood running from a crude platform. Bodies were stacked in a pile. Heads were mounted on pikes.

"Oh gods. What the hell did you do?" Tannin whispered, but Adair hadn't hesitated and was already too far ahead to hear her. Or he was ignoring her, which was also likely.

Flint had turned a sickly green. Ava was deliberately staring somewhere in the distance, glassy-eyed as she walked past the carnage with her fists clenched tightly at her sides.

Tannin caught up with Adair's long strides. "Why?" she demanded. "Why do this?"

"We needed a stronghold." He glanced at her. "Don't make trouble, Tannin. This has been planned for months. Believe it or not, this is the cleanest way. A battle would have cost more lives."

"He's right," Ava said hoarsely. "I've seen this tactic from listening in on my brother's lessons. Cut the head off the snake as it were."

"Aye, metaphorically!" Tannin gestured to the gruesome pikes. "I don't think that was part of the fuckin' instructions."

Adair turned to face her. "And what exactly would you have done?"

"I don't know!"

"Exactly. So hush up. Dana knows what she's doing."

They walked the rest of the way in silence. The residents had seemingly taken the instruction to keep to their homes seriously because the streets were unnaturally quiet.

Before they were even halfway there, they could see the keep. Most of the thatch-roofed buildings surrounding it didn't rise higher than one story, so the taller collection of stone towers and halls stood out a mile away. It even had its own ring of stone walls to protect it.

As they drew nearer, however, the majesty of it faded as the details became clear. Just like everything else in Dunoak, it was in a shabby, sorry state. For all its formidability, the keep hadn't managed to escape the dampness that seemed to hang around Dunoak like an unpleasant cloak. Moss clung to the walls, and Tannin could see that the lower windows were spotted with mould. The path that led into the courtyard of the keep was at least free of mud. They stomped over worn stone as they made their way to an iron portcullis. It shuddered and rose at their arrival. Tannin peered up at the sharp spikes as they passed underneath and quickened her step until she was safely through.

Inside, the courtyard showed signs of the night's violence. Splattered blood had been hastily covered with sawdust, and broken shields had been kicked into the corners.

Wide-eyed faces peered at them from all sides. The keep's servants no doubt, probably wondering if they were about to lose their jobs, their homes or even their heads. Tannin half expected arrows to rain down on them, but clearly, whatever the people here had seen, it was enough to subdue them – for now at least.

As they headed for the largest set of wooden doors, they flew open, thrown wide by a mountain of a man who then strode down the stairs to greet them with unnerving speed.

Well, that's a warg for sure.

"About time!" he boomed.

He was huge. A wall of muscle that dwarfed even Adair by comparison, with a thick, brown beard and tattoos curling across his bald head that had been hidden by his helmet when he'd shared that nod with Dana at the gate. Tannin gave herself a mental pat on the back for picking up on that.

"Hello," Tannin said queasily giving a small wave.

"Tannin, this is Douglas. He's Dana's second."

"I thought you were Dana's second?"

"Only when Doug isn't around."

"Well, well, I haven't seen you since you were a bairn." He cocked his head. "Ye look like yer Ma."

"My grandad used to say that," Tannin replied reflexively.

"Strange fellow that one. Can't say I'm sorry he's not around." He cleared his throat. "Dana tells me you've been in Armodan this whole time. Doing what?"

"Not all the time and uh…I worked in a bakery," Tannin muttered.

"A baker?!" He guffawed. "Oh, your ancestors would be turning in their graves."

"Indeed they would." A slim figure appeared from Douglas' shadow. Tannin's stomach sank into her boots.

"Master Theo," she breathed. If ever there were a person from her childhood she would be glad to never see again, it was him.

"Novice Tannin." He inclined his head slightly. It was respectful yet somehow his sunken eyes still managed to convey the disappointment he had always had in her as his student. She instantly felt seven years old again and shrank into Adair's shadow.

Dana appeared in the doorway behind them. Unlike Adair, she'd changed out of her travelling clothes. Still an earthy brown like the peasant clothes they'd pilfered, Dana's dress didn't look exceptionally extravagant except for the patterns on the hems and the perfect fit of the garment. And, of course, the heavy solid gold that decorated the belt at her waist, the bands on her arms and the rows of piercings that glittered in her ears. Her hair was braided differently too. Two smaller braids lined the sides of her head at the temples, the rest fell loose down her back. The golden torc around her neck had two snarling warg heads at each end that rested on her collarbone.

Golden. She had tried to ask both Adair and Dana about the ceremony to become Golden – subtly, of course, she knew it was a well-kept secret but they wouldn't tell her anything except hint that she had already passed the stage in her transformation from warg-blood to true warg where the Golden ceremony would have taken place. She'd missed her chance. She could never be Golden.

Tannin snapped back to reality in time to hear Dana instruct Douglas to show Ava and Flint to some guest rooms and for the rest of them to adjourn to the council chambers. Tannin gave Flint a panicked look. She didn't want to split up.

He gave her a reassuring smile. "You'll be fine," he mouthed as they turned to follow the man-mountain that was Douglas up the stairs. Tannin watched them go forlornly, wishing she could also disappear.

Corridors and tapestries whizzed by in a blur as Tannin was hustled into what Dana had called the council chambers. A huge, oval table dominated the room where all but three seats were already filled. A few faces were familiar to her even if names escaped her, but to Tannin it was clear these were all important, powerful people. And all wargs. They sat, straight-backed and proud, well-dressed and with swirling tattoos inked on bare, muscular arms or snaking up their necks. Gold glinted at her from every direction.

"Right," Dana said, ushering Tannin into a chair next to her. "I've updated you on most of the information we learned in Armodan, not least that we now have Tannin here with us, but we've got a lot more to discuss."

Dana whizzed through a round of introductions of names and titles without pause and leapt straight into her plans. Douglas joined them as she was midstream.

Tannin could barely keep up with the conversation. She was missing so many details. So many new names thrown around as well as codewords that no one thought to explain to her.

From what she scraped together, the group abided by a solid hierarchy with Dana at the top, closely followed by Douglas. The rest split into groups with Adair at the head of the rangers – a job that would mean spending most of his time away from the city. A dark-haired chiselled-looking warg called Lachlan was the head of the Dunoak defences, and a woman with reddish hair and ink crawling up the side of her face called Catriona seemed to be in charge of coordinating their finances. The rest of the names flittered past Tannin's ears but refused to take root in her mind.

Tannin sat in semi-stunned silence for most of the meeting, but it seemed no one really expected her input anyway. She studied the council chamber instead. The table they sat at was made of thick, polished wood. Carved into the surface was a crude map of the Five Kingdoms. Banners adorned the walls. Familiar purple and gold for the Brochlands, blue for Rill, red for Gormbrae and white for Cascairn. Tannin assumed the green must be for Woodren.

Dunoak wasn't a wealthy city by any stretch of the imagination, but some serious money had been spent on this room, Tannin thought as she examined the decorative weaponry lining the walls. An axe that was far too large to actually be of any use hung on the wall above an empty fireplace. The blade had been etched to depict a battle scene. Tannin assumed one side was Dunoak, and if they displayed it, then they had probably won. She didn't know enough about this soggy swamp kingdom to even make a guess at who they were fighting.

"Tannin?"

Her attention snapped back. "What?"

"We're discussing your training. Your grandfather didn't train you at all?"

"No, I told you, I was a baker." She turned to Dana. "Did you not tell them I lost my memory for, like, six years? I thought I was completely human. I didn't know anything about Remnants or wargs or anything."

"What?"

"Because I got the last dose of that warg-juice at the wrong time or something. I got blood-poisoning." She shrugged. "I didn't even remember I was a warg til last year. That was a fun thing to just find out one day, by the way. Not at all traumatic."

"Warg-juice," Theo echoed in disbelief. Tannin still hadn't worked out what his role in all this was. He wasn't a warg.

"As you all may have guessed, that means our plans have to slow down somewhat until we can shine Tannin up to Golden standard. Unfortunately, Sommer is aware of this. We had a very close call in Armodan. She knows we can't challenge her yet."

Tannin rubbed the scar on her thigh through the thin fabric of her breeches. Close call was one way to put it. Getting absolutely humiliated was another.

"We dig in here. We defend our position. We gain allies," Dana said, stabbing her finger onto the map with each statement as a babble of discontentment filled the room. "We play the long game. In the meantime, I will be taking the mantle of laird here."

"What about the lass taking it?" It was Lachlan who spoke. His cheekbones really did look like they had been carved, Tannin thought as he frowned at her.

"I don't want it," Tannin said quickly. "Dana can have it."

"You don't want it?" Theo echoed her again.

Tannin glanced at him in annoyance. She'd forgotten he did that. Repeating whatever she said and making her feel like she'd said the wrong thing every time.

"Right, honestly? I am just trying to not die," she said earnestly. "Sommer would have killed me in a second if she didn't need me alive. I don't want a bigger target on my back."

"Why does Sommer need her alive?" Catriona spoke from across the table.

Tannin frowned.

I'm right here.

"She thinks she knows where the vials are," Dana sighed.

"Actually," Tannin said suddenly realising, "how did you get made into a warg if he stole the vials before you got the last dose? I mean, I got mine after me and my grandad left. Kind of a last hope thing when we were about to get murdered by redcaps, actually. It messed me right up and I was sick for ages. I didn't remember anything about wargs or Stonestead or anything." Tannin trailed off, aware she was babbling and cleared her throat. "How did you get the last dose?"

"Your grandfather took the core serum. The part that they used to make the different doses. The third doses for all of our year were already made and stored elsewhere. That's all that was left."

"Do you know what he did with them?" the inked woman interrupted brusquely.

"Not a clue," Tannin said bitterly. "Didn't stop Sommer trying to chop me into pieces, though."

"Surely you must know something? It is of the utmost importance."

"What part of "warg juice made me lose my mind" was too difficult to understand?" Tannin's patience had withered. "My grandad didn't even tell me what I was, let alone where he hid his secrets. If I knew, trust me, I would've said when Sommer was stabbing me. I quite like having all my limbs attached."

"Tannin. Catriona. Peace," Dana interjected. "We are fortunate that we can take our time now. This position is defensible and it is out of Sommer's way. She knows we aren't a threat to her yet, so it is my belief that she will focus her efforts on relations in the Brochlands and to the west rather than wasting resources on us, but that doesn't mean she won't have spies. In the meantime, we strengthen our own advantages. Each of you know your tasks, but I will be calling on some of you from time to time to help with Tannin's training as well. You can think of her as a novice, still."

She looked at Tannin directly. "I'll deal with the less physical side of things. I'll sit with you tomorrow and give you a proper overview of our situation. As for your true warg abilities, we know you can do a full change, but have you ever considered a partial change?"

"You mean like this?"

Tannin held up her hand and flexed as her fingers lengthened, blackened and razor-sharp claws sprouted from her nail beds. Surprised murmurs from around the table accompanied her little show.

"Oh." Dana blinked. "How did you learn that?"

Tannin shrugged and let her hand resume its normal form, "I had time when I was hiding out in Attilo's place. Just started playing around."

The familiar ache of loss settled in her chest at the mention of his name, and the memory of those cosy nights in his small apartment. Him fussing over her when she had a bad night. Cooking dinner together. His hugs. The scent of lacewood oil.

Dana cleared her throat dragging Tannin out of her well of memories. "Well, that's one lesson we can skip then. The rest of you, not a word to anyone – even the warg-bloods – about Tannin. I want complete silence on the topic. Every single one of us is responsible for keeping her alive. For now though, I think we've all earned some rest. Once again, good work everyone."

They filtered out of the room, each warg touching their fingers to their forehead as a gesture of respect and a few murmuring congratulations to Dana on the successful take-over.

Theo looked down his nose at Tannin as he passed. "You have a lot of work to do."

After everyone had left, Dana walked Tannin up to her new accommodation. They didn't speak, but Tannin was glad of the silence. Her head felt too full already, and she barely registered where they were going.

"This will be your room," Dana said as they arrived at a wooden door that looked exactly like every other they had passed. She pointed down the corridor. "Flint is down there. Ava is next door. I want you to stay put for now until things get settled. And Tannin, I mean it. I don't have the time or the desire to babysit you any longer. I have so many other responsibilities here, so just please do what I say.”

Tannin nodded numbly. Honestly, she just wanted to sleep. The meeting had lasted hours, and she could feel her pulse behind her eyes as she entered her new room.

The bed with its worn but soft sheets was low to the ground and incredibly inviting. It was so wide she could probably sleep across it if she’d wanted. A heavy, rustic wardrobe and a stone fireplace that stood opposite the foot of the bed made up the rest of the room along with a sink and a dressing table.

Tannin peered out of her window to the large square beyond the keep’s walls. The dirt on the pane obscured any detail, but she knew that was where they had seen the bodies earlier. She wondered if they had been cleared away yet, or if the wargs were content to leave them to the flies a little while longer.

That square was probably just a regular market square once, but now it would be forever tainted. She wondered how long it would take the people here to go back to everyday lives. Back to their shops and smithies and bakeries.

“Dana, is this really the way to do this? There’s a whole city of people out there who have nothin’ to do with this.”

“Do I need to make you swear an oath too?”

“Of course not. I just—”

“Then do as I say and don’t question my methods.” Dana took a deep breath and traced the warg heads on her torc with her fingertips. “We’ve got a lot of work to do.”

Chapter Nine

Home Sweet Home

Tannin

The room she was given was wonderful. She hadn't lit the fire yet, but she could just imagine how cosy it could get. Tannin only wished she had a bigger window. She liked to be able to see out. To be able to get out if she needed to.

A retinue of nervous-looking servants who wouldn't look her in the eye had even dragged in a copper tub and filled it with steaming hot water and scented oils. She had leapt in with many a contented moan. It had been far too long since she'd had a hot bath, and the water was distinctly grey when she had finished scrubbing herself clean. Tannin grimaced. She must've made such a great first impression to the rest of the wargs in all their fancy clothes and gold.

She had devoured the meal that had been brought up for her and just lit the last of her candles when there was a tentative knock at the door. She knew who it was without having to even think about it.

"Come in."

Ava held a candle of her own and had also recently bathed. Her long hair was still damp as it hung down her back, just starting to form its usual rich waves.

"I wanted to see how you shoulder is doing. You said earlier that it hurt."

"The bath helped."

Ava nodded and seemed indecisive if she should go or not.

"You can take a look," Tannin sighed and loosened the strings at the front of her shirt so that she could slip it off her shoulder. The servants had brought her some fresh clothes, which she was thoroughly glad of. Nothing she had in her pack would pass for remotely clean anymore.

Ava examined the wound and talked Tannin through some exercises to test her range of motion. It wasn't any better than usual, but it wasn't any worse either.

"How was the meeting?" Ava asked tentatively.

Tannin was tempted to be patronising and tell her it was warg business, but she didn't have the energy.

"Exhausting," she replied honestly. "I'm way out of my depth."

Ava had that frown that meant she was going to ask a lot of questions. Tannin held up a hand to stop her.

"I really didn't understand what's goin' on. Dana is gonna explain it to me tomorrow. Today, I'm just so tired my brain is like soup."

Ava nodded. "Me too. I'll let you get some rest."

She stood to leave and then hesitated like she wanted to say something more. Tannin waited, but in the end, all that Ava said was, "Good night."

Tannin sank into the soft bedding. She'd wanted to sleep alone for so long, and finally, she had not only her own bed but her own room too. It was blissfully quiet. Too quiet. She found herself hopefully listening for the sounds of Ava's soft breathing that she'd become accustomed to.

I do not miss her, she told herself sternly as she punched her pillow into a more comfortable shape.

I'm just used to her. That's all. That's why I can't sleep.

In the end, she gave up on sleep and grouchily threw back her blankets.

Even with the comfort her accommodations offered, being indoors set Tannin's nerves jangling. She found it hard to believe that she actually felt better in the shitty tent than here in the keep, but the stone walls surrounding her made her feel so trapped. And it really didn't help that she had nothing to distract herself with.

She chewed her lip. Dana said to stay, but didn't actually specify to stay in her room. She said stay put. Surely, exploring the keep a wee bit wasn't off limits? It wasn't like she was leaving the building, and it wasn't that late.

She reasoned that knowing the keep a little better might ease her mind and let her sleep, but as she walked through the dark echoey corridors, she decided it was a mistake and the keep was most definitely just creepy as fuck. Every creak of old wood sent prickles down the back of her neck, and some of the faded portraits lining the hallways looked down right malicious.

Following the winding staircases, some shorter than others, she found herself on strange middle floors like a balcony overlooking a feast hall and servants' corridors that had windows at floor height to rooms she had no clue how to access. The keep had clearly evolved and additional parts built on top of each other until it was the warped behemoth it had become. Eventually, even the way back to her room evaded her, and she had to admit she was lost.

As she rounded a corner, a tantalising scent reached her. Something sweet and buttery. A tentative sniff had her mouth watering, and she followed the scent until she found a stiflingly hot kitchen. It had that same chaotic functional feel that the kitchens in Fletcher's bakery always had. The ceiling was discoloured from smoke and steam, and the utensils hanging from various racks had the creeping first signs of rust. A tray of freshly baked biscuits ready for the next day sat cooling on the counter. Tannin gazed at them longingly.

"Oi! Who are you and wit are ye dain' in ma kitchens?" a woman yelled from across the room. She was almost as broad as the narrow passage between the ovens and the workbench, and the map of stains on her apron told of a lifetime of recipes.

Tannin gave the woman a sheepish grin. "Uh. Hi. I'm Tannin. I was just explorin' and smelled the biscuits..." she trailed off under the woman's stern gaze. Not for the first time that day, she felt like a child again.

"This isnae a place tae be wanderin' aboot. Especially since..." the woman huffed. "Yer one of they new ones, aye?"

Tannin nodded. If the woman knew exactly what the "new ones" were, she didn't seem particularly phased by it. Or she was hiding it well.

"Whoever ye are, ye'll still need feedin'." The woman scooped up one of the biscuits Tannin had been eyeing and popped it on a plate. Thrusting it at her, she said, "Ye can call me Cook. Now oot of ma kitchen and keep oot. I'm very busy and this isnae the place for the likes of you."

"Wait, can I have some tea?" Tannin asked hopefully. "I can't sleep"

"I'll git Alby tae see tae it."

"Alby?"

"He's the odd jobs boy and I'm a very busy woman. ALBY!" Her sudden bellow made Tannin jump.

Moments later, a boy raced into the kitchen and skidded to a stop. He must've only been around nine or ten years old.

Alby and Cook couldn't have been more physically different if they'd tried. Whereas Cook was broad with the complexion – and, Tannin suspected, the personality – of lightly curdled milk, Alby was dark, stringy and his face split into an eager, gap-toothed grin at the sight of Tannin.

"Gotta job for me?" he asked Cook, bouncing on the spot. "Somethin' good?"

"This here girl does."

Alby beamed at Tannin and puffed out his chest. "That's right. I'm the man to call. Anything you want doin', I can do it. Just say the word."

"Can you make me some tea?"

"On its way, ma'am." He actually saluted. "Anything else?"

"Not right now. Wait no, actually can you tell me how to get back to my room? I'm in one of the guest rooms, and I don't really know how I got here," Tannin admitted with a sheepish shrug.

"I'll take you!" he chirped. "And I'll carry the tray!"

After he pelted off down into what Tannin assumed was a pantry, she smiled.

"He's a wee cutie."

"Dinnae go taking advantage now," Cook said sternly. "Ye gie him a job, ye pay him, ye hear me? He don't get a proper wage."

"I won't. I mean I will. Pay him I mean," Tannin promised.

At some point... Where the hell am I gonna get coin?

The boy appeared moments later with a clay mug balanced on a tray. Tannin tried to say she could carry it herself if he could just point her in the right direction, but he insisted on escorting her properly, carrying her mug and her biscuit like they were precious gems while clearly trying not to bound ahead like he wanted to. On the way, he peppered her with questions, apologies for asking questions and then more questions.

He wanted to know where she'd come from, if she were staying, did she ride horses, did she like horses because he liked horses and he was going to become a knight, did she know what happened to the old laird, did she know all the other new people in the keep. Tannin's head whirled with all his questions and she tried her best to be vague.

How much of the slaughter did he see? Did Cook keep him away from the worst of it? Gods, I hope so. He's too young for this.

When they arrived, he hovered near the door, and when Tannin told him she didn't have any money for him, he looked crestfallen despite his protests that she needn't give him anything.

"Next time, I'll have somethin' for you," she promised. "Something good."

"It's okay," he said mournfully and then lowered his voice conspiratorially. "I heard some of these new folks are some kinds of monsters. I can protect you, though. I've got a knife, so if you need protecting you shout on me, right?" He puffed up his thin chest and showed her the pitifully small dagger he had hidden in his boot.

Tannin made the appropriate impressed sounds at the blade while trying to not picture Alby's face when he found out she was one of those monsters.

"Maybe if I do all the jobs for you and the other new nobles, I can get myself a proper sword. If you give me something good, coin and the like. Then I can protect you from all the monsters, right?" He straightened up, trying to make himself as tall as possible.

"Right," Tannin agreed hollowly.

Noble...me...monster...also me.... When did I become this?

"Good night, Miss!"

Chapter Ten

Horse and Hound

Ava

Life in Dunoak was going to take a lot of adjusting to, Ava realised.

The first few days, she jolted awake in the middle of the night with no idea where she was, and it always took a decent half hour to settle her mind again. During the day, she traipsed after Flint and Tannin as they explored the keep, scrambling up and down staircases and pushing each other into spiderweb-covered alcoves.

It only took about two days before they had explored every room. Well, Ava and Flint had at least been into every room. Tannin refused to descend below ground level into the mouldy cellar.

Tannin had told her that they had communal kitchens in Stonestead, and meals were either eaten together or not at all. Only a few of the wargs lived in the keep, and the rest, plus the warg-blood Remnants, had taken over the elaborate homes of the executed nobles in the upper part of the city. Nevertheless, the wargs had kept their meal habits and always showed up for dinner.

Dana kept them updated with the wargs' takeover in short, passing comments during those communal meals. It was never much. Just a quiet confirmation that everything was going to plan. A plan Ava would have liked very much to be let in on at some point, but any attempts to pry were shut down instantly. That was fine. She would find out on her own if she had to. In the meantime, she watched.

Ava found it fascinating to watch the wargs and warg-bloods as they piled into the hall. There was simultaneously unruly chaos alongside a set of iron-clad societal rules that no one could really describe to her. She'd tried to find out the whys and the hows, but every time, she was just told "that's just the way it is". Eating together seemed to be one of those immovable rules.

The food in Dunoak, however, was far from the mountain fare of the wargs and even further from the luxuries she'd enjoyed as a princess. The swamp kingdom of Woodren certainly had some interesting cuisine – most of it smoked or pickled – and after forcing down a stew made from some kind of eel-like creature that lived in the mud, Ava decided that she really wasn't a fan.

Of course, they imported a lot too, so it wasn't only eel on the menu. The swampish sludge linked up with the Shey river that wound all the way through the Brochlands and further to the western coast. With shallow-bottomed boats, goods were brought almost directly to the city gates. Through her own studies and eavesdropping on those of her brother, Ava knew a great deal about trade in the Five Kingdoms.

Not that anyone here appreciates that.

Ava had tried to get Dana to see her worth as an advisor many times now to the point the warg leader was refusing to even see her anymore. Tannin was even less receptive to her advice and attempts to share her knowledge. The only time she ever felt a hint of usefulness was when she tended to Tannin's aches and pains. She toyed with the idea of becoming more of a healer. If that was all they were going to see her as, then she may as well be good at it. She'd already confirmed several useful plants growing as weeds around the keep's tragically under-tended window boxes. She could put them to use if she wanted to. And there was the book. Ava suppressed a shudder. She should never have stolen it. The kind of magic described in there was a level she could never hope to achieve. And others she never wanted to even attempt.

Or do I?

Ava had always accepted that she would never have power in the courts and throne rooms of the world, but that kind of magic promised a different kind of power. Power from the shadows. In a way, that had always been her strength – hiding, watching, learning. She'd stuffed the book under her mattress until she could find a better hiding place for it, but at night, when she couldn't sleep, she found herself rifling through the fragile pages and dreaming of what could be.

"Come on, princess." Flint jostled her and dragged her out of her thought spiral.

"What? Where?"

"We can't just sit around waiting for Tannin to get back from beastie lessons. Luck favours the bold!"

"And exactly where would the bold be going?" Ava asked as she followed him.

He grinned and tapped his nose in response.

"You ever actually had a job?" Flint asked as he strode out into the courtyard.

Ava raised an eyebrow.

"No, you wouldn't have, would you?" He seemed to be talking more to himself than to her.

"What kind of job do you have in mind for me?"

"More for me, but there's an opportunity for you too." He winked. "I'm charitable like that."

"I do not need charity," Ava replied, affronted.

"Call it a favour, then. We're going to the barn. I heard folk talking, and it sounds like the old horsemaster needs a hand. Apparently, he's a right old arse, though, so might turn out to be nothing. He's extra salty 'cause Dana's making him sell most of the old laird's horses."

"Why?"

"Apparently, wargs don't ride at all, and horses don't like them anyway, so there's no point in keeping them. He's refusing to give up his favourites, though." Flint kept walking. "Makes sense. I never thought much about it before, but remember when Tannin's house got set on fire? I brought her to that crypt on a horse, and I thought it was freaked out cause of the smoke, but now I think it was her."

Ava made a non-committal sound in her throat. There were memories attached to that incident that she did not want to think about. How Attilo had tended to Tannin's wounds so gently and carried her up to the castle in his arms. How he had sat with Ava while Tannin slept and reassured her that her injuries weren't as grave as they looked when she had gotten panicky. He had told her she had done a good job on the stitches. And then later that night...with Tannin...in the bathing pool.

"Besides, I also heard that the horsemaster's dog had pups." Flint's eyes sparkled at he grinned again.

"This is mostly an excuse to go cuddle some puppies, isn't it?"

"Absolutely."

The kennels were attached to the stables, and the pair quickly found a low-fenced area filled with straw and mewling balls of fur.

"Aw, puppies!" Flint exclaimed, hopping the barrier and cooing as the babies stumbled over themselves trying to sniff his boots.

The dogs at the castle where Ava had grown up had been working dogs. She had been warned to stay away from them, but she had to admit it was impossible to resist reaching out to ruffle the tiny, fluffy heads that popped up from amongst the hay. Flint knelt amongst them. Ava rolled her eyes at him as he lay down in the hay. The puppies swarmed him immediately, bouncing and trying to lick his face. He laughed. It was such a pure sound that reverberated off the rafters and set the tiny tails wagging in a frenzy. He reminded her so much of her brother, Florian, sometimes. He had loved animals too and doted upon his hunting hawk, Kess. They never found her after he died.

Ava declined Flint's invitation to join him in the hay, opting to lean over the barrier to pet them instead. She might've given up her royal standing, but she was still above rolling around in a barn.

"You are going to end up with fleas if you keep playing around in there," Ava said disapprovingly.

She was going to say more, but a familiar Sense rolled over her skin. It was an almost pleasant, earthy feeling and so distinctly *Tannin* that she looked up instantly to look for her and found the young warg strolling towards them.

"Tannin actually had fleas once." Flint grinned as he noticed they had company. "Remember, Tan? Eve made you take a bath in vinegar."

Tannin gave him a dirty look. "Aye, I do and thank you so much for bringing that up."

"Any time." He blew her a kiss. "Dana let you go early?"

"Aye, she's busy," Tannin replied. "Look at these wee cuties!"

"Very important warg business, I suppose." Flint scooped up the palest puppy.

"See," he said holding up the little golden fluffball. "This is what I'd have expected you to look like as a warg." The puppy wriggled and sank its tiny teeth into his hand. "Ouch! It's even as mean as you are."

Ava was about to ask for the rest of the vinegar story when they were interrupted by the door swinging open and in bounced a large golden-coloured hound.

"This must be mumma!" Flint said and clapped his hands on his thighs. "Hiya, sweetheart! Come here, girl!"

The dog took a couple steps towards him and then stopped, sniffing. Her tail dropped instantly and her head swung around to lock eyes with Tannin. A growl sounded low in her throat.

"Woah," Tannin said putting up her hands. "Good doggy."

The dog's lips curled back into a snarl as she barked, spittle flying.

"No, no. Shhhh. Good dog." Tannin backed away and looked at Flint in bewilderment. "What's wrong with it?!"

"Oh, that is interesting," Ava said. "It's not just horses, is it?"

"Apparently not," Flint replied grimly. "Tan, watch out."

"What are you talkin' about?!" Tannin demanded as the dog barked again, inching closer, jaws snapping.

Tannin backed away until she hit the higher fence at the side of the kennel. Ava gasped as the dog lunged. Tannin yelped, hauling herself up onto the wooden wall. The dog leapt around under her, snapping at her ankles and snarling.

"What's all this?" An older man entered, leaning heavily on a cane. He glared at Flint, who was covered in straw, Ava who was wringing her hands, and then up at Tannin, who was crouched on top of the wall with the dog nipping at her from beneath and growling.

"Here!" he barked, commanding the dog to his side. She went, but slowly and begrudgingly giving Tannin one last warning bark.

"What're ye dain in here?" he demanded.

"What the fuck's wrong with your dog?!" Tannin retorted, not daring to budge from her perch.

"Tannin!" Ava hissed reproachfully and Tannin made a face at her in return.

"Nothin's wrong wi' her. She's protecting her pups." He squinted at Tannin. "Ye dinnae look like one o' them, but the dugs dinnae lie."

"What?"

"Yer one o' they beasts, ain't ye? Get doon aff that fence and git oot ma kennels. Yer spookin' the animals." He brandished his cane at her.

"I'm spookin' them?" Tannin said in amazement. "She tried to fucking bite me!"

"Aye," the man said exasperatedly. "Cause yer a predator near her weans. Now GIT!"

"Maybe we should leave," Ava offered quickly. "We're sorry, sir."

The man snorted. "Ain't no "sir", young Miss. Name's Angus. And this ain't no place for playin' aboot."

"I'm actually here 'cause I heard you might need a hand with the horses and the like," Flint said. "I've worked with horses before."

"So ye know yer beasts now, do ye?"

"Aye."

Angus looked him up and down and grunted.

"And Ava knows herbs and stuff. She can help too. Maybe even with your leg." Flint gestured to the man's cane.

Ava stumbled over her words for a moment. She had hoped for a more sophisticated approach, but it would have to do.

"Yes," she said finally. "Yes, I could do that."

Dealing with aches and pains was something she at least knew a little about. Tonics to add to her bathwater or creams to soothe sore muscles were something she had made all the time back home. If she'd gone to the royal healer every time she'd hurt herself training with Attilo, her secret life wouldn't have been very secret for long.

Angus sniffed, looking at each of them. "Alright then. You two come wi' me. You," he pointed at Tannin who still hadn't come down from the fence. "Git oot and stop botherin' ma dug. And dinnae be goin' near ma horses neither. They can smell a warg a mile off and they dinnae like it, so away wi' ye!"

Ava felt a pang of sympathy for her as Tannin leapt from the fence and darted out of the barn, but it would have to wait. She hurried after Flint and the horsemaster into the stables. She had a job to do.

Chapter Eleven

Warg Law

"So." Tannin threw a honeyed nut in the air and caught it in her mouth as they walked. She'd wheedled until Dana bought them for her. The mountain of information being dumped on her had made her snacky. "What's Sommer's army like, then?"

"Disciplined," Dana replied pointedly as Tannin missed her mouth with the next throw and fumbled to catch her sweet treat before it fell to the ground. "She has different divisions, each with a leader, like we're trying to do here. A core pack of her year group make up her inner circle. We didn't even approach them with the option to desert. It would have been suicide."

"What was your division?"

"I led the first wave warriors. We were always the first ones sent in," Dana said, a dark look crossing her face. "The cannon fodder."

Tannin wasn't brave enough to pry any further, especially when wails of despair reached them. For part of her lessons that day, Dana had taken Tannin into the city. Six warg-bloods, armed to the teeth, accompanied them for the tour. Their path was taking them past the main square where the wargs had slaughtered the rulers of the city. Tannin had naively hoped it would have been since unused. She should have known better.

She had expected the full-blooded wargs to have the most interest in the regular floggings and other gruesome punishments in the square for slander against Dana's rule, but it was the warg-blood Remnants – the ones who never qualified to take the serum – who lapped it up, jeering and crowing as the blood flowed. Especially with the younger warg-bloods, ringleaders had emerged and cliques had formed, always thirsty for blood. Some even took souvenirs from particularly entertaining executions. Tannin would watch in distaste as they flooded into the keep's feast hall afterwards, waving blood-soaked handkerchiefs or locks of hair.

Today was no exception, and the closer they got to the square, the more faces Tannin recognised and the more animalistic fervour that always accompanied the warg-bloods left its tang in the air.

Her dread grew with every step.

"Dana, I really don't want to see," she muttered under her breath. "Can we go a different way?"

"This is the quickest way," Dana replied curtly. "Also, I want you to see. I want you to understand that you will also have to make difficult choices. Sometimes, you have to be cruel to be kind."

The wails reached new volumes as their party rounded the final corner into the square. The heads from the night of the takeover were mounted all around, eyes and lips already lost to the ever-hungry corbies. But they weren't short of company on their pikes. Fresh bodies, speared and slumping, dripped steadily beside them.

"We have to show Dunoak that we have no tolerance for rebellion or resistance to us, but at the same time, that life under warg rule can be beneficial," Dana said as they walked through the grim decorations. "That's why later today, here in this square, we will distribute one gold crown and one sack of grain to each household if they swear fealty. We are here for the long haul, and although we did take over, we now have to rule these people fairly."

"I don't think they'll see this as fair."

"They will," Dana insisted. She dug around in her pocket and brought out a few coppers. She held one up, as if to inspect it in the light, and then flicked it to a dirt-crusted child who had been inching towards them hopefully. "Start small, integrate, support the local businesses and keep the trade routes strong. We don't want to crush the people here. We have to support them if we want them to support us. Do you understand?"

"Aye," Tannin replied slowly, conscious of the fact that Dana wasn't moving to go around the killing platform but was making right for it. "I understand good business, but what are we doin' here?"

"You can make a donkey move by tempting him with a carrot or beating him with a stick." Dana's dark eyes glittered as she held up another coin. "Think of these as carrots..." She flicked it into a jumble of people that would soon become a crowd and basked in their jubilations as she gave the raised platform an affectionate kick with the toe of her boot. "...And this is the stick."

Tannin looked again at the stage and realised that a lump she'd thought was a body waiting to be displayed was moving.

"What's goin' on?"

"Some rich merchant came to me this morning, offering a pitiful sum for us to leave. He's going to regret it, and we will let it be known that we are not to be bought off." Dana's lip curled back from her teeth in a snarl.

It wasn't the first or even the tenth offer the wargs had gotten to vacate Dunoak, but this one seemed to have particularly irked Dana. She didn't usually dish out punishments personally and certainly not on a whim. Whoever the unfortunate soul was must have really, really pissed her off. Others had been dragged to the dungeons for insinuating Dana was too young to lead or for insisting to talk to "the man" in charge. To be fair, Dana was young – less than a year older than Tannin – but she had been trained to lead. That was the path that she'd chosen, or maybe that was chosen for her, Tannin was still a little fuzzy on the process, when she had ascended into the ranks of the Golden. Adair had taken the route of the rangers and Dana had fast-tracked to leadership. It suited her. If she had stayed with Sommer, she would have been something akin to a general.

She looked the part of a general too as she mounted the stairs to the stage after ordering Tannin to stay with the warg-blood escort and away from the cityfolk's attention. She held her head high and moved with a predatory fluidity as she approached the hunched shape. A sharp kick had him sprawling across the wooden planks in a disjointed sort of way that made Tannin think quite a few of his bones had been broken already. Her stomach swirled, and bile threatened to rise in her throat as Dana told the man's story to the assembled Dunoakers in a cool, clear voice. She painted him as greedy and soulless, and the crowd practically danced to her words.

"We are wargs!" Dana hollered to the jeering mass. "You think you can pay us to leave? You think you can strongarm us?"

She drew the short sword she wore at her hip and stabbed downwards. Tannin's view was blocked, and despite her growing nausea, she couldn't help but stand on her tiptoes to try and see. She'd missed what Dana had done, but whatever it was, the audience had loved it and she held something aloft, triumphantly.

"Well, here's what I think of your strong arm!" Dana waggled the thing she was holding.

Oh. Oh, that's disgusting.

Tannin stopped trying to see after Dana threw the arm to the yowling warg-bloods to fight over. She seemed to enjoy encouraging their wildness. Tannin wondered if that was a deliberate intimidation tactic. She strongly suspected that Dana planned everything she did.

After she stepped down from the platform, announcing that the merchant be mounted on the spikes whether he was dead or not, she threw another handful of coppers into the crowd and swept off into a side street. At her escort's jostling, Tannin realised she was meant to follow – at a discreet distance, of course – until they were away from curious eyes. It would give the game away entirely if Tannin was seen to be honoured by the warg ruler's attentions. Her safety was dependent on her being anonymous, the wargs had all agreed.

"So," Dana said casually clearing her throat as Tannin caught up like she hadn't just dismembered a person. "I think it's about time we start work on your Changing. How are your injuries? Do you think they can take it?"

Tannin blinked at her for a moment before recovering. "Uh aye, I think so."

She rolled her shoulder. "Ava said it's about as healed as it's gonna get."

After arriving in Dunoak, Ava had been able to get better ingredients for the various goops and creams she slathered on Tannin's scars. By now, they only really hurt if she wasn't careful. Or if it rained. She had always thought Attilo had made that up. Whenever the heavens opened, the old soldier would always limp more and take a less active role in teaching her and the princess self-defence techniques in the dingy crypt that had been their secret hideout.

"Good," Dana said, pausing to peruse some graffiti for any traces of anti-warg sentiments. "That's one thing off my mind. Although, I wouldn't trust her if I were you."

"Ava? I don't trust her," Tannin replied flatly. "You know what she did to me."

"I also see the way you two look at each other. She's always going to put her kingdom first." Dana gave her a stern look. "You are low on her priority list, even if she is useful for now."

"I do not look at her in any sort of way," Tannin snapped, growing warm under her collar.

"Then we won't have any problems."

Tannin scratched the side of her neck absent-mindedly as she waited for her next instructions. And then her side. She been feeling weirdly itchy for days, sometimes to the point that it took all her willpower to stop herself tearing her damn skin off.

"I think I'm bloody allergic to something here," she grumbled, scraping her nails down her arms.

"Stop that. You'll be shedding. You'll be needing brushed out."

"Excuse me?" Tannin was sure she heard that wrong. "Brushed?"

"Your warg coat needs brushed out or you'll get matts." Dana squinted at her. "Not even had your first shed."

Tannin made a disgusted face. "God, you make it sound like we're actual animals."

Dana raised her eyebrows warningly.

"Being a warg is an honour, Tannin."

"So you've said," she huffed.

"I'll have one of the wargs brush you out after we're done here."

"No," Tannin said quickly. The last thing she wanted was the others knowing how un-warglike she was. "I'll sort it myself."

They walked the rest of the way in uncomfortable silence, but the closer they got to the keep, the more animated their escort became with lots of musings about what was for dinner. The topic made Tannin's own stomach sink a little. It wasn't that she particularly liked eating alone, but for her, dining all together in the big hall was uncomfortably nostalgic. Her memories of childhood dinners all together in the huge, cave-like halls of Stonestead felt like they belonged to someone else. It was jarring and at the same time horribly familiar in a way she couldn't explain so, when they reached the keep, she made her excuses and ducked away down a quiet corridor instead of following the joyful burble of voices to the feast hall. She had more exploring to do, anyway.

A tempting-looking trellis let her climb up onto a lower portion of the roof. From there, it was a relatively easy scramble up onto a flat section between two higher towers. The space looked like it might have once been intended to be a balcony, but someone just forgot to add the door. Moss clung to every crack in the weather-stained stone, and something mushroomy was growing near the ledge she'd just climbed up. Still, Tannin smiled. From here, she could see over the keep's walls to the roofs of the city and even a murky outline of the braes and swamp beyond. And it was blissfully quiet.

Her new secret place wasn't the only interesting thing Tannin managed to find on her solo explorations, and she proudly showed off both discoveries to Flint that evening.

"Look what I got." Tannin waggled the flask she'd found at him as he sprawled on the blanket they'd brought up to the roof.

"Ooh. Where'd you get this?"

"Hidden in the pantry," Tannin said with a scowl. "I deserve a damn drink. This is the worst. I can't believe dogs hate me."

Flint had told her all about his day with the horses, which she didn't care about, and the dogs, which unfortunately she did.

He cocked an eyebrow sceptically. "The worst? Really?"

"Alright, smartarse. It's in the top five then. Attempted murder, death and destruction, crushing pressure of inevitable leadership." She ticked them off on her fingers. "And now, no puppy cuddles."

Flint laughed as she scowled again.

"I'm gonna make that dog love me. You mark my words," she said seriously.

"You're gonna get bit."

"She just doesn't know how lovable I am."

"You sure the caution isn't warranted? The old Laird's personal mount reminds me of a certain champion horse back in Armodan," he said pointedly. "A champion horse that *someone* ate."

Oh. So, he did know about that.

"I have no idea what you're talking about," Tannin said blithely.

"Uhuh. Not a clue."

"Nope."

"Didn't have yourself a wee midnight horsey snack?"

"I am shocked and appalled you would even suggest it."

"*Uh-huh.*"

Snatching the flask from her, he took a swig and grimaced. "Tastes a bit foosty"

"Probably is, but do you care?"

He grinned and brought the flask back to his lips. "Not particularly. Price of whisky here is criminal, and the 'shine just aint Skirts' quality."

"None of this is any kind of quality." Tannin gestured out across the view.

"Told you from the start that Dunoak is a shitehole."

"Ah, but it's our shitehole now." She reached for the flask, but he held it out of reach. "Hey, gimme!"

"Come get it." He wiggled it high above her head.

"You're an arsehole." She jumped for it and missed. "Flint, I will climb you like a fuckin' tree, don't think I won't."

Flint snorted but tossed her the flask in defeat. They sat quietly for a while, looking out over the rooftops as the lights in the windows dimmed one by one.

"It's not *so* bad here," Tannin said finally.

"Could be worse," Flint agreed. "I still miss the Skirts though."

"Me too. The Swords, Fletchers'...Gods, I miss Eve so much...Mrs O'Baird..."

He leaned over and splashed some of the whisky onto the cracked stone. "For Mrs O'Baird. May the old bird rest in peace."

"Pour one out for Attilo too."

"He seemed like a good man."

"He was."

Flint nodded solemnly and splashed another measure out.

"For Attilo. May he rest in peace."

Chapter Twelve

Brushie Brushie

Ava

Ava held her breath as the voices from within Dana's office rose once more. The mention of her name had her pulse thundering. She lay flat on her belly on one of the upper floors, as close to the wall as she could get. Damp had gotten to the corner of this storage room, and with just a little prying, the skirting had come loose to reveal a tiny hole to the room below – not large enough to see anything, but big enough that she could hear Dana's private conversations. If she was willing to tell Tannin about her spying, she would have thanked her for always making Dana shout. It was very helpful.

"We need the money."

"You are not ransoming Ava, and that's the end of it. She's still under oath to me anyway, right?"

"It only a matter of time before the king finds out she's here and sends someone to come get her anyway. We may as well get some well-needed coin."

If Dana raised the issue in an actual meeting with the other wargs, Ava would be as good as shipped off and Tannin wouldn't be able to do a damn thing about it. Ava let herself smile. Although the conversation confirmed her worrying suspicions that Dana was starting to see her as nothing more than a coin pouch, it made her stomach flutter to know that Tannin was fighting for her. It didn't mean Tannin had forgiven her or that she even didn't still hate her. But it did mean that she wasn't ready to lose her.

I'll take that for now.

So far, no one besides Tannin, Flint, Adair and Dana knew who Ava was. But it was only a matter of time before the secrets got out. That Ava was the Brochland's princess and Tannin was the heir to Stonestead. Tannin had jokingly offered to declare Flint a lairdling so he didn't feel left out. He'd insisted he was desirable enough as it was, and a title would only make fending off the ladies that much harder.

"She's useful," Tannin insisted from below. Her voice was accompanied by footsteps, heavy but made soft by the thick rug Ava knew carpeted Dana's office, and Ava could picture the warg leader pacing in annoyance.

It was true, though. Ava's salves and herbs not only continued to ease Tannin's stiff and sometimes still painful shoulder, she had started offering her simple cures to others. A cook's burned hand was soothed with a salve; the horsemaster's dodgy hip was bothering him less after a bath with a pouch of leaves she had painstakingly sorted through; even one of the wargs, Catriona, had begrudgingly accepted a tonic for a vicious headache. Ava had been desperately trying to earn her place. Even though Dana clearly had her misgivings, she had allowed Ava to take over a basement room as a work room. It still needed a vigorous clean, but already news had spread about her being of druid descent, and some of the keep's staff had already knocked on her door with requests.

"What about the warg-juice?" Tannin tried again. "She's been looking into it, trying to find out what it does. She's good at the research stuff. Let her stay and let her try and help. And before you say folk back home couldn't recreate it, she's a druid-blood. It's what they do."

Ava winced. She had said that. It was a foolish bluff, and she had no idea where to even start, but that serum seemed to be too important to not use as leverage. If there was a chance she could recreate it, it was a chance the wargs were likely to take - if they didn't run out of patience.

It seemed, however, that Dana still had just enough left.

"It's not off the table. But she'll stay for now." Her voice was stern and Ava was sure it was accompanied by a scowl. "And stop calling it 'warg-juice'!"

The change in Dana's tone made it clear she was wrapping up.

Time for me to go.

Ava stood, rubbing her hip where it had been pressed against the hard floorboards and dusted herself off. A set of back stairs would take her out to the gardens and no one would ever think she had been anywhere near Dana's office. The keep's lopsided construction was an eavesdropper's dream – not quite as effective as her secret tunnels in the castle had been, but good enough that she was confident that there was nowhere in the building that she couldn't spy on if she needed to.

As she headed outside, Ava wondered idly if Tannin was ever going to warn her that Dana wanted rid of her.

Probably not.

The likelihood that Tannin would ever admit to defending her was close to none.

As she rounded the corner and saw the plot of earth she'd been working on that morning, she frowned. It was a mess. She'd wanted to get so much more of it done today, but she couldn't risk missing out on information in favour of a sentimental project. She dug a ribbon from her pocket and scraped her hair up into a knot. She missed having someone to pin it properly for her. Her appearance these days was never anything more than shabby, and at times, downright appalling. Although she had committed to running away, she did sometimes desperately miss her home comforts. And home. She missed home. Nothing here was familiar.

"Feeling sorry for yourself won't fix anything," she told herself as she lowered herself to her knees and attacked the weeds that were infesting her patch of dirt. She had already taken cuttings and re-potted any plants she knew she could use for her potions, but this was something she needed to do for herself. The more time she spent away from home, the more the memorial candles just weren't enough anymore.

Smooth, round rocks formed a ring around the hole Ava was digging. Vibrant flowers with scraggly roots lay beside her, ready to be planted. She had thrown herself into her work and sweat was dripping from her brow when a tingling Sense pulled her out of her trance.

"Hello, Tannin," she said without turning.

"How do you know it's me?"

Ava wiped her brow and sat back on her heels, giving her a pointed look.

"What are you doin'?" Tannin leaned on the wall and watched her as she teased the last of the large rocks out of the dirt. "Do you know anythin' about gardening?"

"A little," Ava said defensively. "It's a memorial." She tried to dust some of the dirt from her hands. "Or the start of one."

"I was thinkin' about him earlier." The quaver in Tannin's voice made Ava's heart twinge. She sometimes forgot that she wasn't the only one who had loved him. "I'll bring somethin' when it's done. An offering."

"You should bring him some bread." Ava smiled. "He loved your bread."

"I make excellent bread," Tannin agreed proudly and then scowled. "Doubt Dana will let me bake. Not a proper activity for a mighty warg. Plus, I think Cook knows I've been stealing ham for the dogs."

Ava shook her head. Flint had told her about Tannin's scheme to bribe the golden-coloured hound into tolerating her. Ava had tried to impart some wisdom, that it wasn't likely the dog would ever like her, but Tannin was adamant and swore the animal hated her a little less.

Ava went back to poking at the dirt. Personally, she agreed with Dana too. If Tannin was going to lead the wargs one day, she had no place in the kitchen. Not that she would ever say that to her face.

She'd expected Tannin to leave but she stayed, rocking back and forth on her heels uncomfortably.

"You're hovering. What do you want, Tannin?" Ava asked bending back over her plants.

"Just admiring the view."

Ava frowned in confusion and then her eyes widened. She froze with the stark realisation that her current position meant that all Tannin could see of her was her backside high in the air and swaying as she worked. Ava quickly sat back on her heels and gave Tannin a glare. She was almost as bad as Flint sometimes, but Tannin cleared her throat, actually looking a little embarrassed.

Did she mean to flirt with me or is it just a reflex?

"I'm looking for Flint actually. You seen him?"

"I think he's out in the town with the boys."

Tannin groaned and ground her fists against her eyes.

She must've forgotten Eoghan and Collum had invited them all out to some music thing in the town. Flint was the only one who had gone. The lack of a social life seemed to drain him, and he had practically skipped out the door.

"I'm sure he'll be back for dinner. Why? What's wrong?"

Tannin chewed her lip.

"I need a favour," she said carefully.

Ava sighed. "What do you need?"

Tannin didn't answer but motioned for her to follow. They scouted around the outskirts of the keep until they found an old shack of a stable that had most definitely seen better days. Ava let herself be ushered inside and lifted an eyebrow as Tannin double-checked that they weren't being followed.

"And you brought me here because?"

Tannin bit her lip again and her cheeks coloured. "I need…"

The words seemed to fight themselves in her mouth and she gave up. Wordlessly, she held out the thing she'd been hiding behind her back – a wide brush for grooming horses.

"You want me to groom a horse?"

Tannin's blush deepened and she avoided looking Ava in the eye. Realisation dawned.

"You want me to groom *you*?"

"I…" Tannin scowled. "Forget it."

Ava took the brush firmly. "You're shedding, aren't you?"

Tannin nodded. She bunched her hands up in her pockets and her cheeks were adorably scarlet.

"You don't need to be embarrassed," Ava said gently. "I'll help. Besides, I haven't had a proper look at you in your warg form and I have to say I'm curious."

"Alright. Just… be quick about it," Tannin muttered, pulling at her shirt hem.

She slid her shirt over her head and draped it over a beam. She turned and immediately crossed her arms over her chest as she saw Ava watching.

"Stop lookin' at me like that."

"I've seen you naked multiple times, you know," Ava scoffed. "Don't flatter yourself."

"Is that why you're starin'?"

"You wish I were staring."

"Turn around," she snapped.

Ava smirked but did as she was told.

Seeing Tannin glow with embarrassment was strangely satisfying when usually she was so… well, not cocky, but she had a kind of rough-around-the-edges bravado that Ava was loathe to admit she actually found charming.

Ava heard Tannin's deep, shaky breath and then a series of grinding and popping noises that made her wince. A body should not make those kinds of noises. It lasted all of half a minute, and then there was once again silence. Ava turned half-expecting to see Tannin's broken body in a heap after hearing the sounds of her being essentially torn apart by her power. But, standing before her in the stillness of the barn, was a beast. The sheer size was enough to terrify even the most seasoned of soldiers. The beast watched her balefully, and her breath caught in her throat as she finally saw the monstrous truth of it.

Golden eyes the size of her fist regarded her warily as if waiting for her to run, to scream, to faint. Ava cocked her head. Flecks of brown mingled with gold in the same way Tannin's dark eyes had specks of copper when they hit the light.

"It's really you in there, isn't it?" Ava breathed out the words, unable to truly break the quiet lull that had settled over them.

She tentatively held out a hand to touch the massive wolfish snout. The beast didn't back away. She could feel the heat radiating from underneath as she ran her fingers through the thick black pelt. It was gorgeously soft, and the warg leaned into her hand as she instinctively scratched behind her ears. The harder she scratched, the more the beast's eyes rolled back and a low groan sounded from deep within its chest. Ava chuckled and those big eyes looked at her questioningly.

"You like your ears scratched, huh?" Ava cooed smugly. "What a fearsome beast you are."

Tannin gave an indignant snort.

"You can't speak right now, can you?"

Ava's question was met with resentful silence.

"Well, that's certainly an improvement."

Tannin dunted her with her massive head and nudged the brush in her hand.

"Don't be impatient, I'm not done admiring you. I haven't had a good look yet."

Ava clicked her tongue and circled in measured steps as Tannin huffed and pawed at the ground. Ava shuddered slightly at the sight of the beastly claws. It was one thing to know Tannin was capable of tearing a person apart with one swipe, it was another thing entirely to see the proof of it. The thick, black fur didn't fully hide the mass of powerful, corded muscle underneath either.

It's still Tannin, Ava reminded herself firmly. Looking back at the impatient expression on the warg's face, there was no doubting it – even with the claws. She reached out and ruffled the fur on her head, playfully.

"So, do you do tricks?" Ava grinned and got a show of bared teeth and a low growl in response. "Alright, alright."

She started brushing. The brush immediately caught on tangled clumps and Tannin whined as it pulled.

"Oh my," Ava muttered. "We should have done this a long time ago. This is a mess. Stay still."

"Brush, brush, brush," she murmured soothingly as she raked the bristles through the thick fur, marvelling at how much was coming off. Before long, Ava had a pile of fluff at her feet, and the front of her dress was covered in it. "There's a good girl. Brushie, brushie."

Tannin rolled her eyes but stayed still and let Ava brush all down her back and sides until only a few bad tangles remained. Before long, the brush glided smoothly through the lush fur in long smooth strokes. Tannin actually seemed to enjoy it. At times, Ava was certain that if she could purr, she would have.

"Okay. Lie down and roll over."

The beast snorted in response.

"You wanted brushed," Ava reminded her.

Tannin stared at her and huffed again.

"I'm not doing a half-job," Ava stated firmly. "Lie down and roll over so I can get the rest of you."

Tannin whined.

Just when Ava thought she really wasn't going to do it, she flopped to the floor with a long, dramatic groan.

This is definitely still the same Tannin.

"Good girl," Ava cooed again and then quickly ducked a swipe from a massive paw. "Hey!"

Tannin replied with more huffing and snorting.

"Stop complaining."

Finally, when Ava was satisfied and Tannin had become restless, she set the brush down to collect the tumbleweeds of fur into a sack, respectfully turning her back again so that Tannin could shrink back into herself and get dressed.

"I'm not a pet," Tannin snapped as she slid her breeches back over her hips. "Call me 'good girl' again and I swear I'll bite you."

"If you bite me, I won't scratch your ears," Ava teased.

"Fuck you."

"In your dreams."

"Ha. Ha."

"Also, you're welcome," Ava said putting her hands on her hips reproachfully.

"Aye, okay, thank you," Tannin muttered and stooped to help her pack all of the fur she'd brushed out into a second sack.

"All this must've really been bothering you," Ava said, gesturing at the piles.

"It was," Tannin admitted. "I could feel it, like, under my skin all itchy."

"It really doesn't hurt you to Change?"

Tannin waggled her head and sighed. "It's not...pleasant, but it's not agony or anythin'. The first time was bad, but now it's just effort, you know?"

"You are quite magnificent, though."

"What, without my clothes on? Oh my, princess, thought you weren't staring?" Tannin fluttered her eyelashes and flashed her a cheeky grin. Ava's cheeks warmed.

I was not *staring.*

"As a warg, you fool."

"Oh, I know." Tannin flexed her arms. "I'm a fearsome monster."

They finished packing up as much as they could then kicked the stray strands into a forgotten pile of sawdust.

"It won't be long until you have your own warg clothing," Ava remarked as they left the barn with the sacks slung over their shoulders. Dana's stamp was like magic in Dunoak. With her sigil on Tannin's order, her fur would be woven and tailored in record time. Whether it was out of respect or fear, Ava couldn't have said, but she grudgingly admitted that Dana definitely had a talent for getting things done.

"Mm," Tannin replied with an excited grin, hefting her sack to the other side with a grimace. "I definitely won't miss being naked all the time."

Ava couldn't help but mutter under her breath with a smirk, "Shame."

Chapter Thirteen

Sweet Like Honey

Tannin

The bundle had arrived at the keep at first light, wrapped snugly in canvas and string. Even though the seemingly never-ending lessons were taking their toll, she hadn't been able to sleep in when she knew it was arriving. When she'd peeked in to see the deep midnight black fabric, Tannin squealed in delight and raced to try it on. She hadn't expected to have fur so dark when her own hair was so light. It felt like a part of her, though. The tunic was sleeveless and fastened with a line of almost invisible, black fastenings down the front while the kilt underneath had wonderfully deep, hidden pockets. Shinier black threads picked out the edges of the material, but other than that, the entire garment was unadorned. When Tannin slipped on her new clothes, they fit like a second skin. To be fair, it pretty much was her second skin, and that idea alone made her feel weird about it. More than that though, it felt so bizarre to wear something that actually fit properly after so long in borrowed or stolen clothes. This was something that was purely hers. It hugged her body in a way nothing she'd ever worn before had.

She buckled her new belt around her middle, slots for weapons hung from her hips as well as a dagger sheath. She grinned at her reflection as she braided her hair back and thought about what Ava's reaction was going to be.

When she returned downstairs, she was surprised to find Ava already awake and halfway through her breakfast. Her reaction did not disappoint when Tannin set her own plate down and cleared her throat to get the princess' attention. Her mouth actually fell open.

"Well," said Tannin, attempting a dainty spin. "What do you think?"

"I...Well...wow." Ava laughed. "Wow is really all I can say. That is really something."

Tannin slid onto the bench beside her and stole a gulp of Ava's tea, earning herself a "tsk".

"You're up early."

"Haven't gone to bed yet."

"That's not good for you."

"Neither is that." Ava eyed Tannin's plate with distaste.

"What?" Tannin asked defensively.

"That's a lot of butter."

Tannin looked at her plate and then back at Ava.

"Mind your own business."

Tannin slathered a thick layer over her bread before pausing and brandishing her butter knife at Ava. "And not a damn word to Dana or the others about it either."

She was supposed to eat exactly what Dana told her to bulk up for physical warg training, but it was oh so easy to sneak the good stuff. As long as no one ratted her out, she was damn well going to keep doing it.

"I found an interesting section in that book I borrowed from that village—"

"That you stole from that village," Tannin corrected with a grin.

"That I borrowed with the intent of giving it back someday," Ava continued, arching her eyebrows. "Anyway, it discussed how a Remnant's abilities manifest when they come of age, and it got me thinking if that process could be refined, then that could be what was used to call forth more of that latent power."

"Uh-huh." Tannin poured a generous measure of honey over her buttered bread.

"As in the serum. Your 'warg juice', as you like to call it. Of course, it could be wildly different between Inherents and Wielders, and I've started off with my own blood, naturally. There are some compounds that increase the potency of certain mixtures. The difficulty is determining exactly which part needs to be made more potent. Do you understand?"

"Mhm," Tannin said absentmindedly licking honey from the side of her hand as it dripped down all over the place. It was runnier than she'd anticipated.

Shite.

She lapped at the honey before it could drip onto her lap, half-listening to Ava talk.

Ava faltered slightly in her explanation of elemental forces. Tannin frowned at her curiously and saw she was staring, her lips slightly parted.

Oh, I see.

She grinned and licked again. Slowly.

"Does this bother you?"

"Stop it," Ava said sternly.

"Stop what?" Tannin grinned and languidly licked along the length of her finger, giving an exaggerated moan of contentment. "What could possibly be distractin' you?"

"You're a pest."

"You're blushin'."

"Be quiet."

"Make me."

Ava let out a long breath and then the sides of her mouth quirked up in a mischievous smile.

"I think you missed a bit."

"What?"

Tannin's entire body froze as Ava grabbed hold of her hand and gently sucked the last drop of honey from her thumb. Her mouth was hot and wet, and her tongue circled the tip of her thumb teasingly for a second before she released it with a little popping sound as it left her lips.

"There," Ava said with a truly evil smirk as she stood up from the table. "Much better. See you later, Tannin."

Tannin watched her leave with her mouth hanging open. The warg-fire in her chest had sparked into life and blazed wildly as well as another heat that burned distinctly lower.

Gods damn her.

"Well, well, well." A voice from the doorway had Tannin spinning around, blushing furiously to see Flint leaning in the doorway with a cup of tea and the broadest grin possible plastered across his face.

"Not a fuckin' word," Tannin warned him.

"You two are doing it, aren't you?"

"No," she snapped, smoothing her hair back and trying to calm her thundering heartbeat.

"But you want to. And she wants to." He took a hearty slurp of tea and waggled his eyebrows. "So, why is there no 'it' occurring?"

Tannin opened her mouth to object, but he interrupted her by saying, "And before you say that's not what's going on, let me remind you that I just walked in on her sucking your finger. So, let's skip the horseshit, shall we?"

Tannin huffed and hid her burning face in her hands.

Flint slid onto the bench beside her. "Tell me the juicy details of whatever the fuck that was."

"It's…complicated?"

"Oh, come on," he groaned. "Tell me! I'm starved for gossip in this damn town and—" He frowned at her plate. "That is a lot of butter."

"Will everyone leave my breakfast alone?!"

She ended up telling Flint everything. What happened in Armodan. How they'd held each other at the tavern. And all the little comments and teases since then.

"Hm." Flint nodded sagely. "So, basically you're playing games and she's better at it than you."

"I didn't say that!"

"Well, she definitely won today, you wee flustered mess."

Tannin groaned. "Why does it have to be her?"

"Doesn't have to be." He shrugged. "We can go into the town and find you a nice wee butcher's daughter or something to have some fun." He paused thoughtfully. "What about that other warg-blood, the one with the long hair and the—" he cupped his hands in front of his chest.

Tannin smacked him. "Don't be such a pig. And no way in hell. She's awful."

She knew exactly who he was talking about. A warg-blood named Callie, who was the leader of one of the more prominent warg-blood cliques. Yes, she might have been objectively attractive, but Tannin had also seen her try to juggle severed body parts for fun.

"So, what you're saying is she's fair game?"

"Do not," Tannin warned him.

"Alright, alright. But back to my point. Fuck the princess or don't fuck the princess, but stop playing these games with her because you're hopeless and she's winning."

"Ugh."

Flint grinned. "You still look a wee bit flushed. If you're feeling under the weather, I hear honey is an excellent remedy."

Tannin glared at him as he laughed and dodged her attempt to swat him, his eyes twinkling with mischief.

"You haven't commented on my outfit," Tannin said, changing the subject. "Do I at least look like a proper warg warrior now?"

"A mini one," Flint teased.

Tannin rolled her eyes.

"Travel-sized."

"Are you done?"

"Wait, I can think of another," he said with a grin.

"Don't hurt that big brain of yours."

"Wargling."

"Fuck off."

Flint laughed. "Seriously though, you look good."

"Oh, I know." Tannin winked.

"I hear a certain princess thinks so too." Flint's grin widened and Tannin groaned.

This was far from the last she would hear of this.

Chapter Fourteen

Medical Malpractice

Ava

The sickness had started in the lower parts of the city, where the muddy sludge was always ankle deep after it rained. Some people said that rats had brought it in, some people said it was travellers from the outer villages, some said the water was poisoned – either way, within two days of the first reports of sickness came the first reports of deaths.

So far, only the old and those who were already ill had fallen, but panic was setting in fast, and every healer in the city was besieged for cures and tonics but also talismans and charms to ward off the sickness.

Somehow, word of Ava being a druid-blood had gotten out, and queues had formed outside her work room from morning until dusk until Dana ordered the gates to the keep closed and issued a statement saying that they were working on finding the source of the illness. A lot of the blame fell on the wargs. If the wargs hadn't come, we wouldn't be sick type thing. A few warg-bloods had been attacked in the street already, and although they came home unscathed, the same couldn't be said for their would-be attackers. Ava didn't know the exact details, but the rumours were gruesome enough to stop her inquiring further. In any case, every second of her time was dedicated to finding a cure for the sickness. Or at least work out what it was.

She'd treated the scores of people who had come to her workroom with compresses and teas and poultices, but they were temporary remedies and she had been almost tearful with gratitude when Dana had sent them all home. She finally had peace to properly study the samples she'd taken. Her workrooms were silent apart from the rustling of her papers and occasional clinking of jars.

BANG-BANG-BANG

Ava leapt out of her skin and cursed silently, trying to mop up the ink from the pot she'd just upended.

Maybe if I pretend I'm not here, they'll go away.

She stared at the door hopefully but again came the frantic knocks, this time accompanied by pleas.

"Hello? I need a healer. Please! I – I don't know where else to go. Please help me."

"Gods, give me strength," Ava muttered under her breath, taking a moment to steel herself before lifting the latch and cracking the door open.

"I'm not seeing any more—"

Ava's stomach lurched. The young woman must have worked at the keep, that was the only way she could have gotten to Ava's door this late, but Ava didn't recognise her tear-stained face. But that wasn't what made the air leave Ava's lungs. It was the heartbreakingly small bundle she cradled in her arms.

Wordlessly, she stepped aside, opening the door to admit the desperate woman. Words of gratitude spilled from her cracked lips as she laid her child on Ava's workbench. For one heart-stopping moment, Ava thought the child had passed already. His skin was sickly grey and mottled with an almost bruise-like purple around the eyes and mouth. Placing her palm to his chest, however, she felt the butterfly wing flutter of a weak heartbeat, and when she listened closely, she could hear the faint rattle of his breaths. Too weak to open his eyes. Too weak to cry.

"You can help him?" The maid looked at Ava with such hope in her eyes. She truly believed that the warg's druid-blood healer could save her son.

Ava forced a smile.

"I'll do what I can."

The next hour or so was a blur. She knew at a glance that it was the same illness that was ravaging the lower parts of the city but she examined the child anyway. She'd then sent the young maid home with every tea and tonic she could scrape together to fight the fever raging inside the tiny body, but inside she knew it wouldn't last. That child was as good as gone, and she could do nothing. The mother trusted her, and she could do nothing. Half the city believed in her because of her bloodline, and she could do *nothing.*

Hours after the woman had left, Ava gripped the edge of her chair until the room stopped tilting. She hadn't slept. The words in her books were starting to blur together. Books and sheafs of parchment littered the floor from where she'd searched through them in a frenzy once she was alone. Scrabbling for solutions, answers, anything. Spilled candle wax hung from the edge of the desk like icicles.

I'm useless. Completely and utterly useless.

Tears smudged the ink of her notes, and her chest felt too tight. Her breathing came as shuddering gasps.

I should never have come here. Why did I think I could do this? I can't help them. Why did I ever leave home?

Before she could fall apart completely, a sharp jaunty rap at the door made her jump.

"Ava?" Tannin's voice sailed through the door.

"Go away," she called, sniffing. "I'm busy!"

Of course, Tannin ignored her and came in anyway. She was dressed for training in fighting leathers, with her blonde hair tightly braided. Any other time, that look would have done something for Ava.

Is it morning already?

"You skipped breakfast," Tannin said setting a bowl down amongst the chaos of parchment. "You should eat. Flint told me about the wee boy. The staff are all talking about it too."

Ava nodded and a tiny sob escaped her. That was all it took for the dam to break.

"I can't do this. I'm not a healer," Ava sobbed through her hands. "A real healer would know what to do. He could die, and I don't know what to do."

"Sometimes things happen. And you are a real healer. You healed me alright." Tannin patted Ava's knee in an awkward attempt at comfort.

Ava gave her a despairing look. "You have to know that was all guesswork. I didn't have a clue what I was doing then either."

"What?"

"Tannin," Ava said exasperatedly. "I know how to make salves for cuts and bruises. Did you think I became a surgeon overnight or something? Yes, I guessed. An educated guess, but a guess nonetheless. The Belacine and your natural warg resilience did the rest. I am no healer. And people are dying because I let them think I am."

She rubbed her eyes and pinched the bridge of her nose, taking a deep breath. "I am out of my depth. So out of my depth. These people need a real healer, not a liar."

"You're not a liar," Tannin said quickly. "You're trying your best."

"You should have seen the way she looked at me," Ava whispered, tears welling in her eyes again. "She had such *hope*. She really thinks I can save him. And I just froze. I didn't know...I couldn't..."

Ava choked back another sob. "He's the same age as my little brother."

"It's okay." Tannin tried to soothe her.

"It is not okay!" Ava stood, suddenly unable to sit still, and paced. "He's going to die, Tannin!"

As she twirled to pace the length of the room again, her dress flapped. She needed sleep and a change of clothes. The apron she still wore tied around her waist was filthy and smeared with gods' only knew what.

"It's not your fault."

"I thought I could do this," Ava whispered. "But I can't."

"You just need some help."

"Oh yes," Ava muttered bitterly. "And give Dana the excuse she's been looking for to get rid of me."

Tannin didn't say anything.

"You think she's right, don't you?" Ava said accusingly. "You think I should go home."

"You said it yourself, you're out of your depth here," Tannin reasoned. "And you only came to make sure I was okay, and I'm fine now so I don't need you. You can go home if you want to. You're not obligated to stay."

"*I don't need you.*" The words were like a knife straight to the heart. Ava knew she had been allowed to stay as long as she was useful from Dana's point of view, but she'd thought that Tannin saw her as something more. As someone more.

"You don't need me," Ava echoed quietly.

"Don't take that the wrong way."

"Get out of my room, Tannin. I have work to do."

"I didn't—"

"Out!"

Even though she felt no closer to finding a solution, exhaustion eventually won that evening and Ava had dragged her weary body back to her bedroom. She had been sorely tempted to sleep in the workroom, but she needed a good night's rest if she was going to be any use. And damn them all, she would be of use.

She had been asleep as soon as her head hit the pillow, but something had woken her again. She lay still. The keep was as silent as the grave, but an urgent niggling raced up and down her spine.

Something is wrong.

Now wide awake, she slid soundlessly from her bed and tiptoed across the room, scooping up her shoes as she went. She hadn't bothered to get undressed the night before – she had been too tired.

Ava bit her lip as she peeked out into the corridor. She couldn't hear anything or see anything untoward, but her Senses were stirring up into a frenzy of alarms. She tiptoed the few steps to Tannin's door and let herself in.

A slowly breathing ball of blankets on the bed told her whatever had woken her, hadn't woken Tannin in the slightest. Ava shook her.

"Whu...?" Tannin blinked, popping a tousled head out of her nest. "Ava, what are you doin' in my room?"

"Wake up. Something's wrong!" Ava hissed with a backward glance at the door.

"With the wee boy?" Tannin murmured, rubbing her eyes.

"What?" Ava was momentarily lost. "No, someone is here that's not supposed to be here. I can feel it. It feels dangerous."

Ava let Tannin shake off the last traces of sleepiness before urging her again. Tannin gave her hand a squeeze of reassurance with a look that said she thought Ava had lost the plot.

"Okay," she mumbled. "I'll go check."

She shuffled to the door at Ava's insistence to put her ear against the old, warped wood. The bleariness left her eyes instantly.

"I hear voices," she said, pressing a finger to her lips.

Ava could only stand there wringing her hands, every nerve in her body jangling in warning.

"Oh shit," Tannin said softly.

Ava's stomach roiled. Something was very wrong.

"Ava!" Tannin whispered, grappling for her hand. "We have to get you out of here. They're here for you!"

"Me?!" Ava squeaked.

"You're a fuckin' princess, eejit. You're worth a fortune as a ransom. They're already on the stairs. I heard them say your name."

Ava looked around desperately. The window in the room was too small to squeeze through, even if it wasn't rusted shut. Tannin patted herself uselessly for pockets that weren't there. Ava twisted her fingers together. If whoever was coming up the stairs wanted her, they would find her almost immediately.

"We have to run."

Tannin nodded in agreement. "Now. Come on."

With the intruders on the stairs leading down, their only choice was upwards. Together, they raced along corridor and up the stairs just as movement appeared at the other end of the corridor. A window at the end of the landing let in a square of moonlight across the floorboards. Tannin yanked the window open, sprinkling its ledge in splinters and peered over the edge. Below was a tile-covered section of roof from a lower level. Ava could see the wheels in Tannin's brain working and realised what she was thinking in utter horror.

"We cannot jump out the window!"

"It's not that high. Come on!" Tannin urged her as she scooted up onto the window ledge.

Ava peered over the edge.

That is high. That is much, much too high.

She backed away.

"I can't," she half-mouthed, half-whispered.

"You can. Move your arse and get up here!" Tannin growled.

"There has to be another way—"

The words died in her mouth as shadowy figures appeared at the top of the stairs. The tip of a crossbow caught a glint of light as men stepped up onto the landing. They didn't look like the ruffians she had expected. They were dressed finely in travelling cloaks and she noted the shine of their boots.

"Hello there, Princess." The man she assumed was the leader, with long, iron grey hair spoke with a dangerous softness.

Tannin grasped her arm and tugged her towards the window where she was still perched on the ledge, other hand gripping the wall.

"I don't know what you think you're doin', but I'm not gonna let you just take—"

"Don't leave a witness."

Grey-hair said it so casually that the meaning didn't register with Ava until the bolt left the crossbow. It whistled as it shot across the landing.

"Missed me, you fucker!" Tannin jeered as the bolt struck the wall several inches to the right of her head.

Ava didn't have time to shout a warning before the old plaster and stone crumbled. The heavy beam at the top of the window ledge loosened and came down on Tannin's head at the same time the wall disintegrated where she gripped it.

"Tannin!" Ava screamed but it was too late. Tannin had toppled backwards out of the window in a mess of masonry and slammed into the roof below.

"NO!"

Ava was half out the ruined window after her when an arm looped around her throat from behind and yanked her back.

No! Let me go to her!

She choked and spluttered, clawing at her assailant, but her nails didn't breach the leather of his sleeve. His grip was tight. Too tight. She couldn't get any air. The landing started to go dark.

"Shhhhh," a voice in her ear said. "Go to sleep."

Chapter Fifteen

Taken

Tannin

"Is she dead?"

"Has to be right?"

Tannin let out a groan as her eyelids fluttered open.

"Aw shite. Put the poor thing out her misery."

Tannin's eyes snapped open as the guard knelt down beside her, knife in hand. She knew him as one of Dunoak's original guards who had sworn an oath to the wargs.

"Fuck off," she wheezed and swatted him away.

Every part of her body felt bruised and heavy, but she managed to push up onto her hands and knees.

She blanched when she saw the blood splattered into the mud. The heavy beam from the window lay beside her along with other debris. Her head was pounding, and touching it sent spasms of pain through her skull. Breathing hurt. She suspected she might have broken something in the fall too.

The fall. From the window...Oh gods. Ava!

Tannin twisted to look up. Daylight.

She must have been unconscious for hours, her body directing all of its energy into patching her up fully. Well, almost fully. She felt thoroughly battered, but she managed to at least get to her feet. The mercenaries that had taken the princess must've thought she was dead.

Oh, they're gonna wish I was dead.

Out of the corner of her eye, Tannin saw the guard trying to sneak away. She seized him by his tunic. Sketchiness rolled off him in waves and he anxiously looked anywhere but at her.

"Where. Is. She?" she snarled, letting her teeth grow into fangs. She didn't even have to try. If anything, she had to hold back from Changing completely.

"Where's who?"

"Men broke in here last night and took her. You know something. I can smell it on you. Where. Is. She?"

He was so much taller than her, but her grip on his tunic dragged him to her level as she growled in his face.

"I..."

"Do not even think about lying to me," Tannin whispered in a deadly calm. Her control was a trembling thread, and from the look on the man's face, he knew it too.

"They said no one would get hurt!"

"Who?" Tannin growled.

"I don't know any names!" he blabbered. "I just know of them. The villages 'round here pay them for protection and the like. They just paid me to...to..."

"To what? Speak up! I'm gettin' impatient."

"They're dangerous."

"I'm dangerous," Tannin replied, baring her sharpened teeth. "What did they pay you to do?"

"To leave the side gate open and...and to put a silencing rune on the guest wing."

"A what?" Tannin twisted to look up at the wreckage of the wall where she'd come tumbling down with the entire window. No one had heard the racket. She shook her aching head, trying to sew together her thoughts into some sort of coherent order.

"How many men?"

"I don't know!"

Tannin narrowed her eyes.

"Maybe eight here last night! In total, I don't know!"

"Where are they takin' her?"

"They didn't tell me more than I needed to know! Please!"

"Tell me somethin' useful!"

The man stuttered for a moment and then exclaimed, "I know where they'll likely stop to rest! There ain't many roads out of here, and if they're wanting to keep away from the rest of the travellers, then there's a place!"

"Where?"

"About a day and a half's hard ride. Nor'west. Around the swamps. Path links back up with the western roads later on, but most people take the safer route. There's a valley where there's a stream and good shelter. Best bet they'll have gone there. I swear that's all I know! I swear it! Please don't tell them I said anything!"

"If I don't get her back in one piece," Tannin hissed through her fangs, her face so close to his that they could have almost brushed noses. "I will hunt you down, and those arseholes will be the least of your worries. I promise you that."

Not wanting to waste any more time, Tannin reluctantly let him go unscathed and raced back into the keep. Thinking of Ava's terrified expression when she'd seen those mercenaries helped push down the pain. Tannin dressed faster than she ever had and was back thundering down the stairs in less than two minutes, smacking straight into Flint as she careened around the landing. He swore and frantically tried to stop his toast sliding off the plate he was carrying.

"Ava's been taken," Tannin grunted as she pushed past him on the stairs, still buckling her belt around her waist as she jumped the last two.

"What?!"

"Ava. She's been kidnapped. I'm gonna go get her back."

"Alone? Tannin, go tell Dana and get help!"

"That's where I'm goin'. Gonna bring a goddam warg army down on them for taking my princess."

"Dana! DANA!" Tannin barged into her room without knocking.

Dana was apparently a light sleeper and did not take well to being woken up because Tannin quickly found herself flat on the floor with a dagger at her throat.

"Ow! For fuck's sake, Dana. It's me! Ava's been kidnapped. We need to go get her. Get off me and quit messing around!"

"Who? What?" Dana re-sheathed her dagger, blinking sleep from her jet black warg eyes. "Tannin, I could've killed you! Wait, are you bleeding?"

She looked in alarm at the dried blood in Tannin's hair, but Tannin waved her off.

"Ava," Tannin repeated impatiently. "Give me wargs and weapons. I'm goin' after them."

"No, you absolutely are not. How long ago did they take her? Horses? *What happened to your head?*"

"I don't know. A few hours? And aye, I think they had horses."

"In a few hours, they could be anywhere."

"So, we find them," Tannin said in a growl.

"You mean to tell me that after months of you whining that you hate her and you want her dead, you now want me to send valuable resources to go find her?"

"Aye," Tannin said putting her hands on her hips. "And I never said I wanted her dead."

"They're most likely taking her back to Armodan anyway." The tension was leaking from Dana's shoulders, and she stretched to pop her spine. "That's who will pay money for her. She'll be home in no time. I can't spare the resources right now. I'll send word to the scouts to be on the lookout."

"Are you serious?"

"They won't hurt her. She's valuable." Dana turned back to the table, muttering under her breath, "One less problem for me to think about."

"You wanted her gone." Tannin pointed an accusing finger.

"If I had gotten rid of her, I would have sent her home to barter a good relationship with Armodan. Maybe as an apology for all the messes *you* made there. Not have her hauled off in the middle of the night without so much as a single coin for the trouble."

Tannin blinked in surprise at Dana's sudden aggression.

"Think next time before you accuse me of actual crimes, *novice*, because I might not be so forgiving."

"I have to get her back."

"You will do no such thing. I'll send word to Adair and the rangers. They'll look for her, but if they're taking her home, then there's not much we can do." Dana shrugged and then narrowed her eyes. "You are to stay here. You are too much of a target yourself. Hear me? I expressly forbid you from leaving this keep."

Tannin clenched her teeth.

Dana returned her glare as she stalked to the door and yelled, "Lachlan!"

"What are you doin'?" Tannin watched in dismay as the warg answered Dana's summons almost instantly.

"You called?" he said in honeyed-tones, looking past Dana at Tannin curiously.

"Tannin here is thinking about doing something very dangerous and stupid. Make sure she doesn't."

"What kind of stupid?"

"Just make sure she doesn't leave the keep."

"If you don't let me go, you're gonna regret it," Tannin hissed. She didn't add the "when I'm in charge" she was thinking about and was glad she didn't when Dana's eyes once more turned inky black.

"Do not presume to threaten me," Dana growled at the same time Lachlan bared his teeth. "You haven't got any idea—"

Dana stopped herself and took a deep breath. Her eyes returned to grey.

"I'm going to my study," Dana muttered, suddenly looking very tired. "Stay with her. Make sure she doesn't leave the keep," she said to Lachlan as she passed.

As soon as Dana left the room, Tannin turned to Lachlan and raised an eyebrow.

"You think you're gonna stop me?"

He frowned at her, folding his arms across his chest. "Make no mistake, heir or no heir, I will lock you up if I have to. Dana's word is law."

Tannin glanced from him to the door. She had enough space to get to it.

"You'll have to catch me first."

"Don't even think about—!"

She ran.

Tannin darted out of the room and slammed the door behind her. She grabbed a spear from a coat of armour, snapped it and jammed it through the rings of the door handles as they rattled from Lachlan's pounding on the other side.

"I'm not sorry!" Tannin yelled as she turned on her heel and sprinted. That door wouldn't hold him for long.

"What happened?" Flint yelled as Tannin leapt down the stairs. He'd clearly been waiting for her.

"Tell Dana," Tannin mocked. "What a fucking great idea."

"What did she say?"

"She said she's on her own. I'm gonna go get her back."

"How the fuck are you going to do that?"

"I'm a big scary monster, I'll figure it out. I need you to—"

Crashing sounds announced that the spear had been no match for warg strength.

"Flint!"

"Got it! Slow him down! Just go!"

"I'll bring her back!" Tannin yelled over her shoulder as she charged off in the direction of Dunoak's main gate. "I promise!"

"Help her."

I promised.

Chapter Sixteen

Damsel in Distress

Ava

"Touch that again and I'll break those fingers for you."

Damn it.

Ava quickly balled her hands into fists. She hadn't been trying to undo the knot that led from the saddle to her bound wrists, just get a better look for when she did try and undo it. She didn't think Grey-hair could see her fiddling.

It had been a long time since Ava had ridden a horse. She had always enjoyed it as a child, but her current experience was souring her memories of it. They were still riding uncomfortably fast, even hours after leaving Dunoak, and she was constantly bumping into the mercenary at her back. His burly arms grasping the reins on either side of her were as much stopping her from leaping from the horse as her actual bindings. Not that she would have leapt from the horse. She wasn't that desperate. Yet. She would bide her time and escape when the right opportunity presented itself.

And redeem myself for getting caught so bloody easily.

Ava clenched her fists against the bitterness she felt. All those manoeuvres and stances and tricks she'd learned from damp days in her hidden crypt training with Attilo, and she'd used none of it. She'd been so groggy and disoriented when she regained consciousness that she was on the horse with a rope around her wrists and a rag in her mouth before she'd even worked out what was happening. A cloak had been draped around her shoulders with the hood pulled up, and a threat hissed in her ear that if she tried to signal for help, she'd be responsible for her would-be rescuer's death.

They'd been riding at break-neck speed for hours but finally slowed to allow the wheezing horses some respite. Ava hoped they were stopping and she could get down for a while, but it seemed her captors were determined to keep moving.

"Here," Grey-hair said gruffly. He untied the gag and tugged it out of her mouth to offer her a waterskin.

She instinctively tried to reach for it and grunted in annoyance when she couldn't lift her hands. As humiliating as it was, she had no choice but to let him tip water into her parched mouth for her. Eating the morsel of bread from his hand that he offered her next was, however, a step too far and she shook her head in disgust.

"My friend," she said, turning as much as she could to face him. "The girl who fell out of the window. Is she okay?"

He chuckled. A low rumble against her back.

"I'd say you've other things to worry about, princess."

"But—"

"Enough."

Ava swallowed.

Tannin is made of tough stuff, but that fall...she could be really hurt. If she is, it's my fault. Oh gods, I hope she's okay.

Ava pushed thoughts of Tannin out of her mind. Worry wouldn't help either of them. She would escape and find her way back to her. Somehow.

"Where are you taking me?"

"Be quiet."

"Whoever is paying you—"

"You gonna pay more? A runaway princess without a coin to her name? Or are the wargs gonna pay to get you back? Doubt they care much for Brochlands' royalty."

Ava fell silent. Dana certainly wouldn't pay her ransom. Would she send a rescue party for her, though? She doubted it. Would Tannin come for her? Possibly. They'd been friendly and flirting, yes, but that didn't mean Tannin would save her. After all, Ava hadn't saved her back in Armodan. Guilt wormed its way up her throat along with a little bile. She could never make that right. And that was even if Tannin was in any state to come after her.

She could have broken bones, she could be unconscious, she could be...could be... No! She's fine. She has to be.

Ava forced herself to focus.

She could make a few guesses at who had hired the mercenaries. Not her father though – he would have tried to coax her home. She was actually surprised and, yes, also a little hurt that he hadn't already tried. Maybe he didn't want her back after all. No, this abduction in the middle of the night was something more sinister. She had to escape before it was too late, but in the meantime, she was stuck in a saddle with a dangerous mercenary. She shifted in discomfort. Her backside was getting numb, and the hilt of Grey-hair's dagger was digging into the small of her back.

Good gods, I hope that's a dagger.

"Wakey, wakey, princess"

Ava jerked upright at the cruel pinch to her side.

"Ouch!"

Exhaustion had gotten the better of her, and she'd been dozing with her head lolling back onto Grey-hair's hardened leather breastplate.

"Brute," she muttered under her breath, but her irritation was soon replaced by anticipation. They were stopping.

Grey-hair passed the reins off to another of his cohort before dismounting. The man, who was younger but just as equally well-armoured and armed as her riding companion, leered at Ava as if daring her to try and somehow steal the horse from him.

As if I could.

She held his gaze disdainfully until Grey-hair unfastened her from the saddle and lifted her down. She staggered as her feet hit the hard ground. He steadied her before barking orders to get a fire started. His grip on her arm was loose, and without thinking she ripped herself free. He glowered at her as she stumbled away from him, skirting his attempt to seize her again.

A looming shadow told her she had, however, backed straight into the arms of another mercenary, who caught a fistful of her cloak and put a stop to her ill-thought-out escape attempt. Ava cursed.

I should have waited.

"Nice try, princess." The grey-haired man cocked his head and reached out to finger the small pouch that Ava wore around her neck. She usually kept it tucked down the front of her dress, but it must have come loose during the excitement of her capture.

"What's this then?"

"Don't touch that," Ava snapped, trying to take it back, but he swatted her hands away.

"Somethin' valuable?" he teased.

"It's worth nothing to you."

"We'll see about that." He grinned nastily and jerked the pouch so hard that the string snapped.

"Give that back!" She again tried to grab it awkwardly with her hands still tied together.

He held it out of her reach and nodded at the other man to hold her while he examined the little pouch.

"Give it back! It's worth nothing!" Ava pleaded, trying to pull away.

"What the hell?" Grey-hair had opened the pouch and peered inside. "Dirt?"

He dipped a fingertip into the pouch and then touched it to his tongue. He made a face.

"Ash?" He gripped Ava by the chin, interrupting her protests. "Why? What's it worth?"

"It's nothing." She glared at him furiously. "Give it back."

He held the pouch up in front of Ava's face and then wiggled it, threatening to tip out its contents.

"No!" Ava howled in anguish and thrashed. Grey-hair watched her in amusement and then righted the little bag.

How dare he, how dare he, HOW DARE HE?!

Ava lashed out with her feet to catch him hard in the shins. He grunted in pain. Then he chuckled. For a moment, Ava thought that was going to be it, but at a nod from their leader, one of the other men who had sauntered over to see what was going on, drew back his fist and hit her straight in the gut. She doubled over, wheezing. She clenched her fists so tightly that her knuckles turned white. Her eyes watered.

Grey-hair tossed the pouch in the air lightly and caught it again. Ava choked back a sob, whether from being punched or from the loss of Attilo's ashes, she couldn't have said. Both hurt.

"If you behave, you can have it back when we part ways, Your Highness," he said, smiling nastily as he gave a little bow before barking at one of the men to get the princess secured.

Ava didn't reply. She'd also stopped struggling. She had to get that pouch back. She had to.

I cannot lose him again.

Chapter Seventeen

A Knight in Furry Armour

Tannin

Even though it was still midmorning, thick dark clouds obscured the sun. The sky was grey and bleak and Tannin could taste impending rain on the air as her tongue lolled from her fanged mouth and she hopped from one solid-looking patch to another. She'd given up trying to carefully plan her path in favour of a trial and error approach. In her warg-form, even if she did misjudge it, she could usually make another bound before the mud really got a hold of her paws. Some parts had no firm ground at all, and it was all she could do to keep moving. If she paused even for a second, she would sink. It felt like every step she took was another opportunity for the swamp to claim her, and it was a challenge it took on with relish.

She'd taken a shortcut that should have, in theory, taken her directly where she wanted to go, but she'd found herself up to her knees in mud, cursing the entire kingdom of Woodren and its stupid swamps. A thousand tiny paths wound through the tangled, disgusting mess, but they were bordered by deceptively deep mud pools that gave way under the slightest weight. She'd been lucky and only sunk in a little. She shouldn't have doubted the stories they told in Dunoak that one wrong move and you'd drown in the murk. As it was, she hadn't drowned, but she lamented the state that her beautiful, black fur had been in. Her human form wasn't much better, but at least the muck would camouflaged her.

She was trying unsuccessfully to persuade her filthy hair from sticking to her face when she heard something through the trees that wasn't a bird or a mouse or any other forest creature. She poked her head out the top and cocked her head to listen again.

The soft rhythmic pounding of horses' hooves.

"Gotcha," Tannin grinned as she scrambled over her rocky shelter and darted into the thicker trees towards the sound.

Flat on her belly and hidden in the weeds, Tannin crawled as close as she dared to the campsite under the cover of darkness. This site was perfectly nestled in a small patch of forest, hidden from any well-trodden paths, with a tinkling of running water coming from nearby. It was isolated enough that anyone screaming for help wouldn't be heard. In other words, it was the perfect hideout if you'd just kidnapped a very valuable princess and needed a place to rest.

She'd almost given herself away when that arsehole had punched Ava in the stomach. She'd taken a deep breath and tried to calm the urge to Change and rip them all to pieces. She knew they needed Ava alive and probably reasonably unharmed, but still. They had hurt her. She didn't like Ava, didn't need her, still wanted her to go home. But the idea of her hurt was more painful than that fall out the window had been. Tannin chewed her lip.

"Help her."

Those were the last words Attilo ever said, and I'll be damned if I let him down.

Waiting to make her move was torture, but the element of surprise was likely going to be her best weapon. The men clearly weren't worried about anyone coming after them. They even felt confident enough to light a fire and were sitting around it, eating and talking in low voices.

And there was Ava, sat with her back against a thick tree. A rope looped around a branch kept her bound hands pinned above her head, and a thick rag covered her eyes. Rage twisted and bubbled in Tannin's belly at the sight.

How do I get to her? What do I do? Think, eejit, think!

Tannin thudded her forehead against the ground to try and summon a semblance of a plan. Stealth was all well and good, but what the bloody hell was she going to do with it?

Tannin's eyes fell on the horses.

That could be a plan...

The men were relaxed but kept up a regular patrol as the night drew on and their small fire barely permeated the gloom.

When the night was at its darkest, Tannin made her move. She slid a little further through the grass, and then froze again as Ava's head snapped up and she looked around blindly, tugging at her ropes. Tannin cursed silently. Of course Ava could Sense her.

Don't you dare give me away.

Ava's sudden fidgeting didn't go unnoticed. One of the patrolling mercenaries stomped towards her. Tannin couldn't help but snarl through her teeth as he nudged Ava in the ribs with the toe of his boot.

"Settle down."

With all eyes on Ava, probably expecting her to attempt an escape, Tannin darted to where the horses were tethered and sliced the reins.

"Go!" she hissed in a frantic whisper, but the horses just stomped nervously and swished their tails.

"Oh, you stupid beasts! Fine." She pulled the nearest horse around to face her and let the heat from her warg-fire rise. Her eyes stung a little as they Changed while the lengthening fangs caused her jaw to twinge. A low and threatening growl rumbled from her throat. The horse whinnied in fright. Its panic spread to the rest, and soon, they were bumping into each other and shrieking as they jostled to get away.

Tannin released the reins and dived back into the weeds as the shouts from the men rang out.

As expected, they were panicking as the horses trampled erratically through the trees. They needed those horses. Tannin watched in satisfaction as almost all of them banded together to try and corral the terrified beasts. Almost all of them.

Dammit.

The grey-haired leader had stayed with Ava, hand on his sword, glaring into the shadows.

I might actually have to kill him.

Tannin's teeth again sunk into her lower lip. Sure, she'd killed people before and she'd live with that guilt forever, but she'd never planned to kill any of them. Actually planning it was an entirely different beast altogether, and the thought of it alone made her queasy. It felt like a line she didn't want to cross. She edged closer, keeping to the shadows.

SNAP.

He whirled and locked eyes with her as she was mid-step, the traitorous twig still underfoot.

He opened his mouth to yell while reaching for his blade. She was out of time. She pounced before she'd even fully decided to do it and knocked him backwards. Her claws were out and jammed into his throat before he hit the ground. His eyes bulged. Wet, gurgling noises came from his mouth along with a spurt of blood. He pawed at her hand uselessly.

"I'm sorry," Tannin whispered as she disentangled herself from him. "Sort of."

Tannin swallowed the wave of nausea that threatened to overwhelm her as the light left his eyes and he slumped to the ground. Blood pooled in the dirt. It was warm and wet on her hands.

"Tannin?"

The voice was barely above a whisper, but it was enough to jolt her back to reality. She grabbed the knife from the dead man's belt. He hadn't even managed to draw it. A small leather pouch lay beside him, having fallen from his pocket as he crumpled. Tannin scooped it up.

"Tannin?" Ava's voice was more insistent this time, and she yanked at her bindings.

"I'm here," Tannin said quickly, kneeling to tug off the blindfold. Ava blinked at her with red-rimmed eyes. "You okay?"

"Yes...no...I'm fine. I just..." Ava shook her head and cleared her throat before widening her eyes at Tannin in dismay. "Oh, please tell me you didn't come alone."

"Do you want me to lie to you?" Tannin reached up to slice the rope holding Ava's hands above her head, and she groaned as she brought them down.

"You are a fool."

"I'm gonna pretend you said thank you like a normal fuckin' person."

Tannin gently took Ava's hands and started sawing through the ropes tying them together. The whinnying of horses and shouts in the dark made Ava startle, and Tannin's knife slipped onto bare skin.

Tannin hissed and daubed at it with Ava's sleeve as blood beaded, but Ava seemed to hardly notice the scratch along the back of her thumb. Underneath the rope, her wrists were rubbed raw. Tannin grimaced. She had the sudden strong urge to kiss the chafed skin better, but she stopped at the last second, giving herself a shake.

Ava gasped as Tannin pulled her to her feet. "You fell out the window!"

"Aye. I'm alright though," Tannin said wearily. "We've got to get of here."

"You're not alright. Look at you!" Ava touched her fingertips to the blood that still clung to Tannin's mud-matted hair. "You're absolutely filthy."

"Not exactly currently my most pressing issue right now, princess," Tannin replied testily. "Move! We've got to get out of here."

"I—oh, wait!" Ava darted back into the circle of light from the campsite. She ducked down next to bedroll and snatched a leather satchel from the ground.

"What the hell are you doin'?"

"I want to know who these bastards are working for," Ava replied, patting the bag. "There are scrolls in here. And I need to find my—"

Whatever Ava was going to say was interrupted by a furious yell from the other side of the campsite.

"Ah, fuck. Run!"

Chapter Eighteen

Old Nightmares

Ava

"Where the fuck do you think you're going?" The question was accompanied by the schikkk of a sword leaving its sheath.

"She's here!" the man bellowed.

"Shit, Ava, run!"

But Ava was frozen by the predatory look in the mercenary's eyes as he emerged from behind the leafy bush that had obscured him. Again, everything that Attilo had ever taught her was gone from her mind. She was like a rabbit caught in an archer's sights.

"Dammit, Ava!" Tannin grabbed her hand. "Run. Run now!"

Shouts to not let them get away rang out from all sides as Tannin sprinted, hauling Ava along with her, into the trees.

Even with her short legs, Tannin kept the pace brutally fast until they were well under the cover of the trees. They were outpacing their pursuers for now, even if Ava was panting wildly. She felt sure that if Tannin let go of her hand, she'd collapse in an instant.

The ground under their feet was treacherously uneven and almost every stumble had Ava's pounding heart leaping into her mouth. A twisted root snagged Tannin's foot. She probably would have recovered if she hadn't been towing Ava along with her. They fell together in a tumbled heap.

Ava gave a pained groan. Tannin hushed her and cocked her head, listening. How she could hear anything over Ava's laboured breathing was a mystery.

"I think...we lost them," Ava gasped.

"I'll know for sure if you shut up for a minute."

Shouts echoed in the distance.

"I think we're alright, but we can't stop."

Ava nodded her agreement. They set off again, this time creeping in the undergrowth instead of crashing through it. She had a vague sense of the direction they were going, but the terrain was getting denser and wilder the further they went.

"You have any idea where we are?" Tannin asked out of the corner of her mouth.

"No," Ava replied. "Gods, you are such a fool for coming alone."

Tannin glowered at her. "Don't you dare have a go at me. I did the right thing."

"I didn't say it wasn't the *right* thing, and I am grateful, but there's no question about it being the *stupid* thing."

"So, I'm stupid then. Ground-breaking news."

"You could have died."

"So could you."

"Honestly, if you would just—" Dread crept down the back of Ava's neck. "Something's wrong."

"Oh really?" Tannin made no attempt to hide her sarcasm. "Is it maybe the heavily armed angry mercenaries that are after us?"

They reached a slight clearing amongst the dense trees and shrubs where moonlight trickled in, giving them a little light.

"Tannin, stop." Ava peered into the dark shadows between the trees, twisting her hands. Her Senses scraped at her almost painfully, like something was trying to escape from inside her spine. "There's something really wrong. I can Sense it."

"That's wonderfully specific," Tannin said under her breath as she stomped further into the undergrowth.

When she looked back, probably to snap at Ava to keep moving, her expression changed from annoyance to alarm, and she indicated frantically for Ava to get down. Ava dropped to her knees and glanced back over her shoulder. The glow of the mercenaries' torches lit up the foliage. They were closer than she had realised. Closer than Tannin had realised too, clearly. Likely trying to sneak up on them and catch them unawares when they inevitably had to rest. Ava crawled to where Tannin was waving her into a thick patch of bracken.

Tannin swore in a continuous stream under her breath and then her mud-streaked face paled. Her eyes went wide.

"What is it?" Ava hissed, trying to make herself as small as possible. Spindly twigs stabbed at her legs as she crouched in the undergrowth.

Thud, thud, thud.

For a second, Ava convinced herself that the rhythmic pounding was her own pulse. Just for a second. And then her blood ran cold.

Drums.

"Ava." Tannin's voice was detached and mechanical. She still hadn't blinked. "We have to hide."

She seized the princess by the arm and dragged her to the foot of a sturdy-looking tree. "Climb. Now."

"Climb? Have you gone mad?"

"The drums. Can you hear them? I've heard those before. It's redcaps. So fuckin' climb or prepare to die horribly."

At the look on Tannin's face, Ava didn't argue and reached up to grasp the first of the low branches.

Tannin shimmied up the trunk, clearly fuelled by panic and adrenaline, while Ava's slick palms struggled to grip the branches. She'd never climbed a tree in her life. Noticing her plight, Tannin reached back with an arm that was far too muscular for her small frame and hauled her a few feet higher. Warg muscles. Ava silently made a note to ask her more about how that worked when they weren't imminently about to be murdered. They stopped climbing when they reached a point in the bough where they could both perch out of sight. Ava made the mistake of looking down. Dizziness threatened to overwhelm her, and she quickly closed her eyes, pressing her forehead against the rough bark.

Her would-be kidnappers crashed into the clearing from all directions. They'd circled around strategically, and the two of them would have been surrounded. Trapped like animals.

"Find her!" one of them barked. It seemed they had gotten over the death of their leader fairly quickly and a new one had already sprung forth. And the fool was entirely oblivious to the impending danger. The drums were getting louder.

Ava trembled but tried to stay as still as possible as the mercenaries beat at the undergrowth and called cajolingly out for her, alternating between threats and promises. Eventually though, the drums were loud enough for even the dullest of ears to hear. Ava knew little about redcaps, but she knew that if you were close enough to hear the drums, you were far too close. The leaves around them shuddered to the beat, and the men's menacing calls shifted to sounds of alarm.

The rhythm of the drums came from all sides and closed in on the space steadily, hungrily, until all at once, it stopped. Shouts rang out from the men to form a circle and they stood back-to-back, peering into the impenetrable blackness with their weapons poised and ready as the oppressive silence drew on.

A twig snap.

A leaf rustle.

The stealthy sounds of movement encroached from all around.

"They're everywhere," Ava's said in a high-pitched, terror-filled whisper.

Tannin pressed a shaky finger to her lips.

A heartbeat. Two.

And then the redcaps attacked.

It was impossible to count how many there were. Grey skin stretched tightly over jutting bone, and blue-black lips peeled back over snarling howling maws. Ava got glimpses of thin limbs and scraps of leather and what looked like bone as the creatures roiled over each other in the flickering light of their primitive torches, clamouring to reach up and swipe at the mercenaries with sharp nails. The drums started again, this time fast and frantic as the creatures whooped and howled and hissed. They were either fighting or dancing – she couldn't tell – but they were a mass of blurred movement, too swift for any of the blades to hit their mark.

When the beasts hefted their torches high, Ava saw the creatures clearly for the first time and instantly wished that she hadn't.

They weren't big, but with so many of them, it didn't matter in the slightest. They had horribly wide, black eyes and wore crude armour that seemed to be exclusively made from dead things. One had a ribcage lashed around his bony torso, and although Ava hoped it was from a deer or some kind of animal, it looked distinctly human. Others wore animal skulls on their faces like masks or had disjointed looking vertebrae sloping down their backs and swinging like tails. Most held some sort of spear or club. They jabbed, batted, bit and scratched at the men with wild abandon.

Once, during one of her schemes, she had been out in the city on one of her less savoury errands with Attilo and had seen a churning mass of rats in an alley strip a dog carcass of meat in mere minutes. These things gave off the same kind of energy. A hungry, manic swarm. Over their snarls and growls, she could still hear the hysterical screaming of the men as they fell one by one.

The one or two that were still alive after the initial onslaught cried out as the redcaps gleefully dragged them into the depths of the forest.

Tannin and Ava clung to each other as silence once again settled.

They slid, wordlessly down from the tree.

"We go that way," Tannin whispered pointing in the opposite direction to where the redcaps had gone.

Ava nodded emphatically.

Chapter Nineteen

New Nightmares

Tannin

"No, no, no!" Ava actually stomped her foot when they ended up back in the blood-slick clearing.

"We must've gotten turned around."

"No! We went southeast. I'm...I'm sure of it." Ava squinted upwards at the sky to study the stars. "No, that's not right. How did we...?"

"Ugh, I bet it's a trick. Like to make people get lost on purpose so they can eat us." Tannin groaned in despair. "We're gonna go round in circles forever until we die."

"Don't be dramatic." Ava pinched the bridge of her nose and took a deep breath. "If it is a trick, then we have to go deeper to get out."

"You don't mean..."

"Yes. I do. We follow them. Find a weapon."

"Will these do?" Tannin quipped, lengthening her claws.

Ava didn't reply but took a deep breath and started down the trail of carnage.

"You're right. I'm a fool. I'm never doing this again," Tannin said after a while as they crept through the tangled undergrowth. They knew they were on the right path by following the deep scratches in the tree trunks and occasional shoe or scrap of torn, bloody clothing left behind on the thorns. "Next time you get kidnapped, you're on your own, princess."

"Be quiet! Look."

They huddled together behind a low, stone wall and peeked out over the top.

The remains of stone structures that stuck up like broken teeth from the well-trodden ground suggested that dwellings had stood here once, but they had been defeated by time and enveloped by the forest.

The redcaps had certainly utilised the space. Animal bones were woven together with reeds and hung like garlands from the trees where carved wooden figures leered from the shadows. A pile of dead wood, interspersed with feathers and dead flowers, stood proud like an altar. Blood glistened wetly on top.

And, of course, the bodies. Dozens of bodies in various states of decomposition lay strewn around the lair. Some had been stripped of flesh from neck to navel, leaving grotesque, half-skeletal forms with slack mouths, widely staring eyes and empty ribcages where organs had been ripped out. Others had missing limbs or seemingly random gaping holes. Some had been skinned. Tannin sincerely hoped they were already dead when the mutilations had occurred. The stench of death and decay and fear was almost suffocating. This was a place of horrors.

"I read...but I didn't think that...Oh gods...oh gods. They're primally spiritual. I think these are sacrifices. If they find us—"

Aya was being far too loud, the hysteria in her voice almost building to a shriek. Tannin spun and covered her mouth.

"You have to be quiet. Okay? We're gettin' out of here, but you need to keep it together. Can you do that for me?" Tannin whispered desperately. Ava's breathing was still far too fast, but she nodded and stayed silent as Tannin removed her hand.

They both jumped as one of the corpses groaned.

One of the man's legs had been hacked off. He was slumped motionless against one of the stones. The ragged end of his leg was blackened char, and a smoky smell hung in the air. His stump had been crudely cauterized, and that was the only reason he hadn't bled to death yet, but he wasn't far from it.

Ava was trembling as she stared at the man. Her hand shook as she picked up a broken bone from the ground. It was splintered into a sharp point. Tannin knew what she was thinking instantly.

Mercy.

"Ava, wait."

Tannin tried to say that she would do it. Ava didn't have to stain her hands with killing when Tannin's were already bloody with it, but Ava moved quicker than she expected. She didn't hesitate.

She strode to the man, stooped and jammed the bone into his throat all in one swift motion. Blood spouted from his neck as she pulled the bone out and his head drooped silently.

Tannin stared at Ava in shocked amazement. "You didn't have to."

Ava's reply was cut off as an inhumanly, high-pitched screech of fury pealed across the macabre circle. Tannin swore. They'd been seen.

"We've got to go! We've got to go now!"

The redcaps took up a rapid drum beat from somewhere disturbingly close but out of sight. Whooping howls swept through the forest around them, but Ava was back to her frozen, startled rabbit state. Tannin shook her hard.

"Which way is southeast? WHICH WAY, AVA?"

Ava, still with the glassy, far-away look in her eyes, pointed.

"For fuck's sake, Ava, this is not the time for you to have a break-down! Here!" Tannin pushed the pouch she'd taken from the grey-haired man's pocket into Ava's hands. She made a small, whimpering noise in her throat and clutched it to her chest.

Tannin Changed, grabbed the back of Ava's dress in her teeth and swung her up onto her back. The princess screamed as she was thrown, but a tug on her fur told Tannin that she had at least come to her senses enough to be holding on.

Ideally, Tannin would have started off slow, but when the first crude spear slammed into a tree, inches from her head, she bolted. Arrows and spears followed, but even the frenzied goblins couldn't keep up with the speed of a warg.

Tannin ran until she physically could not take another step.

She staggered to an exhausted halt and tilted to indicate to Ava to get down then shrunk back to her usual self in a disturbing series of cracks and popping of bone that she'd come to expect.

"Break," she rasped as she doubled over with her hands on her knees, trying to suck air into her lungs.

Ava clutched her arms around herself. She opened her mouth to say something, but no sound came out and she closed it again. Her lip trembled. She clung to the little pouch like her life depended on it, but when Tannin regained her breath and tried to go to her, she shook her off brusquely.

"Right." Ava put her hands on her hips and was all business in the blink of an eye. "We need to find some fresh water."

She strode to look out at the forest beyond, but before she was out of reach, Tannin caught her hand and squeezed.

"Hey. Are you okay?"

Ava exhaled slowly. "I have to be."

"I was watching. I saw what happened with your pouch so I took it back after I killed that arsehole." Tannin indicated to where it usually rested against Ava's chest. "It's Attilo's ashes, isn't it?"

Ava nodded wordlessly.

"I'm sorry."

"I wanted to scatter them somewhere nice. I was waiting for somewhere that felt right. Somewhere he would've liked." Ava's voice cracked. "There's not much left..."

"We can find somewhere to scatter them together. When we get home," Tannin said gently. "But first, where the fuck are we?"

They found a stream without much difficulty. The previous night's rain had little rivulets of water running from all directions downwards, so they simply followed them. They stumbled their way through the thick foliage until they could hear the unmistakable sound of running water. They both drank deeply, and Tannin dunked her whole head in the stream, shaking her wet hair from her face and spraying Ava with water.

On Ava's intuition, they followed the rushing waters, taking detours where the bank gave way to treacherously wobbly rocks and forcing their way through the wild plant life that choked the forest floor.

Tannin gallantly offered Ava a hand to climb over a particularly slippery patch of knotted tree roots. Ava hesitated.

"Take my hand before you break your leg."

"I can manage."

"I'm not carrying you if you do break your leg," Tannin said stubbornly. "You can drag your sorry arse home."

Ava scowled but grabbed her hand, letting Tannin steady her until they were back on firmer ground.

Ava cleared her throat. "Thank you."

Tannin smiled and nudged her with her shoulder. "I promised Attilo I'd take care of you. I don't need him scowling at me from the great beyond. Or from in that wee pouch."

"I miss him." Ava's fingers traced the shape of the pouch under the fabric of her dress.

"I do too."

They carried on in silence.

"You know, with that man back there...I would have done it. You didn't have to."

"I know."

"And it was definitely a mercy kill. Like you shouldn't feel bad, but if you do, then I get it. It's a big deal to take a life. I mean—"

"Tannin," Ava said seriously and turned to face her. "That wasn't the first life I've taken. I'm fine."

She tried to turn around and walk on.

"Woah, wait a minute. You can't just say that then walk away." Tannin scrambled after her. "Story time, princess."

"Well, I didn't kill anyone directly, but I did pronounce the sentence, so I may as well have done."

"Why did you do that?"

Ava let out a heavy sigh. "It was a lesson. A rite of passage. My brothers learned the same way I did what it meant to rule. To have the power of life or death over someone."

"Sentencing someone isn't the same as—"

Ava spoke over her.

"I had to look them in the eye when I said it. To know what I was dooming them to. When it was my turn, my father told me that I could uphold the law, or I could put my feelings first and show the world that I was corruptible. That I put myself above the law and above the kingdom. Above its people."

Tannin gave a low whistle.

"I had to." Ava paused, her blue eyes locking onto Tannin's brown ones. "It was a hard lesson to learn, but one that a princess must."

Tannin broke the eye contact. "Life of a royal, huh?"

Ava made a noncommittal sound in the back of her throat, then stopped and turned to face her.

"Tannin, what I did to you—"

"You had to?"

"I shouldn't have."

"No, you shouldn't have." Tannin squinted at her. "But you did say you were gonna let me out eventually. Out of curiosity, how long were you plannin' on leavin' me there?"

Ava gave her a long look. "I...hadn't decided," she admitted. "I really messed it up. And now you're banished."

"Meh. Banishment isn't so bad. I do miss Armodan, though. I miss not doing bloody training every day."

"They do seem pretty hard on you."

"It's a Golden thing. I'd be like them if I'd stayed."

"I'm glad you're not."

"Don't think I'd look good with muscles?" Tannin flexed her arms dramatically.

Ava smiled and shook her head exasperatedly.

"Tannin?"

"Yes, princess?"

"Thank you. For coming to save me."

Tannin grinned. "Mhm that's what? 3-0 to me now."

"What?" It took Ava a bewildered second to work out what Tannin meant, but then she was affronted. "Uh, no! I saved you from your infection! And I stopped you drinking Sommer's poisoned wine!"

"Aye, but you were on -1 for leaving me in that dungeon." Tannin smirked. "We'll call it 3-1."

Ava huffed and gritted her teeth. "Accepted."

"And yet, I still came to save you," Tannin teased. "Because I'm just so damn lovely."

"Mhm."

"Which I did at great risk to myself."

"I know, you fool."

"Not to mention—"

"Tannin."

"Aye?"

"Shut up."

Chapter Twenty

In Trouble

Tannin

After a few more hours of walking, Tannin was ready to admit defeat and just pass out in a ditch somewhere. She was actually about to suggest it when a cart came trundling around the bend. Its rattling was music to her ears, and a combination of begging, wheedling and Ava's admittedly impressive powers of persuasion got them a ride back to Dunoak.

Squashed amongst crates in the back of the wagon, Ava pulled the satchel she'd taken from the mercenaries onto her lap. She plucked one of the dozens of scrolls from the bag to investigate. Tannin had no such ambitions and promptly slept on Ava's shoulder the whole way back, only waking every so often when Ava grumbled at her to stop drooling on her dress.

"Hey, wake up."

Tannin grumbled incoherently until Ava's jostling became more sincere.

"What?" she moaned, giving the princess a glare.

"Look at this."

Tannin scanned the parchment with bleary eyes and blinked a couple of times until she realised that it wasn't written in a language she could read.

"What does it say?"

"I don't know. It's a code." Ava's voice was filled with excitement.

"Great," Tannin yawned and tried to nuzzle back in for further snoozings. Ava elbowed her.

"What?" she whined again. "What is it?"

"Look," Ava insisted.

Tannin's eyes grazed the parchment again until she saw what Ava was getting at. The page hadn't been signed in a traditional sense, but inked at the very bottom was a symbol that chased the last traces of sleep from Tannin's mind.

"Triquetra," Tannin breathed.

Even after her nap, Tannin was still exhausted and longing for a hot bath and bed when they finally traipsed back through the city gate.

The on-duty guards organised a hasty escort to take them back to the keep. The warg-bloods they passed on the way eyed them with equal parts curiosity and pity. Dana's mood the past two days must have been particularly prickly. Tannin internally grimaced.

"There was a baby at the keep," Ava pressed one of the guards as they made their way through the city. "He was sick."

"The boy lives," he said gruffly. "He won't be the same as before, but he lives."

"Oh, thank the gods."

"You might want to ask them for a wee bit mercy for us too," Tannin muttered out of the corner of her mouth. Now that the adrenaline of the rescue was long gone, she was left filled with dread.

When they reached the keep, they were taken straight to Dana's office. The woman in question strode in less than a minute later with the air of an impending storm.

The warg leader's expression was unreadably stony as she snapped at servants to clear the room.

"You too, out," she snapped at Ava and then rounded on Tannin. "You. Stay."

Tannin started to protest but shut her mouth at the look Dana gave her.

Ava squeezed her hand. "It's okay," she mouthed.

Tannin did not want to let go but did anyway as Ava left with the servants and she was left alone with Dana. As the coattails of the last of them disappeared out the doorway, Tannin turned to explain herself.

"Dana, before you—"

It was too late. Even though she was half expecting it, Dana's backhanded blow still sent her staggering.

"What," Dana said with dangerous calm, "the hell were you thinking?"

Tannin's eyes were watering and she blinked them clear, holding a hand to her stinging cheek.

"You weren't gonna go after her. No one was! And I got her back, so don't you—"

Dana hit her again. This time, she flew backwards into the wall.

"Do you even know how stupid it was to run off like that?" Dana snarled. Her eyes had turned midnight black and her voice carried a low and dangerous growl. "How reckless? Irresponsible? Do you know how many people I had to send out after you? Adair and I risked *everything* to save you from Sommer just for you to toss it aside like its nothing?"

"That wasn't...I didn't..." Tannin's rehearsed words got lost somewhere in her throat with the way Dana was glowering at her. She'd expected Dana to be angry at her. She hadn't expected to be scared of her. Her face stung from the blows.

"You better start taking this seriously, Tannin, because I am so very close to the end of my patience with you, you understand?" Dana loomed over her as she growled. "Unfortunately, you are still my responsibility. Do anything like that again, and I'll drag you into the town square and flay the skin off your bones myself. Do you understand me? Or maybe I'll take your princess instead. Maybe then the message will get through your thick head."

"What?! You can't do that!" Tannin cried.

Dana lunged for her and slammed her into the wall so hard that the wood behind her crunched. Pain blossomed from the back of her skull. Dana's fingers squeezed her jaw tight.

"Tell me again what I can and cannot do, Tannin," she whispered, digging her nails into Tannin's cheeks. "Go on."

When Tannin didn't say anything, she nodded. "Thought so."

"There is a chain of command, Tannin, and you might have the blood right to Stonestead, but that does not mean you can do whatever you want. The opposite, in fact. You are weak and you are a target, and you are putting everything at risk. I had to leave this whole city unprotected to send people out looking for you."

Dana released her. Tannin sank to the floor, gasping. "You start weapons training in the morning. At dawn. Maybe that will beat some sense into you. From now on, you do what you are told, when you are told and you do not leave these halls without my express permission. Do you understand?"

Tannin didn't trust herself to speak. Her knees shook as she scrambled to her feet.

"Get out."

Tannin fled.

Tannin jerked upright and wiped her eyes with her sleeve as the door to her room creaked open.

"Tannin?" Ava whispered.

Goddammit, did she have to come in right now?

She'd burst into tears as soon as she was alone in her room. Dana was right. Ava was right. She was a fool. She wasn't cut out for this. Every time she tried to do the right thing, it blew up in her face.

Ava didn't say a word about her tear-stained face as she came to sit on the bed.

"I'm sorry you got in trouble. Flint too."

"What?" Tannin flinched. "What happened to Flint?"

She had been planning to go find him as soon as she'd gotten a hold of herself and stopped bawling like a bairn.

"He spent a night in the cells." Ava frowned. "Did you not know?"

"No." Tears welled up again. "Gods, I messed up so badly. Is he okay?"

"You know him. He's fine. What did Dana say to you?"

Tannin shrugged, fiddling with a loose thread in her bedding.

"She came to speak to me too."

Tannin looked up sharply. "Did she threaten you?"

Ava looked alarmed. "No, why? What did she say to you?" Her eyes raked over the marks Dana's nails had made on Tannin's cheeks. "Did she hurt you?"

"It's nothing." Tannin dragged a hand over her tired face. "Not really."

"Don't lie to me," Ava whispered harshly and then said more gently, "She told me to stay away from you. I'm guessing she said similar to you."

Tannin waggled her head and went back to toying with the thread.

"Maybe it would be for the best."

"Is that what you want?"

Ava sighed. "I want selfish things. Maybe it is safer for us to keep our distance. I am a liability, after all. Maybe I should go home."

"After all the trouble I went to get you back here?" Tannin demanded, indignant.

"Which you shouldn't have done," Ava reminded her with a gentle smile. "You're too valuable."

"No one else was going to," Tannin murmured.

From Ava's expression, it was clear that she had already worked that out – that, to the wargs, she was an acceptable loss.

"I'm not your responsibility. Your responsibility is to the people here. They're going to be your people soon enough."

"You are my responsibility," Tannin replied stubbornly. "I promised."

"I thought you would be happy to see me leave."

"Yes, leave. Not be dragged off in the middle of the night. And anyway, that was before I knew the fuckin' Triquetra were after you. Now I want you to stay. Stay where I can protect you."

"I can protect myself."

"No, you bloody can't."

It had come out harsher than she meant it to, and the following silence stretched out uncomfortably.

"They're going to start training me to be a proper warg. To become the leader they want me to be."

"That is probably for the best." Ava offered a weak smile. "Discipline never really has been your strong suit."

Tannin nodded her agreement miserably. The back of her head still throbbed from Dana's idea of discipline.

"Can I...can I stay here tonight?" Ava asked. "Just sleep, I mean. I can go if you'd prefer but...I just..."

"You don't want to be alone," Tannin finished for her.

Ava nodded, seeming a little embarrassed but smiled when Tannin shifted over a bit and patted the space beside her on her bed.

With sleep feeling like a lifetime away, Ava was a comforting warmth at her side.

"You really do have the boniest elbows."

Chapter Twenty-One

Training

The sun had barely risen when Tannin entered the training hall to meet Theo. She'd left Ava sound asleep with a hastily scribbled note on the bedside table, warning her to be careful not to be seen when she left. Dana would possibly make good on her threats if she knew they'd spent the night together immediately after her warnings, however innocent it was.

Dana had clearly told Theo everything and he regarded her with extra sourness, but he didn't say a word until he barked at her to stand to attention.

"Feet a little wider. Straighten your spine, for gods' sake, don't slouch."

When her old school master was finally satisfied with Tannin's posture, he stepped back.

"Remain here until I return," he said and left.

Tannin groaned inwardly but did as she was told. She remembered this exercise all too well from the academy. Experience had taught her someone would be watching to make sure she stayed exactly as she was. It was an exercise in obedience and following orders. One that she'd failed countless times as a child. Already the urge to roll her shoulders, shake out her legs, even straighten her tunic was almost overwhelming, but she clenched her teeth and remained motionless. She wouldn't give him any more reason to be pissed at her.

Tannin had been to the big training hall in the basement a few times now to show off her warg form. At first, she'd had to be generously bribed to descend into the basement, but it turned out it wasn't so bad. Dana hadn't been able to hide how impressive Tannin's warg form was. She'd said anyone who saw her couldn't deny the strength of the mountain spirit in her blood, and Tannin had felt very pleased with herself indeed.

Fighting in her human form, though? That was an entirely different thing, and she could already feel the humiliation that was waiting for her.

What felt like hours later, Theo returned with a sack full of weaponry and armour.

"Swordplay is an art. It takes skill, patience and discipline," Theo said as he rummaged through what he'd brought. "We do not have time to teach you that."

"I thought that's why I was here?"

"I'm not going to waste time teaching you how to fight with a sword. It's not worth the effort. Here." He dumped a pair of axes into her arms as he shouldered past her. "Requires less technical skill and practice than a sword. Let's get started."

Tannin slunk to the kitchens after training, thoroughly demotivated. Meal time had come and gone hours ago, but there was bound to be leftovers somewhere.

"Cook told me to tell you that if you keep stealing ham for the dogs, she's going to string you up in the smokehouse as a replacement," Alby said solemnly as soon as she entered the kitchens.

"She can't prove that was me."

And it wasn't that much ham... Well, maybe it was.

"I saw you take it." His big eyes stared her down in reproachful judgement. "Stealing is wrong."

"Only if you get caught." Tannin winked.

"Cook said—"

"Alright, alright!" Tannin raised her hands in surrender. "I won't do it again. You got any leftovers for me? I missed lunch."

Alby rifled around the kitchen and returned with two hardboiled eggs, a bread roll and a glass of milk. She saluted her thanks before taking it all up to the dining hall. It was empty as expected, except for an older man sweeping diligently. Tannin settled into one of the long benches.

She had expected to be left alone but looked up at the sound of footsteps, hoping for Flint. It was Dana. She quickly turned back to peeling her eggs.

"I owe you an apology," Dana said to Tannin's surprise, coming to sit across from her. "I never should have hit you."

"That's what you're sorry for?" Tannin's eyebrows shot up in disbelief.

"What should I be sorry for?"

"Uh, imprisoning Flint? Or how about threatening Ava? She did nothin' wrong."

Tannin still hadn't seen Flint, and despite Ava's assurance that he was no worse for wear for his night in the cells, she still owed him one hell of an apology.

"For one night for impeding my orders, and for goodness' sake, Tannin, I was never going to hurt either of them."

Tannin took an obnoxiously large bite instead of answering, glaring at Dana as she chewed.

"You will though," Dana said in a soft whisper. "Hurt them, I mean. If you don't stop messing this up. You're going to do something you regret, and the people closest to you are going to pay the price for it. If you care about her, you should stay away from her. Flint too." She stood. "Your place is with the wargs, whether you like it or not."

She left without another word.

"Not," Tannin muttered resolutely under her breath, pushing herself away from the table and leaving the rest of her food uneaten. She had lost her appetite. She wanted to find Flint. The sight of his big, dumb grin was exactly what she needed to soothe the gnawing anxiousness in her gut.

When she found him, he was indeed grinning widely, strolling in the direction of the stables, but he wasn't alone. He was hand in hand with...

"Callie?" Tannin blurted incredulously, scraping the name from the back of her memory.

"Oh hello." The warg-blood flashed her a smile. "Tannin, isn't it?"

"Tan! There you are!" Flint dropped Callie's hand to pull Tannin into a brief hug. "I was worried about you!"

"I'm alright. Ava too."

"Aye, I saw her last night, and she filled me in this morning while you were away training. I know she left out the juicy bits though, so tell me everything."

Callie's eyebrow cocked at the mention of the training. Tannin shot Flint a "shut-up" look. She was supposed to be a no-one. No-ones did not get secret, private lessons. Callie's little half-smile told her he had only confirmed a suspicion she already had.

"I have to get back. I just wanted to see that you were okay. Ava said you got in trouble?"

Flint laughed. "Oh aye. Dana was raging and had me chucked in a cell, but I had just the cutest gaoler."

He winked at Callie and she giggled in return.

"Right..." Tannin said, failing to hide her bewilderment. "Uh, talk later?"

"Aye. I've got work to do anyway." He gestured over his shoulder with his thumb at the stables.

"I'll walk you back in," Callie offered Tannin brightly as Flint waved his goodbyes.

The short trek back to the main building in Callie's company was so awkward it was painful. Tannin had hoped to make quick escape, but she had no such luck.

"Can I give you a little advice, Tannin?"

"Can I stop you?"

"Look, I'm not stupid or blind. None of us are. I'm pretty sure I know who and what you are," Callie said matter-of-factly.

Tannin winced.

"Oh please. You arrive with Dana, you lurk around the keep all the time, and out of all of us here, a scrawny little thing like you that no one seems to know gets a seat at the table in council meetings? Come on."

Tannin ignored the insult.

"So?"

"*So,* for someone like you to be pining after a stable boy? It's embarrassing to everyone who has to see it."

"*Excuse me*?"

"You follow him around like a little lapdog." Callie gave her a pitying grimace. "It's sweet to an extent, but can't you see he's not interested in you?"

"I'm not interested in him either," Tannin said affronted. "We're friends. He's...he's like my brother."

"Tell yourself whatever you need to get over him." Her lips curled in a patronising smile. "But the more pathetic you look, the worse the rest of us look. Keep that in mind, hm?"

Tannin stared at her open-mouthed as Callie gave her arm a comforting little squeeze.

"Good talk."

Between Dana's warning and Callie's oh-so-well-intentioned advice, her non-wargness had started to get into Tannin's head. Over the next few weeks, she found herself spending less time with her friends and more time throwing herself into her training.

"Do not throw it!" Theo bellowed as he wrenched Tannin's axe from the straw-filled practice dummy's head.

"But I got him!" Tannin protested gesturing at the cloth face with the leering grin painted on it, which had now been split neatly in two. "And I have another." She held up her other axe and waggled her eyebrows.

Theo slapped it out of her hand.

"And now you're unarmed," he snarled.

"But he's dead." She pointed at the dummy, which was now drooping.

Theo smacked the side of her head in response.

"There will hardly ever be just one, novice," he reprimanded. "Go retrieve your weapons. Start again. No throwing."

"No throwing," Tannin muttered mockingly as soon as his back was turned and then scolded herself. She had promised that she was going to try harder, but she was hot and irritable. They'd only been at it for an hour, and she was already drenched in sweat, and her arms were aching from swinging at dummies. She personally thought it was impressive that she managed to throw the damn thing in the first place, let alone get the dummy right in the face.

Theo kept her even later than usual before he finally let her leave with an aching back, leaden legs and a growling stomach.

She craved fresh air after so long in the stale basement, so she filled her pockets with a random assortment of leftovers and climbed up to her usual spot on the roof. Peace and quiet. That's what she wanted. What she needed.

She clambered up with ease despite her sore muscles but almost let go of the wall in shock as she crested the top and was met with the view of startlingly pale, gyrating arsecheeks.

"Oh my god!" Tannin shrieked. "FLINT! What the fuck!"

This place was supposed to be empty. This was her place.

"Oh fuck, uh, hey Tan." Flint grinned at her sheepishly as he covered himself and his equally naked partner with a blanket. "Didn't hear you there."

"Flint...what the...THIS IS MY SPOT!"

"Oh, is this your special place?" Callie said, eyes glittering. The way she said it made it sound so childish.

Tannin's mouth opened and closed as words failed her. She made a disgusted noise in her throat.

"Tan, wait, I'm sorry! Just...gimme a minute." Flints voice faded as she shimmied back down, leaping the last few feet. The fall was a little too high to be comfortable, but she landed without injury even if she did stagger a bit.

She continued grumbling under her breath as she stalked into the gardens. Ava had actually done quite well with the plants. They weren't looking as sad and bedraggled as they had when they'd arrived. She was there now with a pair of pruning shears, snipping at leaves. She raised an eyebrow as Tannin stomped past and plonked herself on a bench.

"What's wrong with you?"

"Flint," Tannin huffed, "and Callie. On the roof."

Ava winced. "Ah, yes."

"You knew? When the hell did that happen?"

Ava gave her a pitying look. "You know, for someone with heightened senses, you are remarkably unobservant."

Tannin pointed back at the roof top. "They are defiling my spot!"

"Don't worry. I think that's the first time they've been up there. They're usually in the storage cupboard, but Cook is doing a stock check."

In response to Tannin's questioning look, she added, "I can hear them from my room. It's directly above."

"Ew," Tannin muttered.

"At least someone's having fun." She looked at Tannin out of the corner of her eye. "Anyone around here caught your interest?"

Besides you, you mean.

"I'm not having this conversation with you," Tannin said flatly. "Anyway, I'm too damn tired to think these days, let alone anything else."

"You'd better save your energy for tonight then." Ava snipped a few more leaves.

Tannin groaned. "Ugh. I don't wanna."

Dana had invited the leaders from the towns and small cities around Woodren who had pledged to support the wargs' occupation of Dunoak for a feast and ceilidh as a show of comradery and not at all as a power flex.

"You might have a good time." Ava shot her a smile. "I know I'm planning to."

"Oh?"

"Someone's asked me to save them a dance."

"Who?"

Ava just gave her a sly smile and snipped another leaf.

"Ava, who?" Tannin demanded.

“I've got some more things to do before tonight. I'll see you there.”

“Hey!”

In the time it took Tannin to scramble off the bench and after her, Ava had swept around the corner and disappeared. She must've legged it as soon as she was out of sight. Tannin scowled and considered chasing after her.

Who the hell asked Ava for a dance?

Chapter Twenty-Two

Ceilidh

Tannin

The dinner and ceilidh that night were supposed to be a show of friendship and alliance, although Tannin strongly suspected that it was more about asserting dominance; especially with the terrified looks the visiting local lairds shot at Dana every now and again and the way she ate it up with a self-satisfied glow.

Tannin didn't feel like dancing, even though the fiddle and drum were beckoning her. Across the room, Ava was dancing with some girl. Tannin's jaw tightened as the girl's hands slipped lower down Ava's back, beyond where anyone could say it was innocent.

"Ooh, green is so not your colour," Flint panted, pink-cheeked and glistening with a fine layer of perspiration, as he flopped down on the bench beside her and helped himself to her goblet. He gave her a disgusted look when he realised there was only water in it.

"What? I'm wearing blue?" Tannin looked down at her new dress, suddenly self-conscious. "Does it look bad?"

She'd taken to wearing dresses more often now that she wasn't working in the bakery and wasn't at risk of setting her skirts on fire, but that didn't mean she didn't miss her scruffy breeches. Dana was also quick to remind her that she would, at some point, have to start making an effort and dressing like the heir she was.

Flint shook his head in amusement. "I'm not talking about your dress – which looks lovely, by the way, you're as cute as a button – I'm talking about your jealousy."

"I'm not jealous," Tannin said a little too quickly. "She can dance with whoever she wants."

"Mhm. Funny how I didn't even need to say what I meant." Flint gave her a crooked grin. "I knew wargs were meant to be territorial, but if you glare any more daggers at that poor girl, she's going to start bleeding."

"Oh, shut up."

"Should've asked her yourself."

"Mhm. I've just remembered I'm not talking to you." Tannin resolutely turned her back on him.

"Oh, come on. I said sorry," he whined. "And you don't own the roof anyway."

"Territorial, remember?"

He let out a dramatic sigh. "Is it the roof or who I was with?"

"Both," Tannin said. "And the sight of your pasty arse."

"I have a lovely arse," he declared. "Shapely, I've been told."

"Don't make me laugh. I'm mad at you." But she couldn't help but smile.

"I think the time for talking might be up anyway." Flint winked as Ava caught sight of them and squeezed her way through dancing couples to reach the table.

Flint bowed graciously with many a hand twirl as he took his leave and Ava bobbed an amused little curtsey at him in response.

"What's wrong, Tannin?" she said planting her hands firmly on the table.

"Nothing."

"Tell me."

"What makes you think something's wrong?"

"Because there are at least four unattended bottles of wine, and you haven't tried to swipe any of them. And you're sitting here on your own and not dancing," Ava said matter-of-factly, crossing her arms. "So, what's wrong?"

"Wouldn't you rather go dance with that girl you were with before?"

Ava chuckled and threw her arm around Tannin's waist as she slid into the seat beside her.

"Ooh, I like you jealous." She was flushed with both the dancing and a little too much wine, but her flirty grin turned serious. "It's not just that though, is it? It's the lairds being here. You..." She tapped Tannin on the forehead. "Don't like that this is getting serious."

"Maybe." Tannin scowled. "I feel like I'm playing a part. Really badly. I dunno who I'm supposed to be right now. Or what I'm supposed to do. They're not supposed to know who I am, but I'm supposed to know them? Am I supposed to talk to them or not?

What do I even say? Oh, and all the warg-bloods know who I am, by the way. They're just not allowed to say they know. Who the fuck even am I, anyway?"

Ava stood facing her. "Tannin Hill. Beast of Armodan. Heir of Stonestead. Gigantic pain in my neck. Whoever you are and whatever you are." She grinned, seized a nearby bottle and pushed it into Tannin's hands. "Stop brooding, drink up and come dance with me. Let yourself enjoy this."

Tannin let herself smile and brought the bottle to her lips.

How can I say no to such an offer?

They danced for hours, changing partners occasionally for a spin or two but always coming back together to clasp hands and swirl each other round. With all the bodies crammed into the hall, it rapidly became swelteringly hot.

Goblets and tankards were passed around with abandon, and they greedily slurped a dangerous mixture of wine, ale and spirit as the dancing became wilder and less coordinated.

Tannin's skin tingled wherever Ava touched her. Waist, hip, shoulder, fingertips. Every touch sending shivers rattling though her, making her crave more. They pressed together when the music upped the tempo, dancing in a way that back home in Armodan would have been scandalous but compared to the warg-bloods' semi-fornication to the rhythm of the music was reasonably tame.

Eventually, more and more couples left the dancefloor as time went on in favour of drinking at the long tables pushed against the walls or disappearing upstairs or even just into shadowy alcoves for a different kind of dance.

As the music slowed, Ava tried to teach Tannin the steps to an elegant waltz between swigs from a hip flask no one was quite sure who it belonged to or what it contained.

"Left foot...no, left... left! Tannin, how many feet do you have? If I'm telling you it's not that one, then it's obviously the other."

"This is a stupid dance," Tannin declared, ready to give up.

"It's not stupid if you relax and let me lead," Ava insisted and jerked her back in close, but she forgot half the steps herself and they stumbled into each other, half with laughter and drunkenness and half with Tannin's clumsy footwork even as the fiddle and accordion faded. They remained on the floor. Even when there was no more music, they still clung to each other swaying lightly.

"Let's go get some air," Ava eventually breathed against Tannin's neck. She nodded numbly.

Outside was still reasonably warm, although Tannin wasn't sure if that was to do with the weather or the astounding amount of drinks they'd had. Ava refused to let her climb up to her spot on the roof to watch the sun rise like she wanted to. That was fair. She was a bit wobbly.

Tannin wasn't sure how long they had stayed outside for, but at some point, they stumbled back in and clung to each other trying to smother their giggles as they navigated the staircases of the keep to eventually collapse onto Ava's bed.

She should've said good night. She should've gone to her own room and gone to sleep. She didn't.

Tannin's fingers interlinked with Ava's and she traced the line on Ava's thumb where the knife had sliced her when Tannin had cut her free.

"It scarred," she said absentmindedly.

"It'll be a reminder," Ava replied before scoffing. "Like I could ever forget."

"I was so fuckin' scared when you got taken. I thought I wasn't going to see you again."

Ava shuddered and then looked into Tannin's eyes. "I don't know what would have happened if you hadn't come for me. You know, there was a moment I wasn't sure you would? If you even could, I mean. That was a hell of a tumble you took."

Tannin propped herself up on her elbow frowning. "Was I supposed to just let them take you?"

"You wanted me to go. You said it a hundred times. And then you came for me even after I didn't come for you in time. Before. In the Gaol." She was still holding Tannin's gaze. "But you did anyway. And then you came for me again when I got caught by those mercenaries. And I can't take anything back, but I can promise, from now on, I will always, always come for you."

Tannin pressed her lips together hard to keep from smiling, but Ava's eyes narrowed, and before she could say anything, Ava cut her off. "Don't you dare make the joke I know you're going to make," she warned.

Tannin put a hand to her heart in mock offense. "How dare you? You think I would ruin this tender and intimate moment with a crude sex joke?"

"Yes. I know you and your dirty mind, you coarse little gremlin."

Tannin laughed. "Gremlin, is it? Ohhh, princess, you forget I know you too." Her lips quirked into a devilish smirk. "And your weaknesses."

Her fingers suddenly scrabbled against Ava's side, making her squawk. She gasped half-curses in between giggles and unstoppable laugher as Tannin tickled her without mercy.

"Stop! Please!" Ava gasped, finally managing to evade Tannin's torture for long enough to speak.

"You sorry for calling me a gremlin?" Tannin teased, relenting in her assault.

Ava growled and pounced, knocking Tannin flat on the bed and pinning her hands down on to the quilt.

"You are an evil, evil person," she gasped. "Tickling is….illegal!"

Tannin laughed, fluttering her eyelashes up at Ava's flushed and furious face. "Illegal? Is that so?"

"I will get my revenge. Just you wait."

"I'm not ticklish."

"I will find something, mark my words."

"Oh, words marked," she teased and then wriggled. "Alright, let me up."

"No. Not until you promise no more tickling."

"But you make the cutest sounds!"

Ava glared.

"Fine. Don't let me up." Tannin smirked. "I'm enjoying the view anyway."

From her position lying flat on the bed, with Ava leaning over her and holding onto her hands, she had a fantastic view straight down the front of Ava's dress where the laces had loosened. Ava followed her line of sight and then tutted. She readjusted herself so that she could pin Tannin's arms to her sides with her knees and sat up to fix her dress.

"You're ruining my view."

"Tough." Ava tilted Tannin's chin up with her fingertip so that she was looking her in the eye and not still trying to peek down the front of her dress. "No more tickling."

Tannin conceded. "Alright, alright. I promise."

"For now," she added under her breath as Ava released her and she scooted partially out from under her so that she could sit up. Ava still straddled her legs. They couldn't have gotten any closer to each other without actually embracing. She could have moved but she didn't.

"What was that?" Ava raised an eyebrow.

"Nothing," Tannin sang with a grin.

Ava sighed in mock exasperation and tucked a strand of hair behind Tannin's ear. She let her hand come to rest on her shoulder. Tannin could feel the warmth of her hand through the material of her dress.

"You really are a monstrous, little gremlin," she said quietly, her stunningly blue eyes never wavering from Tannin's.

"Then why do you look like you want to kiss me?" Tannin whispered back, still grinning.

Ava's smile faltered. "Tannin…"

"Don't lie and say you don't want to."

"It's not that I don't. Just…it's complicated."

"Look, it's never going to not be complicated. With you, with me, either of us with anyone."

"That's true." Ava traced Tannin's jaw with her thumb.

"We are who we are, we can't change that, but I want this and I know you do too. It doesn't have to be anything serious if you don't want that, but will you stop stalling and *damn well kiss me already*?" Tannin said. "You—"

Ava's lips crashed against hers as she kissed her hard.

"Shut," she murmured against Tannin's smiling mouth, "up."

Chapter Twenty-Three

I Need Your Blood

Ava

Sneaking around with Tannin was the most fun Ava had had in a long time. Stolen kisses in shadowy alcoves and secret, lustful looks across hallways. Tannin's days were always occupied with the other wargs, but the nights, they had all to themselves. They'd agreed to never spend the entire night. Even so, they sometimes melted into a boneless heap and didn't move until the morning rays peeked in through the small window.

The previous night had been one of those times. Of course, Flint had caught on to them almost straight away and had pulled Ava aside to have a private word.

"Do not break her heart again," he had warned her without preamble and with none of his usual humour.

The "again" had stung.

She had promised that she wouldn't, and he had left it at that. He reminded her so much of Florian yet again, and the loss chafed at her heart. Flo would have said exactly the same to anyone she was involved with. Justus wouldn't have bothered. They had never seen eye to eye, and he had always been jealous whenever Flo spent time with her instead of him. He used to break her dolls when no one was around or spread mean rumours about her. That was one of the reasons she started keeping to herself in the first place. She had always had Attilo and had cared about him deeply, but now she didn't just have one person to care about. Tannin, Flint and even little Alby who seemed to have taken a particular liking to her and kept popping his head into her workrooms to see if she needed help, were all people she was not willing to lose.

Like I lost Flo and Attilo.

Ava had seen to it that the security in their wing had been heightened ten-fold since her kidnapping, with alarm runes painted by her own hand hidden in every crevice and along the doors and windows. If a group of human mercenaries could get into their rooms, then so could others. Not to mention any agent of Sommer's. Dana had obviously realised that too, and patrols, locks and barriers had all been checked and enhanced for peace of mind, but Ava had taken it to the next level. Armed with her borrowed druid book, she'd fortified every weakness she could find. Not that she had told anyone, of course. She found that she still couldn't quite trust the wargs or warg-bloods and couldn't be sure that one of them hadn't sold her out.

Ava had been toying with going even further. The book detailed recipes that she'd once considered far too dangerous to even consider, but now? She never wanted to feel helpless again. With all the talk of the warg's secret serum – "warg juice" as Tannin called it – Ava couldn't help but wonder if there was an equivalent for a druid blood.

I need to run some tests.

"I'm fairly sure that's not right." Ava frowned at the spread of cards on the table.

"That's because you don't understand the game, dear." Flint graced her with a dazzling smile.

Tannin and Flint were sat at one of the long tables in the hall, playing a popular card game, both cheating outrageously.

"I understand perfectly fine." Ava rolled her eyes. "It's a simple game. But look, there can't be three fives here. There were already two on the table."

"Shut up, Ava." Tannin frowned at the cards in her hand. "I'm trying to think."

"But—"

"Sh."

Tannin decided on her move and placed a card, moving another on the table and chucking a few stone counters into the cup in the middle. She turned to Ava.

"Alright, what do you want?"

"You can finish your game first."

"Not with you hovering. What do you want?"

"I need your blood."

Tannin started. "Excuse me? Why? And also no."

"Just a little bit. I want to see how warg blood compares to a warg-blood Remnant's – one of your people who didn't get the serum. I just need a proper warg's now, and can you imagine me asking one of the others?" She laughed lightly. "So yes, I need your blood. Come down to my room in around an hour?"

"Wait, I didn't agree to—"

"Excellent. See you in an hour. I'll set everything up."

"Ava!"

"Enjoy the rest of your game. Flint is about to win, by the way, even with that extra four you have in your hand." She nodded towards his pile of cards. "Two sixes and then add two pebbles takes your fives. No way back from that."

Tannin frowned at the table in front of her.

She scowled and flicked a pebble in Ava's direction. "Go away."

Ava grinned as she left the hall.

"You are a weirdo, princess," Tannin muttered, tapping one of the jars and then yelping as the frog inside blinked at her. "That's alive!"

"Of course, it's alive," Ava grumbled. She'd asked Tannin twice now to sit down, but she was still perusing Ava's shelves. "I don't make a habit of killing little creatures. Now, come over here, sit down and *stop touching things.*"

Tannin made a face at her but did indeed sit down where Ava indicated. Her freckled nose wrinkled. As much as Ava had cleaned her workroom, the smell of mustiness never left. To a warg, it must have been intense, she mused, making a mental note to write that down later.

"So, what creepy witch stuff are you doing to me today?"

"Not the fun kind." Ava winked at her and Tannin rolled her eyes. "I need just a vial or so of blood and then you can go."

"Which of the warg-bloods donated? I can't see any of them being too keen to do this." Tannin walked her fingers over the edge of the worktop and reached for one of the pots of dried herb on the surface. Ava rapped her on the knuckles.

"I made a trade. The blood for some, uh, recreational herbs."

Tannin stopped pouting and massaging her fingers to gape at her.

"And before you say anything, no, I didn't grow them, and no, I don't have any more."

"Where did you get them?" Tannin demanded.

"Another trade," Ava said with a tired sigh. "It's exactly like back in Armodan. I never had coin, remember? It's a skill to know what people want and what they'll give me for it."

It had taken her weeks to sus out likely traders of illicit materials. Flint had helped.

"So, what are you trading me for my blood?"

"Ah that's different," Ava said primly. "You're donating out of the goodness of your heart."

Tannin snorted. "I much prefer bribery."

Ava leaned in, close enough to kiss, and ran a fingertip along Tannin's jaw.

"I'm sure I can think of a little *reward* for you later."

Tannin waggled her eyebrows, pretending to mull it over.

"Okay, deal. I'm all yours."

Ava gave her a tiny kiss on the tip of her nose. "Good."

All playfulness, however, vanished as Ava began to prepare her knives. She kept them razor sharp. She positioned Tannin where she wanted her and then brought the knife to the soft inside of her arm. Tannin grimaced as the blade nicked her skin.

"Ouch."

"There, there," Ava crooned as she held a heated bronze cup under the cut. "Do you need me to kiss it better?"

"Maybe," Tannin said, watching the steady trickle filling up the vial. "Maybe I need more than kisses to feel better. This is a cruel and vicious wound, after all."

"I cannot get any more of those herbs," Ava said, catching Tannin's meaning.

Tannin gave a dramatic sigh.

"Okay. All done," Ava said as she held a scrap of cloth to the tiny incision she had made in Tannin's arm.

"Are you going to tell me what you're doing with my blood?"

"Creepy witch stuff."

"Tell me."

Ava sighed. "I already told you I'm trying to work out what makes your blood different from the warg-blood Remnants'. If we can remake it, then we have something Sommer doesn't."

"I'm pretty sure it took a team of warg-bloods decades to come up with that serum."

"It doesn't hurt to look."

"It hurt me!" Tannin pointed out waving the blood spotted scrap of cloth.

"For goodness' sake." Ava strode over to stand next to her and lifted Tannin's arm to her mouth, planting an exaggerated kiss right beside the cut. "There. All better. Now go do something more useful than playing cards."

"I already have archery lessons with Catriona later – which I'm terrible at, in case you're wonderin'."

"The wargs should be giving you more responsibilities and not just worrying about turning you into a warrior. Not every ruler has to be a fighter," Ava said with a frown.

Her personal library back in Armodan was filled with tales of past rulers too quick to sound the war trumpets, and their ultimate ruin. She'd always found it frustrating that her brother's tutors spoke often of great battlefield victories, but monarchs who reigned peacefully for decades were relegated to nothing more than footnotes. If she hadn't been listening through the keyhole, she might've spoken up about it.

"You know you're talkin' about wargs? Of course I have to be a fighter." Tannin raised her eyebrows sceptically. "You really think that I should be makin' the decisions?"

"With instruction and advice of course."

"Meaning you."

"Clearly. I'm the only one here with any experience, and yet none of you take me seriously."

"Maybe you're just a better witch than you are a princess."

Ava squinted at her with suspicion, looking for traces of mockery.

"You should go prepare for your lessons."

"What, no kiss goodbye?"

Ava sighed and leaned over, yanking Tannin forward by the front of her tunic to plant a firm kiss on her lips. Tannin smiled into it. When Ava started to pull back, Tannin's fingers entwined in her hair stopped her retreat. Soft lips grazed over her jaw and down the side of her neck, making her groan.

"I'm going to make you late if you don't stop that," Ava murmured, her pulse spiking.

"Then I'll be late."

Chapter Twenty-Four

Mistaken Identity

Tannin

Tannin breathed in the cool night air in triumph. She deserved this after all her hard work in training. Even Theo had begrudgingly admitted that she had made strides in the right direction. She hadn't had a night out in so long, and when Collum and Eoghan had invited Flint, and by extension her and Ava, to come watch them play at a local tavern, she had jumped at the chance. It took a little wheedling, but Dana agreed that she had earned it.

Her and Flint met up with Collum and Eoghan just past the gates of the keep. Ava had too many witchy potions to brew and had declined the invitation. The brothers had come dressed in their stage costumes with matching brightly coloured jerkins. Collum carried a wide flat drum under his arm while Eoghan had a carved wooden flute tucked into his belt.

Tannin wolf-whistled when she saw them, and both bowed dramatically. She was looking forward to hearing them play. Flint had told her Eoghan had a beautiful singing voice.

Collum audibly grimaced as the four of them entered their most frequented tavern. A dull hum of conversation flitted through the stagnant air. The night was still young, and with most of the regulars still closing up their shops or grabbing a later dinner, many tables stood empty. The few patrons scattered around the room were not yet drunk, although they were making a decent attempt to get there.

"Ooft, this place could do with livening up," Collum said.

At the sight of the musicians, a round of drinks arrived at their table. The boys were getting paid coppers for the night, but the first round was on the house.

"Well, get on with it then." Flint grinned as he grabbed a chair, put his feet up on the table and tucked his hands behind his head expectantly.

Eoghan and Collum were artists. Their years as travelling musicians had them instantly in tune with their audience, and they played them just as expertly as they did their own instruments. They knew when to perform a round of popular drinking song that had everyone, drunk or otherwise, thumping their fists on the tables and when to sombre it down. Flint and Tannin sang loudest of all, and the latest song had them competing to down their drinks. Tannin lost ungraciously, and as forfeit, had to get the next round.

She made her way to the bar with liberal use of her elbows to squeeze through the crowd that had gathered around the stage.

The innkeeper's eyes widened at the sight of her. She held up two fingers, and he immediately scrabbled for two fresh tankards. He had offered her a very, very good discount when she *accidentally* revealed her wargishness to him earlier that evening. Sometimes, being a terrifying monster was extremely helpful, she thought as two overflowing tankards were slid onto the counter in front of her. With the amount of coin she had saved, she only felt slightly guilty abusing her heritage. She'd told Flint on no uncertain terms not to tell Ava about it or she'd never hear the end of it.

"You keep some…interesting company for someone of your status."

Tannin flinched at the familiar voice in her ear and turned to glare at her old teacher. He wasn't alone. A group of young-warg bloods had also spilled into the tavern, including Callie, who was now happily sitting on Flint's lap. Tannin groaned.

"Do you lot conspire to ruin my fun or does it just happen organically?"

"Tannin—"

"He's paying," Tannin said to the barkeep with a jerk of her head towards Theo before grabbing the tankards and stomping back to the table.

Unlike herself, the warg-bloods did not hide what they were, and the nearest tables eyed them with caution and subtly shifted their chairs further away.

"Aw, don't worry," Callie crooned catching the eye of one of the men nearest. "We don't bite."

"Oh aye, she does," Flint responded with a wink, giving Callie a playful pinch and making her squeal.

Tannin mimed throwing up over the side of the table.

The warg-bloods were a rowdy bunch. Soon, the regulars trickled out of the tavern, faster still when the two musicians took a break.

"Dunno about you, but I need a drink," Eoghan said as he approached the table.

"Me too."

"Flint? Do you – Oops, he's, uh, busy." Eoghan grimaced and turned away at the sight of Flint and Callie's amorousness. "What about you, T? Fancy another?"

Tannin drained her tankard and slammed it down on the table. "Absolutely. I'll come with you."

"You don't have to—"

"Shut up. Save me from this." She indicated to Flint, who was kissing down the side of Callie's neck.

Eoghan grinned. "Guess I could use some help carrying the drinks."

Tannin followed Eoghan to the bar. While they were waiting, a young man sidled up and clapped him on the arm.

"Good show, mate."

"Thanks."

With a face as bland as flour and his dusty brown clothing almost camouflaging him against the bar, Tannin wouldn't have given him a second glance.

"Shame about the crowd though," he said in distaste, glancing over at the table where the warg-bloods were playing a game that involved stabbing knives between their fingers. "It's weird, innit? That they're wargs?"

Tannin shrugged noncommittally. She knew they weren't actual wargs like he thought they were, but she couldn't exactly say anything without outing herself as one of them.

"There's a rumour going about that one of them is, like, warg royalty."

"Aye, I heard them say it's like a wee warg bairn, and that's why there's so many of them here. To protect it, like." Another equally bland-looking youth had joined them. This one had a crooked jaw like he was missing quite a few teeth.

Tannin inwardly winced. She was pretty much no better than a child.

"There's bets on who it is. I stuck a crown on that boy that's always about the keep."

"Nah, he was here ages before them."

"No one knows when they started showing up. Or how many of them there are."

"I heard it was a girl anyway."

"There were soldiers here from Armodan this afternoon asking about a girl. I bet that's what they were after. The royal one."

Tannin startled.

Armodian soldiers? Here?

"Nah, you boys hear what happened in Armodan, though? Apparently, one of them went on an actual rampage. It's one of those feral ones. They never caught it and they're still after it. That'll be why they're there."

"You think it's here?"

If they refer to me as "it" one more fucking time...

Tannin gripped her empty tankard hard and felt the metal start to bend in her hand.

"I heard from the blacksmith that the nobles think it is and called them in."

"Doubt the wargs will be happy when they hear that."

"Aye, but if the soldiers get rid of this royal bairn and the feral one, then all these monsters might follow and finally leave us alone."

"That's a shite plan."

"How else we gonna get rid of them? It's a fucking infestation."

Tannin's tankard was a warped mess in her hands.

"What we talking about?" Flint had finally stopped sucking on Callie's neck to come join them at the bar. His hand giving her arm a warning squeeze told her he'd noticed her strangling her tankard. She glanced at him and then subtly chucked it under a table and out of sight.

"Wargs," another man said and then spat on the floor. Their conversation was attracting more unwanted attention.

"They're not that bad." Flint cast a nervous glance at the table of warg-bloods and then caught Tannin's eye. She gave a tiny shake of her head. If they made a scene, things could get bloody. But at the same time, they should leave before she lost her temper and put this arsehole's head through the damn table.

"We're talking about the mad one from Armodan. The soldiers are gonna root it out."

"And apparently a royal one."

"My bet's still on the kitchen boy."

The latest to join the conversation spat on the floor again. "Hope they burn the fucking thing. I'll help them build the pyre."

Flint turned so quickly that his beer clattered to the floor.

"What did you just say?" he snarled.

"I know you're fucking that bitch, but what do you care about some warg runt—"

Tannin would have absolutely punched him if Flint hadn't beaten her to it. His fist smashed straight into his mouth, and the youth fell backwards into his friends, a stunned look on his face and blood dripping from his busted lip. Tannin made a mental note to be impressed later, but in that moment, she had to haul Flint to the side to stop a bottle being smashed over his head.

"Alright, time to go." She ducked as Collum yelled a joyful battle cry and slugged the bottle wielder in the face.

She turned and smacked straight into Callie. Her lips were twisted into a vicious, almost murderous smile.

"No," Tannin said firmly and then pointed to the individual warg-bloods gathered behind her eager for a fight. "No, no, no and especially you, *no*."

The last remark was directed at a slight girl with deceptively angelic face who had drawn a knife. They looked at her in confusion.

Fuck.

She forgot she was supposed to be playing a no-one.

Oh well.

"Theo! Get them under control before someone actually dies," she barked at the older man. No matter how it all started, she knew she would get the blame from Dana simply by being in the same room.

To her surprise, he actually inclined his head and rounded on the warg-bloods, hissing at them to sit back down. They did. And every single one of them stared at her.

"We've gotta go," Tannin muttered to Flint as they scrambled out of the way of flying fists.

"You don't say."

"You bloody started this!"

"Pffft, like you wouldn't have."

One drunk unwisely tried to intercept them and quickly found himself on the floor, wheezing from Tannin's knee slamming into his belly.

Otherwise, they reached the door unscathed. A backwards glance told them that Collum was having the time of his life while Eoghan was sitting on the bar, yelling encouragements. He gave them a cheerful wave over the brawl.

"They're fine, let's go."

"We've got to go tell Dana that Armodian soldiers are here in Dunoak."

"What the hell are Armodian guards doing here?"

"Uh, looking for me? Obviously. King Florian is full of horseshit."

They speed-walked back in the direction of the keep. Without sunlight unforgivingly showing all of its decrepit decay, the streets actually looked somewhat quaint. Tannin felt the adrenaline from the fight seeping from her bones. She slowed her pace.

The night was cool and clear. Even the usual city stink seemed to have vacated for the night, but it was far from quiet. Tannin cocked her head, ears twitching. Those were not usual sounds.

"There's something goin' on. Listen."

They followed the sounds towards the square in front of the keep. Tannin gasped when they finally had a view of it.

The square was swarming with guards. Some of them in Dunoak colours, some in the distinctive red she knew so well.

The Armodian guards trying to gain access to the kitchen side entrance were currently receiving the beating of a lifetime from Cook. She wielded her rolling pin as effectively and brutally as a seasoned warrior as she blocked their way into the kitchen.

"It's not a boy!" one of the guards yelled, shoving a roll of parchment into the face of another guard. "I've seen her with my own eyes. This is her!"

It was one of Tannin's wanted posters.

Meanwhile, Cook had lost her rolling pin and was beating back the Armodian guards barehanded, but she couldn't take them all and a few made it passed her into the kitchens. They returned a few minutes later, dragging a howling Alby with them.

"Oh no," Flint whispered.

"I told you it's not him!" the Amodian guard bellowed.

"Can you be sure?"

"Of course, I'm fucking sure!"

No way I can take them all on. Not alone.

"I'm calling for help."

Alby was shrieking. Cook was roaring whilst simultaneously smacking two guards' heads together. Shouts of protest erupted from the quickly gathering crowd.

Tannin darted into the shadows, threw back her head and howled. It was an unmistakable warg howl that shook the cobbles under her feet and silenced the rabble in the square as they cowered.

Well, that should do it.

"We've got to get to Alby before they hurt him."

"This way." Flint indicated a seemingly direct route through the chaos to where the guards still held the kitchen boy.

"Why the hell isn't Dana out here already dealing with this?!" Tannin hissed as they ran. "Surely she knows and—Ah, fuck."

A guard had stumbled right in front of them, and upon looking up and meeting her eyes, his face went slack and then a triumphant grin stretched across his face.

"Here!" the guard yelled and Tannin cursed. He yanked his sword free and pointed it straight at her heart. "This is her! She's the warg!"

His shout attracted the attention of more guards, and a dozen more weapons left their sheaths.

"You can't prove that," Tannin said with a shrug even though her heart was racing.

"Tan, your eyes are glowing," Flint said weakly.

"Oh right." She stared upwards and blinked hard several times until she was sure her eyes had lost their wargish, golden colour and turned back to the guard. "Like I was saying, you can't prove shit."

"Demon," he hissed.

"Fuck you."

A quick glance over her shoulder told her she was now the focus of all of the guards – Armodian and Dunoakers alike.

Dammit.

A sharp warning cry rang out. Tannin nearly jumped out of her skin as an arrow hissed past. An overeager Armodian archer on a rooftop opposite notched another arrow. Tannin's pounding heart took on a new rhythm as heat flooded her limbs and her inner fire roiled. She let it take hold. Red-clad guards surrounded her as she contorted and crunched her way into her monstrous form.

"Wait, wait, wait!" Flint cried trying to race around and holding his arms out like his lanky body could shield her from the panicked guards. Two of them caught him and held him back with grunts that it wasn't safe.

"This is what we warned you about!" The guard who had had her wanted poster yelled in the direction of the Dunoak guards and gathered civilians. "This is the beast who ravaged the city of Armodan!"

He advanced, pointing his finger at her, his other hand gripping his sword. Tannin stared him down in amusement. He could holler all he liked, but she could hear the blood sloshing in his veins as his heart raced like a wee rabbit.

"She did not!" Flint protested.

"Say what you like about wargs in general," the guard continued. "But that one is too far gone."

"Leave her alone!"

"And who are you to defend that monster?" The guard rounded on Flint. "Did you see what it did? How many people it killed? And for what? For NO REASON!"

Tannin bared her teeth. She had had damn good reasons at the time. It didn't matter to anyone that she hadn't meant to kill anyone at all and was just trying to survive. It didn't matter to anyone that she was filled with regret and nightmares from that day. It didn't matter to anyone that she was sorry.

The guard now turned to the rest of the people. "This beast is out of control, and what happened in Armodan will happen again here! You will never know peace while it lives!"

The guard's accusations mounted and grew fevered as spittle flew from his mouth. He would have the whole city thinking she slaughtered babies and drank their blood in a minute.

Tannin caught Flint's eye as the guard continued to rant and rave. His eyes widened and he mouthed "No" at her.

He knew her too damn well.

He knew that she has had just about enough of this guard pointing his finger in her face. She leant forward and neatly, *daintily*, bit it off.

"TANNIN!"

Fuuuuuuuuck.

Tannin snorted and pawed the ground as two familiar figures shoved their way into the square. The nine-fingered guard stared at his hand in disbelief. The pain clearly hadn't kicked in yet.

Tannin growled as Dana and Douglas came to a halt right in front of her, but it changed quickly to a small yelp as Dana reached up to grab her furry pointed ear and yank on it hard.

"Change. Back. Now," she ground out through gritted teeth.

Although she was loath to give in so easily, keeping her warg form was exhausting. Reluctantly, Tannin contorted and shrank back to her human self.

"Hi Dana," Tannin said weakly. "Before you start, if it wasn't for me, Alby could have died."

"Tannin, you cannot possibly fathom how much I do not care about one tiny human," Dana retorted.

"He's not one of you?" one of the guards blurted.

Dana gave Tannin one lastan bitter vicious glare before bearing down on the guards who quickly lowered their weapons. Douglas stood motionless, but the glare he gave the guards promised violence.

"Him?" Dana said, glancing at Alby who was enveloped in Cook's strong arms, crying uncontrollably. "He is as human as dirt. Stop trying to burn my kitchen boy. You have ten seconds to explain yourselves, and it better be good. What is the meaning of this?"

"That," the nine-fingered guard choked out, "is the Beast of Armodan."

He had gone deathly pale and, although he was taking the loss of his finger in his stride, his knees were quaking.

"I am aware," Dana replied drily.

"I am so not in the mood for this. King Florian promised I could leave freely, so what are you even doin' here?" Tannin demanded.

"We aren't here on King Florian's orders." He leered even as his tunic darkened with blood as he clutched his hand to his chest. "Private contract."

Another interrupted. "We *are* here on King Florian's orders, and this act of bounty hunting is unsanctioned." Now that Tannin looked closer, there did seem to be two parties. This latest guard's uniform was far more pristine, and his light brown hair was neatly combed. Even before Tannin chomped him, the other man had looked bedraggled.

"These men do not act on behalf of Armodan or the Brochlands," the neat guard announced.

He glared at the nine-fingered guard, who was losing steam quickly. He clutched the arm of the man next to him and submitted to being lowered to sit down as he called for a healer.

"What orders?" Dana hissed. Her eyes were blazing with fury. Tannin's insides squirmed thinking of how that was probably going to be directed at her later.

"Princess Avalyn," the guard said in a booming voice.

The words echoed in the form of whispers throughout the square until the noise was deafening.

"Are you or are you not holding the princess against her will?"

"Decidedly not," Dana replied sourly. "If she were here, then it would be of her own volition."

"In that case, I have a letter for Princess Avalyn of the Brochlands," he said firmly. "I am to place it in her hands and no one else's."

Dana narrowed her eyes.

Before she could confirm or deny Ava being in Dunoak, the main doors to the keep were thrown open once more and Princess Avalyn herself descended. She hadn't changed her clothing or hair, but the young woman who graced them with her presence was most definitely no longer just Ava. Tannin watched as she squared her shoulders and strode out of the crowd. Of course, she had been watching and listening in.

"Your Highness."

A portion of the guards dropped to their knees. Tannin suspected those were King Florian's real messengers.

The neat guard with the letter cleared his throat to speak, but Princess Avalyn cut him off by holding out her hand for the scroll.

Once more, he tried to gather his words, but an imperious look and a raised eyebrow from the princess had him sheepishly handing over the letter instead.

Avalyn didn't say a word. As soon as the scroll was in her palm, she turned on her heel and walked back across the square with her head held high as if daring someone to stop her. With her hair and skirts billowing out behind her, she was the essence of royalty. Even when she disappeared into the great hall, the guards still stared reverentially after her.

"I believe you have completed your mission," Dana said with the ghost of a smile playing across her features. "Now, we're going to talk about what happens to people who cause trouble in my city."

Chapter Twenty-Five

Disowned

"You *bit...*" Ava pinched the bridge of her nose and closed her eyes. "...his finger off?"

"It's rude to point," Tannin replied with a shrug.

"You are unhinged."

"At this point, are you surprised?" Tannin threw her hands in the air. "And don't try and distract me. I want to know what that letter was."

Ava had returned at once to her workrooms to read the letter in private. She had then instantly thrown herself into work to distract herself. She didn't want to think about the gravity of those words. Not right now. Possibly not ever.

Flint and Tannin had bowled into her room as she was prepping a poultice for a guard's unfortunate rash, and they were determined to not leave her alone until she divulged the contents of the letter.

Ava threw some seeds into a bowl and aggressively ground them into powder. She needed to do something with her hands or she was going to tear her hair out.

She let out a long exhale and gripped the edge of the table. The letter had been written with decorative, swirling letters in coloured ink and gilded edges. The contents had, naturally, also been decorative nonsense, but hidden in the soft wording was a clear message. She'd honed the skill of reading between the lines a long time ago, and she recognised her father's words on the page as clearly as if he was standing before her. His eyebrows would come down low over his eyes, and within his thick beard, his lips would press together until they disappeared. When he was shouting, that was okay. It was when he spoke softly that she knew she was really in trouble.

She'd seen no evidence of her mother's influence on the message, but that was hardly surprising. She had become a shell of the woman she once was since Flo's death. She walked the halls like a ghost and excused herself from all matters of state to tend to her gardens. In a way, Ava now understood that. Since Attilo, the act of nurturing something into life had brought her unexpected comfort.

"Ava?" Flint prompted.

"My father, uh, disowned me."

"What?!"

"Read it for yourselves." Ava thrust the parchment at Tannin and grabbed more pots and jars from her shelves. She really did not want to talk about the letter, but she knew the two of them well enough to know that they were not going to let it go.

Tannin squinted at the thick coil of parchment. Her mouth moved as she sounded out the words while the furrows of her forehead became more pronounced.

"Ava, I don't understand what this means – just tell me what it says."

"It says," Ava began, "that if I've sided with you, then I've sided against Armodan and my title is forfeit." She put down the jar she was holding and tipped her face up to the ceiling, eyes closed, and exhaled. "Basically, that if I'm not home by the end of the month, then I can forget going home at all."

"So, it's not set in stone. You can still—"

"I'm not leaving," Ava said firmly, even though Tannin was very close to hitting a nerve.

Doesn't she want me to stay with her?

"Is it because of that stupid oath? Fuck the oath." Tannin waved her hands exaggeratedly like she was casting a spell. "I hereby release you from it."

"It's not the oath." Ava finally turned to look at her. "I don't want what's waiting for me in Armodan. You know I never wanted that life."

And I want to stay with you.

"It's one thing to say it. It's another to actually give up the life of a princess," Flint reasoned. "You sure you don't want to think this through?"

Ava picked up a tin watering can and sloshed water into the yellow petalled flowers she'd grown in a pot on her window ledge. They didn't really need watering. She could hear Flint and Tannin mouthing and gesturing to each other behind her back. She set down her watering can.

"If I went back, I'd be alone."

It wasn't just that neither Flint nor Tannin would be there. Here, in Dunoak, Attilo wasn't a blatantly missing piece. He'd never roamed these halls. Armodan without him would be unbearable and, like a missing tooth, she wouldn't be able to stop herself poking at the wound. He would be a haunting memory every day.

"Flint's right. This is your family we're talking about. You should think about this properly," Tannin said. "And get some rest. You need sleep."

"I need results."

Results won't tell me to leave.

"You're gonna burn out."

"I don't care!"

"Hey, I have a question." Flint interrupted their brewing argument, a sly smile spreading. "Going back to the finger biting incident."

Tannin narrowed her eyes at him. "What about it?"

"What happened to it?"

"What?"

"The finger." Flint made a face. "Did you swallow it?"

Tannin paled. "No! I mean...I don't think I did. Oh gods, did I?"

"Ava, in your opinion, since Tannin isn't really human and if we assume that that guard is, would that be canniba—"

"Don't you fuckin' finish that question. It is not!"

"It could be," Ava replied with a smile, catching Flint's wink. The distraction was a welcome relief and she latched onto it gratefully. Anything to avoid thoughts that would poke at that growing painful place in her heart.

"I do not like this conversation," Tannin declared, crossing her arms.

"It's a valid one," Flint reasoned.

"I'm not listening to this." Tannin covered her ears. "I'm not a damn cannibal!"

She began to hum to drown out any further teasing while Flint sauntered over to lean on the desk next to Ava.

"I'm just messing with her," Flint whispered from behind his hand. "I saw it on the ground."

Tannin's head snapped up. "You bastard."

Ava shook her head at him, trying to hide her smile. "I am appalled at you, Flint."

"Aye, but I made you laugh, so I win." He grinned and caught Tannin's hand as she tried to punch him in the arm. He pulled her into a bear hug even as she squirmed.

"Get off me! You're the worst!"

"The cutest wee cannibal there ever was," Flint sang.

Ava watched them in amusement. She so often felt like a useless appendage when the three of them were together. She didn't think Tannin had noticed it, but Flint certainly had. Like just now, he made the effort to drag her into their nonsense. To make her feel included.

Doesn't he want me to stay?

Ava's throat tightened.

"Alright, you children, I've had too many distractions already. I need to get back to work."

Tannin extricated herself from Flint's crushing hug.

"Do you ever even take a break? We were gonna go have another drink in the hall, but we can bring it down here instead. Have a wee after party." She flopped down and stretched out luxuriously on the ratty sofa that Ava had in the corner of her work room and fluttered her eyelashes. "Why don't you come lay down for a bit and relax?"

"No, get out. Both of you."

"Tannin!" The bellow came from above and the three of them winced.

Ava shuddered as the runic wards she'd carved into the stairwell flickered to life a few moments before Dana's heavy stomps could be heard thundering down the stairs.

"Fuck," Tannin groaned just as the door crashed open.

Ava grimaced. She'd just replaced that lock.

"What the hell was that mess?" Dana demanded, striding into the room and glaring at Tannin.

Ava purposefully did not look at the reddish splatter on the sleeves of her white tunic. However much time she spent around the wargs, she still couldn't get used to their casual approach to violence.

"Not my fault is what it was," Tannin retorted, taking a subtle step back. Ava couldn't blame her. Dana angry was a sight to behold, and the last time Tannin had been on the receiving end, Ava had found her sobbing her heart out with nail marks down her cheeks.

This time, however, Dana's anger was directed elsewhere.

"How dare they?!" Dana seethed. "They think they can come here and make demands of me?"

"Maybe they just don't know you. Us," Tannin replied carefully.

Dana scoffed. "Well, after this they bloody will. We started to build a reputation here without bloodshed, but it's high time we showed them that we are not to be taken for fools or to be walked all over."

This is her definition of without bloodshed? Oh gods. I'd hate to see what she considers bloody. I doubt the blood in the square even ever gets time to fully dry.

"And you." Dana rounded on Ava. "Did you bring them here? Did you talk to someone?"

Ava swallowed. Dana seemed so much bigger in the small space of her workroom.

"I did not," she replied, lifting her chin and hoping she sounded confident.

"You're not to leave the keep," Dana said firmly. "At all. Either of you. For any reason." She glanced at Flint. "You, I don't care about."

He shrugged. "Fair."

"Tannin, the whole damned city will know about you by now, and gods' know, a lot of people want you dead. The heir to Stonestead or just you personally. So, for the love of all that is Golden, stay in the keep."

"Am I in danger?"

"Absolutely. Swear you will stay behind the walls of the keep."

"But—"

"Swear it!"

"Alright, I swear!"

"You too." Dana glared at Ava. "I've had enough trouble with you already."

"I swear it."

Ava had absolutely no intentions of leaving the safety of her runic wards now that her identity was out in the open. She was still worth a staggering amount of coin to the right people, disowned or not.

Dana seemed satisfied with their obedience, so Ava chanced her luck.

"What are you going to do with the Armodian guards?"

She did not like the smile that crept across Dana's face. She didn't like it one bit.

Chapter Twenty-Six

Picnic

Ava

Dana had been unfortunately correct about the danger to Tannin's life. Would-be assassins seemed to be around every corner. Their bodies had been hung from the main gate next to the Armodian guards Dana had executed. Ava could see them sway gently in the wind from the keep windows.

Only one of the assassins had gotten anywhere close to her. Ava shuddered a little at the memory. She'd woken up as her Senses assaulted her with violent shivers and her runic wards were triggered. She'd been under no illusion that she'd be any help whatsoever in the event of intruders, so she'd tweaked them so that they not only alerted her but dissolved strategically placed pieces of wood that fell to smash vases or knock over pieces of furniture and bring the well-armed nightly patrol running.

That night she'd stood, dagger in hand, listening to the sounds of the scuffle that followed. When, at last, there was silence and she'd been brave enough to poke her head out into the corridor, she had found Tannin looking groggy and bewildered standing in her nightshirt, axes in hand, and Lachlan, muscles bulging, with his spear skewering the would-be assassin to Tannin's bedroom door.

Since that night, sleep had been elusive even on the days she did get to bed before the wee hours of the morning. Tannin, as well, had started taking the danger a lot more seriously. Ava had come clean to the wargs about all the protections she had put in place, and surprisingly, had received a slap on the back from Dana rather than the usual hostility she was accustomed to. It seemed the wargs were warming to her after all.

Their attitude was mirrored by the string of gloriously sunny days they were treated to. The mood in Dunoak had also mellowed to the point where Tannin and Ava had been given the okay to leave the keep with a well-armed warg-blood escort and only during the daytime. Needing some time to just enjoy themselves, Tannin, Flint and Ava planned to meet Collum and Eoghan on a grassy brae just outside the city for a picnic.

"You can come along next time," Ava promised Alby as he helped the three of them pack a basket full to the brim with crusty bread, jam, cheese and leftover roast meat from dinner the night before. The boy didn't reply. He kept close to Ava's side and didn't look at Tannin once even when she tried to speak to him. He had really taken the whole warg thing to heart.

As they left though, Tannin reached into her pocket and flicked a gold coin in the air before catching it again. Alby's eyes went wide as she tossed it to him.

"For all your hard work."

It would be a treasured addition to the sock full of coppers he had conspiratorially confided in Ava that he kept under his mattress. He was still gazing at the gold, glassy-eyed, when they left.

"Oi! If you're a big strong beastie, why am I carrying all the heavy stuff?" Flint grumbled, hefting the basket to his other shoulder as they left.

"Shush, we've got to keep up appearances," Ava sighed. Dana had seemingly relaxed her aversion to Ava and Tannin spending time together. Either that or she realised it was futile to try and keep them apart. Ava was reasonably confident that Dana didn't exactly know the extent of how much time they spent together, but it still worried her what would happen when she did find out.

"That's right. I'm just small and helpless." Tannin fluttered her eyelashes at him, and he stuck out his tongue at her

"Oh, come on! Everyone bloody knows who she is."

"Aye, but it's still a secret even if everyone knows. Like, they know but they're not allowed to say. So, we're not saying it either."

"That's so dumb."

"And yet you're still carrying the basket."

Today's warg-blood escort, thankfully, did not include Callie and her crew, but rather three, burly young men that Ava didn't know the names of. She'd seen them around, but they tended to be more interested in wrestling each other than anything else. They trailed them at a respectable distance as they walked through the city.

They were meeting the brothers at the city gate to walk the rest of the way together. As they rounded the last corner, Tannin announced that she could already smell the apple tarts fresh from the market and the punnet of strawberries they had brought with them. Ava's mouth watered.

They found a good spot in the shade of a thick-branched tree halfway up the brae, out of the harshness of the midday sun, to lay their blankets and sprawl out. Their warg-blood escort also flopped down in the shade a few trees over.

Flint uncorked a flagon of ale with his teeth and passed it around as they laid out their feast.

"We heard there's important folks gonna be in town tomorrow," Eoghan said.

The unasked question was directed at Tannin and she nodded.

"River traders are comin' to visit. They've got a sort of a town a wee bit south of here."

The brothers exchanged a look and Flint audibly groaned.

"What kind of shite should we prepare for?" He popped a strawberry into his mouth. "Like scale of one to ten, how shite? Actually, if it's a ten, don't even tell me."

"Awk, it's not that. It's just..." Collum looked to his brother for help.

"That sounds like kelpies, and the kelpies are...dangerous business," Eoghan said.

"That sounds like you have experience." Ava frowned as a daisy fell out of her hair – one of the many Tannin had stuck into her thick waves without her realising.

"I always thought kelpies had something to do with horses? Like horses in the water and then they drown you? Those were the stories my ma always told me anyway," Flint said.

Ava looked at Flint out the side of her eye. She'd asked Tannin for Flint's history after he'd turned up at her secret crypt with a half-dead Tannin and a lot of questions last year. She had had frustratingly little information, and when pressed, had said he didn't seem like he wanted to talk about it, so she'd never asked. All she had said was that Flint never really mentioned his mother. She'd run off with a lover when he was still very young – before he had even learnt his letters – and he, in turn, had left his father's house when he had barely stopped growing. He'd always joked that it was to find his fortune and fame. Ava had tried to pry and found him just as evasive as Tannin had said.

"Aye, there's truth in those stories to be sure."

"So, what are real kelpies like then?"

"The waterways are their business, but they're also fierce horsemasters, you've got that right."

"Can horses even swim?" Tannin interrupted.

"Nah, they pull the boats, like."

The boys painted a vibrant picture of canals all through southern Woodren. Ancient waterways connecting hundreds of small villages, with tree roots wound into pathways that the horses walked on to pull the boats. It was said that only those with kelpie blood could navigate the twisting trails and treacherous waters.

Ava was fascinated. Kelpie-bloods were some of the most elusive Remnants, and she had read very little about them. She wished she'd brought a quill to take notes.

"They'll make a deal for almost anything, but you've got to watch your wording. If you fuck with them, they'll drown you. It's gruesome-like. They get the horses to do it – bet that's where the stories come from like yer ma said."

"Aye, so they'll tie your legs and chuck you in the water, but the rope is attached to the horse. They make it run, so you're pulled through the water." Collum lay on his back with his legs in the air and mimed thrashing in the water.

"But your arms are free, so you can sometimes make it to the surface to get air but only a wee bit. Man, it takes 'em ages to die." Eoghan's grimace turned to a grin. "You can make good coin betting on it, though."

"Oi, oi, speaking of!" Collum held out his hand.

Scowling, Eoghan slapped a golden crown into his palm.

"Oh, whatcha bet on?" Tannin eyed the gold with curiosity.

"On you darlin'." Collum winked.

"What?"

"Well, we knew it was one of yous that was...y'know," Eoghan said in a hushed voice. "Timing and all that. Then that big lad at the tavern, and yous are all staying at the keep – didnae take a genius."

Between the brothers and the warg-bloods, Tannin's identity was quickly becoming the worst kept secret in Dunoak. Ava was privately a little smug that she had kept her secret better.

"And you thought it was me?" Tannin turned to Eoghan. "Who'd you think it was?"

Eoghan jutted his chin in Ava's direction.

"What about me?" Flint complained, outraged. "Don't I seem like I could be a big, scary warg?"

"It's more them two seem like they've got secrets, like."

"Aye, we all know your secret now too, your Majesty," Collum said, waggling his eyebrows.

"Technically, it's 'your Highness'." Ava grinned. "But I'll let it slide."

The brothers chortled.

"So, any other secrets you two are keepin'?"

"Oh, so many secrets," Ava said with light amusement, laying back on the blanket to gaze at the clouds.

Flint snorted. "Oh aye. Except it's the same secret, and it's that they both want to fu—"

Tannin kicked him.

"Ow!"

He kicked her back but with a grin. She threw a handful of grass in his face.

"Oh mature, That's – bleughh!" He spat out the grass that had gotten into his mouth as she threw another handful.

She lifted up yet another fistful, threateningly. "Not another damn word, you gossipmonger!"

He placed a hand over his heart in mocking solemnity. "I will take your secrets with me to the grave."

"Oh no." Tannin sat up abruptly. "Oh *no.*"

"What?"

"I do know where the goddam stupid fucking vials are."

Ava also sat up quickly. "You do? Tannin, that's huge."

It was vital that the Dunoak wargs got to the vials before Sommer, but Ava couldn't avoid the knot of anxiety that twisted at the thought. If they got the vials, they didn't need her to recreate the serum.

"I have to tell Dana," Tannin groaned. "Urgh. Picnic over. Duty calls."

"What is it?" Collum asked.

"I'm sorry, I can't tell you. Ava, Flint, you can stay if you want, but I have to go back." Tannin stood and brushed grass from her skirt. "Actually, there's no point in you coming 'cause Dana won't let you in the council chambers anyway, but I'll tell you everything later, alright? Save me some strawberries."

"You're leaving right now?"

"I can't just sit still now I know...the thing that I know I know." She cast a pointed look at the brothers. "I mean it about the strawberries, though. I still want some."

She waved as she walked back down the hill but sped up into a jog as she reached the bottom. Her warg-blood escort weren't far behind.

"Weren't they supposed to protect you, too?" Flint frowned.

"In theory," Ave replied drily. It was disappointing but not surprising that the protection Dana offered her was conditional.

"Fuckers," Eoghan said casually. "So, a princess, eh?"

"Unfortunately," Ava went back to laying on the grass, letting the dappled sunlight kiss her cheeks.

"Avalyn of the Brochlands." Eoghan exhaled. "Weren't you supposed to marry prince what's-his-name? From Rill?"

Ava's eyes snapped open. "Prince Erlan. What do you know of that?"

He shrugged, looking at his brother for assistance. "Everyone knows that. It was going to be a big thing and then it never happened. Is it 'cause you ran away?"

"I didn't run away."

"Aye, you did," Flint countered. "Very much did the running away thing. Turned up at my door in the middle of the night and everything."

"I didn't run. I...took a spontaneous long-term trip," Ava said but it sounded so ridiculous even she couldn't help but smile.

"So, we've got a runaway princess, a monster in disguise..." Collum cocked his head at Flint. "A dashing rogue."

"Uh huh," Eoghan said catching his meaning and nodding excitedly.

"What?" Ava asked suspiciously.

Eoghan grinned.

"This is going to make an excellent song."

"Don't you dare!"

Chapter Twenty-Seven

Warg Juice

Tannin

Tannin slowed a little so that her bodyguards wouldn't think she was trying to run away from them, but she buzzed with excitement. Finally, she knew something useful.

The guards at the entrance to the keep nodded to her as she passed, but the ones at the entry to the council chambers barred her entry. Apparently, Dana was already in a meeting. She ignored them and barged in anyway. Dana wouldn't want this to wait.

"And that's why the city's boundaries are—" Dana stopped mid-sentence as Tannin threw the doors open and strode in.

"Everyone out," Tannin said in a commanding voice, surprising even herself.

"What do you think you are doing?"

"I remembered. The important thing. The thing I thought I didn't know but I do," Tannin said breathlessly, half from excitement and half from her jog.

Dana was silent for a moment and then said quietly, "Everyone out."

Murmurs of disapproval noises hummed through the chamber. Tannin plucked at the back of her shirt where it was sticking to her.

"I said out," Dana repeated, louder. "We will pick this up later."

"The warg vials are in Armodan," Tannin said as soon as the last of the footsteps had faded.

Something had clicked into place in Tannin's memory at Flint's phrase.

Some secrets we take to the grave, my dear.

"Tell me everything."

"I think," Tannin began carefully, suddenly realising that she had no proof of what she was about to claim. "I think that he sewed the vials into his own body. I think they're buried with him in a graveyard in the Skirts."

Dana's nose wrinkled. "What makes you think that?"

"I caught him one day. Sewing up a big cut in his side." Tannin drew a line across her abdomen to demonstrate. "Some secrets we take to the grave. That's what he said. He wouldn't tell me what had happened, and now, I think he did it himself. I know he sewed it up himself. At the time, I thought he had just had an accident or got himself into a fight."

"That's all you saw?"

"The vials aren't big, I remember them," Tannin insisted. "They would have fit in the wound he had. And it's absolutely the kind of thing he would do."

Her grandfather had always had a twisted sense of humour. He had sewn the vials into his side, she was sure of it. Which meant the vials were buried in the graveyard outside of the Skirts of Armodan.

"I need to think," Dana said, rubbing her temples.

"We could send a really small group on a secret mission," Tannin replied in a hushed voice, made eager by the secrecy. "One that people wouldn't look twice at. I can't go since I'm, y'know, banished but I can draw a map. Show them exactly where he's buried."

And then they can dig him up and cut him open.

Tannin swallowed hard. It wasn't a pleasant thought.

Dana gave a measured nod. "I'll make a plan."

"I actually think I know who we should send."

Tannin met Flint in the barn. He had wanted to check in on the dogs before the Kelpies arrived. He would end up very busy stabling their horses that they would no doubt bring with them. Ava had disappeared off to her workrooms after they'd come back from their picnic.

"So," Flint said making a resigned face when Tannin told him about the warg-juice vials. "We're going graverobbing then."

"Well, I'm not," Tannin pointed out, tossing another piece of pilfered meat to the dog who was prowling at the bottom of the fence she was perched on. "I'm banished. I can't just go waltzing back, they'd kill me on sight. But...I thought you might go."

She suspected she could even come down off the fence by now, but she wasn't going to risk her ankles just yet. Her efforts were definitely paying off, though. There had been no snarling today. The dog, seemingly realising she had no more food for her, huffed and sat down heavily.

Flint scratched the dog's ears.

"It would be dangerous. People know your connection to me," Tannin added, "But it would raise the least suspicion, and you know your way about the best. You don't have to, of course."

"Of course, I'll go. Kind of glad of it, actually."

"You want to go back, don't you?" Tannin rested her elbows on her knees. "I miss it too."

"I could check in on Eve on the way. And the wee one."

Tannin's heart did a little skip and then flopped. She missed Eve. She missed Eve a lot.

Tannin exhaled. "You'd have to be so careful, Flint. I mean it, no schemes, no detours. In and out."

"I'll be a wee mouse," he promised. "No one will know I'm there."

Through the wide open door of the barn, they had a good view of the road the visitors would most likely take, and so, they were some of the first to know when the kelpie-bloods arrived.

When they did, there was no mistaking them. Mounted on a dozen black horses, the kelpie-bloods rode into the city in utter silence, like mist seeping across the swamps. The huge beasts' hooves should have sounded like thunder on the cobbled street. Tannin looked at Flint in alarm.

"Well," he breathed, "that is something."

As the riders approached the keep, they dismounted with a grace that told of experience. The doors to the keep opened, and Dana emerged, glittering with gold and flanked by Douglas and Adair. Tannin hadn't seen Adair in ages. He'd been out with his rangers, trawling for news. She hadn't even known he was back.

"Shouldn't you also be there?"

"Aw fuck. Aye, I should."

Still wary of the dog, Tannin scrambled along the top of the fences of the stalls until she could leap for the door.

"You look ridiculous."

"Shut it. Move your arse. You should be there too for the horses, remember?"

Tannin raced to join the wargs, with Flint loping along behind her. Dana gave her a relieved look out of the side of her eye as Tannin slunk past the wargs to the back of the group.

She was the only one not wearing gold, she noticed peevishly. Tannin pressed her lips together to hide her pout. Surely, Dana could lend her some even just for appearances' sake.

Actually, she wasn't the only one. Ava stood just inside the main door, cloaked in the shadows, observing the welcome. Tannin waved at her to come out, but she shook her head and slid further into the darkened hallway.

The woman that Tannin assumed was the leader of the of kelpie-blood visitors handed the reins of her mount to a younger woman and stepped forward, touching her fingertips together in what Tannin guessed was a sign of greeting. Like the rest of the group, the woman was dressed in the browns and greens of the swamp lands. Her wrinkled, brown skin could have so easily been mistaken for ancient tree bark. Her mist-grey hair fell to her waist and looked like it should have had moss growing in it instead of beaded braids. The group looked startlingly out of place in a city, even one as overwhelmingly mud-soaked as Dunoak. These were people who were part of the landscape itself. Tannin shivered. Even the densest of minds couldn't deny they exuded some kind of old magic.

"I am Iona of the Alderglen Kelpie-folk. Which one of ye fair young 'uns is Dana of the Stonestead Wargs?"

Dana stepped forward to greet her, and her wizened face split into a large smile. Instead of accepting the hand Dana held out for her to shake, the older woman grasped her by the shoulders, pulling her downwards to plant a large, wet kiss on either of her cheeks. Tannin stifled a chuckle as Dana tried to remain unruffled by the sudden intimacy, but she was clearly rattled. Tannin liked seeing her rattled.

She managed to regain her composure as she called for bread to be brought. Cook herself proudly strode forth with a fresh loaf. The scent made Tannin's mouth water.

"Ohhh, that looks like a good one," Tannin murmured under her breath with envy as she watched the old woman struggle to tear the dense loaf apart.

The wargs stood solemnly as Dana and Iona both ate from the loaf and exchanged small talk about the journey and the weather while the new arrivals unloaded their carts. Part of the arrangements for the visit was that it was also to be somewhat of a trade festival.

The kelpie-bloods were given permission to have their stalls right along the walls of the keep. Before they had even finished setting up, city folk were already swarming, eyes gleaming at the fresh intrigues they had brought.

Tannin's curiosity was drawn to one of the young women unloading the carts. The shape of her face and eyes bore a close resemblance to the old woman. A granddaughter maybe? Her skin glistened as she hauled sacks from the back of the cart, her arms taut with muscle. She paused for a moment and lifted the hem of her shirt to wipe the sweat from her brow, giving Tannin a glimpse of the sculpted abs underneath.

"Close your mouth. You'll catch flies," Ava murmured into her ear.

Tannin flinched. She had been too pre-occupied to hear Ava's approach.

"Like you weren't looking too," she shot back.

"Far more subtly than you were, that's for sure." Ava shrugged and smirked. "Anyway, I prefer blondes."

Tannin raised an eyebrow, but before she could respond, a harsh shout erupted, followed by a scuffle that dragged their attention to a less pleasant sight.

Two of the Alderglen men had a third by the arms and were struggling to hold him. Dana was mere paces away, holding a stone knife at arm's length in distaste. Iona stood beside her. Tannin did a double-take.

The friendly-faced, old woman persona was long gone, and if that glower had been fixed on Tannin, she knew her knees would have been quaking.

"An unprovoked attack?" The kelpie-blood leader's voice was deadly calm. She cocked her head to peer at the attacker's features closely. "Ye were not invited to this gathering, Findar."

"It was not unprovoked!" the man called Findar yelled. "They murdered the laird here! Took Dunoak for themselves! It won't be long before they come for us next!"

Spittle flew from his lips as he raged.

Iona gave a thoughtful nod. "So, ye were going tae what? Assassinate the lass? Aye, they took Dunoak, but fair and square as far as I see. But see, here's what I'm not hearing..." Her mouth twisted. "...how any of that affects business."

"But...if—"

"Ifs and hearsay?" Iona chuckled. "That's what ye come tae me with in yer defence? If ye were going for a brave gesture, at least go for the big 'un." She nodded at Douglas and tutted.

Iona turned to the gathering crowd. "This man is not one of my party. He is an interloper, a thief, and has disrespected our hosts. He has neither my protection nor my favour." She turned to Dana. "It's custom that ye can claim his horse for yer own since the deed was against yerself, though I've heard yer lot don't care for the beasts."

"We do not."

"Then ye'll have the horse's price in coin." Her tone left no room for debate. "This isnae a representation of my folk, and I'll no have it said that we didnae put it right. Our traditions demand a drowning."

"No!" gasped Findar. "Aunt Iona, please!"

Iona ignored him. "Do ye have a source of water? Honestly, a bucket will do."

Findar had sunk to his knees, eyes wide, still muttering his pleas for mercy.

"That's not a good death." Dana's nose wrinkled in distaste.

"It's traditional. But as ye suffered the slight, we can amend the method. Have ye a preference, dear?"

"A blade will do."

"As you wish." Iona moved swiftly, taking the stone knife from Dana and thrust it straight into Findar's stomach.

The blade squelched as she rotated it and dragged it through the soft flesh of his abdomen. He didn't cry out, but his mouth stretched open in a silent scream until the knife was pulled free and he was allowed to sink to the ground.

"Leave him tae bleed, then." Iona wiped her bloody hands on her skirts and harrumphed. "Waste of a boy, that one. Worst of my sister's brood. Shall we go inside? This breeze is getting tae my old bones. I'll take a nettle wine if ye have it, there's a good girl."

She swished past the wargs and into the keep, mossy green shawl flapping behind her.

Chapter Twenty-Eight

Good Business

Tannin

This was shaping up to be far more interesting than Tannin had expected it to be. Murder tended to do that. Not just that, though. Dana was scrabbling for control, which made Tannin gleeful. It was all she could do not to outright laugh when Dana had to scurry after the kelpie-blood leader into her own keep.

Iona had insisted on a full retinue accompanying her to oversee the official business, so Dana had invited at least an equal number of wargs to even the scale. The numbers meant that they held the meeting in the feast hall rather than the council chambers.

"Right," Iona said having nestled into a chair by the fire in the long dining hall. Between two long bony fingers, she clutched a glass of whisky that she'd settled for in the absence of nettle wine. "The auld laird wasn't a friend, but he wasn't no enemy of mine neither. We had a good ol' fashioned trade agreement that I'll let ye have a gander at if it so pleases ye. Transport mostly. Our boats can take the swamps and get goods to and from the Shey."

"We didn't invite you here to discuss trade," Dana said, holding herself up as tall as she could manage in her seated position. "We invited you to discuss fealty. The immediate surrounding villages have already pledged to Dunoak."

"And I'll say straight off I'll no be givin' it. We don't need owt from ye that we cannae get ourselves. That's no tae say we cannae be good neighbours."

Dana's smile tightened. "I understand your position, but our ambition here is greater than just this city, as I'm sure you know."

"Oh, I know a lot of things." Her eyes flicked to Tannin who was perched within listening distance, and then back to Dana.

"Then I'm sure you know the benefits aligning your people with ours would bring."

"And the trouble it would bring."

"If trouble were to come your way, you would want our protection."

"It better no come our way if it knows what's good for it."

Dana's jaw clenched momentarily before she relaxed and swirled her own glass of whisky. Tannin's was already empty. She'd been absent-mindedly sipping at it as she watched the two powerful women talk.

"What was the arrangement with the previous laird here?" Dana asked.

At a click of Iona's fingers, a young man hastened to pass her a roll of grimy parchment. Just like the woman Tannin had been admiring outside, he too could also could have passed for a relative of their leader.

"It's all there," she said with a wave of her gnarled hand and lifted her glass for a refill.

Dana perused the document. "What's this about insurance?"

"Pirates." Iona's face twisted. "It's gettin' worse-like." She continued with a shake of her head, "Water's the fastest way to travel and don't they know it."

"Can't you defend yourselves?"

"Aye, most times, but if they get ye, they get ye and once yer got..." She opened her palms and shrugged. "That's why there's an insurance. I'm risking my folks and my boats. Not tae mention the further ye get down river, the more they dislike us folk. And I'm no just meaning me and mine. You and yours willnae be welcome there either. The coastal parts just ain't safe for Remnants no more."

"What do you mean?" Tannin blurted.

Remnants in danger? Triquetra?

"There's stories. Stories I don't like. We've never been friendly-like with the sea folk, but now, young 'uns have been disappearing and the like. I heard there's a turncoat selling out those with the old blood. There's stories of Remnant blood being sold across the seas. Raiders have started coming for it too. They think it'll give 'em powers if they drink it. Fools."

Iona spat on the floor. Dana's face scrunched in disgust.

"Well, you're paid absurdly well for your time in any case," Dana said drily looking back at the numbers.

"Good business is worth it." Iona gave her a toothy grin.

Tannin watched the leader of the kelpie-folk with interest. She reminded her of Skirts traders – determined and crafty.

But trading was one thing she knew she did well. She always got a few extra carrots, a copper knocked off the price of thread or a better deal on the trinkets the princess had paid her with. Half the trick was just being cheeky enough to ask for it. The other half was playing games.

"We've got what you need," Tannin interjected, a grin spreading across her cheeks.

Oh, this is a game I can play.

"Stay out of this," Dana snapped, earning herself an amused glance from the older woman.

"Trust me," Tannin said as her confidence bloomed. "I have a solution I think everyone will like."

Iona's crooked teeth showed as her smile widened. "This could get interestin' yet. What've ye got tae say, wee 'un?"

Tannin leaned back in her chair and crossed her legs, trying to mirror the woman's relaxed pose. "Oh, just that we could solve this wee problem of yours."

"You've already got my attention, lass, don't try and be clever," Iona snipped.

"You don't have control of the waterways. You're losing to the pirates. Slowly, but you said it yourself it's getting worse."

Iona's bony fingers twitched in agitation.

"You need that control back. I'll bet you've lost customers because you can't deliver. I bet some of your customers have even contracted the pirates to move their goods instead of the kelpie-folk. You're just going to become more and more unreliable until you're pushed out of business."

"If you've got a point, make it quicker."

"If there's one thing wargs are good at..." Tannin grinned. "It's hunting."

The room hummed with hushed whispers.

"Ye cannae hope tae get them all."

"We can get enough." Tannin shrugged. "Send a message and all that. That the kelpie-folk trade is not to be messed with. That they have powerful allies."

"We'd still need insurance for larger commissions."

"We can discuss that."

Tannin's eyes flicked to Dana. She wasn't sure she could make those kinds of promises, but the words were already out of her mouth. Dana's lips thinned but she gave a nod.

"We'd need payment in advance."

"On delivery."

“Half up front.”

“Quarter and that’s being generous.”

“Quarter and some pirate heads.”

“That we can make happen, can’t we?” Tannin looked to Dana again. “We’ve got some rowdy warg-bloods itching for a hunt. I’ve definitely got a particular few in mind. Let them scratch. We’ll gift the heads to our new friends.”

“When I say heads, lass, I dinnae mean any old head ye can pass off as a pirate. I want the figureheads from their boats. I know every last one by heart.”

“Don’t trust us to get the job done?”

“I dinnae trust anyone and neither should you.”

“We need something else.”

“Of course, ye do.”

“Information. You hear things on the water. In the interests of good business, it would be the smart choice to pass those things on. Especially about a certain wargish queen making moves in the Brochlands.”

“Would it now?”

“Profitable even.”

“How profitable?”

“Depends on the value of the information.”

“Hmm.” Iona licked her lips and considered Tannin’s proposal over her clasped hands. “I’ll draw up a new agreement to these terms. You can accept or refuse. Sign it in blood.”

She heaved herself to her feet and nodded towards the door. “I’ll send some of my boys round with it in one week.”

“You’re not staying?”

“I dinnae ever sleep on solid ground if I can help it. It’s how I’ve stayed alive so long.”

The kelpie-folk packed up as swiftly as they had set up, and by the end of the day, the only trace that they had ever been there were deep hoofprints in the mud.

A surreal feeling in the hall lingered for a long time after they had left – like they had taken some of the usual jovial atmosphere with them and left an uneasy feeling behind in its place. Tannin was running the meeting over and over in her head, trying to pick out something she’d missed, something that was making her feel all anxious.

Should I not have stepped in? Did I do something wrong?

It wasn't until much later in the evening when she heard raised voices that it dawned on her where the unease was coming from.

Douglas was furious.

"It is beneath us to scrape for their trade like this, when we should be taking what we want."

"We don't have enough power to act like that yet," Dana replied solidly.

Douglas stepped further into her space, crowding her with his bulk, but Dana didn't step back. She tilted her head up to meet his eye.

"We are wargs," Douglas snarled. His nostrils flared in anger.

"We are a small number of wargs in a small city that needs allies. We do not have the strength to make such demands."

"You are making us weaker. For the future of our people, we need stronger leaders, stronger representation. Stronger than *you*." He gestured at Tannin, who flinched. "She's no better."

"Then what do you propose?" Dana's voice dripped with malice. "Do you have the stones for what comes next, Douglas?"

Douglas scanned the room. Tannin wasn't the only one who had stopped to watch them, and the room awaited his answer with bated breath. The air was thick with expectation.

He straightened to his full, formidable height.

"Dana, I challenge you."

Chapter Twenty-Nine

Challenge

The warg-bloods' fervent desire to see a fight meant that the arena was set up in a spectacularly short time. The whole of Dunoak was stirred up into a frenzy at the chance to see a warg in their "true" form, and shops and taverns shut their doors as everyone swarmed out of the city.

Roughly hewn planks of wood formed a crude fence around a flat area outside of the city. The recent warm weather had dried up the ground to the point it was hard underfoot. People surrounded the square well in advance. Tannin had to really work to secure a space at the front.

She'd dragged Ava with her as she'd squeezed through the crowd and looked around for Flint, who was supposed to meet them there.

"Where is he?"

"Playing bookmaker most likely," Ava said derisively, flicking her hair over her shoulder. "Are we sure we want to be this close? Couldn't this be dangerous?"

"Aw, don't worry, princess, I'll protect you," Tannin mocked, slinging an arm around Ava's waist.

Ava shrugged her off and made a face. "I'm not sure I want to watch this anyway. I've already seen what wargs can do, and I've no desire to see it again."

"Ah, but this is warg v warg…Well, proper warg v warg."

Her own bout against Sommer didn't count.

That was an arsekicking, not a duel.

"Is there even a referee or a judge or anything?" Ava twisted her fingers together like she always did when she was uncomfortable.

"I don't think they're really sticking to any hard and fast rules. It's just win by any means necessary."

"Not quite, wee 'un."

The two of them spun round to where Lachlan stood lounging on one of the barriers. Tannin was grateful that he didn't seem the type to hold a grudge after she had managed to run away from him and go after Ava.

"There's two rounds. First round, they stay in their human forms and use traditional northern weapons until first blood is spilt." He waggled his head. "Used to be that they said the sight of the blood triggered a bloodlust that then made them into beasts, but that's all poppycock. They usually even take a break after first blood if it's just a friendly duel. They can't use the spirit of the mountain beast until after first blood. It's a binding pact."

Tannin thought back to her fight with Sommer. That wasn't exactly how it had happened, but when she'd agreed to fight with a sword, it was true she had felt some kind of block or unwillingness to transform.

Catriona chimed in from Lachlan's other side. "Once first blood is spilt, though, they can choose to use their other form. Most do. Usually, it's whoever can summon the beast spirit first has an advantage, and then, it's either until surrender or death. First blood counts whether it's a wee scratch or a proper gutting, so there's ways to tip the scale. I've not seen a death match myself, but I reckon it'll go to it today. Aye. Death it'll be."

Tannin had been sneaking into the kitchen to grab a snack when she'd seen Douglas and Catriona embrace that morning. She had suspected that they were sleeping together, but when he dipped his head to press his forehead to hers, the inked patterns that climbed the side of her face had perfectly linked up with those that covered his shaved head.

"Who do you want to win?" Tannin asked Lachlan cautiously. He gave her a curious look out of the side of his eye.

"Right now, all I want is to see a damn good fight. I want to see some blood." He lowered his voice. "You might want to be paying attention though, lass. Could be you out there soon enough."

Tannin blanched.

He gave her a wink and her stomach unclenched only slightly.

She didn't want to think about what would happen to her if Dana lost. Douglas sure as hell didn't want her to lead. Would he get rid of her? She didn't think he was the type, but she didn't think he'd challenge Dana either. If she ran from Dunoak, how far would she get until either Douglas' wargs or Sommer caught up to her? Or bandits or bounty hunters? Where would she even go? What would she do? She wouldn't survive a month. Her mouth ran dry. The crowd around her seemed to press in from all sides. She couldn't breathe. She rubbed her throat hard, trying to convince herself there wasn't a rope looped around it, choking her air.

"Tannin?" Ava's voice sounded far away.

Ava's hands were not as soft as they had once been back in Armodan, but were still comforting as she squeezed Tannin's own.

"Whatever happens here today, we'll work it out. Okay?"

Ava could read her like a book. Tannin nodded stiffly.

"Aye." Tannin exhaled. "This has all just got serious really fast. You ever see a duel?"

Ava shrugged. "Plenty of friendly ones with blunted swords. I used to watch my brothers with their men in the courtyard. I've seen duels in the tournaments too when I was younger but not in recent years. I let my family believe I had no taste for them and would rather spend my time in quiet contemplation." An amused smile played across her lips.

"I still can't believe you got away with that."

"Why not? I'm an excellent actress. Actually, I think they were all rather glad they didn't have to pay me any attention."

"Did Attilo ever duel in the tournaments? Before he was your bodyguard, I mean."

"I don't think so. The tournament knights are all glory hounds, and that was never his style. I imagine he trained some of them, though."

"What do you think he'd have made of all this?"

"I think even he would have been out of his depth here. He certainly wouldn't let us have front row seats to this."

"He wouldn't have wanted to watch?"

Ava chuckled. "He confessed to me once that a lot of blood makes him queasy. Made." She cleared her throat. "But he wouldn't have wanted me, well, you as well I suppose, being too close either in case something happened. It's strange, not having someone watch out for me like that. Having so much freedom. It's...a little frightening to be honest."

"If you need someone to tell you what to do, I'll gladly boss you about." Tannin grinned. "You're still indentured to me after all."

"Not what I meant," Ava said rolling her eyes. "And, no, I am not. I'm under oath. There's a distinct difference."

"Whatever, you're still mine."

Ava scoffed, but a hint of pink appeared across her cheeks. Tannin felt warmth rise in her own face as she realised what she said. She was about to explain that she didn't mean it like that when she saw familiar faces across the square.

Flint was smiling that sly, satisfied smile that Tannin knew meant he had probably made a lot of coin out of this duel already and it hadn't even started. She pointed him out to Ava and returned his wave. From the press of the crowd, he wouldn't be able to squeeze his way over to them before it started. There was already movement from within the two tents that had been set up at either end of the field for the fighters. Two men roamed the length of the arena, sprinkling it with sawdust.

The blare of horns quietened the crowd for a split second before the fighters emerged and the spectators erupted into cheers. Wargs, warg-bloods and regular Dunoakers hollered and crowed from the sidelines. They didn't seem to want to show too much support one way or another, although it sounded like Douglas got a bigger cheer from the warg-bloods.

Tannin had expected them to wear armour or at least fighting leathers, but Douglas appeared bare-chested with his tattoos on display, stretched over hard muscle and little more than a loin cloth. He raised his spear to the sky to thunderous applause.

Dana wore only slightly more – an extra band of fabric wound around her chest – as she also raised her weapons into the air with the roar of the crowd. She had the same twin short swords she had had in Armodan grasped in each hand.

"No armour," Ava muttered.

"I noticed."

"It's a show of confidence. Of bravery. I've seen these fights fought entirely nude," Lachlan remarked. "One of the most underhanded first blood wins I've ever seen." He cringed a little and his hands moved instinctively to protect his groin at the memory.

The two fighters took their time making a lap of the ring until the audience was almost frothing at the mouth with impatience. A drummer hammered out a furious beat as the two approached each other in the centre.

The beat stopped. The combatants bowed. Douglas held out his spear, and Dana clinked the tip of it with one of her swords.

The drum started up again with a slow, heavy thudding. Tannin's stomach squirmed in apprehension and excitement.

Dana could die, she suddenly realised. Like, actually die. Her heart did an unpleasant swoop.

The tempo increased. Dana took a defensive stance. Douglas mirrored her. They circled each other as the beat reached a frenzied speed.

Dana lunged first and the crowd erupted.

Tannin had no idea how Douglas managed to dodge the attack, but he did and quickly followed it with his own. They went back and forth at such a speed their movements blurred, but it was a coordinated, careful kind of chaos. They were holding back. She could feel it.

Tannin could barely follow the flurry of attacks, but she saw the first drop of blood hit the earth as clear as day. She could almost hear it sing as it fell, and collectively, the wargish part of the crowd sucked in a breath.

Dana didn't even spare a glance at the shallow cut Douglas' spear had made across the back of her hand. She didn't give him a moment to breathe and doubled down on her vicious strikes. Blades flashed and clanged against each other with abandon. The careful spell of first blood had been broken, and now they hacked and slashed at each other fiercely – both going for the kill with each fresh attack, neither giving the other the space or time to transform.

Tannin gripped the barrier so hard she thought it might splinter under her fingers. Her own blood thrummed in her veins as she yelled and jeered with the rest of them. The scent of sweat, sawdust and blood filled her nose and sparked something primal. She could feel the violence deep in her bones. The drops of blood flying from the tip of Dana's blades were like garnets as they splashed to the ground. Douglas's spear glittered in the sunlight as he swiped again at Dana's throat. Tannin no longer cared who won. The fight was a beautiful, terrible dance and she was swept up in it.

Douglas caught Dana with a vicious blow to the chest with the butt of his spear, and she flew half the length of the square, sprawling in the sawdust. Tannin's heart leapt into her mouth as the crowd exploded into cheers and howls.

This is it. She's lost. She's dead.

Logic crept back into Tannin's mind long enough for her to feel sinking dread at the thought of Dana's death when the warg's head flicked up and her face was a mask of triumph. It had been a ruse. A plan. To get space. To get a split second's worth of time to—

Dana exploded from her crouch in a whirl of fur and claws, her limbs still contorting and crunching as she threw herself at Douglas.

His spear came up to meet her and plunged her side but not before she tore a colossal chunk from his chest and dug her claws into his arms. His spear was wrenched from his hands as she pulled back and shrank, snapping the spear in two and freeing it from her flesh.

Douglas was on the ground, wheezing and clawing at his torn chest. Dana stood over him, dripping blood, with the broken remains of his weapon in her hands. One motion from her and they would be jutting from his throat in a second. She said something that Tannin couldn't hear over the yells of the crowd. Douglas gave a slow nod, then a firmer one, raising both hands in surrender.

He hauled himself to his knees, still under the threat of his own spear, however loosely Dana held it in her hands, and tipped forward to press his forehead to the dirt at her feet.

Chapter Thirty

Bloodlust

Tannin

Colours seemed especially bright. Sounds, too loud. Tannin's eyes darted after a fly that managed to find its way into the tent. Someone bumped her shoulder, snapping her attention from the fly. There were too many bodies in the confined space. Too hot.

All of the wargs, Tannin included, had bounded into Dana's tent immediately after the fight had ended. Following a raucous round of congratulations, wine had been poured and Dana made her victory toast. The words had been lost on Tannin. More about honour and what not. She couldn't keep still. Her bones were jittery.

"Ooh, someone's suffering from bloodlust," Dana crooned. Her smile was wide and her eyes bright even though her skin was clammy and she clutched at the wound in her side. Ava would have to sew that up for her later.

Where is Ava? Did I leave her outside?

"What? No, I'm not."

"Oh really?" Dana quipped and held up her sword where streaks of crimson still glistened on the blade.

The room shrank to the tiniest drip of blood as it ran down the length of the blade. Tannin followed its progress, entranced. She could have sworn it made a tinkling, ringing sound. It was a beautiful red. All the rubies in all the crowns of the world couldn't match it. Her own blood sang in response, that tell-tale burn in her eyes and pressure on her lower lip as her warg side strained at her control. She could almost taste the coppery tang of that blood drop on her tongue.

Dana snapped her fingers in front of Tannin's face, shattering the trance-like state she'd found herself in. She shook her head hard and covered her mouth where her fangs were jutting out.

"Shite," she mumbled.

"It's the bloodlust," Dana remarked, her grin of victory still too firmly plastered across her face to summon any kind of a rebuke. "You can never tell how hard it'll hit until it does. Adair, take her with you when you go hunting will you?"

She laughed a deep belly laugh that reverberated round the tent. It was almost a howl, and Tannin fought the urge to throw back her head and join her. Victory was heady in the air. She wanted to whoop and leap and dance and tear into something with her teeth and—

"Okay, enough of that." Adair grasped her shoulder, laughing, and steered her out of the tent.

"Bring us back some water fowl or something we can spit roast," Dana called after them. "Tonight, we celebrate like WARGS!"

"What's going to happen to Douglas?" Tannin asked as she ducked under a low branch. She and Adair had taken the easier eastern trail, leaving the other hunters to take the southern trail looking for bigger game.

"He's sworn an oath of service, but he'll be out of Dana's inner circle. He'll be relegated to grunt work." Adair sniffed in derision. "He chose that over an honourable death."

Tannin thought back to the tender embrace she'd seen between Douglas and Catriona.

"Maybe he's got something to live for," she mused and then gave a sly grin. "Guess that means we're one *Doug-less* in the inner circle then."

Adair opened his mouth to reply, but then made a shushing motion instead and crouched down in the weeds. Tannin copied him, dropping to the ground. He'd seen something. Something they could hunt. Her nerves were still a rattling mess of bunched-up tension, and she hardly dared breathe as she waited for whatever he had seen or heard to reveal itself.

There.

The sound. Slow steps, the rustle of leaves. Breathing.

The boar was a solid mass of bristle and muscle. Tannin's warg eyes watched the skin pull and crease as it walked, betraying the immense strength underneath. She could taste the heat of it on the air.

"Yessss," she breathed softly, creeping forward through the grass, her clawed fingers digging into the earth.

"No," Adair said, catching the back of her tunic and tugging her back into the undergrowth. The rustling made the boar pause, its beady eyes frantically scanning for threats. Its great sides heaved with its breathing for a moment before it shoved its snout back into the dirt, routing around and snuffling.

"I want it."

"It'll gore you in a second. A beast like that needs a team. Coordinated attack and even then, you risk someone coming back in pieces. We go around. With any luck, there will be some birds near the water." He poked her in the chest. "You, of all people, should be aware of the dangers."

Tannin glared at him. That was a cheap shot. She had been barely days old when her father had been killed by a boar, it was hardly a core memory.

"I don't think I can just let it go," Tannin said in a slightly strangled voice. "Adair, I *want* it."

"No," he said resolutely. "Shake it off. We go around."

She followed him for a few moments, but the pull of the warm flesh so close by, unaware and pulsing was too much. It was a prickling, aching need she couldn't ignore.

She glanced back just as the wind brought the earthy stink of the boar straight into her face. A low growl sounded in the back of her throat, so soft it was almost a purr.

Adair heard it too late. His arms closed around thin air as she sprang into the trees.

She scaled the trees until the boar was directly beneath her, pawing the ground and desperately searching for the threat it sensed was close. Pity it didn't think to look up. She landed claws first on its back and hung on with all four paws as it tore through the swamp, shaking and thrashing in its attempt to dislodge her. She could have ended it there. Claw or fang straight through its spine. She knew she could do it. The beast below her was powerful, immensely powerful, but the strength in her own limbs told her she could take it apart if she wanted to. But the thrill of the fight was too much to end so soon. She let it throw her off, and she rolled into a cat-like crouch. The boar didn't waste any time on circling or intimidation. It ran straight for her, aiming its sabre-like tusks at her flank. She dodged, letting a claw slide along its side, splattering dark blood onto the fallen leaves. She crooned as mockingly as she could with her limited vocal chords. It had the desired effect. The boar went wild. It bellowed in anger, crazed eyes lolling in its head and attacked again. She slammed into its side with all her weight. It was like shoulder ramming a brick wall. The impact jarred her joints right down to her toes, but the beast fell, skidding on the now wet leaves, its little legs waggling in the air.

Tannin grinned a terrible fanged grin as she loomed over her fallen foe. She'd satisfied her need for fun, and now it was time for blood. The boar seemed to know it too and let out one last pitiful wailing shriek as she sank her fangs deep into its belly.

"I'm going to be picking bristles out of my teeth for a week," Tannin whined as they walked back towards Dunoak.

"You're lucky that's your only complaint," Adair huffed. They carried the boar between them, but clearly Tannin's adrenaline was still pumping because she didn't seem to be feeling the weight of it as much as Adair was. "It could have killed you."

"Y'know, I don't think it could have. It didn't feel like it could."

"That is because you're young, restless and were filled to the brim with bloodlust and stupidity."

"Wow, rude. How about a 'well done, Tannin' or a 'you did good, Tannin' or even, gods' forbid, a 'thanks for dinner, Tannin'."

Adair dropped the boar's front legs abruptly and Tannin almost fell over it. She swore and caught herself before she ended up face first in its disembowelled insides.

"Stop it," he said pointing a warning finger at her. "I almost lost my sister today. You think I wanted to watch you almost die too? This is *not* something to be proud of. You lost control."

Tannin blustered over a denial that wasn't true while he glared at her until she fell into a slightly embarrassed silence.

Adair's jaw clenched and unclenched.

"I'll carry it the rest of the way," he said finally, heaving the carcass across his shoulders and stalking off, leaving Tannin to trail after him.

When they approached the gate, the guard on duty whistled at the sight of the beast slung over Adair's shoulders, impressed. "Damn."

"Didn't go down easy, that's for sure." Adair grinned. "I'll make sure to send a plate out for you."

It took a second for Tannin to register what he'd said, and when it did, she was furious.

"What are you doin'?" Tannin hissed, outraged as soon as they were passed the gate. "This is my kill and you're takin' the credit?"

"This is not your kill anymore. You want to explain to everyone how you could take this down on your own? You are not ready to be the heir and you know it. Is your pride going to overrule all our hard work in keeping you safe?"

Tannin's pride was certainly thinking about it.

She watched in mutinous silence as Adair was again and again congratulated and fawned over for the boar. It was true if she said she'd killed it, half of them wouldn't believe her and the other half would put it together that she was not only a warg but a damn powerful one at that. She would have to step up and claim her heritage. Tannin scowled. Yes, it made sense she couldn't claim her victory, but it didn't mean she was going to accept it graciously.

"There you are!" Flint grinned at her from one of the long tables that had been dragged from the feast hall outside to where the bonfires were crackling. "You should see the pile of coin I made today. Phew! You know, for a minute, I thought she was actually gonna kill him? She's a damn scary lady that Dana. Are you even listening? What's up with you?"

"I killed that boar," she told him, still glowering over at Adair as he handed it off to the butchers to get it mounted above the fire. "And he gets all the credit for it."

"Awk, come on. Does it even matter? Bet it still tastes good." He nudged her with his elbow.

"It would taste even better if I got credit for it," she grumbled.

"There's some waterfowl already cooked if you're hungry already. And don't say you're not 'cause I know you get all grouchy like this when you're hungry."

Tannin made a face at him but couldn't deny he was right when her stomach gave an audible rumble. Following the smell of roasting meat from the other fires took them directly past the now mounted boar. The closer they got, the more concerned Flint's expression became.

"Tannin, that thing is huge. Look at its tusks!"

"I know," Tannin's lips stretched into a smug grin. "It was fun."

Flint blinked at her. "You are fucking terrifying, you know that?"

She grinned. "Aw, you say the sweetest things."

"I'll eat with you, but then I'm gonna turn in. I can't stay and enjoy the celebrations."

"What?!" Tannin asked. "Why?"

"We're leaving for Armodan tomorrow," he said in a hushed voice. "At first light."

"Oh." She hadn't realised they would be going quite so soon. He could be gone for weeks. "Can you do me a favour?"

"No promises."

"Can you put some flowers on Attilo's grave for me?" she asked quietly. "And for Ava."

His eyes softened. "Of course."

Chapter Thirty-One

Always a Princess to Me

The party was set to leave the next morning before the sun rose with everyone sworn to secrecy under oath. Ava and Tannin watched from the window as the party made ready to leave. Flint sent them both a wave and a wink as he saddled up a horse for Eoghan and Collum. Dana had agreed that travelling with musicians was also a good cover if anyone became too curious. Musicians travelled all the time. Not that the brothers actually knew what the mission was. Flint had just mentioned a trip, and they had jumped at the chance for an adventure.

"Can't say I'm not happy for her to be gone for a while," Tannin muttered under her breath as Callie mounted up next to Flint. She and two other warg-bloods were going to provide protection. "He has the worst taste in women."

"He seems happy enough," Ava replied, massaging her temples. She had overdone it a little partying with the wargs last night. It wasn't her first hangover, but she could tell the headache would take more than her usual tonics to shift it.

"Do you wish you were goin' with them?"

"Could ask you the same."

Tannin folded her arms and leaned against the window frame, seemingly unbothered from the night before. "Kind of? I loved Armodan. Well, I loved the Skirts, but also your father will have me killed me on sight if I go anywhere near the city, so I think I'm fine here for now."

"He wouldn't exactly be happy to see me either."

Tannin scoffed.

"No, really, I didn't leave Armodan in the most civilised manner," Ava said, tugging on a lock of her hair. So far, she had avoided telling anyone the full story. "I was being watched so closely after everything that happened. It took some...creativity to be able to leave."

"Mmhm. Spit it out. What did you do?" Tannin leaned back clearly enjoying watching Ava squirm.

"I caused a small distraction that turned into a rather large distraction." She twisted her hands in her lap. "Tapestries are more flammable than I initially considered."

The ancient, bone-dry fabric had gone up in seconds.

At least, it was some of the uglier tapestries.

"You set the castle on fire?"

"I also stole quite a few valuable elixirs if you remember. The Belacine I used on your shoulder? I told you it was expensive. I may have downplayed that a little." Ava swallowed hard. "It was one of a kind and priceless."

When she had heard the guards talking about recovering the Beast's body, she hadn't even given the theft a second thought. If that's what it took to save the girl she loved, then so be it. Her uncle kept all sorts of concoctions in what he thought was a secret cabinet. Ava had perused the glittering bottles so many times that she knew exactly which ones to take.

"Wow. You are a terrible princess."

"Not anymore." She had been waiting for Tannin to ask as the deadline for her return to Armodan loomed, but it had come and gone without a word. If she had wanted to retain her title, then she should have been home a week ago. The cruel part of her mind told her that her father was probably relieved. "I've been disinherited now. Did you forget?"

"I didn't forget. I thought you'd bring it up if you wanted to talk about it. Do you want to talk about it?"

They're better off without me.

"No."

Tannin smiled and nudged her with her shoulder. "You'll always be a princess to me."

Ava narrowed her eyes. "What do you want?"

"Who says I want something?"

"You're only nice to me when you want something."

"Excuse you, I'm a fucking delight."

Ava rolled her eyes at her.

They watched as the party trotted off out of the courtyard and kept watching until they had disappeared from view.

"Although," Tannin began with a wicked smile. "My lessons are cancelled. What shall we do with the rest of our day?"

A day in bed was even better for her mood than any tonic would have been. Ava stretched luxuriously before resuming stroking Tannin's tousled hair. In the light that trickled in from outside, it looked like strands of gold.

"You know, even though I wanted to go back home..." Tannin said, tracing her fingertips over Ava's arm "...I'd rather be here with you than there without you."

Ava swore, in that moment, her heart actually swelled. How long had she been waiting to hear those words? Her cheeks ached with the width of her smile.

Tannin pressed a gentle kiss to her lips before pulling back, closing her soft, brown eyes and leaning into Ava's hand that was still stroking her hair.

"Do you know that you're beautiful?" Ava murmured.

"Well, they say beauty is in the eye of the beholder." Her lips quirked into an impish smile. "And you have the most beautiful eyes."

Ava blinked once.

"You did not just say that."

Tannin cackled, clearly very pleased with herself, even as Ava smacked her in the face with a pillow.

"How on earth am I attracted to you?" she asked, despairingly.

"Oh, come on, that was good," Tannin chided as she wrestled the pillow away from her.

"It was not."

"Admit it! That was good!"

"You are awful." Ava rolled over so she was facing the other way and wrapped the blankets tight around herself, hiding her smile. Beside her, she could still feel the vibrations of Tannin chuckling at her own joke.

Warmth spread through her once more as she played Tannin's voice in her head. She would doubt the words later, but for now, Ava let them bathe her in happiness.

"I'd rather be here with you."

Chapter Thirty-Two

Elevens

Tannin

Tannin was yawning as she took her usual seat in the council chambers. Alby had banged on her door absurdly early, announcing that Dana had called a meeting and to be in the council chambers in ten minutes. She wasn't the only one who was fighting off traces of slumber.

"A break-away group of Sommer's wargs are travelling East. To Dunoak," Dana began without preamble. "They will be here by tomorrow."

"Who is it?"

"Most are from eleventh. A few from the year below."

Eleventh. Tannin frowned trying to remember if she knew anyone from that year. Her own year had been called the fourteenth. The fourteenth batch of true wargs. Fourteenth and the last, she thought with a jolt. Her grandfather had taken the serums. There was no fifteenth.

Elevens would all be three or four years older than her. Adair's year. She shot a hasty look at him across the table to see if he had reacted to the news that his old yearmates were coming, but his face was as blank as stone.

"Do we...like these wargs?" she asked carefully

"If they'll swear fealty and join us against Sommer, then sure, we like them. I'm not going to lie to you, we need the numbers."

Her expression softened and she said, "This next bit is all politics and clever words."

"What is our stance then? What are we offering them to join us? Do you think they know Sommer's weaknesses?" Tannin asked, tiredness forgotten. This was the only shred of an advantage they had gotten since leaving Armodan.

The rest of the council exchanged awkward glances.

"You're not going to be at the meeting this time."

"What? Why?"

"What I'm saying is, you should sit this one out."

"What? Why? I did well at the meeting with the kelpies. I thought I was supposed to be gettin' more involved. People already know who I am. I should be steppin' up not sittin' out!" Tannin looked around at the other council members. None of them would meet her eye. Theo twisted a gold ring on his finger.

"It's more of a tradition that anything else, but if we want to make allies, then we should keep to the familiar processes and standards..."

Tannin nodded slowly as realisation set in.

"Golden only party, huh?" she sneered.

"Don't take it the wrong way. It's what they will be expecting. You can still come to the feast later on."

"Oh, how gracious of you to allow me to attend." Her chair screeched along the floor as she shoved it back. "After all this time, I'm still not enough for you, am I?"

"Don't make a scene. This is politics, Tannin, sit down."

"Oh, go shove it up your gilded arse."

Tannin rested her elbows on the stone wall and tried not to cry. After she'd stormed out of the council chambers, she'd just started walking without any kind of destination in mind other than *away*.

She wasn't stupid enough to go too far and venture into the chaotic rabble outside alone, but she took herself as far from the keep as she could. The streets here were narrower and reminded her of the overhanging, claustrophobic comfort of the Skirts, if only slightly. She'd come to a stop where a low wall surrounded a rare patch of greenery and a tiny bird was pecking around the base of a bush. It was so small. A part of her wanted to catch it and crush it in her fist.

She frowned and blinked hard.

What the fuck is wrong with me? I don't want to crush a bird.

She smoothed her hair back from her face where it had come out of the knot she'd shoved it in when she'd been roused from her bed, made to go to that stupid meeting all to be told she wasn't good enough. That she never would be.

Fuck them. Fuck them all.

She stayed leaning on the wall, watching the bird until she no longer felt she needed to cry and the sting of tears had settled into a low ache in her chest.

If Flint had been around, she would have been trying to convince him to run away with her right now. Forget wargs, forget Dunoak, forget Sommer, just go. Ava would be too sensible to agree, so they'd just have to drag her along with them like when they went to that village festival. A mild kidnapping.

Where would they go, though? The Brochlands were a no-go. Absolutely fuck going north or to Rill. Gormbrae? Tannin sighed. Nope, they'd have to take a ship far away from the Five Kingdoms altogether. To the lands across the sea. Where none of them knew anyone, and more importantly, no one knew them.

She'd been here before. These thoughts. When she was stuck in Attilo's rooms, plotting her escape from Armodan, and even before, when she'd been plotting running from her grandfather's debts. These were the thoughts that went round and round in her head, never giving her answers. She had nowhere to go.

Tannin realised that her traitorous feet had been taking her back in the direction of the keep while she hadn't been paying attention. She scowled and sharply changed direction. Maybe she'd go to a tavern. Getting drunk and picking a stupid fight sounded like exactly what she wanted to do right now.

"Tannin!"

The unexpected voice had her stopping in her tracks and turning so quickly that she stumbled.

"Callie? What the hell are you doing here? You're supposed to be halfway to Armodan! What happened? Where's Flint?" she demanded.

Callie's tunic was streaked with mud and her hair was a mess. A reddish smudge that looked horribly like blood stained her cheek.

"Tannin," she gasped through her tears. "It's Flint. Oh gods... Flint. It's so bad! Y-you have to come now!"

"What? Is he okay?!"

She shook her head, choking back sobs. "You have to come now."

"We should get help. The others—"

"Please just come! It's bad! He doesn't have a lot of time. We need to go now! Please!"

Callie took off at a sprint with Tannin yelling after her to wait.

He's doesn't have a lot of time...

She hesitated for a moment, but as soon as Callie was out of view, Tannin swore and took off after her.

"Callie, stop!" she shouted but the other girl didn't even slow. Not even when she charged through a side gate out of the citadel and into the outer city.

Tannin hesitated again. She had never been out this far alone.

"We have to get the others if something is wrong!" she yelled.

"Tannin, we don't have time!" Callie screeched back at her, continuing to run father away. "Flint doesn't have time!"

Tannin swore and looked back. It would take her at least fifteen minutes to run back to the keep, gods' knew how long to get those eejit wargs to listen to her, and then another fifteen minutes at least to run back.

Tannin was already losing sight of Callie again. She made her decision. For Flint, she couldn't risk it.

Tannin's lungs were burning when Callie disappeared though a warehouse door that was cracked open barely wide enough for her to fit through. The inside was cloaked in shadow. Tannin slowed to a halt. The building was weather-worn and dilapidated just like the abandoned buildings that surrounded it. A warning sign hung squint from one last nail holding it in place.

Danger. Unstable building.

"Callie?" Tannin called tentatively.

"In here! Quickly!" Her voice was frantic.

"Flint, are you there?" Tannin shouted.

This doesn't feel right. This doesn't feel right at all.

A moan came from within. Definitely male.

"Flint?" she called again, inching closer. "Flint, are you here? Are you okay?"

She stepped over the threshold. "Callie? Answer me, dammit! I'm gettin' nervous."

The inside of the warehouse was a mess. Rafters had tumbled down and littered the floors while abandoned crates were stacked high on all sides. A covered wagon stood in the centre of the room. It was the only thing that looked even remotely in good repair. Tannin edged towards it.

The door slammed shut behind her. She whirled, her axes already in her hands. Theo's lessons about never going anywhere unarmed had been drilled into her so effectively that she had slung her axe belt around her hips to even go to the council meeting that morning. She was eternally grateful that she had when she saw the figure that now blocked the door.

"Hello, Tannin." The man standing there – young, tanned and lean – would have been easy to dismiss if he hadn't been cleaning his nails with the tip of a dagger.

"What the fuck is this? Where's Flint!" Tannin yelled. She spotted a smirking Callie lurking by the crates and rounded on her, eyes narrowing. "I'm gonna kill you. Where is he?!"

"Well, well, well," a voice crowed from atop a pile of crates. "Look what we have here."

Tannin whirled and stared up at the grinning face. It tugged at something in her memories, but she couldn't dredge up a name. There was no doubt that the man was a warg though as he slid from the crates and landed soundlessly, catlike. His hair was shorn close to his skull and his eyes seemed too small for his face. Beady. She looked again at the man with the dagger. The glint in his eyes was also unmistakably predatory.

Tannin swallowed. The elevens had arrived early.

Chapter Thirty-Three

Surrender

Tannin

"What do you want?" Tannin asked, keeping her distance as the man who had jumped down ran a hand over the lid of a crate.

"You, of course." Another voice. Female this time. Tannin whirled again. A blonde girl grinned at her as she sauntered out from behind a fallen beam. "We're here to take you back to Stonestead. Your challenge with Sommer still stands, and she wants to put an end to it before you start making any more trouble."

"Hard fuckin' pass on that one," Tannin said, hefting her axes.

The three laughed, and as their voices bounced throughout the ruined warehouse, Tannin's heart sunk further. They had her surrounded.

"Don't be an idiot. You're coming with us one way or another."

She shook her head vehemently and gripped the axe tighter. "I'll take each of you. One at a time. I challenge you."

Her defiant statement was met with more laughter.

"It's doesn't work like that," Beady-eyes said with a grin. "Now, do yourself a favour and drop your little toys and get on your knees."

"Go to hell," she snarled. "I'll fight you all then. Come on!"

There was no way she was going down without a fight. They might kill her, but by the gods, she would take as many of them out as she could on the way.

"I'd rather die here in a fight than be dragged back home just to be executed by Sommer any day."

"One last chance," the tanned warg with the dagger said with malice.

She just had to get around them, find a way out of this warehouse, and run like hell back to the keep. In here, alone, she was nothing, and from the look in the warg's eyes, he knew it well.

"You want me? Come get me." She lifted her axe.

"Oh, I would but I just hate unnecessary work. Plus, Sommer wants you alive." He tilted his head and watched her closely. "I think you'll surrender."

"Why the hell would I do that?"

"Because of this." The man with the beady eyes who had leapt from the top of the crates had moved to lean against the wagon.

Tannin turned warily.

He yanked the cover free and her blood froze. It was a cage. And inside…

"Flint," she breathed. She had hoped with all her heart that Callie had lied and Flint was still safely on the road.

He was alive. Bruised and beaten but alive. Eoghan and Collum too. The three of them crammed together behind the iron bars, barely conscious.

"Oh, fuck you," Tannin groaned in dismay. "Fuck you all so much."

"Don't go with them," Flint croaked woozily. "Tan, don't do it."

The warg smacked the bars and told him to shut up.

"So, what will it be?" He smiled. "Will you come quietly? "

She glared.

"Where are the others? The warg-bloods?" she asked Callie directly with a snarl. "Did you kill them?"

"You don't even know their names, don't act like you care," Callie retorted.

"What? Like you acted like you cared about Flint?"

"Oh, enough," the tanned warg growled. "You'll have plenty of time to trade barbs on the journey. Throw those axes over here, dagger too, and get down on your knees."

"Get fucked," Tannin growled. Those iron bars might be holding her friends prisoner, but they also put a barrier between them and the wargs. They had at least a little time. She shifted into a defensive position.

"Ooh someone's been training," Callie cooed.

"Tannin, don't! Just run!" Flint yelled, flinging himself against the cage door with a burst of energy. The tiny space was far too small for the three of them, and Collum winced as Flint knocked into him.

Beady-eyes moved too quickly for Tannin to even think of intercepting him. He seized Flint's hand where it was clamped around one of the bars and jerked his arm through the gap. Flint's eyes went wide as the warg turned his attention back to Tannin.

"You have five seconds," he said with a sigh as if the whole situation had become tedious. "One."

He increased pressure on Flint's arm, bending it back against the bar.

Oh gods, he's going to snap it.

"Don't you dare!" Tannin took a step forward, axes raised.

"Two-three," he said cruelly, applying more pressure. She would never get to him in time. And a broken arm would just be the start. She couldn't bear it. She couldn't...

Tannin's mind scrambled for any way out. If she tried to fight, they'd kill him, Eoghan, and Collum and probably just take her anyway. The best she could do was maybe, maybe, take out one of them on a very good day with an insane amount of luck. And her friends would still be dead. There was no way out.

"Wait!" Tannin yelled as Flint cried out. "No! Stop! I surrender!"

She slid her axes across the floor and raised her hands. "I surrender, stop!"

"Dagger too."

She wrenched it free with shaking fingers.

"I'm sorry, Tan," Flint ground out. "I'm so sorry."

"Tick tock," the blonde girl jeered in amusement.

Tannin growled in frustration and threw her dagger aside. It clanged off stone and echoed as she raised her hands.

"I surrender," she repeated quietly.

"No, don't—!" Eoghan's voice was quickly cut off. Tannin didn't look to see the cause as she sank to her knees.

"I knew we could work something out," Beady said cheerfully, releasing Flint's arm and motioned to the others, whose approach was heralded by the jangling of chains.

Tannin ground her teeth and clenched her fists to stop herself from bolting as she saw the thick shackles the tanned warg carried. Everything in her body was screaming at her to run, but the image of Flint's terrified face kept her rooted to the spot. She kept her eyes fixed on a crack in the floor in front of her as the warg reached her. The others closed in in a tighter circle around her.

The heavy metal was cold as it touched her skin. The surface of the manacle was etched with symbols. Runes. She understood what they were as soon as the latch was closed and locked around her right wrist. Her inner flame felt like it was being smothered under a horribly cold, damp blanket. She gasped involuntarily. The wargs chuckled.

"Binding runes. They're very effective at making sure you'll stay in your human form for the journey," the tanned boy said grasping her other arm.

"What about these runts?" the girl asked.

"We've earned a bit of fun, I'd say." Beady-eyes leered. "How fast do you think they can run?"

Tannin's head snapped up and the movement caused the warg to fumble the latch for her left wrist. "You said you wouldn't hurt them!"

"No, I didn't. I lightly implied it." He cocked his head. "Can't deny us a bit of sport now, can you?"

She could see it so clearly in her mind. They would release them, make them run, only to hunt them down and tear them open for the sheer enjoyment of it. And she wouldn't be able to stop them.

Not going to fucking happen.

She wrenched herself out of the tanned warg's grip where he was still in the process of locking the left manacle. It fell loose and she swung it like a flail straight into his face.

CRACK!

Blood spurted from his nose. She used the momentary distraction to shove off the ground and launch herself at the next nearest warg. The runes still locked onto her right wrist stopped her from Changing, but she could still damn well make a nuisance of herself and buy some time. Tannin threw a handful of grit she'd swiped from the filthy floor into Beady's face, momentarily blinding him, then leapt onto the girl's back.

Tannin tried to pull her chain around the girl's neck and strangle her with it, but the warg was fast and slammed her back into the wall. Tannin grunted in pain but held on. She'd lost her grip on the chain, she couldn't Change, she had no weapons and the warg was seconds from throwing her off and beating her to a pulp. As a last resort, she did the only thing she could think of. She sank her teeth into side of the girl's neck. She felt the scream reverberating through her teeth and up into her skull as she tore a chunk of the soft flesh from her throat.

The girl staggered, clutching at her throat as blood poured through her fingers. Tannin released her and dropped to the ground, rolling into a crouch.

Two of the other wargs were already Changing, their bodies contorting as their new shape fought to take control.

Tannin didn't even spare the seconds it would cost to take a deep breath before she gripped the manacle on her wrist and *pulled*. Something snapped in her thumb and the manacle flew to the ground.

If she had spared her hand a glance, she would have seen the skin and flesh torn clean off the back and side, hanging by a few thin strands. It would have been agony if she had felt it, but as soon as she was free of the shackle's grip, the fire in her chest roared into life and all she felt was pure, blistering heat.

Chapter Thirty-Four

Demon

Ava

Ava was worried. She'd looked everywhere, even climbing up onto that godsawful roof terrace that Tannin liked so much, but she wasn't there. Whatever Dana said, Tannin was not in the keep.

"Don't you think that—"

"Enough!" Dana snapped. Worry had made her bold, and Ava had followed Dana into her office, even though the warg had made it clear she was done with the conversation. "She'll be sulking somewhere like a child because she didn't get what she wanted. My guess is that she won't even show for dinner out of spite."

Ava opened her mouth to respond but Dana cut her off with a snarl, stalking towards her. Ava stumbled back through the doorway.

"Stop. Pestering. Me."

The door slammed shut in her face.

Dana was, unfortunately, correct. Tannin didn't show for dinner. Ava sat alone. None of the wargs or warg-bloods spared her a glance, let alone included her in their conversations. Without distraction, her fear ran rampant. Something must have happened.

Where is she?

Maybe it was because she was already highly strung, but when the doors to the dining hall crashed open, Ava couldn't stop the scream that tore from her throat. The doors had swung open with such a force that they smashed off the walls with a sound like thunder. Stone dust billowed from the cracks they left.

The last of the fading daylight illuminated the dark and smoky hall, and the sounds of merry feasting dropped away sharply as the demon that had entered the hall stalked between the tables. Mouths dropped open as it passed. People scrambled out of the way as it made for the top table. Ava couldn't blame them. The figure could not have been more blood-soaked if it had bathed in the stuff. Each step shook a small torrent of ruby red droplets onto the stone floor. Blazing gold eyes, too large for the small face, were filled with fire as they glared daggers at the top table.

The limbs were too long. Distorted. Even as Ava watched, sinew shifted underneath and bones ground audibly against one another. Seeing her in her warg form was one thing. This...this was...she didn't have any words.

No one dared breathe, and the only sound was Tannin's bare feet slapping wetly on the stone floor. She stopped when she reached the table, stretched out with a human hand tipped in obsidian claws and hooked a jug of wine, the sharp tips raking over the crystal surface with a screeching sound that set Ava's teeth on edge. Dark wine joined the blood splattered on the floor, flowing out of the corners of a fanged mouth. Ava jumped as the jug shattered on the floor, tossed aside without a second glance. The beast shuddered as if relishing the sound of destruction.

Tannin wiped her terrible mouth with the back of her hand, smearing the blood and revealing pale freckled skin underneath. Those golden eyes fixed themselves on the wargs at the top table.

"It appears," she rasped in a voice that was so painfully familiar. "The elevens were never going to join us."

There was movement. A metallic sound.

The bloodied figure moved like lightening, slamming the man who had tried to draw his weapon to the ground before anyone could so much as blink. A warg-blood. Ava had seen him around the keep plenty of times and never paid any attention. Her Senses had never been triggered by any of them. She watched in horror as Tannin's demonic form crouched on his chest, back claws ripping through his tunic.

"Traitor," she purred with deadly softness.

Traitor? How could I not know? How could I not have seen—

Razor-like claws flashed, and the warg-blood's breathless protests became pain-filled yells as they raked down his face.

She stood as he wailed.

"Tannin?" Ava squeaked but her throat was so tight that hardly a sound left her lips.

Dana and the wargs were on their feet, armed but bewildered, as the beast addressed them.

"Anyone else working with Sommer has until I count to five," she said. A claw dragged over the table as she continued, "to get your scheming, traitorous carcass out of this hall before I start painting the walls with your guts."

"One."

Silence stretched like a bowstring pulled taut.

"Two."

Three further warg-bloods scrambled to comply, hauling the injured man up and struggling for the door. Tannin followed them, grinning horribly.

"Three."

"What is going on?" Dana demanded but Tannin ignored her, stalking the traitors out of the hall.

"Four."

Ava found the use of her legs and scrambled after them. She wanted to call out to her, but her throat was still clamped tight around her words. Her palms were sweating.

I knew something happened. I knew it. Tannin, what did you do?

Outside the keep, a large crowd had gathered. A silent, horrified crowd. Their eyes tilted upwards. Ava followed their gaze and then gasped.

Set atop three spears, blades driven deep into their skulls, were three monstrous heads.

"Five."

Chapter Thirty-Five

Aftermath

Tannin

"Tannin, open the door."

She ignored the knocking and wormed her way deeper under her mountain of blankets. It was too hot under all the layers, but it was the only place she wanted to be.

After expelling the traitorous warg-bloods, she'd told Dana to do what she wished with them, returned to the hall, hooked a claw through the head of the suckling pig that had been a trial run in preparations for the elevens' arrival the following day. She'd dragged the whole thing upstairs to her room. The trail of blood and gravy she'd left would probably horrify the servants when they saw it.

As soon as she was alone, she'd ravenously stripped it to the bone, even crunching a few between her teeth to get at the marrow. She'd never been so hungry in her life, but as soon as her hunger was sated and she looked at her hands – human again and crusted with gore – she immediately felt sick.

She'd bathed frantically in icy water, not bothering to call for hot water to be brought up, flicking pinkish soap bubbles all over her floor. Her injured hand had healed impossibly quickly in her warg state and was now covered in shiny, tender scar tissue.

Still damp but clean, she'd dragged the spare blankets from her cupboards, piled them high and buried herself beneath them.

She'd been there ever since, and no one had come to bother her until now. Tannin hadn't given any response, but it seemed she wasn't giving up. The princess was as stubborn as ever. A few moments later, the soft metallic scratching sounded followed by the squeak of hinges told her that it didn't matter if she answered the door or not. Tannin gripped her blanket tighter.

I'm going to kill Flint for teaching her how to pick locks.

The mattress depressed slightly as Ava sat beside the blanket pile.

"Come out," she said in the soft tones Tannin had heard her use on the timid stray cats that skulked around the keep.

Absolutely not.

Tannin curled into an even tighter ball.

"Okay," Ava said with a long exhale.

Tannin felt her hand rest on her back through the many layers and pat gently.

"The boys turned up and told us what happened up at the warehouse. They're all okay, by the way, shaken but okay."

Tannin balked. She hadn't even given a second thought to her friends. All thoughts of anything had fled her mind the second she had Changed.

Flint.

How could she have forgotten about him? Had she just left him there in a damn cage surrounded by bodies?

The headless bodies.

Oh, fuck fuck fuck. Why did I do that?

Ava started to peel back the layers of Tannin's nest, ignoring the groans of protest until the light of the candle fell on her face. Ava smoothed her hair back and made some soft, reassuring sounds.

"You don't have to talk about it just yet."

Tannin scooted up until her head lay in Ava's lap and let her continue to stroke her hair.

"What happened today?" Ava asked gently after a while.

Tannin couldn't explain it. She'd been seized by the unbearable heat that raced through her veins, and she'd let it overtake her. She'd been present but not present at the same time. She'd killed the nearest one first. The one who had wanted his sport. She'd knocked him to the ground and dug through his chest with her front paws, spraying his companions with his insides as he choked on his own blood. The girl was next, and she finished the job she'd started by tearing out her throat entirely. The one who'd tried to chain her...she'd torn his limbs from his body and left him to bleed.

And then she'd taken their heads. Well, all of the warg heads. There wasn't much of Callie's left to mount after she'd crushed her skull in her jaws. It had been so soft inside. Jelly-like...

Tannin leapt off the bed and stumbled against the sink just in time to retch into it. She retched until her stomach muscles ached from heaving, and then she sank to the floor. She was shaking as she allowed Ava to guide her back to bed and tucked her back into her blankets with a stream of placating words.

What have I done?

Tannin felt numb to her core and hardly slept a wink. Ava had offered to delay Dana from interrogating her, and Tannin had gratefully accepted. She could barely string two thoughts together, let alone have that conversation. However successful Ava was, though, eventually Dana would barge in to question her. As reluctant as she was to leave her sanctuary, she was even more reluctant to talk about what happened.

As soon as she left her room, however, she could hear people talking downstairs.

"...and then she tore out her throat with her teeth. Her human teeth!"

Nope. Nopenopenope. Not dealing with that.

Every time she heard voices, she changed directions and ended up somewhere close to the kitchens. The bubbling sizzle and murmur of voices was a comfortingly normal sound. Still, she didn't want to see anyone. The pantry ended up being her refuge.

It stayed a peaceful haven for several hours, during which she happily scrunched herself up with a tin of Cook's homemade biscuits until eventually the door eased open

"There you are," Flint looked down at her. "What are you doing in here? Everyone's looking for you."

"You just answered your own question."

"You can't just hide in the pantry."

She ignored him and held out the tin. "Want a biscuit?"

He sighed and shook his head. "Obviously, I want a biscuit."

Flint squeezed in beside her, his knees pressed hard against his chest in the tiny space. He winced as he settled.

"Nothing too bad. Ava's given me stuff for it," he said in response to her questioning look as he plucked a biscuit from the tin. "Bruised ribs."

"Bruised face."

"Aye. Chipped tooth too." He grinned at her and she saw there was indeed a chunk missing from his tooth on the right side.

"I'm so sorry," Tannin whispered.

He shrugged. "I think it gives me a charmingly roguish look."

"You could have died. You could have actually died, Flint." Tannin's lip trembled. "And I'm so sorry. I just left. I...I don't know what I was thinking. I just..."

"Don't you dare cry." Flint reached out to wipe away a single tear that had already leaked out and then pouted. "'Cause if you cry, I'll cry. And if I cry, I'll ugly cry and nobody wants that."

Tannin gave a weak chuckle.

His look turned serious. "Tan, you seriously fucked them up."

"I know," she wailed. "I'm a monster."

"Is that why you're hiding away down here?"

"I'm not hiding."

"You're a terrible liar."

"I'm a terrible everything."

"You're a decent killer."

Tannin stared at him, open-mouthed and furious.

"Why does it bother you so much this time? Is it because they're wargs and not humans?"

"Shut up!"

"What then? Why does it bother you?"

"Because I liked it!" Tannin yelled. "I enjoyed it! Flint, I loved it. The power. The killing. Because I'm a fucking monster."

Tannin hid her face in her hands.

"Do you even realise what you did?"

"Uh, yes," Tannin replied sourly.

"No, really. Tan, you were gonna give yourself up for us. Sacrifice yourself. And then you took on three wargs. Three! And won!"

"So?"

"People fucking love that shit. You're a legend already. Do you know what this will do for morale here? For your reputation? Eoghan and Collum have drafted about ten songs already."

"You really think people are going to be okay with the monster that did that out there?" Tannin gestured in the vague direction of where the pikes were mounted. "Some savage, fuckin' beast."

"Honestly, I want to shake you sometimes for being so dense. Aye, Tannin. You took on three full wargs and risked your life for your friends, and they're not going to forget that. People follow power. And you are..." He gave a long exhale. "You are damn powerful. You have got to bloody well stop sulking and own up to what you are."

“Which is?”

Flint suddenly laughed. “Oh, you should hear what they’re calling you now.”

He told her.

“That is awful,” Tannin said in disgust.

“It’s fantastic.” Flint grinned and slapped his thighs. “Right, enough of the pity party. Let’s go get you obscenely drunk.”

Tannin managed a smile and held a hand to her heart. “Aw, my favourite.”

Chapter Thirty-Six

A Toast

The first face Tannin saw when they entered the crowded feast hall was Dana's. They locked eyes instantly.

"I can't do this," Tannin said, her feet already backtracking. "I'm goin' back to the pantry. Bring whisky."

"No, you're not." Flint linked arms with her. "You are going to celebrate your victory and stop moping."

"Tannin." Dana had reached them.

Tannin flinched. "If you're gonna hit me, just get it over with."

"I'm not going to hit you." Dana shook her head in amazement. "All this time thinking you're useless."

The door was flung open and Adair strode in. His hair was mussed and his cheeks flushed. People staggered out of his way as he barrelled towards them. Tannin squealed as he wrapped his arms around her middle and lifted her into the air with an uncharacteristic whoop.

"A berserker. Our wee Tannin is a goddam berserker!" Adair bellowed as he dropped her again. "I suspected the mountain spirit was strong in you when you killed that boar, but oh, I did not see this coming."

"I'm a what?" Tannin said, staggering backwards and ducking his attempt to hug her again. "Get off! Are you drunk?"

"Yes, he is but can you blame him? We have been waiting months for you to step up and become the warg you were supposed to be. Months to get the tiniest shred of usefulness out of you." Dana gripped Tannin's shoulders and shook her slightly. "This is what I've been trying to get out of you. Well, not this exactly but something! This is what we need. This is what the heir to

Stonestead was meant to be. Gods, to think I almost gave up on you, but yes, Tannin. Yes!"

Dana grinned feverishly and clapped her on the shoulder, the motion making her flinch again. "Tannin, look at this. Look at the people. Our people. Your people."

Tannin stared at her in confusion. "The drunk people?"

"You don't get it."

Dana grabbed a few discarded goblets from a nearby table and sloshed a generous measure of wine into them. Pressing them into Tannin and Flint's hands, she hopped up onto one of the benches and bellowed for quiet.

"We lost some good people today," she began.

Tannin had a moment of confusion before she remembered that Flint, Callie and the brothers weren't the only members of the Armodan party. There had been two other warg-bloods with them.

Dana raised her goblet to the ceiling. "To fallen friends!"

"To fallen friends!" echoed back around the room in a boom of voices.

Dana called each of the names, and again, the words were echoed back. Tannin couldn't match a face to either name. She felt horrible about it.

"May they rest in peace." Dana took a deep swig, smacked her lips once then continued, "But today is also a day of celebration! Today, we celebrate victory! Today, we celebrate the spirit of the mountain!"

Fists thumped tables and feet stomped making the candles shudder in their holders.

"Today, Tannin," Dana reached down to seize Tannin's arm and drag her up onto the bench with her, to her embarrassment, and proclaimed, "showed us what she is made of! She is the heir to Stonestead! A true carrier of the mountain spirit! A warrior! A leader! A queen!"

Dana's voice had heightened to a roar as she lifted her goblet in one hand and Tannin's arm in the other in a show of victory.

"So, raise a toast! To the fallen! To the wargs!" She grinned at Tannin, her incisors too long and her eyes blackening. "To the Feral Queen!"

By the time she staggered out of the feast hall to the rest of the rampant celebrations with the wargs, Tannin was already past tipsy and the cool night air was deliciously refreshing on her flushed skin.

"So, what is a…bear…" Flint struggled over the word as he stumbled against her. "…bear-thing?"

"Berserker?" Tannin slid her arm around his waist. Half to steady him, and half to steady herself. "A monster of monsters!" she proclaimed. "Fiercest warriors ever."

Flint laughed. "And that's you?"

"I'm fieeeeerce." Her grin faltered. "They do always die in the stories, though. Like…badly."

Flint's reply was drowned out.

The entire city seemed to have taken to the streets. Music clashed and muddled from every direction, flowing through the throng of people dancing to whatever beat they could work out. A steady push of bodies made it clear that there was an end destination to the revelry.

Bonfires had sprung up in the field where Dana and Douglas had fought for the lairdship. Writhing figures surrounded them, caught up in their dance, oblivious to the daredevils leaping through the flames.

The closer she looked, the more Tannin realised that the leapers were all wargs and warg-bloods, their faces painted with swirls and streaks of colour. The bravest leapt the largest fire and gained the largest cheers. Flames lapped at their ankles, and smoke seeped from singed hems.

The energy was infectious and Tannin found herself yearning to join them.

From somewhere near the fires, a chant started up, slow at first but then louder and louder.

"Wargs…wargs…wargs …Wargs!…Wargs!…WARGS!"

"You want some monsters?" one of the wargs yelled, ripping his shirt open and spraying buttons everywhere.

One by one, they contorted and Changed.

Tannin watched, entranced. Silhouettes contorted in the firelight. Lithe limbs radiating power stretched and tensed as they leapt around the flames. They were horrifyingly beautiful.

Wood was thrown to the fire until it looked like the flames would lick the very stars above them. The wargs seemed content to dance around it now instead. No one in their right mind would try to leap it.

No one in their right mind…

"Go on." Dana gave her a crooked smile. "You know you want to. Go show them what you've got. Show them who the Feral Queen really is."

Tannin looked from her to the fire to the wargs. Her face split into a grin.

She kicked off her shoes and took off at a sprint towards the biggest bonfire. Just before she reached it, she let her own flame loose and dropped to all fours. Limbs lengthening and muscles straining, she leapt straight for the blistering flames. And then she was flying.

By the time she landed on the other side, she was in her full warg form. Terrible, monstrous and slightly smoking from the edges of her singed fur but otherwise unscathed. With eyes blazing like fire themselves, she drew herself up to her full height in front of the awestruck crowd. She threw her head back with a roar so fierce it shook the panes of nearby windows loose from their frames. The sound of shattering glass filled the air as the last notes of her thunderous howl trailed off.

Silence fell as she transformed back, shaking off the last shreds of fur and fang in front of the wild-eyed crowd. They seemed to be waiting for something.

She raised her fist to the darkening sky with a victorious yell. The crowd exploded into cheers and frenzied whoops. Faceless figures, silhouetted by the fire, bowed down to her. Drums took up a rousing beat as chants of "TANN -IN! TANN-IN!" flowed through the air and fresh bottles were cracked open.

Tannin grinned.

Oh, I could get used to this.

The dancing lasted for hours. Tannin was vaguely aware that her feet had started hurting a while ago, but she couldn't bring herself to stop.

Tannin laughed as Flint spun her round at breakneck speed and she lost her footing. She stumbled and slammed into the person behind her. She would have ended up on the floor if the person hadn't caught her under the arms.

"Ooft! Sorry!" Tannin gasped, righting herself. "Oh, there you are, princess! I sent someone to go find you ages ago!"

"I got—" Ava paused to hiccough, then continued, "...side-tracked. With Eoghan and Collum."

She pointed, and sure enough, the brothers had found Flint. The three of them were dancing some sort of jig – albeit a little gingerly.

"Patched 'em all up good." She nodded to herself satisfied. "Then we had a drink. An' then another."

Tannin squinted at her. "You're drunk."

"Absolutely," Ava agreed solemnly. "And you're a queen. I didn't see that coming when we first met."

"Mhm," Tannin said, relieving Ava of the goblet of ale she was in danger of spilling. "You mad I outrank you?"

Ava's eyes twinkled with mischief in a way that made Tannin's stomach flutter. "You think I mind being underneath you?"

A low groan made its way out from Tannin's throat.

"You say some dangerous things, princess."

"I've come to appreciate danger." Ava slid closer and wrapped her arms around Tannin's neck. She smelled like bonfire smoke.

"Well, we have a knack for getting into it."

Ava snorted. "No, you do. I'm just along for the ride."

"You didn't have to come with me."

"Yes, I did," Ava said with a dramatic sigh. "You are my little bad luck charm, and I had the utter misfortune of falling in love with you."

Tannin momentarily forgot how to breathe and then choked on her own spit.

The colour drained from Ava's face as she realised what she had said.

"I didn't...you...what?" Tannin shook her head as if trying to physically unjumble all of the questions she wanted to ask.

"I have to go," Ava whispered, eyes wide. She stumbled back a few steps and disappeared into the crowd. Tannin stared after her with her mouth hanging open.

She looked at Flint, bewildered.

"She's in love with me?"

Chapter Thirty-Seven

Gold or Blood

Tannin

"We need some powder or something to cover those freckles."

"What's wrong with my freckles?" Tannin demanded.

"They make you look young," Dana said matter-of-factly. "No one is going to follow a child."

"You aren't much older than me!" Tannin scowled but let Dana and Catriona paint her in a variety of different ways to try and find something suitable. She didn't like any of it.

"Welcome to the life of a leader," Catriona quipped as she daubed a coloured stain onto Tannin's lips. "So much of it is about appearances." She tilted her head to the side. "This colour is too dark."

"I don't think it's too dark," Dana disagreed with Catriona, as she had been doing for most of the morning.

Tannin groaned. "How about I always appear as a warg? Then you don't have to worry about my bloody make-up. Or clothes. Or teaching me what to say."

She wished Ava was there. She knew how to deal with this kind of thing. But the princess was avoiding her. She'd somehow managed to avoid being alone with Tannin in the few days since the celebrations however hard Tannin tried to track her down. She cursed Ava's ability to Sense whenever she was near and make a quick getaway. She swore she'd chase her down when she had the time.

But first, she had her very first council later that morning as queen.

Once she had escaped Catriona and Dana, she washed her face clean of all their efforts and tried not to think about her new status. She re-dressed in her usual common clothes but stares still followed her wherever she went.

She squared her shoulders and made a conscious effort to ignore them. She wasn't hungry, but she knew she would be later and wouldn't get the chance to eat for a while, so she forced herself to make her way to the dining hall.

"Nervous?" Flint elbowed her lightly in the ribs as she stared at her plate. She hadn't managed one bite of her breakfast. She had no idea what she was going to say. Dana had tried to get her to write out a proper speech, but the words just wouldn't come and her stomach was looping unpleasantly with nerves.

"You know what helps?" he continued, helping himself to her bacon. "Picture them all naked. Then it's not so scary."

"Ew, no." Tannin dragged a hand through her hair. "I don't even know why I'm nervous. It's not like it's gonna be any different to the million other boring meetings."

"Aye, but you're in charge."

Tannin exhaled and made a noncommittal noise in her throat.

"Right. Just cause you're in charge now doesn't mean you have to do everything. They're gonna help. Delegate. Boss people around. Buy me shiny presents with your new queenly treasury."

"Ha. Ha. Ha. We don't have a treasury."

"Spoilsport."

"I need people to start taking me seriously. Maybe Dana is right. I need a new look."

"Ooh, what kind of look are we talking?"

"I don't know. Like, I understand the importance of appearances, but none of it...feels right. None of it feels like me."

"How do you feel when you do the thing?"

"The thing?"

Flint curled up his hands in an imitation of claws. "Grr."

She made a face at him.

"I dunno. It's certainly not pretty make-up and dressing up. It's all blood and guts and glory and...aye, okay, grr."

"So, try and be that then." Flint shrugged. "It's not that complicated."

"Be the monster I'm supposed to be?"

"Why not?"

"I'm not even Golden," Tannin said quietly.

"I thought you didn't care about that stuff?"

"Obviously, I lied. They've got their wee, exclusive club and I'm not in it. How am I supposed to feel?"

Flint shrugged. "Get rid of it then? You're really not getting this whole 'you are queen' thing, are you? You know you can just outlaw it."

Tannin blinked at him.

"What?" he asked, reaching around to pinch her last piece of bacon.

"I couldn't do that...could I?"

"You. Are. The. Queen," he said slowly and deliberately and then added, "Eejit."

"Huh." Tannin mulled it over. "If I outlaw you stealing my food would that make any difference?"

"None at all, mate." He grinned. "I gotta go but good luck today. Knock 'em dead."

Halfway towards the door, he turned and called back, "But don't, y'know, actually knock 'em dead. I know that's like your speciality but try not to."

"You're not funny."

"I'm hilarious."

Tannin took a fortifying breath. The wargs of Dunoak were assembled before her. She had even summoned Douglas away from his work digging new sewage tunnels for the expanding populous. The other wargs gave him a wide berth, lest they be tainted by his fall from grace.

"Welcome," she started.

The room exploded into cheers and the thuds of fists on tables and stomping of feet on the stone floor before she could continue.

She'd deliberately chosen a larger chamber than their usual council rooms. She wanted every warg in attendance. She wanted to know what she was dealing with – what she had in her arsenal – and which of them would actually accept her as their queen. Especially with what she was about to do.

"It is time to address the issue," Tannin said squaring her shoulders and standing before her assembled wargs, pride swelling in her chest. "I am not Golden. I never have been and I never will be. That is something that you will all have to get over."

An awkward intake of breath sounded from all corners of the room, as if she had just confessed something embarrassing.

"We could re-create the trials," Catriona suggested. "Perform the rituals here to make you Golden."

A cacophony of voices followed her statement.

"But the ceremony—"

"It wouldn't be traditional."

"We'd have to make do."

"We have to do something to bring her up to our level."

Bring me up to their level!

A growl escaped Tannin's throat, and several wargs faltered over their suggestions.

"No."

"What? But you must—"

"I said no. I will not be doing any trials or worrying about becoming Golden when we have a thousand other things to think about. As a matter of fact, there is going to be no such thing as the Golden in Dunoak. I hereby renounce the whole idea of the Golden."

Tannin continued over the small outcry her words brought, as if no one had made a sound.

"If you follow me, you surrender your gold. No exceptions."

"You cannot—!"

"I can't what?" Tannin challenged. "What can't I do? Cause where I stand, I can do whatever I want. And what I want is no more Golden horseshit. Sommer is the Golden Queen. I am not."

She glared around the room, catching Lachlan's eye.

"Do your pretty wee golden bands make you feel important, or is it the blood in your veins? We're all wargs, aren't we? Where does your strength come from, huh? Gold or blood?"

When he remained silent, she stood, planting her palms on the table. "Answer me."

"Blood."

"And you?" Tannin turned to Catriona, who sat to her left. What runs in your veins? Is it pretty, shiny gold or is it the blood of a warg?"

"Blood," Catriona said more firmly.

"What give us our power? Trinkets? Or blood?"

"Blood." A few voices sounded at once.

Dana stood at Tannin's side.

"The blood of a warg!" Dana proclaimed. "The spirit of the mountains!"

Breathless, Tannin signalled for silence. "No more Golden. No more Golden and no more hiding. Let them know we're here, and let them know we're going to fight for what's ours! Not with gold but with teeth and claws! WITH BLOOD!"

"With blood!" Dana bellowed.

Lachlan, Catriona, all of Dana's inner circle took up the chant. "With blood!"

"Blood! Blood! BLOOD!"

The word caught like wildfire, and as the echoes bounced back, it sounded like a thousand voices took up the call. Tannin herself joined, and together, they howled the word until the rafters rattled and gold jewellery was torn off and dropped at her feet. The fervour that it churned up inside her, and that she could see in the eyes of the other wargs, was intoxicating as they thundered as one.

"Gold or blood?" Theo remarked under his breath as he passed. The wargs had filtered out of the chamber, but the air still vibrated with their exhilaration. "Nicely done."

I think that's the first compliment he's ever given me.

"You always underestimated me," Tannin replied, glowing with pride. "Maybe I'm not the blood heir for nothing."

She'd had all the gold collected in a sack and had Alby safely lock it away. He'd had to make multiple trips, his thin arms straining under the weight of it. It would still have its uses – to pay the kelpies, for one thing. She had signed the agreement Iona had sent as her first official act as queen. Denouncing the Golden had been the second.

Tannin was the last to leave after the meeting when a flash of fabric caught her eye as a figure slunk around the corner.

Oh, no you don't.

"Oi!" she called as she darted after the creeping spy.

"Oh, hello," Ava blustered. "I was just..."

"Eavesdropping."

She gave her a sheepish smile. "Old habits."

"You've been avoiding me."

Tannin stalked towards her, making her step back. Tannin followed until Ava's back hit the wall. Ava gave a gasp as Tannin stepped in close and pressed her hands to the wall on either side of the princess.

"You've been avoiding me," Tannin repeated.

"I have not," Ava said airily. "You've just been busy."

"Mhm."

"It sounded intense in there."

"Very intense. You should have been there."

"My place is behind the scenes. You know that."

"It was. You could stand beside me, you know."

Ava shook her head. "We should still keep this, us, quiet."

"I don't care what people think. Come be a queen with me."

Again, Ava shook her head and then smiled coyly. "Power looks good on you."

"Oh, does it now?"

Over the thundering of her own pulse, Tannin heard Ava's breath catch as her gaze flickered to her lips.

"Do you have anywhere you need to be right now?" Ava murmured, clearing her throat.

"I have a little time." Tannin grinned. "You wanna talk about what you said the other night?"

"I don't want to do any talking at all."

"I still don't think I want to be queen," Tannin said, propping herself up on a pillow as they lounged in bed. She had missed the meeting she was supposed to be at and had sent Alby scuttling back downstairs with her apologies. "Too many responsibilities."

Ava scoffed, "Oh please, you're going to love barking orders and making people kneel for you."

The princess was, objectively, always beautiful, but with her hair mussed and the tantalising glimpse of pale skin under the blankets, she was stunning.

"Would you kneel for me?" Tannin smirked.

Ava arched an eyebrow. "Only if you asked very, very nicely."

"I'm the Feral Queen. Haven't heard? I don't do nice."

"I still can't believe you did that to those wargs."

"A lot of people can't. I'm just gonna have to be so horrible that they believe it."

"You don't really look like you could have torn the heads off three wargs." Ava admitted, stretching back into the pillows contentedly. "You're too adorable."

Tannin swatted her.

"Shame you can't just carry those around with you to show them off."

"Oh." Tannin's face split into a wide grin. "Oh, that's given me a really, really bad idea."

Chapter Thirty-Eight

A Crown for a Queen

In the following weeks, people arrived in Dunoak in their droves. News of the Feral Queen had spread like wildfire, and the guards had their work cut out for them organising the huge makeshift camp that had grown up around the walls. The wargs walked with a new-found sense of pride, and finally, Ava shared in it.

Tannin had done what Dana never had, recognised that Ava had actual experience in leadership. She had granted her a seat at the table. No more getting covered in dust, listening at holes in the floor. The people of Dunoak had been given a voice too. Tannin had a separate council set up with a mixture of those with wargish blood and those without to discuss city and day-to-day matters. With her regular training and other duties, Tannin usually delegated those meetings, but Ava never missed one.

Wargish warfare wasn't her strong suit, but Armodan wasn't a successful city by accident. She had grown up hearing about the slew of background planning that went on just to make it function. This was something she knew how to do.

Dana had had the right idea with expanding their sewage system to cope with the increasing populace, but she had severely underestimated how much work had to be done. The camps outside the main city were a bubbling cauldron of disease just waiting to spill, and Ava had diverted all of the workforce away from fortifying the city walls to digging trenches.

Her efforts to unlock the secrets of warg-juice were also halted in favour of a testing method to make sure their wells were still pure. The bout of sickness that had overtaken Dunoak, however brief it had been, still haunted her. They never did find the cause.

Although she had honed her craft significantly during her time in Dunoak, Ava wasn't too proud to acknowledge her own limitations. For larger injuries or grievous illness, Ava always sent people to the healers in the city. Within the keep walls, though, she thrived. No one else seemed to really care that Ava was in fact Princess Avalyn of the Brochands as long as she could cure their ails.

With all her experimenting plus the countless cuts, scrapes and sniffles that required her attention, little Alby's near-constant presence in her workrooms was thoroughly welcome. She didn't let him near anything that could be dangerous, but he eagerly fetched herbs from the markets for her and stirred the bubbling pots of acrid smelling liquids. Tannin had the same budget as Dana had for Ava to play with, but she had far more tricks. For the Feral Queen, the merchants and shopkeepers were always willing to supply 'free samples' in the hope of encouraging her patronage, and Tannin gleefully encouraged the practice. Under normal circumstances, Ava would have cautioned against such methods but without her ingredients, she couldn't make any cures.

With all the changes going on, Ava and Tannin rarely had time to themselves anymore, but in true wargish tradition, they did still try to have meals together. Unfortunately, Tannin was resolutely still a morning person, so in order to break their fast together, Ava had started conditioning herself to keep up with Tannin's ludicrously early starts. She did not like it one bit. It made her grouchy and Tannin teased her about it relentlessly.

That morning, she was extra irritable, and when Alby informed her there was a visitor, she groaned. She was not in any mood for pleasantries or forced niceties.

"Has he identified himself? Has someone checked him for weapons?" She regretted the harshness of her tone as Alby's expression faltered.

"Yes, Miss Ava."

"Good." She forced a smile. "I'll need your help later today. I need someone strong. Come see me around midday."

His blazing smile was back in an instant. He assured her he would be there, that he was strong, that he could help, and then he zipped off in the direction of the kitchen before she could ask him anything further about the visitor. The boy was a ball of energy even at this absurd time in the morning.

Ava straightened her dress, touching the leather pouch that lay against her breastbone. She still hadn't scattered Attilo's ashes. Nowhere had felt right so far, not even her memorial garden. She sighed. A worry for the future. Right now, she had to deal with the strange man standing in the entrance hall.

He wasn't what she had expected. Even though he was probably wearing the best clothing he had, his scuffed boots and blackened fingernails gave him away as a craftsman. He tugged off his faded cap as she approached and twisted it in his hands.

"Good morning," Ava said cautiously.

"I've got a delivery. I was told to come here when it was done. She said – Her Feral Majesty that is – she said to come straight away." His eyes darted as he spoke in a way that made Ava wonder just how rough the guards had been with him. Since the incident with the elevens, and considering Tannin was an assassination risk in general, they had been extra thorough in recent times.

The man stepped aside to show her the crate he had brought with him. She narrowed her eyes.

"What is it?"

He shifted on his feet. "I wasn't to say to no one. I had my instructions. Commission, it was."

"Open it."

"Beggin' your pardon, Miss. I have my instructions."

Ava set her jaw. She was very tempted to play the "Do you know who I am?"' card but before she could, a clattering announced someone rapidly descending the stairs.

"Ooh, is that what I think it is?" Tannin practically bounced into the hallway in excitement. The craftsman looked like he was about to keel over but nodded faintly.

"Tannin, what on earth did you—" Ava's question died in her throat. Tannin winked at Ava's stunned reaction, making butterflies flood her insides.

Her eyes weren't warg-gold, but she'd darkened them around the edges in thick, black kohl that made them blaze anyway. Her lips were stained the colour of fresh blood. She'd also streaked charcoal down her cheeks in thick lines. The effect was striking. That's where they had been going wrong. Dana and Catriona had been thinking make-up for a queen, but what the Feral Queen really needed was war paint.

As the craftsman pried open the crate at Tannin's demand, she leant in to whisper in Ava's ear.

"Like the look?"

"I do." Ava tilted her chin up with a fingertip so she could better see the patterns. "You look fearsome."

"I am fearsome." Tannin grinned. Even her human teeth looked somehow sharper than usual.

When the craftsman had finally wrestled the lid off of the crate, Tannin tore into the packaging with slightly more ruthlessness than was called for, despite Ava's chidings to be careful. As the entirety of the thing inside was revealed, Ava couldn't help but grimace.

"What," Ava asked in repulsed awe as she peeked inside, "is that?"

"You like it?"

"That is..."

"Horrific?" Tannin suggested with glee. "Awful? Terrifying?"

"I was going to say disgusting." Ava's nose wrinkled. "Please tell me that is not what I think it is."

Tannin trailed a fingertip over the monstrous construction. "What better way to show off my new title?"

The crown that she'd commission was a thing of ugly beauty. Fangs as long as her forearm jutted up from the broken jawbones of the wargs she'd killed in a macabre mimicry of a crown's points. Iron or steel lined each tooth, weaving through the cracks in the bone, holding it all together in a metallic sheen of webbing. A feral crown for a Feral Queen.

"Is it...to your satisfaction?" the man asked. He had bowed back-breakingly low when Tannin had opened the package and only now dared to raise his head.

"It's certainly impressive," Ava said, squinting at the construction. "You did want to solidify your dreadfulness."

"It's just as grotesque as I imagined it," Tannin whispered, turning the crown over in her hands before setting it on her head. Her blood-red lips split into a terrible smile.

"It's perfect."

Chapter Thirty-Nine

Old Friends

Tannin

Tannin was not used to being the centre of attention. As well as being constantly pestered by the warg-bloods for gory details of the now infamous slaughter, there were the gawkers too. Always peering in windows and camping outside the keep to try and get a glimpse of the fearsome beast. Douglas had eventually managed to shoo them away once Tannin had snapped and given permission to threaten them with a horse whip.

Even up on her spot on the roof, she had to be careful not to venture too far towards the edge or she would be seen by the undeterrable lurkers.

"It's just like back home," Flint remarked as they stood, looking out over the ramshackle mess of tents and hastily constructed wooden shacks beyond the city limits. "Except we're the nobles now. When did we get fancy?"

"I dunno," Tannin responded, adjusting her cloak. It was a deep blue, as soft as fur and, barring her warg wool clothing, probably the most expensive thing she had ever worn. "It's getting bigger every day. We won't have enough stores to feed all these people."

"I was going to say that's not your problem, but I guess it is, Your Majesty." Flint smirked.

Tannin gave him a sour look. "Just keeping this bloody city alive is so much work. We don't even have time to talk about what Sommer is up to or what the hell we do next. Life in Armodan was so much easier."

"Easiness is overrated." A voice reached them right as Dana's head crested the stone roof. "Power is far better."

"Hi, Dana," Tannin said with a grimace.

Dana tracking her down meant there was work to be done. She'd barely had half an hour's peace. Dana confirmed her suspicions by announcing she was needed downstairs.

"A group arrived today pledging to the Beast of Armodan, not the Feral Queen. Know anything about that?"

"Huh," Tannin said with a frown.

"Who do you even know still in Armodan?" Flint asked, mirroring her expression.

"Who doesn't actively want me dead? I have no idea. Only Eve. If Eve walked all this way with that teeny wee bairn, I'm gonna smack her."

"Who's Eve?" Dana asked sharply.

"We worked together in the bakery."

Even though she fervently hoped Eve was safe somewhere in the Brochlands' countryside with Graeme and the baby, the possibility of seeing her again made Tannin's heart sing.

"None of these people look like bakers. They look like bandits to be honest. Their leader and a few others are waiting for you in the great hall."

When Tannin shot her an apprehensive look, Dana added with an exasperated sigh, "It's just another meeting and I can't do it for you, so let's go."

"Duty calls," Flint sang, pushing off the wall where he'd been leaning. "Cards later if you're free?"

Without waiting for an answer, he sauntered off leaving Tannin with Dana and a looming appointment with a group of supposed bandits.

Tannin peeked around the huge door. Bandits was a near enough description, Tannin thought as she took in the rugged, travel-worn group. They were almost all male and looked unarmed, as expected, but each one of them exuded some sort of aura of violence whether it be bulging muscles and scars or just piercingly soulless eyes.

As intimidating as they were, they looked with deference upon the shorter figure in the centre when she spoke. Her gruff voice was like music to Tannin's ears.

"Nyesha!" Tannin's joy at recognising her turned to horror when she turned around. "Oh, *fuck.*"

She spoke without thinking – a gut reaction to the rows of twisted scar tissue running from the corner of Nyesha's mouth, up underneath a patch where her left eye should have been to where her braids were missing along the side of her head.

Tannin gaped. Those rows of scars. Claw marks. From when she'd tried to cut the noose down. She hadn't been in control, but she didn't think...she didn't mean to...

Apprehension twisted in her gut. Was Nyesha here for revenge?

The half of her mouth that wasn't marred with claw marks curved upwards.

"Alright, lass? Or should I be calling you Your Majesty now?"

"I—" Tannin stammered. "Oh gods. Your face. I am so sorry —"

Nyesha cut her off with a wave of a hand. "A scar is a reminder. These remind me of the day I didnae die. Ye saved my life and I'll honour that debt."

"Oh, you don't owe me anyth—"

Nyesha dismissed her babbling with another wave of a hand. "Blood is blood."

"I thought I was done for up there," she said quietly enough so that only Tannin heard her. "I'd have given my eye, my leg, what's left of my damned soul not tae die that way."

She grasped Tannin's hand and squeezed it hard before all trace of that bitter emotion sank back behind her iron walls.

Tannin couldn't help it. She threw her arms around the older woman's waist and hugged her tightly. Nyesha went as stiff as a board and gave her an awkward pat on the top of her head. She was clearly not a hugger. Tannin let go and Nyesha cleared her throat.

As she stepped back, she noticed one of the figures behind Nyesha. Tall, gangly, with a shock of red hair that she recognised from her time in the city Gaol. The guard grinned at her uneasily and gave her a little wave.

Tannin blinked. "What are you doin' here...uh...?" His name escaped her.

"MacDubh." He bobbed a bow. "I'm with Ny."

Tannin looked between the two of them. "How in the hell did that happen?"

"I could ask ye the same, lass." Nyesha let out a gravelly laugh. "How on earth did a wee gutter rat like you end up a queen?"

"Tannin." Dana raised an eyebrow.

"Right, introductions I guess." Tannin bit her lip. There was no way to phrase it that was going to sound good. She took a deep breath. "Nyesha is a gang leader from the Skirts of Armodan. We did a job and then we were in prison but not because of that job. For other stuff. And then there was the…ahem…gallows, and I did that…" She gestured to Nyesha's scars. "…And I haven't seen her since, but I saved her life. So, she's here to help."

Dana looked from Tannin to Nyesha and back. Her expression said she was not happy at this new development. Her mouth twitched like she wanted to say something, but in the end, nothing came out.

"I would've come sooner, but I had some things tae take care of back in the Skirts. I've left a trusted lieutenant in charge."

The last time they had spoken was deep underground in the city gaol when they both thought they were living their last days on earth. Nyesha had told her of her rise to power in the gang circles and the subsequent betrayal by a man she thought was her friend. Tannin had, of course, also met the traitorous Hamish when she first dipped her toe into a life of crime. He had been charming and dangerous and was quick to give a golden-toothed smile, but behind the façade, Nyesha had painted a picture of a ruthless and violent man. Tannin had worked that out for herself when he tried to kill her and burnt her house to the ground on behalf of the Triquetra, of course, but she hadn't realised it extended to his own people too. He had been taken by the paranoia that Nyesha was going to take control from him. He set her up and sent her straight to the gallows.

Tannin hadn't seen or heard from the older woman since that day. The day she would really rather forget. She still had nightmares. And the last she heard Hamish was still alive, well and pretty much running the Skirts from the shadows.

"What about Hamish?"

Nyesha smiled a smile that stretched her scars and was full of vicious secrets.

"As I said. Things to take care of."

A flash of gold from Nyesha's throat caught the light. On a string around her neck hung a single golden tooth.

"What did you do to him?"

"How strong's yer stomach?" Nyesha countered.

Tannin exhaled. "I think we need something to drink."

Nyesha brought MacDubh and another of her brutes with her to the council chambers. Tannin summoned her own inner circle as well as a healthy amount of ale.

As the rest of her people arrived, Tannin made the introductions with pride. Dana, Catriona, Lachlan and Ava. Adair was, again, out with his rangers. Ava arrived last. Nyesha's unmarred eyebrow quirked as she entered. Then her eye narrowed.

"Actually, that job we did was when I met Ava for the first time." Tannin jabbed her thumb in Ava's direction. "She stole the sightlens, by the way."

Ava nodded to Nyesha and her crew. "A pleasure."

Nyesha folded her arms and jutted out a hip.

"Princess Avalyn." She drew out each syllable with no small amount of derision layered on each.

Of course, she bloody knows who she is.

Tannin groaned internally, but to her credit, Ava barely flinched.

"Princess?" MacDubh yelped and quickly sketched a sloppy bow. Tannin noted, with irritation, that Ava got a deeper bow than he'd given her. Technically, she outranked her right now.

"She's with us," Tannin assured Nyesha, but the coldness of her stare remained.

"Is she indeed?" She spat on the ground and glared. "I recognise yer face and I remember yer voice, *Ava.*"

Oh.

Nyesha looked to Tannin and arched her eyebrows. *Eyebrow.* Her unasked question hung in the air. *You forgave her?* Tannin swallowed.

Nyesha has a sharp memory for grievances.

Having been in the cell across from Tannin, Nyesha had heard her pathetic pleas for help and Ava's ice cold refusal. The glare she gave Ava though was pure poison.

"Uh, Ava?" Tannin murmured. "Maybe sit this one out?"

Ava swallowed hard and nodded.

Nyesha watched her leave and waited until the door was closed to turn back to Tannin.

"What the fuck is she doin' here?"

"Long story." Tannin fluttered a hand. "Drink?"

Goblets were filled as everyone took their seats, and Nyesha waited until everyone had settled before speaking.

"Ye trust these folks?" she asked out of the corner of her ruined mouth.

"As much as I trust anyone." Tannin cocked her head at the red-haired ex-guard. "About trust..."

"Nah, wee MacDubh is awright. Aren't ye, Mackie?"

The boy flushed at the nickname.

"After it all went down that day, the lad found me bleedin' but still kickin'." She chuckled. "Dunno if he was originally plannin' on sendin' me straight back up on that platform, but after I stopped the eejit gettin' trampled durin' yer wee show, he took me to a healer instead. Just went on from there really. I'm teachin' him the ways, like."

"He's your apprentice?"

"More or less." Mackie grinned. "Pays better than being a Gaol guard, that's for sure."

"As much as I'm all for reminiscing old times," Dana interjected. "I'm sure we're all curious as to what you're doing here."

"As much as I am here tae honour a debt, this place ye've got here…" Nyesha inhaled deeply. "It's got the scent of potential."

Tannin cocked her head with a smile. "You didn't strike me as the type that wants to be one of my foot soldiers or – gods forbid – a guard. So, what do you want?"

Nyesha jutted her chin in the vague direction of the growing muddle of makeshift buildings beyond the walls.

"Ye haven't got control of your outer city."

A ripple of discontent made its way through the wargs. Tannin had learnt that any criticisms had to be well sugar-coated to not be met with outright hostility.

"It is under control," Catriona snapped, reaching past Nyesha for the ale jug.

"Pfft, save yer pride, lass. I might not see as well as I used to." She gestured to her missing eye. "…but even I can recognise a mess when I see one."

"We're working on it, but we haven't got the men for it and it just keeps growing," Tannin said with a wistful glance towards the window. Ava had more of less given her the same feedback, but solutions were making themselves scarce.

Nyesha clicked her tongue. "That ain't the right attitude. It ain't about numbers. It's about control. Ye've got control of the top level, aye, but the lower levels? In the grit and the dirt? They dinnae care who's in charge up here. You know that, lass. In the Skirts, did ye care about the fancy nobles? Nah, they need someone there in the dirt with them who's not afraid tae get bloody."

"What are you suggesting?" Dana asked sharply at the mention of blood, but Tannin had already worked out the direction Nyesha was looking to.

"You want to be laird of the outer city."

"Laird is a fancy title and all, but no. What needs done out there shouldnae have an official title. Shouldnae have a name."

Tannin swallowed. She knew first-hand what kind of person it took to do that job. Clach had been that person in her world. He'd pushed her grandfather to drink over insane debts, blackmailed her, forced her into crime, tried to have her falsely arrested for murder...And she'd stabbed him to death. She hadn't thought about him in a long time and she really hadn't wanted to.

"I don't need anything from ye. I dinnae need gold. I can fix the mess ye've got oot there, and all ye need to do is not ask questions, deny all knowledge, and keep yer enforcers oot of my business. Can ye do that?"

Tannin glanced to each of her circle. They were there to keep her from making rash decisions after all. From their uncomfortable expressions and pursed lips, it was clear that no one was thrilled with the plan. Tannin sipped her ale, giving them time to object, but no one said a word. In a way, that was good. Deny all involvement, as it were.

She caught Dana's eye. An almost imperceptible nod. It must pain her to accept non-warg help in her own city.

Except it's not hers. It's mine.

Tannin puffed out her chest.

"I have conditions."

"Of course, ye do."

"We've got a trade agreement with the kelpie-bloods of Alderglen. That, along with the distribution of their goods, is to be protected and upheld."

Upheld. Tannin suppressed a little wiggle. When had she become someone who used words like upheld?

"Agreed."

Tannin leant back in her chair and swirled her glass. She knew from experience that an offer like this didn't come without the glint of coin somewhere.

"You're a business woman first and foremost. I know you've got a plan to make money out of this." Tannin smirked. "I want a percentage of the profits you make."

Nyesha laughed outright. "Still a greedy, wee gutter rat at heart, aren't ye? I'll give ye five percent."

"Twenty."

"Ten."

"Twenty."

Nyesha stopped smiling as Tannin's grin broadened. "Now that's askin' a lot."

"This is my city."

"Fifteen."

"Deal and you still have to pay your taxes like everyone else."

Nyesha snorted.

"And I want your counsel when I ask for it," Tannin said, any trace of humour leaving her voice. "I need someone with your..."

"Experience?"

"Unnerving knack for criminal activity?"

Nyesha chuckled and clinked her glass against Tannin's.

After a long swig, she wiped her mouth and said, "I'd certainly advise against certain company for a start."

"You mean Ava?"

Nyesha's one remaining eyebrow rose. "It could be an accident, y'know. Things happen and—"

"Do not finish that sentence," Tannin said sharply.

Nyesha blinked in surprised. She opened her mouth to respond, but Tannin was quick to cut her off.

"I said..." Tannin let her eyes blaze gold for just a second. "...do not. She is off limits."

Nyesha inclined her head ever so slightly in acceptance. "I'll let it be known."

Tannin could have sworn she even looked a little impressed. Glancing around the table, she realised that any doubt anyone had as to the extent of her and Ava's relationship had been swept away in that one statement.

Ah, fuck it.

She was a queen, dammit, and she would be with who she wanted. She caught Dana's disapproving frown out of the corner of her eye. She could frown all she liked. Dana didn't have the power to scare her anymore.

Tannin turned fully to face her, lifted her goblet in a silent toast.

Off. Limits.

Chapter Forty

A Game of Queens

Tannin

Tannin watched as Ava traced the grooves in the table that made up the crudely carved map. She had told Tannin before of a beautiful map table her father had, inlayed with different shades of marble for the five kingdoms and golden waterways weaving between them until they reached the gleaming sea. Her brow was furrowed up in concentration as she gave Tannin an impromptu geography lesson before the rest of the council arrived. She always looked her most beautiful when she got all serious.

If only there hadn't been a meeting today, they could have made excellent use of this table, Tannin mused. She suppressed a grin. Now, there was a thought. The two of them on top of the whole damn world.

Tannin rounded the table and slid onto Ava's lap.

"Do you mind?"

"Not at all." Tannin tipped her head back to wink at her. "Best seat in the house."

"You're not listening to me, are you?"

"I am." She wiggled her hips against her under the guise of getting comfortable, relishing in Ava's sharp intake of breath. "Intently."

Getting Ava flustered was a challenge Tannin undertook with great enjoyment, and succeeding at it was the highlight of her day. The princess, however, was never one to back down from a challenge.

Hot breath tickled Tannin's ear, and the touch of Ava's lips on her skin made her shudder in delight. She leaned in, fully prepared for whatever filthy comment Ava could come up with. Instead, Ava's teeth nipped at her earlobe, sending a flood of heat and shivers down her body, and all the clever comments she had been saving up flew out of her brain.

"Excuse me, sorry, Your-Majesty-Your-Highness-Your-Wargliness," Alby peeped as he stuck his head around the door. Tannin quickly vacated Ava's lap. "There was a delivery that they said couldn't wait and to bring it to you immediately. From the Golden Queen. Life or death. I'm sorry. Excuse me."

The Golden Queen. Sommer. This is anything but good.

Dana and the rest of the council arrived as Alby set a small box on the table. He wouldn't meet Tannin's eye. It hurt. He still wouldn't talk to her, and when he did, it was all bows and titles and terrified apologies. She swallowed the hurt.

"What's that?" Catriona asked, looming over the table in an effort to see better.

"How would I know?" Tannin snapped, reaching for it.

The wooden box was plain and unremarkable, apart from the mountain range sigil stamped upon it in pure gold. Tannin recognised it as the symbol Sommer had chosen for her budding kingdom.

I should get a sigil.

She slid a claw out to wedge it open, enjoying the impressed murmur from the assembled wargs. They knew she was more than proficient with her Change, but she still liked to show off a little. It was her one skill, and she'd be damned if she hid it away.

She tossed the lid aside and rummaged in the straw filling.

Tannin's questing fingers found something solid. She held it up and exhaled. "Fuck."

"Why did Sommer send you a pipe?" Dana demanded. She tried to reach for it, but Tannin jerked it away. "What does it mean?"

"It means she has the vials." Tannin rubbed her temple with her free hand. "Sommer can make more wargs."

"You got that from a pipe?"

"Considering we worked out my grandad sewed the goddam vials into his fuckin' skin, and I put this in his pocket when I buried him? Aye, I'd say the message is loud and clear. There's a note too." Tannin showed her the elegantly written letter that had accompanied the pipe.

Sorry for your loss.

"She's such an arsehole." Tannin ground the parchment into a crumpled ball and chucked it across the room.

"We've got to step things up," Dana said, her expression severe.

The council members voiced their agreement.

Tannin tightened her grip on the pipe.

"Let's do it."

That very day, the Feral Queen claimed the entire Kingdom of Woodren for the wargs. There were no other actual contenders because Woodren never had an official ruler. It kind of felt like cheating, even though there was nothing anyone could do to oppose her. That didn't stop complaints and threats filtering to the keep every day. They'd doubled the house guard and the patrols on the walls, and Nyesha had done a good job of silencing unrest in the lower city. Even so, Tannin couldn't quench the feeling of uneasiness, especially since she'd simultaneously announced a levy on surrounding towns. It felt uncomfortably similar to the way roving gangs in the Skirts would shake down businesses for protection money. Why should any of them care about her stupid claim to a kingdom in the north that they'd never heard about? As a matter of fact, why did she even care?

Because Sommer is not going to stop trying to kill me for it, that's why.

Tannin groaned and rubbed her eyes. Those kind of thoughts were not going to help with the mountain of things she had to do today, including holding a grievance hearing. Her rule over the rest of Woodren was tenuous at best, and if the smaller lairds and chieftains looked at her and saw doubt, then she'd lose whatever power she had faster than she could blink.

And I've just told them all they owe me more money. Great.

The procession into the main hall was nothing short of regal, with her advisors paving the way across the stone floor and Tannin herself bringing up the rear, fanged crown sitting proudly on her head. She almost ruined it by giggling at the absurdity of it but managed to stop herself by pinching herself hard.

The room was split in two, carved apart by the aisle they walked down, packed with onlookers on either side. Their eyes gleamed with horrified awe as the Feral Queen passed on the way to the podium. To her throne. Some of them were complainants, some witnesses, but most were purely spectators eager for some sort of drama.

The complainants were, of course, not just regular townsfolk but local lairds and chieftains who were important enough to warrant an audience with the now legendary queen.

As Tannin settled into her throne, which was in reality just the biggest chair the keep had to offer, she had to reach up and stop her massive crown from wobbling. It was heavier than she remembered, and a knobbly point was grinding into her skull above her left ear. She'd have to get that fixed.

"Alright." Tannin cleared her throat. She was probably supposed to give an address or something, but she hadn't prepared anything.

Oh well.

"Who's first?"

Very few of the lairds who came forth actually had anything worth hearing. In the future, she would delegate this task to one of her unlucky advisors, but at least once or twice, she had to show her face. Small disputes with other lairds were little more than childish bickering. One had accused his brother of murder though, and one lady had an unfaithful husband that she wanted beheaded. That was at least a little entertaining, especially when Tannin had refused to sentence him to death and she had to be removed from the hall, squawking like an indignant goose.

Tannin's patience was wearing thin by the end of the day. The latest complainant was sawing through her last nerve with every word he spoke, even more so since his grievance was against her.

"Alright," she said, placing her palms on the arms on her chair and letting her scroll filled with numbers and accounts lay on her lap. "Just so we're clear. You don't want to pay the levy because you can't afford it? Then why can Laird Elford, who has half the lands you do, pay without question? Why do the people of Fenglade, who have half the trade that your people do, pay fewer local taxes? And if you collect all this extra coin, what do you have to show for it?"

She was so glad Ava had coached her for this. The princess knew exactly what to look for to find pressure points, and she was correct in saying that pride was almost always a sweet spot.

He opened his mouth to argue, but she shut him down immediately.

"Your lands and people can afford my levy. What they cannot afford is your own personal extravagance at their expense. I'll send one of my own people to revalue your revenues, and if need be, the funds will be extracted from your personal accounts and holdings," Tannin said, satisfied with the way his mouth went slack and his face purpled in indignation. "Grievance denied."

He turned, aghast, to the other lairds who sat around the edges of the hall.

"Are we really going to let this child do this to us? To dictate her own laws! She is nothing but a thief!"

"Oh, go fuck yourself."

"Tannin!" Dana hissed from the side lines.

"My apologies." Tannin gave him a dazzling smile. "I respectfully invite the esteemed laird to go fuck himself."

Dana slapped a hand to her forehead.

The hall erupted into combined laughter and outrage with the laird himself spitting with fury.

Tannin ran her fingertip around the lip of her goblet, slowly lengthening one claw and letting it scrape the glass with an ear-splitting wail, interrupting his tirade and silencing the hall.

"Oh, sorry were you sayin' somethin'?" She arched an eyebrow.

The blood drained from his face at the sight of the claw, poised menacingly on the goblet's rim. He tried, once again, to speak but she interrupted before he could.

"No?" She let her hand settle back to normal, lifted the goblet and gestured at the door. "Then I think we're done here. Pay the damn levy."

"You need to execute that man," Dana muttered under her breath as they left the hall. Her cheeks were red with indignation. "He could spread dissent."

"We can keep an eye on him." Tannin lifted her crown from her head and massaged the painful spot above her ear where it had been digging in. "I'd rather not start lopping off heads all over the place just 'cause someone was rude to me."

"It's about respect."

"If he starts any more shit, I'll send Nyesha in to break his knees. How 'bout that?"

"You need to be careful," Dana warned her. "Your softness is a weakness, and it will come back to bite you."

Tannin treated her to a fanged smile. "I bite back."

Dana scoffed. "Cute, but you will regret letting him live."

Tannin left her to go get changed before her afternoon training session but not before Flint caught up with her. He had gone the extra length to look especially dapper for her first hearing and had matched his shirt to the pale blue of his eyes. Ava had said she would come too, but Tannin hadn't seen her in the crowd.

"You were such a bitch," Flint crowed gleefully.

Tannin grimaced. "Was it too much?"

"Oh no, Tan," he said draping an arm across her shoulders. "It was *delicious*."

Chapter Forty-One

Enemy of my Enemy

Tannin

Alby might have stopped talking to Tannin except in mortifying deference, but any spare time he had, he spent almost glued to Ava's side. The next time Tannin saw Alby, when he came to tell her Dana wanted to see her, he had even made himself an unofficial apprentice badge. She was going to compliment it, but the boy had already sprinted away. Ava had told her that he felt betrayed that she had lied to him and scared that he had never known what she was. He was deathly afraid of monsters, and the poor boy had seen the warg heads up close when they had taken them down from the spikes.

Tannin dejectedly took the stairs to Dana's office and knocked.

"You know you are, technically, now in charge. You can just come in if you want to," Dana said as she opened the door.

Tannin flopped into a chair opposite her. "I can't be a polite queen?"

"You're many things, Tannin, but polite is not one of them. Every town from here to the border has pledged to pay the new levy. Good work." Dana poured her a glass of something from a tall decanter.

In response to Tannin's raised eyebrow, she said, "Gormbraen spirit. Firewater. It came in last week as a tax payment. I thought it was appropriate."

"Nyesha is doin' a good job," Tannin said accepting the glass. "Although, the ears are a bit too gruesome for me."

A garland of severed ears, from those who had tried to avoid Nyesha's tax collectors, hung like bunting from the toll tower on the main road into Dunoak. They never managed to avoid them for long. At least Tannin had managed to talk her down from taking hands instead, but it was still a gut-churning sight to behold.

Despite the harsh measures, the outer city was gradually becoming more civilised under Nyesha's iron fist and Tannin's rule. She had followed Dana's example in being seen out with the people, supporting their businesses and helping with some charitable causes. The people of Dunoak had become accustomed to their wargish leaders and treated Tannin with a respect she had never expected. Flint had been right. Between the outlandish stories of her power and Eoghan and Collum's musical tales of her heroism, she was quickly becoming a legend in her own right. The weight of it pressed down a little more on her shoulders with every passing day.

Tannin took a sip of the drink Dana had poured her. It was almost whisky-like and she shrugged her approval.

"Why is Gormbraen firewater appropriate?"

Dana tossed her a letter. The ruby-red seal had already been cracked open and hung heavy from the thick parchment. It was signed Laird Cormack and bore the seal of the Gormbraen king, King Modric, at the bottom.

Tannin noticed that the letter had been addressed to her and chose to ignore the fact that Dana had opened it anyway.

"Who's Laird Cormack?"

"A very influential member of King Modric's court. He's also known as the Falcon. Maybe you know him by that name. They say he has eyes everywhere and that he is a brutally efficient tactician in battle."

All these lairds and generals and captains claimed to be great tacticians and fearsome warriors. Tannin had yet to meet one that wasn't also a pompous arse.

"And King Modric?"

"You should know who King Modric is," Dana reproached her.

"I know he's the king. That's about it."

"His blood has ruled Gormbrae since before it even was Gormbrae. He's also sometimes called Modric the Red. The legend was that he used to be fair-haired. By the time he reached manhood, however, he had already spilled so much blood that his hair turned red. He's not someone to mess with lightly, and he chafes against the Brochlands' hold over them."

If that legend is true, then my hair should at least be a wee bit red by now.

Tannin made a noncommittal sound as she scanned the letter, filtering through all the complimentary nonsense until she got to the good part.

"An alliance?" she blurted. "With Gormbrae? I'm from Armodan. What are they thinking?"

"You're not, though. You're from Stonestead. And King Florian still wants your head." Dana's hard eyes studied her face. "It's a logical offer if you think about it. Enemy of my enemy, if you like."

Tannin turned her attention back to the letter, sceptically. "They're inviting us to the Falcon's Rest – what a pretentious name – the Laird's fort on the border with Woodren...Hmmm, I guess that's close enough to home to bail if it goes wrong..."

Tannin muttered mostly to herself as she re-read the invite.

"They want us to help attack the Brochlands, don't they?"

"I'd assume so."

"In exchange for help against Sommer? Is Gormbrae even strong enough to stand against her?"

"A better question to ask is, how strong would Sommer be without allies if we helped Gormbrae take the Brochlands? Rill is rich, yes, and they could make life very difficult for us if they did deploy their resources on the Shey river, but against Woodren, Gormbrae, and the Brochlands if we helped take it, they'd have to stand down. Not to mention our claim on Cascairn. Sommer would have no one."

"Unite the kingdoms against Sommer." Tannin tapped her chin with her fingertips. "That's a huge leap."

"It's a goal to aim for," Dana said. "One that isn't outlandishly unachievable either. We use Gormbrae's desire for the Brochlands for our own gain. They're not going to stop until they take it, even if they have to scrape up scraps of land piece by piece. They'll want our support from the East, and we can use this alliance to infiltrate their high councils and influence decisions to our advantage." Dana leaned forward, eyes shining. "This is a real opportunity."

Tannin stared at the letter in her hands without really seeing it. If the wargs helped Gormbrae take the Brochlands, then her banishment would be over.

I could go home.

She could go back to roaming the chaotic streets of the Skirts with its overhanging, wilting houses and myriad of strange shops and market stalls. Her favourite inns and taverns. Her and Flint could flick roastnut shells at the guards from crumbling staircases and run away laughing their heads off when they were spotted. They could go drink at the old ruins near the graveyard for old times' sake.

"I can't turn on Armodan," Tannin whispered. "I can't turn on the Brochlands."

"Tannin," Dana said, reaching over to take her hand in an uncharacteristic show of affection that made Tannin nervous. "There is not a person left in Armodan who wouldn't mount your head on a spike. If not for King Florian, then for Sommer. She's got her claws sunk deep into that city. Everyone saw her almost kill you without even trying. You need to let it go and realise that you have your own city now. Your own kingdom, in fact."

Tannin stared at her distorted reflection in the firewater and swirled it.

Mrs O'Baird's house had probably been built up into something new by now, but in her mind, it was still a smouldering pile of ash. It was true, she had no friends left in Armodan. Even her old acquaintances in the vegetable markets from when she did Mrs O'Baird's weekly shopping would rather see her dead than share a pleasant "good morning". It wasn't home anymore. But it had been.

"You aren't that girl who called Armodan home anymore. You were a penniless baker, and now you're a wargish queen."

"Assistant baker, actually," Tannin corrected.

"You're helping my point. Armodan was a different life. It's time to let it go."

Tannin mulled it over as she sipped at her Gormbraen spirit. It really wasn't bad at all.

It couldn't hurt to hear what they have to say, could it?"

She tipped the rest of it down her throat. "Alright, when do we leave?"

Chapter Forty-Two

Blood Magic

Ava

"Will you just tell me what is going on!?" Ava said in exasperation.

Tannin hadn't been able to sit still all evening. She'd gone from jiggling her foot as she sat on Ava's workroom sofa, to pacing, to twirling a strand of pale hair through her fingers. All while biting her nails.

Eventually, Ava had taken her by the shoulders, sat her down and demanded to know what was going on. Between Tannin's obvious agitation and her own Senses drilling into her brain, she was getting anxious.

As difficult as it was for Tannin to get started, once she did, she didn't stop. Not even to breathe, it seemed. She rambled out her entire meeting with Dana. About the letter. About Gormbrae, About Armodan. About home. About how it would mean actively siding against Ava's family.

Seeing Tannin so worried about how she would react made Ava feel intensely guilty that she had already heard the whole thing from the storage room above. She decided to keep that secret to herself.

Ava schooled her features into the appropriate levels of surprise and turmoil as Tannin finished her explanations. The poor girl looked deflated.

"I suppose it is logical that Gormbrae would see potential in your budding rule," Ava said, trying to make her tone comforting. She had already thought it all through and put her feelings aside to deal with later.

Or never. Probably never.

"It gains them reputation through you as well, which could earn them more support from their own people…" She waggled her head. "Yes, I can see why they reached out."

Tannin blinked. "You do realise if we did ally with them, we'd be fighting against the Brochlands. Against Armodan."

"Yes, I am aware."

"Okay." Tannin narrowed her eyes at her, clearly not buying Ava's nonchalance. "Do you know this Falcon, then?"

"I've met him once I think when I was younger. King Modric sent ambassadors every once in a while to keep the peace. We did the same, of course, but always on our terms. There was always a dinner, and then they would disappear into my father's study to talk."

"Now they're at war."

"It was a long time coming."

"And now you're on the side that's maybe gonna support Gormbrae."

"Yes."

"Doesn't that…bother you?"

"Yes, it bothers me!" Ava snapped and then immediately softened when Tannin winced. "But Dana is right. That's neither your life nor mine anymore. We can't go back. We both need to let it go."

"But—"

"Do you want me to be upset? Would you like me to get angry and tell you not to meet them?" Ava challenged. "Do you want me to talk you out of this because you're scared?"

Tannin pouted. "Maybe."

"Well, tough. This is the best choice for Woodren and the wargs. That's what you have to think about now."

Ava shoved her hands into the pockets of her skirt before Tannin could see that they were trembling. Her own personal feelings had no place in this decision. That was the truth of it.

I made my choice.

"Can't you ever just tell me what I want to hear?" Tannin huffed.

Ava smirked playfully, thoroughly glad of an opportunity to get away from painful topics. She reached out to brush Tannin's hair away from her face where it had come out of its braid. All of the wargs and warg-bloods wore their hair braided. Not that it didn't suit her, but Ava found herself missing Tannin's scraped-together knot that she used to wear during their evenings together in the crypt. It had made her look softer somehow.

"Hm? I bet I can come up with something you'd like to hear."

"I know you're changin' the subject," Tannin chided and then paused, a sly grin forming. "Continue anyway."

Ava cupped Tannin's chin in her hand and traced her thumb over her bottom lip. "It'll have to be later. I have things to do today."

Tannin's face fell. "What things?"

"Things that aren't you. Now leave."

She released her with a wink.

"You are such a tease," Tannin grumbled as Ava guided her to the door.

"Always." Ava grinned and gave Tannin a quick kiss on the top of the head and then gently, lovingly, shoved her out.

With autumn drawing to a close and the weather taking a turn for the worse, the trip to Gormbrae was organised at break-neck speed before the threat of snow would make the return journey impossible.

As Tannin rolled an extra cloak into a tight bundle and squashed it into her already over-full pack, Ava sat on her bed and tried not to correct her. Even if her stomach hadn't been in knots, Tannin's chaotic approach to packing would have stressed her out.

"You sure you're okay about this?" Tannin pressed for the hundredth time, rolling up the sleeves of her loose, grey shirt before continuing to wrestle with her baggage. She could have worn much finer clothes if she'd wanted to. In fact, Ava knew that there were lovely dresses hanging in her wardrobe, but Tannin seemed determined to "save them for a good occasion". She wouldn't listen to Ava telling her that a queen needed no occasion. It was something her mother used to say.

"I am worried," Ava confessed.

"I knew it." Tannin abandoned her attempt to fasten the clasp of her pack. "I knew you didn't want me to do this."

"It's not that I don't want you to go. It makes perfect sense to try and curry favour with the southerners, but I've got a strange feeling about it. Something isn't sitting right with me, but I don't know what. Maybe it's just because it's all so rushed. And I don't like the idea of you going alone."

"I'm not going alone. Dana's organised a proper party. Even Theo announced this mornin' that he's coming too. Dana isn't too happy about changin' plans at the last minute, but he knows the most about other kingdom's customs and things or so he says. He might be useful, even if he is an arse."

"You know what I mean."

"You can't come with me," Tannin murmured. "They're enemies of your kingdom. It would slightly send the wrong message if we showed up with you in tow to talk about alliance."

"Obviously." Ava rolled her eyes and then braced herself for what she was about to say. The more she had worried, the more the yellowed pages of her stolen druid book called to her. This time she had listened. She had shuddered at some of the rituals it had described but some...some she could stomach.

"I think I have a way we can stay in contact."

"Don't tell me you bought a pigeon."

"I mean a secret way."

"You bought a secret pigeon."

Ava gave her a withering look. "I did not buy any birds."

"Ooh, a creepy witch way."

"Exactly."

"How afraid should I be?"

"Nothing should go wrong."

"That did not answer the question in the slightest." Tannin narrowed her eyes at the hint of apprehension in Ava's tone. "What are you gonna do?"

"Nothing too dangerous," Ava assured her with a flutter of her hand. "I do need your assistance, though. Tonight."

"Did we have to do this at midnight?" Tannin grumbled, stifling a yawn. "I was up at the crack of dawn."

"It's a full moon, and there's some debate about whether or not moonlight aids in druidic potency." Ava shrugged. "Besides, I enjoy the poetry of it."

Ava strode past the beginnings of her memorial garden to the back of the keep where the weed-choked plants were still sorely neglected and the paving was cracked with stringy blades of grass forcing their way through the stone.

"Are you telling me you're keepin' me from my bed for the aesthetics?"

"If you want to put it like that. Now come here, sit, be quiet." Ava's bag clinked when she set it down. She had been surprised that such a dark magic had such commonplace ingredients. She had been able to source everything she needed in one trip to the market. She had gone herself this time. She wouldn't let little Alby be tainted by any part of this.

Tannin did as she was told and sat cross-legged on one of the pathways. "Are you gonna tell me what we're doing?"

"*I* am making speaking stones."

"What's a speaking stone?"

"You really can't work that one out for yourself?"

Tannin made a face at her.

"A speaking stone," Ava said, reaching into her bag and setting out various jars and clay pots before clarifying, "is a stone that will let us communicate while you're away."

"How does that work?"

"It's...blood magic, I suppose you could call it." Ava's forehead scrunched up with concentration as she struggled to find the right words. She could have recited passages from her druidic text from heart, but it would have been completely lost on the warg sitting in front of her. "Blood can carry power, as you know, but also intention. And if you connect it with the correct runes in the correct way, then you can influence that intention to carry information. Does that make sense?"

"Are we talkin' about my blood or your blood? Are you gonna stab me again?" Tannin demanded, leaning backwards and eyeing Ava's bag as if it were likely to bite.

"Both. We need a pair of stones if we are to communicate."

"So that's a yes on the stabbing," Tannin muttered sourly.

"Look on the bright side. This time you get to stab me back," Ava said lifting an ornate dagger from her bag, "Well, carve really."

"*Carve!?*"

Ava shushed her and opened the book. With something as intricate as this, she wanted the instructions right there in front of her. The comforting old-book-smell of parchment, dust and mildew mingled with the night air as she flipped it open.

Swirling patterns were a common decorative motif across all five of the kingdoms, but it wasn't widely known that most of them were of druidic origin. Ava knew very little of the history and the creation of runes and had put feelers out for any books or scrolls that could possibly give her more information, but she'd heard little back.

The rune that was inked across the page she flipped to was swirled. Three swirls interlocking in a triangular form, to be precise.

"Three is always an important number," Ava informed Tannin, as she peeked at the drawing with a frown. "Especially for something involving living things. Mind, body and soul. Earth, air and water. You can't do anything with only one part. It's all connected.

We make the stone like so." Ava trailed a fingertip over the drawing and down to a list of instructions written in elaborate wording. "And then a touch of fresh blood – that's what they mean here by living blood – should complete the link when we want to use them."

As they stared at the instructional diagram, what they were actually about to do started to sink in.

This is too far. This is crossing the line.

"This is gruesome." Tannin raised her eyebrows. "You sure you don't want a pigeon?"

"We don't have to," Ava whispered. "It is a little extreme. I just...I thought...You're going to be so far away, and if something goes wrong, sending a message can take days or you might not be able to send one at all, and I still don't feel quite right about this journey..."

Now, in the light of the moon, Ava hesitated. This ritual would forever bind them together. But she still couldn't identify where the uneasiness was coming from. She'd gone over every inch of their travel plans, going so far as to sneak into Dana's office to triple check. Everything was under control.

But so far out of my control.

She bit her lip. She'd often worried that she was unjustly paranoid but between kidnappers, assassins and the filthy world of royal politics, life had proven that anything could happen.

But also, a part of her wanted to do this just to see if she could. To prove that she could.

Tannin laid her hand over Ava's, silencing her inner turmoil.

"Just tell me what to do."

"You're sure about this?"

"Absolutely not, but let's do it anyway."

"Story of our lives," Ava murmured as she dipped a quill into a pot of ink. "We'll practice the symbol with ink on parchment first, then ink on skin and then..."

Tannin swallowed audibly. "And then with the knife."

She nodded. She paused with the nib hovering over the parchment to trace the symbol with her fingertip and then began to draw.

They both practiced sketching the symbol a few times until it looked like the one in the book and both their fingertips were stained black.

"You've practiced this symbol before, haven't you?" Tannin said looking at Ava's neat diagram.

Ava nodded.

"Remember that book I took from one of the villages? I haven't done the full ritual if that's what you're asking. Or any other blood magic. There's no one else I would do this with."

"I'm touched. Does Dana know about it?"

"No. I give her enough that she finds me useful, but I'd be a fool to readily offer up everything I have."

"Scheming as always."

"Being pragmatic," Ava corrected. "Are you ready to try on skin?"

"Mhm." Tannin took up the quill. "Where should I draw on you to practice?"

Ava chewed her lip for a moment before lifting her skirt to bare her thigh. "Here. It's a big enough area to draw it a few times."

Tannin touched her inky fingers to Ava's skin, quill poised. Her breath caught as her fingertip traced along Ava's thigh. Her dark eyes looked black in the moonlight.

Gods, Tannin. Not the time.

"Will you focus, please," Ava insisted, shattering whatever pleasant thoughts Tannin was having. A drop of ink splattered onto the path. "We don't have time to waste."

Tannin grinned at her sheepishly.

It took surprisingly few tries for her to get the symbol perfect.

Ava only needed one attempt, but even with urgency and dread of what they were about to do, she found herself also being a little distracted. The moonlight. The intimacy. The warmth of Tannin's skin under her fingertips. Not to mention her skirts were bunched up tantalisingly around her hips.

Ava exhaled and sat back on her heels. She was almost feverish with apprehension and excitement of performing this new magic, and her emotions were getting the better of her.

Get a grip.

Tannin poked the black symbol on her leg.

"That's it then. Time for the real thing."

Ava reached for her dagger. She'd sharpened it that afternoon.

"Do you want to go first?"

Tannin shook her head. "You're the expert here. I'll copy what you do. Where does it go?"

"Left arm. The veins there go straight to your heart."

Tannin swallowed hard and held her arm out.

Ava's stomach squirmed and heart thudded.

"It will scar, you know. You'll have this mark forever."

"Good thing it's a pretty symbol then isn't it," Tannin grumbled. "Just do it."

Ava took a deep breath, placed the cup under Tannin's arm to catch the blood, and began to carve.

As Ava set the two cups on the ground next to each other, her hands shook. The blood inside looked black and ominous.

Neither of them had made a sound throughout the process, but the drawn look on Tannin's face spoke volumes. Ava felt the same. If this didn't work, they had just mutilated themselves for nothing. And it had really, *really* hurt.

Ava held out two brooches. They were no more than cheap baubles she had picked up in the city. A matching pair. She'd prised the replica precious stones out of them and left just the metal casing and pins.

"I thought this would be the easiest approach. It won't stand out. No one will know what they really are."

From what she knew, this kind of ritual wasn't common even amongst the druid-bloods of the south. It was still a risk, though.

"Hold these for a moment."

Tannin stared at the tiny, copper measuring spoons Ava had just placed in her hands. "Spoons?"

"It's as near to the correct size as I could get without raising suspicion. Hold them steady."

"Cook is gonna kill you if she finds out about this."

With bated breath, Ava poured a dash of her blood concoction into one, and Tannin's into the other. It hissed as it touched the cold copper.

"And now?"

"And now we wait for it to crystalise."

They sat in silence, the only sound the occasional rustle of dry leaves or the distant wails of the city's nocturnal creatures. Ava shivered and it had nothing to do with the temperature. Her arm throbbed under the bandage tied around it. Although hers must've hurt too, Tannin's face betrayed nothing but expectation as the first signs of crystallisation began to appear.

She trusts me...Gods, I hope this works.

Ava placed the hem of her skirt over the spoon to muffle the sound and struck hard with a mallet she'd pinched from the stables.

When she lifted her skirt again, the copper spoons were bent and misshapen but the freshly made speaking stones came free. Tannin picked hers up between her thumb and forefinger and squinted at it. Ava held hers in the palm of her hand. Perfectly round, curved like the bowl of the tiny spoon and blood red. It could have passed for a polished ruby.

Ava pricked her finger with the dagger and pressed it to the warm, glassy surface of the stone.

"How do we know if it works?" Tannin whispered.

Ava took her hand and jabbed the pad of her thumb. Tannin's cheeks puffed out as she suppressed her yelp and Ava pressed the fresh bead of blood to the corresponding stone.

Owwww, that hurt.

Ava gasped. Tannin's mouth hadn't moved, but her voice reverberated inside Ava's skull so clearly that the stone almost slipped through her fingers.

Ava turned to her, eyes bright with triumph.

It works.

Chapter Forty-Three

Journey South

Tannin

Tannin pressed the needle of the brooch into the pad of her thumb, wincing a little, and squeezed until a drop of fresh blood beaded. She furtively checked she was still alone before smearing it across the face of the brooch and waiting with bated breath. Ava should have been doing the same. They agreed on midnight again – when most of Tannin's group would likely be asleep and she could "speak" without attracting attention.

Hello?

I'm here.

Tannin puffed out a long breath.

It still works.

Of course, it works. How is the journey?

Boring. Long. My feet hurt. You?

Nothing new.

She had already told Ava all about the Kelpie paths they'd found. Exactly like Eoghan and Collum had described, the party had come across clearly man-made canals, bordered with thick roots and branches woven into pathways. They were beautiful and impressive but absolutely dripping with foreboding. As the group took care to avoid them, Tannin swore they were being watched from the undergrowth.

How do those massive horses walk those paths?

Maybe they didn't. Maybe that was just a story. Who knew what was true and what was myth anymore?

Thankfully, once they left the wet, mushy swamps behind them, the walk wasn't so bad, even if it was so cold that frost clung to the grass in the mornings. Their hunts weren't often successful this late on in the season. A few rabbits here and there. A scraggly fox with patchy fur had been trailing them for the past two days, hoping for scraps. It didn't even bother to hide.

They'd brought enough supplies with them to not go hungry themselves, and Catriona sang old Cascairnian folk songs when they sat roasting sausages on the fire in the evenings. It was almost homey.

Days of walking had left Tannin feeling mostly bored, but as the Gormbraen border drew closer, tedium turned into nerves.

As they settled in for the night, Dana plopped herself beside Tannin, holding a hot, skewered sausage. She kept it out of Tannin's reach.

"You have to pass a test first. Tell me about the Falcon, and if I'm satisfied, then you can eat."

Tannin groaned. "Again?"

"Again."

"Okay. Laird Cormack, known as the Falcon, is the laird of Falcon's Rest, which is a fort on the Woodren-Gormbrae border. He has lands stretching from the Woodren border halfway to Ravensmore. He's got one son called Benwald, a sister and a nephew. Suspected but not confirmed druid-blood heritage. He kisses King Modric's arse so thoroughly that he's considered his right-hand man..."

Tannin screwed up her face, trying to remember more details. "He's got a pet falcon because he's dedicated to the theme. What else? Coat of arms is crossed swords and a falcon – again surprise surprise – uhhh...Okay, I'm out. Gimme food."

Dana moved the sausage further away. "How many men has he got?"

"About five thousand?"

Dana waggled her head. "Close enough."

"Yesssss," Tannin groaned as she bit into the meat and then cursed colourfully as she burnt her tongue.

"Maybe try and limit the swearing while we're at the Falcon's Rest?" Dana suggested, giving her a decidedly disapproving look.

"No promises," Tannin replied with her mouth full of smoky, spiced sausage.

"We'll get some good food in Gormbrae at any rate. They're also said to have some of the best wine."

"Mm." Tannin swallowed and then stared into the fire. They would arrive the following day, and she felt overwhelmingly underprepared.

Dana sighed. "Don't be nervous. It's going to be fine. You're going to be fine."

"What if I fuck it up?"

"You won't."

Tannin arched an eyebrow.

"Alright, if it looks like you're going to fuck up, I'll swoop in and save your arse from embarrassment, how about that?" She nudged Tannin with her shoulder, coaxing a smile out of her.

"But, honestly, I don't think you'll need it." She patted Tannin's knee. "I'm proud of you for how far you've come."

Tannin was silent for a moment and then blinked back tears.

When was the last time someone was proud of me?

Dana coughed pointedly to cover the sound of Tannin's sniffing. "I have something for you, actually. There's no need for anyone to know how useless you are when you're not in your warg form."

"Thanks," Tannin said drily.

Tender moment gone then, I guess.

"I'm not insulting you. I'm being practical. Here," Dana said handing her a leather bundle. "I had these made for you. We won't be taking in weapons, of course, so you can't have a shield, but these are fortified with steel inside and they're subtle enough that you can wear them under your clothing. You can defend yourself at least a little bit if it does go wrong. Remember your training, but trust us to handle it if anything happens. I don't want you getting into a fight."

Tannin shook out the bundle to reveal a set of bracers coated with intricately decorated dark brown leather.

"Oooh." Tannin ran a fingertip over the carved patterns. "These are pretty!"

And they must've cost a fortune.

Dana helped her lace them on and sheath her arms from wrist to elbow. She could feel the hard interior, and with the weight of them, she was fairly sure she could deflect blows from a sword or even arrows if she was quick enough. As an added bonus, they also hid the rune Ava had carved into her arm that she'd so far managed to keep secret. The healing had been quick, but Ava was right. It would leave a scar. She flexed experimentally.

"Do not take those off," Dana said sternly. "They might save your life. I mean it. I promised to make sure you stay alive, even if you do make it damn hard sometimes." She reached out and ruffled Tannin's hair and received a swat in return.

"It's not my fault people keep trying to kill me!"

"It is at least partially your fault."

Tannin glowered.

"Get some rest," Dana said, standing and stretching. "We've got a big day tomorrow."

"Like I'm going to be able to sleep," Tannin grumbled to herself as she tucked herself in for the night. Nerves were going to keep her awake even with the delightfully cosy fur lining of her bed roll.

She gave a last look around to check no one was looking and chucked the last of her sausage into the undergrowth. A last donation to their wee fox stalker. She sent a little prayer with it.

"Please, *please*, don't let me fuck this up."

Chapter Forty-Four

The Falcon's Rest

Tannin

Tannin wiped her clammy palms on her skirts. She'd had a special dress made for this meeting – first impressions are worth gold, Dana had said – and Tannin had to admit it was a damn nice dress. Deepest midnight black with swirling patterns on the bodice and hem embroidered in green thread. The sleeves billowed and hid her armoured bracers underneath. Nestled in her hair, she wore a simple, iron circlet. She'd talked Dana out of having her wear a gold one.

No gold. Ever.

She had actually wanted to bring her horrible fang crown, but Dana had persuaded her to leave it behind in favour of a prettier one. A crown made from the remains of people she'd killed wasn't the best introduction to friendship, she'd reasoned. Tannin had protested. Yes, her fang crown was awful, but it was hers. And wargs were awful anyway, so it was hardly the wrong impression. She loved her fang crown. It made her feel fearsome, powerful...taller. The last thing she wanted was for people to look at her and see a child. She wanted them to see the monster she was underneath. To see what she represented. But in the end, practicality won. The fang crown was a little difficult to transport.

They had enough to carry as it was, and since wargs and horses did not mix, they actually did carry it all. The twinge in her back was soon forgotten, though, as they made their way further past the border into Gormbrae.

The landscape was probably lush and green in the springtime, but the path they walked crinkled underfoot. The reds, golds and browns of autumn leaves still hugged the branches of the trees, even if she could taste the impending winter on the wind. It was beautiful, and Tannin lost herself in the colours until Dana nudged her to point out the loch.

"We're almost there," she said. "We should see the fort soon."

The still water of the loch glittered like glass, and they caught their first glimpse of the Falcon's Rest through the trees.

Its spires reached high with web-like walkways spanning between towers. The pristine white walls put the clouds to shame. To call it a fort was an insult, Tannin thought, this was a palace.

There was no other word for it. She was jealous as hell.

"Their fort is better than our keep," she whispered at Dana.

"Because they have money," Dana replied under her breath. "So, play nice."

The only way to enter the imposing structure was via the wide, stone bridge they were approaching. Tannin didn't need to look over the side to know that it fell away to a nauseatingly steep drop. Rather than braving the sight of the ravine, Tannin turned her attention to the landscape that their high position afforded. It was clear why the Gormbraens had built here. Not only was the fort itself impenetrable, but it allowed for an almost completely unobstructed view for miles. On the distant roads, barely visible, she could make out the smudges that were checkpoints and strongholds.

An escort, from one of the checkpoints they'd passed, rode ahead of them with a banner that announced their arrival.

My banner, Tannin thought in a moment of surrealness. *I have a banner.*

It was a huge, billowing thing, midnight black with a white fang stitched into it surrounded by an intricate border. The council had decided on the design together, and for once, they had actually agreed.

"This is so weird," she muttered aloud.

"Just remember what we talked about and don't be intimidated. Yes, we want their support, but we won't die without it so don't promise anything," Dana instructed, slapping Tannin's hand away from her mouth to stop her biting her nails. "Keep calm, stay professional."

"What happens if this is a trap?"

"Then they regret it."

The first shock they had as they crossed the long bridge to the entrance of the Falcon's Rest was that it was not just the Falcon who greeted them in the high-ceilinged entrance hall. That fiery red hair, even though it was streaked with white at the temples, could hardly be mistaken. If that wasn't enough of a giveaway, the bejewelled crown on his head would have been.

That is a king. I was not told about a king. I am not prepared for a king.

"Welcome, Your Majesty!" King Modric's voice was rich and buttery as he spread his arms wide. "Welcome to the Falcon's Rest!"

He beamed as they approached. Tannin shot Dana a panicked look.

"King Modric." Tannin followed Dana's lead in dropping into a curtsey. "We weren't expecting you to be here."

Dana kicked her ankle, the movement hidden from view by her own swishing skirts.

"I mean, we didn't expect to be graced by your presence for this visit," Tannin corrected. Ava had been coaching her on how to sound more refined, and she cursed herself for just blurting the words out. She knew she could do better. She would do better. This was all for Dunoak. For Woodren. For her people.

"Such a rare opportunity requires a personal touch." His lips parted as he smiled, showing chipped and crooked teeth. "Plus, I don't need much of an excuse to visit my old friend."

He clapped the man to his right on the back. Laird Cormack wasn't as tall or broad as the king, but they looked to be of a similar age – the Falcon's hair was almost entirely grey, but he stood proudly as his green eyes scanned the Dunoak party with intense interest. He didn't wear as many jewels or adornments as the king, but rings still shone from his fingers and a thick disc of gold with a falcon emblem hung from his neck.

"Thank you for inviting us to your home," Tannin said just as Ava had coached her. "We are honoured by the invitation."

"The honour is mine." Laird Cormack's voice paled in comparison to the king's boom, but it had a melodic lilt that was pleasant to the ear.

The laird clicked his fingers. A young man appeared by his side with a silver platter on which stood a pristine loaf of bread decorated with leaves and roses carved into the crisp crust.

"I've been informed that you like to honour the old ways," Laird Cormack said with a hint of a smile playing on his lips like he was enjoying a private joke. "May I break this bread with you?"

"Aye." Tannin cleared her throat and awkwardly stepped forward to accept her half of the loaf as he tore it in two. Her worn-in, comfy boots didn't go with her elegant dress, and the neat slippers she wore were pinching her heels.

It was a shame to ruin such a pretty design, she thought as crumbs trickled to the ground. She tore herself a small chunk and passed the rest to Dana to distribute amongst their party. After the king and the laird had eaten their piece, the Dunoak party followed suit.

Could have done with some butter.

"Come!" King Modric rumbled. "Let us dine properly! The staff will see to your belongings."

Tannin shot a questioning glance at Dana, who nodded encouragingly. Tannin shrugged before dropping her heavy pack on the floor and following Laird Cormack into the Falcon's Rest.

Jealousy washed over her again in waves as they followed him through to a lavish feast hall, which could have held half of Dunoak's keep within its walls. The high ceiling was painted with frescos of past battles and royalty. Tannin craned her neck to try and make out some of the gold-edged detailing.

"You all must be hungry and tired from your journey," remarked Laird Cormack. "I've heard you do not ride?"

"No, we walked," Tannin replied still staring up at the ceiling.

The hall could have seated hundreds of guests, but only one long table stood in the centre with places set for each of their party. The king, of course, took the head of the table with Tannin and then Dana on his right side. The Falcon took the left while the rest of the Dunoak visitors sorted their own places down the length of the table.

"I'll save you a long speech." Laird Cormack smiled down the table. "I shall therefore only welcome you again to my halls. Anything you desire, simply speak it and it shall be done. I look forward to discussing our alliance with you all tomorrow, but tonight is for full goblets and fuller bellies!"

He clapped his hands twice, and the two doors at the end of the hall emitted a flood of servants carrying platters, tureens and jugs of wine. Tannin's mouth started watering as they set dish after dish on the table. The laird and the king himself provided a running commentary of each delicacy as it arrived.

"One of the most beloved dishes of Gormbrae, something of a national dish if you will...fresh from our very own loch...If you have a sweet tooth, might I recommend the baked pears?"

Tannin nodded enthusiastically, to which Modric himself poured a lake of heavy cream into a bowl for her alongside the syrupy fruit and then topped up her wine glass. Dana had been right in saying that Gormbraen wine was some of the best. It went down dangerously smoothly, and Tannin was starting to feel giddy.

"And this over here is actually horsemeat. Have you tried horse before?" Cormack indicated to a tureen filled with a rich brown stew.

Tannin swallowed her mouthful with difficulty and wiped pear juice from her lips. "Once. Can't say I'm a fan."

"It can be rather tough, but we have an excellent chef here. I'm sure you'll soon have many new favourites."

She skipped the horse meat – too many bad memories – but it was true the spread was incredible, and she had to stop herself from completely gorging herself. It would be a pretty bad first impression if she made herself sick on the first night. The food was so rich she expected to probably have some stomach issues the next day anyway, but she couldn't bring herself to care too much when it tasted so damn good. The rest of the party seemed to enjoy dinner just as much, and soon, everyone was half slumped in their chairs, groaning with contentment.

"Before you retire for the night..." Laird Cormack clapped his hands once, something that Tannin noticed was his preferred method of communicating with his servants. Surely enough, a uniformed woman appeared at his elbow with a tray laden with glasses and a decanter. He distributed the glasses and lifted his own delicately between two fingers. "...a toast. To our budding friendship."

King Modric lifted his glass high. "To new friends."

Tannin accepted the dram gladly. "To new friends."

The Gormbraen firewater burned deliciously. An excellent end to an excellent meal. This was going well. She was doing well. Tannin caught Dana's eye over the rim of her glass. She raised her glass a fraction higher and Dana mirrored her, shooting her a secretive smile.

To us.

Chapter Forty-Five

A Change of Plans

Tannin

The suite Tannin had been given wasn't quite as opulent as Ava's old rooms in Armodan, but it was still utmost luxury.

A room fit for a queen.

A four-poster bed, hung with heavy, dark red curtains and covered in silken sheets beckoned her from the bedroom. A writing desk stood opposite a set of lush couches, and a large fireplace stood in the sitting room. Soft fur rugs covered the floors, and the windows looked out into an inner courtyard.

Tannin stretched and gave a contented groan as she sank into the mattress. The rain made a soothing patter as it struck the windows. The servants had heated the bed for her with coals in a metal contraption to the point where it was deliciously toasty even on top of all the blankets.

I so want one of those for back home.

Sleep itched behind her eyelids. She'd be very glad to get out of her fancy clothes and have a good wash before bed. She glanced around to check there weren't any servants still lurking around before she stretched again, right to the tips of her fingers and flexed her claws.

Dana had warned her against even the slightest Change that could be construed as a show of aggression, but she was alone and in need of a little reassurance. She found the deadly weapons at her fingertips very reassuring. Besides, flexing her claws was as satisfying as cracking her spine after a long day, and it had been a very long day.

Tannin stopped dead and stared at her hand. It was human. She tried again. Nothing. The thing she called her warg-fire was still crackling in her chest, but when she examined it closely, it didn't feel alive. Not like it usually did. It felt like it was behind glass and she couldn't get to it. Panicked, she tried her other hand, her legs, her fangs, even her goddam tail. Nothing.

She grabbed her brooch with the hidden speaking stone in it and stabbed her thumb a little too aggressively with the pin. Blood ran down her wrist as she pressed the tiny cut against the cold stone.

"Ava, something's wrong," she whispered at the brooch cupped in her hands, but her pleas were met with silence. "Ava! Answer me, dammit!"

Of course, there was no answer. They had agreed to talk in the morning since she would been at the feast all night. It was now well past midnight.

I have to find the others. I have to find then now.

She seized the door handle and wrenched it open, coming face to chest with an armoured guard.

"Can I help you?" he asked, clearly surprised and clearly guarding her door.

"Uh, no. I...uh," Tannin scrabbled for words. "I just need to see Dana about somethin'. Nothing to worry about. Just a wee thing. Won't be long."

"I shall escort you." He bowed.

Fuck.

If there was a guard right outside her door, then that meant something was definitely wrong. It wasn't beyond the realms of possibility that the laird had had the wargs drugged during the feast. The rules of hospitality should have protected them, but some people were willing to risk the omens.

This had the scent of a trap all over it. Tannin stole a glance at the guard walking beside her. He seemed perfectly at ease, but a tendon strained in his neck. As they walked, she caught him looking at her too. Sizing her up. His fingers grazed the hilt of his sword.

He knows I know.

"What's that?" she cried suddenly, pointing over his shoulder.

When he turned to look, she seized a vase from a side table and cracked it over his head. He went down like a stone and lay unmoving on the floor amongst the strewn petals. Tannin sprinted down the corridor, pausing at each corner, back pressed to the wall, listening. Even with adrenaline pumping through her, exhaustion weighed on her like a heavy blanket. She couldn't keep this up. She had to find help right now.

"Fuck," she breathed as she heard voices.

She darted across the corridor and into an alcove, squeezing herself into the small space behind a statue, hidden in the shadows. She was grateful for her slight frame as the guards sauntered past. They would see the other guard if they kept going straight. The one she'd knocked out. Or killed. She really wasn't sure how hard she'd hit him. Maybe they'd take a different route.

"Spread out! Find her!" The shout came sooner than she'd expected it.

Fuck, fuck, fuck.

The guest chambers Dana had been given were just one corridor over from her own. She raced the last stretch, wrenched the door open and threw herself inside. She made to slam the door shut, realising at the last second that it would tell the guards exactly where she was. She thrust her arm back through the gap, and the door smacked against her bracer instead of the doorjamb. It made a clunk, but a soft one, and Tannin breathed a sigh of relief. That would've really hurt if she hadn't had the armour beneath her sleeve.

Thank you, Dana.

She cast around the room, expecting Dana to still be awake, but it was dark and silent. The creeping shivers up her spine told her the room was empty. Still, she tiptoed through to double-check.

Maybe she already knows something is wrong.

The rest of the party had been given barrack-style accommodations with rows of narrow beds in a larger hall on the lower floor. That was Tannin's next stop.

Tannin crept through the corridors. When she got to the barracks, it was dark and silent. Too silent. At least one of their party should have been awake to keep watch like always. Gods knew the rest of them snored loud enough to wake the dead. But she heard nothing. Tannin tiptoed through the room, and sure enough, the beds were empty. All but one.

"Theo!" Tannin hissed, spotting his head poking out from under a fur blanket, "Theo, wake up! Something's not – ugh!"

She'd grabbed hold of the blanket to rip it off him and touched something wet. The coppery tang hit her nostrils a second later.

"Oh no, no, no," Tannin mumbled as she again reached for the blanket and peeled it back. Theo's head rolled to the side as she did, and she had to clap her non-bloodied hand to her mouth to keep from screaming. His throat had been slit so severely that his head was hanging on by mere threads of sinew.

As Tannin backed away, an involuntary squeak made it past the hand she kept over her mouth. Her head was swimming and she blinked hard to fight the wooziness.

Theo was dead. No...Theo had been murdered.

Dana. I have to find Dana. We have to get out of here right now.

She peeked out and waited until a group of guards had thundered past and then backed out of the room and eased the door closed. No one had to know she'd seen the body.

"Hey!"

Tannin's head snapped up, and she locked eyes with the lone guard who had doubled back at the end of the corridor.

"Don't—" he began but she had already started running.

He swore and tore off after her, yelling for the rest of the guard. The clamouring of armour answered his call.

She was light and fast, and as long as she didn't hit a dead end, she was sure she could outrun them even if the rugs slid out from under her at some points. If she fell, they'd catch her. If she stopped for even a second, they'd catch her. Her only hope was to keep moving and try and lose them and then get help.

"Shit, shit, shit!!" Tannin skidded around the corner, barely managing to stay on her feet and barrelled into hall where they had dined earlier that evening.

She'd expected the hall to be empty. It wasn't.

"Dana?" Tannin slid to a halt.

Dana was frozen with her goblet halfway to her lips, across from the king and the laird, who were reclining in their chairs. Cormack jerked bolt upright at the sight of a wild-eyed, out-of-breath Tannin. The rest of the Dunoak party stared back at her sheepishly.

"What the actual fuck—?!"

Tannin didn't get to finish as the squad of guards crashed into the room behind her. She reflexively seized a discarded goblet and threw it as hard as she could into the nearest man's face. It shattered on impact with his head, and he went down hard.

She scrabbled for another weapon, something to throw, anything, anything at all, but they were on her before she could take another step. She fought, screaming and furiously trying to Change, as they wrestled her to the floor and held her there with her face pressed to the stone. Her circlet lost its grip in her hair and rolled under the table.

"Dana!" she screeched but Dana remained motionless at the table. "Dana, fuckin' help me!"

"Tannin, calm down!" Dana insisted as the rest of the guards stowed their weapons and stood at ease. "This is for the best."

The party hadn't even drawn weapons to defend her. An icy claw gripped her heart. They had all known.

"What? Get off me!" She struggled until she could only lie there, panting. The knee pressing into her back made even that difficult. "Dana, what are you doin'? What's goin' on? Why can't I Change? Help me dammit!!"

"Calm down, Tannin. They're not going to hurt you."

"I thought you said she drank it?" Dana muttered to Cormack.

The laird rose and peered down at her.

"She did." His eyebrows pinched together as he frowned. "A warg must need a much higher dose than I expected. Summon the artisan." His last comment was directed at one of the guards.

"What's goin' on!?" Tannin bellowed from the floor.

"We've made a deal." Dana rubbed her eyes, suddenly looking very weary. "This was supposed to be a lot less traumatic. You were supposed to take a sleeping draught."

"You what?!"

"One day, you'll see that I'm doing you a favour," she said. "You're going to be fine, but you're not coming back to Dunoak with us. You're staying here. The council and I will take care of the wargs. It's the best solution."

Tannin gaped at her.

"Fuck your solution! You can't keep me here!" Tannin thrashed and bucked and swore at the guards pinning her. "Get off of me!"

"Calm yourself!"

"Traitor!"

Tannin's tear-filled eyes searched out each of the party for that final sting of betrayal. They knew. They all fucking knew. Except Theo, she realised. He'd only insisted on coming at the last minute...and lost his life for it.

"You're dead! You hear me? Dead!" Tannin spat, struggling like a wild animal. "You murdered Theo!"

"Tannin," Dana said, traces of sadness colouring her tone. "You know you can't compete with me. And certainly not with Sommer. You made a good go of it, and I am proud of you. I really am."

"Proud of me? Go to hell!" Tannin screamed. "How long have you been planning this, you murderer?"

"The details aren't your concern," King Modric said, sweeping through the hall to stand with Dana. He looked down at Tannin with a fond curiosity. "I just hate to see good resources wasted. Who knows? Maybe we'll have a use for a warg berserker in the future."

Dana nodded and gave Tannin a small smile. "I'm sorry. This is for the best."

"Why don't you just kill me yourself, coward?"

"I'm *saving* your life. Sommer has the vials, so she doesn't need you alive anymore. She'd kill you in a heartbeat and we'd lose everything we worked for. I'm doing this to protect you. I have the King Modric *and* Laird Cormack's assurance that you'll be well looked after. You'll have everything you could want."

"And be out of the way so you can steal my crown?" Tannin snarled. "No one is going to accept this. They won't accept you."

Dana smile wistfully. "That is something that I didn't expect. I didn't expect you to win the people quite as spectacularly as you did. But in a way, that's also good. They'll fight even harder for a martyr. Especially one who fell so heroically in battle like you did."

It took Tannin a second to work out what she was saying.

"You're going to fake my death?" Tannin spat in outrage. "How dare you?! ARGH!"

The Falcon must have made some sort of gesture because Tannin was yanked from the floor. She howled in frustration, almost wrenching her shoulders out of their sockets in her attempts to get at Dana. She would kill her with her bare fucking hands if she had to.

She grunted as she was flipped onto the table and made another attempt to slip free, but her limbs were again inescapably pinned down.

"Get it done," the king muttered to someone off to the side.

From the floor, she hadn't seen the artisan come in. He'd clearly been roused from his sleep and squinted in the light of the hall. His tousled hair had the beginnings of grey, and crow's feet crinkled at the corners of his eyes. He unrolled a canvas of tools on the table beside Tannin and glanced down at her with what looked like genuine sympathy and discomfort as she continued to struggle.

"What are you doin'?" she gasped as he selected something from his set of tools.

She saw the flash of a blade and shrieked but instead of piercing her flesh, he slit the fabric of her sleeves and then the leather of her bracers. He peeled it back to reveal the metal underneath. The metal that was scrawled with runes.

Binding runes.

Binding runes that she'd willingly put on.

"I did tell you those were for your protection," Dana said softly. "This is all to keep you safe. Keep you alive."

"You're fuckin' sick." Tannin stared at the symbols.

The artisan leant over her again and uncorked a glass flask filled with a blueish-black liquid. It could have been ink but the feeling of foreboding, sending ice deep into her bones, told her it wasn't.

"Touch me and I'll kill you!" Tannin hissed at him and he recoiled.

He faltered slightly, but under the stern observation of both his king and his laird, the artisan took a breath and continued.

"I am sorry," he murmured. "This will only hurt a moment."

"We agreed she wouldn't be harmed," Dana rebuked, catching the guilt in his voice.

"The pain will be temporary, and unless you have a better idea to keep a warg contained, then we will proceed with the plan that you set in motion," Modric said with a sneer. "The bracers need to be properly sealed."

Sealed? They were going to seal away her warg side completely. Leave her little fire stuck behind that pane of glass where she could see it but not use it.

Tannin's resolve broke.

"Dana!" Tannin panted in despair. "Dana, please! I'm begging you! Don't do this! Please!"

"That is your problem, Tannin. And it's exactly why you couldn't be allowed to rule." Dana leaned over her and tilted her head to the side with a sigh. "Wargs don't beg."

She nodded to the artisan. "Proceed."

As the artisan tipped the inky potion onto the etched symbols, he chanted low under his breath. At first, nothing happened as the liquid filled each of the grooves, but when the binding ruins became whole in blue-black, it felt as though they sank through the metal, scalding her. The seams melted together. Tannin screamed as the burning hot metal fused with her skin. Pressure like the metal bands around an overfull barrel compressed her chest as her little warg-fire was crushed into the recesses of her ribcage, dampened and weak.

A bitter scent filled the room as it swam before her eyes, redness blurring the edges of her vision.

"Is it done?" someone asked in an echoey, distorted voice.

She mumbled as the guards released her. She tried to rise but slumped. "I'll kill you all...Kill you. I swear."

Cormack brought his hand to his mouth in response like he was blowing her a kiss. A white powder rained down on her.

She couldn't avoid the tingling specks that landed on her face, and she was breathing too heavily to try and avoid breathing it in.

The tingling spread from her lips and tongue and down her hoarse throat. They zapped through her limbs, making them warm and sluggish, the tension leaking out of her muscles.

Her tongue felt heavy and thick and didn't respond the way she wanted it to. She squinted, and Dana's face came into focus. Tannin's lip curled back in a snarl.

"I...am going...to kill you," Tannin promised in a halting whisper, "and then...I am going to piss on your grave."

Chapter Forty-Six

Missed Messages

Ava

The speaking stone brooch she held in her hands was crusted with blood. Ava swore and tried again, stabbing into a fresh fingertip and smearing the stone with red.

It wasn't working.

She took a breath. Just because she couldn't contact her right now didn't mean Tannin was in any trouble. She could be busy. Maybe someone was there with her and she didn't want to use the stone. It was unlikely that she was still asleep – Tannin didn't sleep in. It was more likely that the fool had lost her brooch. Or broken it. Ava exhaled. She would try again at midnight and again tomorrow morning. Then she would worry.

Worry isn't useful right now.

Ava forced herself to go to breakfast. The hall seemed so much emptier even though it was only a few people missing. Adair sat in Dana's usual seat. He had taken over laird duties since both Tannin and Dana had gone to the Falcon's Rest, but Ava thought it was a strange choice. Adair spent most of his time out of the city with his rangers, watching the roads and picking up information. He was barely ever in Dunoak. Lachlan would have made more sense as a temporary replacement. Even as he sat with Adair, he looked a little put out. His golden-brown eyes focused on his spoon as he stirred his porridge. Ava's own bowl had long gone cold.

"Aw, you miss her already. Don't you?" teased Flint as he joined her, awkwardly folding his long legs onto the bench.

Should I tell him? No. Too soon.

"Well, I've got something to take your mind off it." He stuffed half an oatcake into his mouth and continued, "I'm taking you out tonight. You can't stay in your wee basement forever, and since Tannin isn't here to bully you, I'm taking up the mantle."

"I actually have to—"

"Ah, ah!" Flint reprimanded her in a spray of crumbs. "No arguments. You're coming out to have a little fun with us for once."

"But—"

Ava was cut off as Flint reached out and flicked her ear. She stared at him in shock. Just a few months ago, no-one would have dared do that to her.

Then again, a few months ago, I was still a princess.

"Did you just *flick* me?" she asked, playing up her outrage at his audacity.

"You were gonna say something stupid." Flint shrugged. "I'll come pick you up after dinner."

As usual, Flint's idea of fun included a substantial amount of drinking. Eoghan and Collum met them at a tavern she had never been to, but since the barmaids gave them a cheerful wave, she gathered that the boys were frequent patrons. Ava wondered just how often the three of them went out. And where Flint got the coin from. His job at the stables paid coppers.

The tavern reminded her more of a pigsty, with its straw-covered floors and...interesting scent, than a drinking establishment. It was one of the cheapest, but it still cost money. She glanced at him out of the corner of her eye. She'd spent so much effort spying on the wargs. Maybe it would have been useful to keep an eye on him too.

Ava tried to just sip at her glass. For one, the ale was bitter on her tongue, but also she wanted to keep a clear head for the morning and also trying again to speak with Tannin that night. The rousing fiddle music from the tiny stage in the back, however, was not conducive to a quiet time, and soon she had been roped into a series of drinking games. Ava wasn't sure how one was supposed to win these "games" because after the second or third, it certainly felt like they were all losing. The brothers, dressed in dull greys and browns instead of their colourful performer garb, avoided the stage that night and dedicated their full energy to telling stories that got progressively wilder after each drink.

"What about you, Ava?" Collum slapped her back and she ended up coughing out her mouthful of ale.

"What about me?" she spluttered.

"You must have some stories!"

Ava glanced around and gave Collum a warning look. Although her secret was out, she didn't want to remind anyone about it. That would just bring trouble.

"How's about how you and Tannin met?" Eoghan's green eyes sparkled with mischief. No doubt Flint had been gossiping and had told them exactly how friendly the two of them were. She shot him a glare.

"Oh, I know this story!" Flint ignored her glare and slapped his hands on the table. "Ava was being baaaaad!"

"So was Tannin!" Ava blurted and then at the brothers' snickering added, "Not like that!"

"They were breaking and entering!" Flint said in an exaggerated whisper to a chorus of ooohing.

"No! It was...I was...oh, alright, yes. I didn't break in, though!" The alcohol was going to her head. She grinned. "I snuck in."

"Tell the story properly!"

"Alright! We both wanted this...valuable item," Ava said carefully. She didn't want to give away too much. "I got it first and then Tannin fought me for it when I was making my getaway. She's vicious. I had back-up though and stole it back."

"You gave her a black eye!"

"That wasn't me! That was someone I hired. She was soooo angry." Ava shook her head at the memory. It had all gone so wrong, and even though she'd ended the night with the sightlens in her hands, it was shattered and unusable. She had, however, found something just as valuable that night. "She's adorable when she's angry."

"Awwww," Flint cooed, throwing his arm around her shoulder. "Who knew crime was so damn romantic?"

"Why were you breaking in places?" Collum wasn't distracted. "I thought you were—"

He broke off in a hiss of pain as his brother's boot met his shin. Eoghan gave Ava a wink.

"I had hobbies." She grinned. "I'm not as boring as people think."

"We don't think you're boring, do we?" Flint slammed his hands on the table again. It wobbled on its uneven legs, threatening to send their tankards flying. "In fact..." he gave her a crooked grin. "...weeeee like to drink with Ava!"

The brothers' joined in the song and Ava groaned.

"'Cause Ava is our mate! We like to drink with Ava, she can down her drink in eight!"

"Seven!"

"You're going to be the death of me," Ava hissed at Flint, even as she lifted her glass to her lips.

"Six!"

"Oh, but you'll die happy." He grinned back.

"Five!" Onlookers joined in the chant.

Ale dripped down the front of her dress as she glugged. She didn't want to find out what the forfeit for failure was.

"Four!"

"Three!"

"Two!"

Cheers erupted as she triumphantly held up her empty glass.

"Ugh." She swayed on her feet. "I'm going to regret that."

It was past midnight when they stumbled back to the keep. Flint had sung filthy tavern songs, completely out of tune, all the way home. If she'd known the words, Ava might have joined in. She was more relaxed than she had been in a while. Flint had been right. This had been what she needed.

It was past midnight when she shoved him, fully clothed, onto his bed and blew him a kiss as she left.

It was past midnight when she collapsed onto her own blankets. The ceiling spun and she squeezed her eyes closed.

It was past midnight.

Ava's eyes flew open. Midnight. She rolled out of bed, skinning her knee on the floorboards in her haste. She rushed to free the speaking stone brooch from the loose skirting board in her room. She had toyed with the idea of leaving it in plain sight, but a gem that size would have made a tempting prize even without the precious magic it carried.

"I didn't forget," she mumbled under her breath. "I'm here. I didn't forget."

With bated breath, she pricked her finger. She was only a few minutes late. The room was still spinning around her as knelt there, waiting.

The minutes ticked by.

"I'm here," she whispered again. "Where are you?"

But, for the second time, no matter how much blood she pressed to the cold, unyielding surface of the stone, she was met with only silence.

Chapter Forty-Seven

Wake Up

Tannin

Wake up.

The thought pierced the fog in her head like a shard of light. A commanding voice in her head that jostled and prodded at her consciousness.

"Ava?" Tannin licked her dry lips and blinked. There was no one there.

Above her was a fabric canopy – a tent? No. She glanced to the side and saw carved bedposts rising to meet the velvety fabric. She was in a luxurious, four-poster bed. A bed that wasn't hers.

Her muscles were achy and cramped. She pushed herself up a little and was immediately swallowed by the unmistakable feeling that something was wrong. She stared at her hands and then her arms. Her upper arms were mottled with purple bruises. And her forearms... Stinging bile rose in her throat at the sight of the smooth metal encasing them. There was no seam. A tiny cry escaped from her lips as she tried to pry at the edges, but it was flush against her skin and she couldn't even get a fingernail under the metal. Her fingernails. She frowned at them in the dim light.

Wrong.

The dirt that encrusted them from days of travel was gone. They were evenly filed and buffed to a shine. Her hands were soft, and a sweet flowery scent reached her nose as she inspected them closer. She didn't remember bathing. Someone else had bathed her. Decidedly unnerved, Tannin peeked under the layers of blankets and furs. Her eyes widened.

Oh gods. Very wrong.

The nightgown was of the finest ivory silk, adorned with delicate lace and covered her about as much as a decent sized handkerchief would have. She yanked her blanket back up to her chin. Her heart hammered in her chest.

“No, no, nononono.”

This is not happening.

Tannin closed her eyes for a moment and took a deep breath.

The betrayal came rushing back in a crushing wave. Tannin growled low in her throat, dragging her eyes open and attempting to leap out of bed. Her heavy limbs didn’t work properly and only succeeded in tangling her in the bedsheets.

She flinched as the door swung open, but it wasn’t a guard. It was a girl. A servant by the look of her crisp uniform and the stack of linen she carried. She strolled in, and upon meeting Tannin’s shocked expression, froze. The servant obviously hadn’t expected her to be conscious. She looked utterly petrified as the door snapped shut behind her. Tannin had so many questions. She wanted to scream and rage and demand answers, but all that spilled from her mouth was a tiny voice.

“Where are my clothes?”

The girl’s mouth opened and closed a few times, never quite managing to produce a sound, before she turned on her heel and fled.

Tannin swore as she resumed trying to extricate herself from her sheets and tumbled out of the bed to hit the rug covered floor with a thud. Searing pain lanced up through her forearms as she tried to push herself up. Her shoulder ached so badly she thought she might be sick.

Don’t panic.

Her body protested as she pulled herself up and staggered on wooden legs through her room. She’d been half expecting a dungeon cell, but they’d placed her back in the luxurious suite. She stumbled out of the bedchamber and into the sitting area.

It was just as elegant and pristine as before, but this time, she saw it for what it was. A very pretty prison. She staggered against the door to the corridor and scrabbled at the handle. It wouldn’t budge. She was locked in.

She hammered at it with her fists, kicked it, slammed her stupid bracers against it, trying to break them off and rammed it with her good shoulder until she was newly aching all over. She yelled until her throat hurt and then she stifled a sob.

Don’t cry. Don’t let them see weakness.

She sniffed and took a fortifying deep breath. There must be another way out.

The window.

She tripped over a rug in her haste to try get to the window and fell. All the noise she was making appeared to have alerted someone. The scrape of the lock from behind her had her scrambling backwards.

She stopped when she saw the figure that entered the room. It was the same girl as before. She was roughly the same age as Tannin, with wavy brown hair escaping from her neat, little bonnet. Tannin snarled, pushed past the girl and seized the door handle again, but it had been swiftly re-locked.

Goddammit

"Let me out!" she yelled, pounding her fist on the door.

"His lairdship has tasked me with your needs," the girl squeaked. "He wishes you to remain in your chambers until he sends summons. Is there anything you require?"

It sounded like she had been rehearsing her little speech all day.

Tannin looked at her incredulously. "How 'bout the damn door key?"

"My apologies." She bobbed in a little curtsey. "That is outwith my duties."

"What day is it? How long was I asleep?" Tannin demanded. "Where is Dana? Are the wargs still here? Let me talk to them!"

The poor girl was shaking and looked like she might faint. Tannin took a deep breath and pressed her hands together to try and calm down.

"Are the wargs still here?" she asked slowly.

"My apologies, Miss," the maid squeaked. "I cannot say."

"Cannot or will not?" Tannin growled, stalking towards her.

"I do not know anything. And…and you should know, the guards will not open the door…whatever they hear."

Tannin halted.

Whatever they hear…

That's why she's so scared. She's expendable.

And utterly useless as a hostage, Tannin realised.

Tannin narrowed her eyes, to which the girl flinched.

"What's your name?"

"Orlaith, Miss." She curtsied yet again. "His lairdship has tasked me with your needs."

"You said," Tannin said drily.

"Is there anything you require?" she asked, her voice trembling almost as much as her hands, which she tried to hide behind her back. "I can have refreshments brought?"

She'd be damned if she was going to accept this confinement without more of a fight, but Tannin's stomach growled loudly enough for them both to hear.

"Fine," she said with a sigh, rubbing her eyes hard. "Do that then. And give me my damn clothes back!"

If anything, she just wanted the girl occupied so she could go back to trying to escape out of the window. To her dismay, she found that not only were the tiny panes reinforced with steel borders, but the damn things were locked so tight they didn't even open a crack to let in fresh air. As soon as she realised it, the air in the room felt stagnant and cloying in her throat.

There was the balcony. Tannin rattled the doors unenthusiastically.

"I don't suppose you have the keys for these either?"

The girl shook her head and mumbled an apology.

"You may choose whatever you like from the wardrobe. Everything has been made to your measurements."

"That is so creepy. Where are my own things?"

Burnt probably, Tannin lamented when girl didn't give her an answer.

"I will assist you to dress if you wish."

"No," Tannin stammered. "No, I don't need that."

She strode to the wardrobe and yanked it open to find a selection of beautiful gowns. Every colour and fabric she could think of hung before her, stitched to perfection.

She groaned but reached for one of the less complicated ones anyway. The girl, Orlaith her name was, had been right. The blue and white dress was made exactly to Tannin's size. She fought the urge to cringe as she wormed her way into it, but it made her skin crawl. She ignored the elaborate shoes and instead chose to investigate the rest of her prison barefoot. If she found a weakness, she wanted to be able to run, and she sure as hell wouldn't be able to in heels.

And if she couldn't run, she'd fight.

She instinctively cast around for a weapon, but Laird Cormack had clearly prepared this room with her in mind. The furniture was firmly fastened to the floor. Even the damn candlesticks were bolted down.

How did I not see this before?

The worst she could do was throw the decorative pillows from the couches across the room, which she did with relish just to ease some of her frustration.

She'd been hoping to get another chance at the bedroom door when the refreshments Orlaith had ordered arrived, but to her disappointment, the food arrived via a lift and pulley system in an inconspicuous-looking cupboard by the door. Tannin mouthed a stream of curses. No way out there.

The platter was laden with cheese, cold meats and fruit but had come without cutlery. Nothing she could use as a weapon. She supposed she could empty the food onto the floor and then smack someone with the plate. If only that would help her get out of this room.

She didn't touch any of the food that the servant girl laid out on the table, but her thirst was too strong to refuse the jug of water. She sipped at it suspiciously. Nothing tasted off, and when she didn't keel over after a few minutes, she drained the whole jug and then paced the length of her room. A savage little part of her wanted to shout that she wasn't going to play his stupid games and to just throw her in the dungeon and be done with it, but she drowned it out. She hadn't worked out the Gormbraens' game yet, but there certainly was one and she had a better chance of escape if she wasn't in a cell.

She strained her mind for the catch as she paced, biting her nails. Why keep her alive? And if so, why treat her like an honoured guest? What was the catch? What was the game?

Why did Dana do this to me?

She dug her nails into the soft fabric of her couch. Then she got up and paced. She drank some water from the refilled jug. It gurgled loudly in her churning stomach. Eventually, she slumped exhausted onto one of her beautifully embroidered couches and screamed herself hoarse into a pillow. She was so tired but refused to get back into the bed. That felt like giving in. Felt like defeat. She wasn't going to sleep in the fancy bed or eat the fancy food. She was going to get out of here.

Tannin rubbed at the cold metal encasing her forearms from wrist to elbow. One day. She promised herself. One day, she'd repay Dana for this sick little trick of hers.

Chapter Forty-Eight

Guided Tour

Tannin

"I know you're awake."

Tannin opened her eyes to glare at the Falcon, who was lounging in an armchair opposite her. She'd woken up to the sound of him entering but had refused to acknowledge his presence. His green eyes watched her intently over his steepled fingers as she awkwardly manoeuvred herself so that she was sitting upright. She was still stiff, doubly so for sleeping on the couch rather than in the bed.

Not that she'd done much actual sleeping over the past two days. It was more that she occasionally slipped into unconsciousness between bouts of trying to hammer the door down.

Her eyes flicked to a pair of guards hovering by the door. Armed and armoured. Glinting helmets hid their faces. She wondered if that was due to the vase-to-the-head incident.

"What—" The words caught in her dry throat and she coughed. Her head swam. She probably should have eaten more.

"You're going to have many, many questions, I know." Laird Cormack raised a hand. "I will explain how this is going to go."

He poured a glass of water from a crystal decanter and slid it across the low table towards her. He then held up one finger.

"First off, know that you will not be harmed here."

A second finger.

"Second, you are not permitted to leave, and any attempt to do so will result in my displeasure."

A third finger.

"Violence on your part towards any of my staff or guards will not be tolerated."

A fourth finger.

"And lastly, I wish that you become a member of my court here. I believe we can mutually benefit from this arrangement."

Tannin blinked at him.

"What the fuck are you on about?" she rasped.

A small smile quirked the edges of his mouth. "Dana did warn me that you had a foul tongue."

"What—"

He spoke again before she could repeat her question.

"I will explain everything." He cocked his head. "If you are feeling civil, I can even explain during a tour of the fort."

Of all the things she was expecting, a guided tour was not one of them. Tannin considered it for a moment and then nodded. A tour of the fort would be useful. Very useful.

"Very well, then." He slapped his palms on his thighs and stood.

Tannin followed him to the door.

She had been eyeing the guards malevolently when Laird Cormack turned to her again. His smile didn't match the steely look in his eyes. "Oh, and please do not do anything tedious. I am being more than generous, but my patience is not infinite."

Guards surrounded them at all times, the two from her room plus two more. If she even looked like she was going to make a run for it, she wouldn't get far. She supposed she could attack the laird. She cast a sly look at him out of the corner of her eye. The sword that hung on his hip looked mostly decorative, and he didn't look like he was wearing any kind of armoured protection. Druid-bloods weren't known for their durability either, but she had no weapons.

Like I could even do much damage in this stupid body.

She would wait and bide her time. Let them think she was a meek, little girl and that the rumours about her vicious warg side were much exaggerated. Gain his trust.

"Your shoulder is troubling you?" he asked. An expression of mild concern crossed his face as he indicated to how she held her arm tucked tight to her chest.

Dana must have told him about her weaknesses. The sting of betrayal never ceased.

"Your guards weren't exactly gentle with me the other day," Tannin shot back.

"My apologies." He dipped his head. "As you know, that was never the intention. I will send someone to your chambers to see to your injury later."

Tannin was tempted to tell him not to bother, but honestly, she could really do with a salve or something. Plus, if she was going to escape, two working arms would probably be useful.

Cormack set a relaxed pace as they walked down the same corridors she'd raced through on the night of her capture. Passing by in silence, she could actually take a moment to notice the suits of armour filling each alcove. It felt like they were watching her.

She fought a satisfied grin when she saw that the vase she'd cracked over the guard's head hadn't been replaced. She wouldn't be able to use that trick again with these new armoured guards, though. She'd have to find a much better weapon.

"The king isn't joining us for this tour?"

"His Majesty has returned to Ravensmore for the winter. He will rejoin us in the spring." Cormack smiled down at her. "He was here only to begin our arrangement officially. You should be honoured that he graced us with his presence."

"So very honoured," Tannin replied through gritted teeth. So far, she had not detected any viable means of escape. The Falcon's Rest was a formidable fortress, both inside and out, and her hopes were dwindling.

"I have agreed to take you on here as a ward. Do you know what that means?"

Tannin shook her head.

"It means you are under my care and my responsibility."

"But I can't leave."

"You are to stay within the walls of this fort."

"Against my will," she said sourly.

He sighed at her petulance. "I would like to make the most of this arrangement. In time, we could become friends."

Tannin snorted.

"You'll be given the title of Lady, and I will have no mention of your previous activities or identity. You are my ward here and nothing more. Understood? You are not the first young ward who has come to me for education and to find a suitable match."

Tannin looked at him in utter horror.

"Don't worry, my dear, I have no intention of that just yet. You will find the Rest a little empty in these first few months, but when spring arrives, it will bring a host of tutors and other young folk like yourself. I hope by that time you will have settled and can integrate into my court, within reason of course, and come to enjoy your time here."

Tannin had felt the blood drain from her cheeks when he said "first few months". She had absolutely no intention of staying that long, but she didn't tell him that. Instead, she opted for nonchalance.

"What a neat little plan you've all thought up. What's your stake in it?"

"Wargs are not an adversary to be taken lightly, and since your cousin has made her intentions to ally with the Brochlands clear, I would be remiss not to have my own warg advantage. Plus, having you here does not only benefit Dana. I believe you yourself could be a great ally if we were to become friends. In the future, I may be in a position to grant you your freedom."

Tannin clenched her jaw and glowered at the black and white marble of the floor. She might have been fooled by Dana, but she wasn't that gullible.

You are so full of shite.

"Who knows what the future holds?" Cormack continued. "I like to keep my options open. You can live a life of luxury here. I intend to provide you with any and all comforts you desire. I can even arrange for a proper education if you like."

He led her out onto one of the high walkways that spanned between the towers. Tannin closed her eyes to feel the wind on her face and took a deep breath. The ball of tension in her chest loosened slightly.

Fresh air.

The rain of the previous days had left the sky cloudless and clear, and from the walkway, she could see for miles. Tannin paused to rest her elbows on the ledge and look out over the water of the loch. She poked her head over the side. It was a long way down.

"If you're thinking of jumping, I'd think again. The water is too shallow to survive the fall, even for a warg," Cormack said with an amused chuckle.

"I can't swim anyway," Tannin muttered and then cursed herself. She shouldn't be giving away weaknesses no matter how small.

The laird gave her a subtle smile.

"You know, a few days ago, I stood right here." He draped an arm around her shoulders, ignoring her cringe, and pointed down and to the right. "And watched your party arrive."

He turned her so that she could see the winding road that headed northwards into the lush countryside. Against the clear blue skies, black banners flapped in the breeze.

My banners.

The traitorous warg party was heading back to Dunoak. Tannin's heart sank further. They had never planned to stay. The alliance was already set up. They were just delivering her.

She growled, shoving the laird's arm off her. "Did you bring me up here to torment me, you fuckin' arsehole?"

She heard the guards nearest to her move but kept her furious gaze on Laird Cormack. He held up a hand to halt them.

"I will allow some anger on your part, but I will not be disrespected in my own home. I brought you up here to say your goodbyes," he told her sternly. "And since you are now in my care, it is in your best interests to refrain from insulting me."

The way he said it made the glib comment she was going to make stick in her throat.

She looked back at the banners disappearing from view. They had actually left her. She was alone. Completely alone.

Laird Cormack turned to continue walking, tucking his hands behind his back. Her heart was heavy, but the armoured presence looming over her told her she wasn't being allowed to wallow. She was expected to follow.

"That brings us to the next stop on the tour. The terms of my agreement with Dana are to keep you contained, safe and cared for. Other than that, the rest is flexible and open to...interpretation. The offer of a title and place in my court that I've presented to you is my own, not Dana's. There are alternatives routes I could take. I want you to understand the extent of my generosity."

He let Tannin ruminate on that as they took the stairs back down from the walkway. When they reached the bottom, a guard heaved open a heavy, metal-bound door without prompting. It screeched open to reveal a dark, stone staircase leading further down. They were already on the ground floor. Tannin could very much guess what was further down.

Her throat clamped shut and her legs refused to move. She was not going down there. Not down into a dungeon. Not ever again.

A torch taken from a nearby bracket was lit and illuminated the top of the stairs. Tannin still didn't move.

"Come."

She didn't move until a hand on her back literally steered her towards the door, and her stumbling feet followed before she could decide to make a fuss.

A pathetic whimper crawled its way out of her throat as the heavy door swung shut. The hand on her back kept her moving, and all of her focus was concentrated on breathing as she took one leaden step at a time. Guards' broad bodies blocked the way behind her.

Cormack was clearly trying to scare her.

She hated that he was succeeding.

They passed several more guards, who bowed their heads as they passed, and arrived in a room with a platform and two posts. The air was suffocatingly stagnant. Their footsteps echoed long after they had come to a stop.

"What are you doin'?" Tannin asked, her voice sounding impossibly small in the cavernous room. Although she had never been to any of the public punishments in Armodan, she knew damn well what whipping posts were. They had stood right next to the gallows.

Cormack gave her an icy smile and then clapped his hands together twice. The sharp sound made Tannin flinch. The guard who still had his hand on her back chuckled.

Motion at the far side of the hall was heralded by the clanking of chains. A set of guards entered from another corridor, towing a hapless prisoner between them. He couldn't have been more than twenty. His swollen face was ashen in fear behind the purple bruising. Heavy chains shackled his wrists and ankles. He stumbled as he was dragged up onto the platform between the two posts.

Tannin was momentarily overwhelmed with relief that she wasn't going to be the one receiving the beating, but then it dawned on her that she was going to watch.

"Wait," Tannin pleaded. "You don't have to do this! I get it. I understand!"

"My dear, this little whelp has earned his punishment all by himself," Laird Cormack said and then tilted his head to the side. "But I'd like you to pay attention all the same. I did promise you an education."

The Falcon tucked his hands behind his back once more and paced the length of the platform. His elegantly tailored, grey robe was long enough to stir the dust on the floor into flurries.

"This boy was once the son of Sir Richmund. A member of one of the most influential families in the north of Gormbrae. If it were not for his father's wealth and standing, he would have been executed like the rest of his little friends in their so-called rebellion."

A cry and then a thud came from the platform at the laird's words. The young rebel hadn't known his friends were dead.

"Not that they would have ever been successful, of course, but it was an insult. But don't worry, at least one of their bodies was put to good use." He gave Tannin a horribly cheerful smile. "I was going to settle for thirty lashes today, but for your own education, Lady Tannin, we'll make it a round fifty."

"You can't—!"

The guard with his hand on her back switched and gripped the back of her neck instead. He gave a firm squeeze. She grunted in discomfort.

The Falcon placed a finger to his lips in a shushing motion. "Careful. That sounded like it was almost going to be disrespectful. If there's one thing I cannot abide in my house, it is disrespect. Begin."

"Enough," Cormack said, finally stopping the blows.

The guard's grip on the back of Tannin's neck had meant she hadn't been able to turn away. She flinched at every crack of the whip, and when the prisoner cried out after the fourth or fifth strike, she had almost cried out with him. Now that the screams had stopped, she could hear the drip of blood even over his ragged breathing. It was a wonder he was even still conscious.

"I assured his father he would go free." He summoned a guard with a gesture. "Cut him down and leave him at the edge of the village. If the wolves haven't an appetite, then he's a free man...Shall we then?"

He swept out of the chamber and back up the stairs. Tannin was steered after him. She was vaguely aware that her face was wet, but as they arrived back in the warmly lit hall above, her tears felt jarringly out of place.

"Well, I think that concludes our evening," the Falcon said with a charming smile as if they had just seen a rather rousing play. He addressed the guards, "Soon, Lady Tannin may explore within the walls of the Rest as she wishes, accompanied of course. Malcolm, she is your responsibility."

One of the faceless guards blanched. "Sir?"

"Something a little more your speed, I think," Cormack replied, a dangerous glint in his eye. "After all, it took you months to track down that little rebel. You will remain here and make sure the lady has everything she needs, though I doubt she'll give you much trouble."

His smile turned to something much more akin to a leer as he regarded Tannin again. His eyes lingered on the bracers encasing her arms before he reached out to brush a fresh tear from her cheek.

"A little bird doesn't need a cage when her wings have already been clipped, now does she?"

Chapter Forty-Nine

Return of the Queen

Ava

The sight of Tannin's banners should have filled Ava with joy, but all she felt was sick. The speaking stone had been deathly silent since the party had arrived at the Falcon's Rest, and they were now returning far earlier than expected. The banners wound their way silently through the streets towards the keep. Tannin had promised to roar at the gates so that Ava would know the second she was home.

She descended the stairs in a trance-like state as the keep stirred itself into a frenzy at the unexpected arrival.

"They're back early!" Flint took the stairs two at a time to reach her. "Do you think that's good news or..." He trailed off at the look on her face. "Something wrong?"

The bodies were brought in, wrapped in bloodstained, white sheets. No one needed to ask who the smaller one was. Only one person on that trip was that small. Flint sank to his knees at the sight of the carefully wrapped body, cradled in Dana's arms. The wail that came next was like nothing Ava had ever heard. The sound ripped itself from his body so viciously it didn't sound human.

Time had passed strangely then. Ava stayed standing at the bottom of the stairs, one hand gripping the banister, as the rest of the party solemnly followed Dana. Catriona was last, broken arm held in a makeshift sling, face drawn and grey.

That won't take long to heal. A week at most. I could make a proper sling. Herbs for pain. Which ones? I don't...I can't remember...

Ava didn't know how long she stood there, but it seemed like only seconds later that the warg, dressed in fresh clothing, was touching her shoulder and murmuring, "You can see her if you want to."

She meant the body. Tannin's body.

Flint was already there when she went into the council chamber. The table had been draped in white cloth. His eyes were red. His shoulders shook. He seemed to fold in on himself as he took in the body that lay on the slab. Ava tried and failed to utter any words of comfort. She felt like she might never speak again. Flint's hand slid into Ava's and squeezed tight as another sob wracked through him.

If not for the blue tinge to her lips and the stark white of her bloodless skin, Tannin might have been sleeping. Except, Tannin always curled into a ball when she slept. Not like this. Flat on her back, arms at her sides. She wouldn't be comfortable like this. And she was so still. Even in her sleep, Tannin mumbled and fidgeted.

Beside her, Flint's sobs were getting more violent.

"Come on. You need a stiff drink." Catriona disentangled their hands and let him sag against her. She touched her fingers to Ava's shoulder. "I'll let you have some time alone."

The silence of the chamber after they left was deafening. When she reached out to touch Tannin's pale cheek, it was ice cold. Her fingertips stroked along her skin, from freckle to freckle. Ava squinted. She had traced those constellations a hundred times before, but the distance between them was off. A cluster that should have lain just below the hollow of her throat was too high up.

With a hasty glance over her shoulder, Ava nudged the white fabric of Tannin's funeral gown aside. The scar on her shoulder was there, but when she ran her fingers over it, the texture wasn't right. It was too neat for having been ripped open like it had been. This was a careful slice.

Suspicion rippled in her mind like a disturbed pond. Something was amiss. Ava hastily dried her tears. There was one mark on Tannin's body that no one else knew about. Ava eased up the lace-trimmed sleeve of the body's left arm.

Her breath caught in her throat. The chilled skin was as smooth and unmarred as the day Ava had marked it. The realization was like someone struck a bell within her skull. The reverberating din was loud enough to pierce the veil of grief and finally let her feel what her Senses had been screaming at her since she first saw the body.

It's not her.

Ava's mind and Senses were on fire.

It's not her. It's not her. IT'S NOT HER.

But there was no way to prove it. Anyone who saw the body, who wasn't intimately familiar with it, would swear it was the fallen queen. They would say she was in denial. Driven mad by her grief.

This is a coverup. A betrayal. There's no way Dana doesn't know this isn't her.

Ava's breath caught in her throat. She couldn't let Dana know that she knew. That would be as good as signing her own death warrant. Bitter rage mixed with relief swirled in her gut. Tannin wasn't dead. Dana was a traitor. They were all traitors. And they would kill her in a heartbeat if they thought she knew about it.

Ava didn't know if the second body was truly Tannin's teacher, Theo, or not. She hadn't ever spoken to him. The killing blow that had felled "Tannin" had been cleverly hidden with bandages under her white gown –Dana sorrowfully told her that a war hammer had caved in her chest– but nothing could hide the fact that Theo's head was not fully attached to his body. The same would happen to her if she revealed what she knew.

Ava was familiar with grief. It had plagued her family for years. It was a part she could play. She would play the part of her mother. She would disappear into herself. Become a shell. No one would look her way while she schemed. And scheme, she would. Dana would not get away with this.

When Ava finally left "Tannin's" side, after what she guessed would be an appropriate length of time to process her heartache and loss, she sought out Flint. She couldn't keep this from him.

He was slumped in an armchair by the fire. A forgotten glass sat on the table beside him as he swigged straight from the bottle. He looked at her with bleary, bloodshot eyes and shakily held out the bottle.

Ava sighed and accepted the offering.

I'll tell him when he's sober.

Chapter Fifty

A Gilded Cage

Tannin

After the demonstration in the dungeon and the stark, gut-wrenching realisation that she really was not going anywhere any time soon, Tannin had reluctantly surrendered to sleeping in the bed she'd been given, eating the food she was brought and even dressing as was expected of a Lady. She had convinced the serving girl, Orlaith, to get her a proper nightshirt instead of the flimsy, lace handkerchief, but that was about as much success as she had been able to enjoy.

Once the shock had worn off, it had been replaced by a deep, burning fury. She could bide her time, but one day, she would kill Laird Cormack and she would damn well enjoy it.

Tannin perched on her window ledge, glaring at the blue skies outside. Orlaith had told her she would wrinkle her dress if she didn't sit properly, and Tannin had told her to mind her own business. She had tried to pick the simplest of all the dresses she'd been given, but even then, it was far more elegant than anything she would have chosen and she had to get help to lace up the back.

A sharp rap on her door startled her out of her daydreams of escape and revenge. She frowned as the scrape of a key in the lock followed.

What is the damn point in knocking?

Malcolm, her assigned keeper, poked his helmeted head into the room. Well, she assumed it was him. Tannin wondered what he looked like under there. His armour hid every part of him right down to his gloved hands. The distortion of his voice from within his helmet made it impossible to even gauge his age.

As he opened the door fully to admit an old man and a skinny boy, Tannin vaguely considered the possibility that it wasn't Malcolm at all but some other anonymous metal sentry. She could have sworn she felt his sneer from the other side of the room, however. He had clearly taken his new job as a grievous insult, and considering the Falcon's words, it probably was. She would find no ally in him.

Tannin waited, watching blankly as the older man set down a large canvas bag on the low sitting room table and dropped his jacket over the arm of the couch. The boy hung back, watching the man keenly while making it a point to not even glance in Tannin's direction. His cheekbones jutted out of his face, giving him an almost skeletal look.

"So," the older man said, finally addressing her. "You're my patient then? Come. Sit."

Tannin rubbed her shoulder. She'd forgotten that Cormack said it said he would send someone to look at her injury.

Took his sweet time about that.

"Guess so," she muttered as she slipped off the window ledge to sit on the couch as he indicated. The couch was much harder than it looked, as she had found out when she had slept on it her first two nights. As she sat down, the overfilled cushions barely sank under her weight.

"I am Professor Marwick, resident healer of the Falcon's Rest." He gestured to the skinny boy. "My apprentice, Finn."

Tannin made a noise of acknowledgement but didn't extend a greeting of her own. The professor peered at her with rapt interest through the tiny glass lenses perched on the end of his nose that made his pale, watery eyes look huge.

Seeming to remember himself, he cleared his throat. "Forgive me, my lady, it is not often that one has the honour of examining a warg. I have many questions."

Tannin glared at Malcolm, but he simply lounged against the door.

"I just need a salve," Tannin ground out through her teeth.

Humiliation crawled across her skin, leaving her feeling uncomfortably hot. What a way to represent her kind. A powerless prisoner in a pretty dress, who needed coddling. Gods, she wished the ground could just swallow her.

"Well, I will be responsible for your general health whilst you are with us," he beamed at her as if it was a gift she had given him. "I need to know all about you. Finn, my boy, take notes. How old are you, my lady?"

"Eighteen."

"And you are a warg of Stonestead."

"Is that a question or are you just stating it?"

"Would you stand for me please, my lady?"

Again, the minutes ticked by in uncomfortable silence as he studied her. She had started to fidget when he spoke again, but he addressed his apprentice, not her, giving a cursory estimation of her measurements.

The professor cocked his head in her direction again. "Would you say you are average amongst wargs?"

"You'd have to ask them," Tannin replied. She tried to keep her tone light since she still wanted something from him, but the way he was studying her like one of Ava's slimy things in a jar made her skin crawl.

"Do you have allergies? Any long-term sicknesses or ailments?"

"Just a sore shoulder."

"Anything in your family history?"

"No."

"As a warg, you can perform a full functional shift into another form?"

"Well, not right now I fuckin' can't," Tannin snapped, flicking her bracers but his eyes lit up anyway and Finn's quill scratched audibly.

"When did you first achieve another form?"

"Is that relevant?"

"Of course, I need to know everything I can about you to treat you to my full abilities."

"There's nothing to know other than I got bloody stabbed and it hurts."

He seemed reluctant to stop asking her about warg things and actually do what he was there for, but after a long sigh, he asked, "When did the injury occur?"

She kept her answers brief. She was particularly vague on who and how it had been treated – a random healer in Dunoak, she said. He had her slip her dress off her shoulder and poked at her scar, ignoring her grimace.

"Hm."

"Like I said, it's fine. It's just sore." Tannin tugged her dress back into place.

"How did this happen?"

"I got stabbed," Tannin said flatly, "with a sword."

Professor Marwick chuckled. "Ah yes, we've all heard varying versions of the story. Why don't you tell me what really happened?"

"I'm not in a storytelling mood."

He smiled. "I am only curious. Will you indulge me?"

His hand was on her shoulder again, the pad of his thumb pressing on her tender scar. Tannin swallowed.

"Is this an interrogation?"

"Of course not."

"Then forget it," she said shrugging his hand from her arm. "And forget the salve. I'll just deal with it if this is what it costs."

The professor tutted and took off his glass lenses. His eyes now looked too small without them.

"From what our good laird has told me, you are going to be with us for quite some time. I think you'll find that cooperation will make your stay a lot easier on all of us."

Tannin clenched her teeth to stop herself from responding as the professor stood and shook on his jacket.

"I will have a balm delivered later today." He stopped to turn to her again before he left. "But we will speak again. There's still much I'd like to know."

"He's creepy," Tannin muttered to Orlaith after Professor Marwick and his apprentice had left.

"I...couldn't say, Miss."

"Oh aye, you could."

"Miss Tannin, if it pleases you." Orlaith addressed the floor when she spoke. "His Lairdship has granted permission for you to leave your chambers."

"I can leave?" Tannin brightened.

"Your chambers, yes," Orlaith said hurriedly. "Sir Malcolm will escort you wherever you wish within the walls of the fort."

"Sir Malcolm," Tannin echoed as she drained the last of her tea. "Didn't know he was a 'Sir'."

"Oh yes, Miss." Red crept into her cheeks. "He is quite the knight."

"Uh-huh." Tannin rolled her eyes.

Time to get the hell out of here.

Tannin tipped her head back to feel the sun on her cheeks, even though the winter wind nipped at her exposed skin. Armed with a thick cloak, bordered with dark fur, she gravitated towards the gardens. The fresh air gave at least the sparse illusion of freedom. Evergreen shrubs and trees provided some welcome life to the otherwise barren gardens with its shrouded benches in leafy, private nooks. She claimed a bench, rubbing her hands together to bring a little warmth to her fingers and smiled a little as Malcolm stomped his feet against the cold. She hoped he was uncomfortable.

He followed her doggedly along with at least one other visible guard. There were also other watchers dotted around the hedges and up on the walls that they clearly thought were hidden from her. She gave a quiet chuckle. They were forgetting that even with her warg side locked away, she was still a warg-blood Remnant, and she could both hear and smell them on the breeze. She reckoned that with a bit more time, she'd be able to tell them apart by their scent – some distinctly less pleasant than others – and work out how many they were and their routines.

A cleared throat from nearby let Tannin know she'd been sitting on the bench with a glazed expression for a little too long.

"Time to go, little bird."

Tannin glowered. She'd have to pay Cormack back for that comment that had inspired the guards to gift her this pet name. Her obvious annoyance had only encouraged them, and now they hardly called her anything else. Unless someone was around to hear them. Then she was "my lady". She couldn't quite decide which she hated more. She definitely hated that she had to be back in her rooms before sundown. At least outside in the garden, she could pretend she wasn't trapped.

"It's not sundown yet," she pointed out, chin lifted in challenge. Her cage may have been gilded but it was still a cage.

"Inside. Now."

Tannin had tried to goad him into talking to her for her own amusement multiple times, but he seemed determined not to be drawn into conversation with her other than to bark orders.

She sighed.

Gods, this new life is going to be boring. Was this what Ava's life was like when she had to be Avalyn?

Tannin mused and then a thought struck her. She knew exactly what Ava would do in her situation. She'd definitely seen a library during her tour.

"I'll go inside, but you promised I had 'til sundown."

"Don't push your luck, little bird."

"I just want to get a book."

"A book?"

"Aye, those squarish things with the pages?"

Malcom crossed his arms. He had zero sense of humour.

Tannin quickly remedied, "I'll be in and out the library quick. One book."

He groaned, but she took that as agreement.

Tannin had been sure she knew the way to the library. However, one decadent tapestry looked much like another after a while and she begrudgingly had to admit she was lost.

"The laird's private wing is off limits." Malcolm stepped in Tannin's way as she attempted to turn into a promising looking corridor.

She frowned. "I'm trying to find the damn library. I know it's here somewhere."

Tannin glanced back up at the spiralling stairs at the end of the forbidden corridor.

Private wing, hm? I bet my stone is up there.

She crossed her arms, staring at him impatiently. He seemed to be waiting for her to ask properly. She gritted her teeth.

"Where is the library?"

There was a long pause.

If he was waiting for her to say "please", he would be waiting a long time.

"One floor up," Malcolm said finally.

"Right," Tannin muttered and stalked off.

On her way, she passed open doors leading into what looked like either dining or meeting rooms. One looked similar to the hall she and the other wargs had dined in on the first night, only smaller. The memory was accompanied by a painful lump in her throat that she unsuccessfully tried to swallow.

As she turned away from the hall and the unpleasant thoughts it inspired, she spotted the fresco.

"Oh."

It reached from the stone floor all the way up to the vaulted ceiling. Figures in sweeping, hooded cloaks, holding handfuls of flame towards the sky. Behind the figures was a triangular, overlapping symbol that was at this point so horribly familiar.

"Oh, I am fucked."

How on earth did they never connect the Triquetra to Gormbrae? Them taking out influential remnant members of society in Armodan pre-attack made so much sense. Tannin wondered if Ava had connected the dots. Maybe she had and dismissed it already? Why did they target Remnants, though? Was this a druid-blood thing? Did they even just target Remnants? They had never really looked at any human deaths. Tannin simply didn't know.

There were too many questions. Too many people playing too many different games. She was getting a headache from the futility of trying to work it all out.

The library also didn't provide much in the way of motivation. It was underwhelming to say the least. She'd expected shelves of colourful tomes reaching to the domed ceilings and gold railed ladders to climb up to them. Instead, she was met with a few bookshelves covered in dust and a rickety old desk.

"Half an hour, little bird, then it's back in your cage you go," Malcolm informed her.

Tannin flipped him off behind his back and turned to peruse the spines.

"What would Ava do?" she muttered to herself. "Learn about the enemy. Read a book. Creep about. Steal my blood…"

Most of the books seemed horrifically dull, but eventually, she found one that, during a quick flip through, at least had pictures in it.

"Alright, I'm done." She waggled the book at Malcolm, who was tapping an impatient foot. "I was getting hungry anyway."

Tannin tugged the thick tome across the window ledge and propped it up against her knees. It was mostly druidic history. She'd flicked through some of the pages already after her evening meal had been cleared away, but it was hard to force herself to actually sit down and read.

She'd have to find something to amuse herself here.

What do nobles even do for fun?

She wriggled into a more comfortable position and adjusted the pillows she'd taken from the bed. The salve that had been sent up via the pully system with her evening meal had worked far better than the one Ava made, and she could still feel the warm tingles seeping into her skin and deep into the muscle. For the first time in a long time, not even the ghost of an ache remained in her joint.

Tannin's attention snapped back to the book as she turned the page to a diagram that was nothing short of filthy. She grinned as she looked it over. It was…interesting. It reminded her of the dirty book she'd caught Ava reading when they were researching the Triquetra back in Armodan. She chuckled at the memory of how embarrassed the princess had been.

The book she held in her hands had some of the same stories Ava had told her once about the time before Remnants, when the Fair Folk themselves roamed the Five Kingdoms. Gormbrae's border had changed since then, but the south had always been home to the druids.

According to the history she held in her hands, the druids used to be fearsomely powerful. They could see power and magic in the air, in plants, animals and stone and in other Fair Folk. And gods, could they use that power.

Ravensmore, the capital city of Gormbrae and seat of King Modric, was raised from the dirt by pure druidic magic alone according to the book and became home to the strongest of the Fair Folk clans.

Tannin rubbed at her eyes. These stories should have been so much more interesting, but the narration was dry and every sentence whittled away at Tannin's will to keep reading. If she had literally anything else to do, she would have given up.

She sighed. She wished she could sleep.

Chapter Fifty-One

Putting the "Fun" in Funeral

Ava

Dunoak was set for the biggest, wildest party it had ever seen. Towering ale barrels filled the entrance hall to the keep, and visitors poured into the city from the surrounding villages and towns. Iona and her kelpie-bloods had even made an appearance that morning. They set up their stalls, selling a host of carved mourning beads, floating lanterns and a potent spirit of their own design, while Iona herself passed on their condolences. Ava listened in on her brief meeting with Dana where, after her sympathies had been offered, she made sure that Tannin's agreement with the kelpie folk still stood. She took the first round of carved, wooden heads that the warg-blood hunting party had brought back. The younger ones had all but been queueing up to be a part of Tannin's plan to hunt down the pirates for the kelpie-bloods. They were just as feverish now as the preparations continued.

Wargish funerals were not ones of sorrow or mourning but a celebration of life. The life and death of the infamous Feral Queen was a celebration that no one would ever forget.

The pyre had already been built at the very top of the brae. The smoke tower it would produce would be seen for miles around as the queen's spirit was carried to the mountains. Ava glared at it. It was a sham. A disrespectful, traitorous sham. And what was worse, Ava thought, looking at the musicians and entertainers that filled the streets, was that Tannin would have loved it.

Another delivery of spirits arriving for the evening's festivities masked Ava's exit as she pulled the hood of her cloak down low. She needed to get away from the keep, from the lies and the deceit, before she exploded. She couldn't keep this in. She wanted so desperately to tell someone, but Flint had not been sober since the bodies had been brought home. Despite dumping copious buckets of cold water over his head, Ava had still not been able to get a coherent conversation out of him. He was mostly either passed out, vomiting or both at the same time while Ava made sure he didn't choke to death.

Ava left Flint snoring under Alby's watchful eye, and she snuck her way out of the keep. With the revelry and excitement, no one paid her a second glance as she weaved through the crowds. White ribbons hung from doorways and were woven into tree branches and around signposts. People wore them in their hair, tied around their wrist or pinned to their lapels. A mark of mourning for their queen.

Ava didn't wear a ribbon. She'd dressed in her dourest, most unremarkable clothing and moved slowly, unconcernedly. As a princess, she had been coached on body language. As an eavesdropper with an agenda, she'd picked up even more. She knew how to make herself invisible. She was a shadow. She was—

Ava let out a surprised gurgle as the back of her cloak was seized, the neckline cutting into her throat, and she was hauled into an alley. Air whooshed from her lungs as she was spun and her back slammed into a brick wall. Catriona's tattooed face scowled, inches from her own.

"We need to talk."

"W-what?" Ava choked out. The woman was around Flint's height, but she felt so much bigger as she loomed over her. Flint never loomed.

"Don't play games with me," the warg growled. "I've been watching you."

"I don't know what you're talking about."

Catriona's fist slammed into the wall beside Ava's head, sprinkling her with dust.

"I know you know!" she hissed. "Cards on the table, princess."

"You first," Ava replied. She sounded braver than she felt. If Catriona hadn't been gripping her cloak, her knees might've given out.

The woman's smile was grim. "You're a smart girl. Listening in when you think no one's watching. Oh aye, I know all your wee hidey holes. And I saw you with the body. I saw how you checked it over. What were you looking for?"

Ava's blood froze in her veins.

"I know you know what we did." The raw regret in her tone caught Ava off guard.

"What did you do?" she prompted, keeping her voice low like she was speaking to a cornered animal. Catriona could still decide to tear her head off.

Catriona's tongue darted out as she licked her lips and scanned the deserted alley.

"She's alive," she murmured.

Ava nodded. "The body is a fake."

"Aye." The warg exhaled. "There was nothing I could do for her. I only had pieces of the puzzle."

Ava waited for her to continue.

"We knew Dana would do something like this. That's why Douglas challenged her. Reckless eejit, he should have waited but he got ahead of himself."

"Douglas?"

"Aye, keep up. I thought you were meant to be smart? Dana is more like Sommer than she wants to admit. She likes the power too much. No way she was gonna give it up. She wanted Tannin to just do as she was told, but then she took to it. Like a wee duck to water. Dana knew she couldn't compete with a berserker if the challenge came. So, she got rid of her."

"But the body is a fake."

"Aye, she didn't kill her. She's at the Falcon's Rest." Catriona's lip curled back in disgust. "Dana exchanged her for the alliance with them."

"You...want to help her?" Ava said slowly. "Why should I trust you?"

"We are wargs. We left Sommer's army because we believed in a true blood heir. Not because we wanted to follow Dana," Catriona snapped. "What she did to our queen wasn't just dishonourable. It was underhand and cowardly. Everything a warg leader shouldn't be. I couldn't help Tannin that night. Numbers weren't on my side. But whatever I can do now, I will."

Catriona's face was open and earnest. Ava's Senses were calm.

Ava cleared her throat. "If we are to be on the same side, may I suggest releasing me?"

The warg glanced at where her grip on Ava's cloak still pinned her to the wall. She let go with a scoff.

"Wherever you're sneaking off to will have to wait." Catriona again glanced around the empty alley. "Ceremony will start at sundown, and you'll be missed if you're not there."

Catriona was right. As winter approached, the nights were growing longer and by mid-afternoon the sun had vanished.

Threads of white-clad figures wound their way up the brae where the pyre stood higher than any cairn. It had been an extraordinary effort to get Flint up, dressed and then to tow him up the hill. He leaned against Ava, swigging from a hipflask she'd yet to confiscate as the body was brought forth. Ava couldn't imagine how she would feel if she thought that really was Tannin being laid on the pile of wood. She had lain awake at night with those thoughts. How was she going to fake this?

As those closest to her said their goodbyes to the queen, some left tokens or gifts to burn with her. Ava clutched her offering of Tannin's favourite tea tightly to stop her hands from shaking. She wondered what the poor, unknown girl under the disguise would have liked. One of the druidic tomes Ava had managed to acquire through her trades spoke of corpse-moulding. A benign mortuary art used to make a loved one more presentable. A corrupted version of that magic was what had carved Tannin's face onto the body, Ava was sure of it. Ava clenched her teeth as she sprinkled her rose tea over the shrouded corpse.

"We are gathered here today..." Dana's voice thundered over the hushed crowd as the flames took hold. "...to celebrate the life of a great warg. Our Feral Queen!"

Howls of equal part jubilation and anguish filled the air. Dana waited until they subsided.

"She died as she lived! Unwavering until the end." She paused to let the words ring out. "We were attacked on the road to Gormbrae to secure an alliance. To secure your future!"

"Assassins sent from the Golden Queen were tasked with making sure none of us made it home. Your queen could have run. Could have saved herself. She did not. She chose to stand with her people and fight! We owe our lives to her sacrifice!"

Ava clenched her fists in her pockets.

Her sacrifice, indeed.

"Our queen fell that day." Dana let her words become sombre. "And we will remember her."

A murmur rumbled through the audience.

"We will remember her."

Dana accepted a torch and touched it to the pyre.

The light scent of rose was the first to hit Ava's nose as the fire caught the fragile petals. It was quickly burned away, replaced by wood and incense. Then roasting meat.

Attilo's body had smelled the same. However much she scrubbed, the scent had lingered on her skin for days. Ava swallowed hard against the nausea that was creeping up her throat.

Illuminated by the growing flames, Dana stood tall. "It is my honour to lead you in her stead and to uphold her legacy! The Feral Queen lives on in all of us!"

As the cries rang out, Dana stooped to retrieve a box at her feet and held its contents aloft. Ava's eyes grew wide in horror as she recognized the awful thing.

Dana's shadow lengthened as she raised the fanged crown to her brow.

"Let the Feral name never die!"

Chapter Fifty-Two

Midnight stealth

Tannin

For such a large fort, the Falcon's Rest was depressingly empty. Orlaith had told Tannin that in the warmer months, the place would be full to bursting with people who came for feasts and summer tourneys. Apparently, a lot of matchmaking went on during those times too. In wintertime, however, the fort was mostly dead with a skeleton crew of staff to tend to the few year-round residents and occasional guests who decided, unwisely, to spend the winter. When the snow began, it would make journeying down from the fort almost impossible, and anyone who stayed was committed to staying until the spring. It was one of the reasons Tannin had so readily agreed to visit immediately. So that they wouldn't get trapped here.

Ha. Ha.

Even with the risk of being snowed in, a few nobles still lingered around the place. Tannin found it entertaining to watch them totter about in their fancy clothes and clucking over everything and nothing. She stood on a stone balcony, breathing the icy air and watching them in the courtyard below. They seemed to be waiting for something. From high up, it was like watching little brightly coloured birds waiting to be thrown seeds.

"It's all very exciting, isn't it?" babbled a woman wrapped in richly dyed furs.

"That's one way of putting it. I'd call it expensive," her companion replied.

"Oh, come now." The woman slapped his arm lightly, making the decrepit fox's head on her shawl wobble. "He's a prince."

"A disgraced prince," he replied with a sniff. "I'll bet he's only here to try and scrap back some respectability."

Suspicion twinged in the back of Tannin's mind.

Surely not...

"It is curious though, that Prince Erlan would be coming here right as the Falcon allies with the Feral Queen. I'd have thought he'd be as far as he could from wargs considering that run-in he had with the Armodan beast."

Erlan? Tannin gripped the window's stone ledge. *Here?*

I'll kill him.

"What does it matter? He's disgraced. He's here as little more than a messenger to take information back to his father, and he's lucky they even let him do that. He was supposed to be married to the Brochlands girl, you know. Such a humiliation that was."

The man sounded gleeful at the downfall of the prince, and Tannin allowed herself to smirk. Seeing him humiliated was a shite alternative to seeing him dead, but at least, it was something.

"I've heard the Golden Queen has even taken up residence in Armodan now." The woman with the sad fox shawl grimaced. "Everyone's a warg-lover."

The man shook his head in disapproval. "A fight between wargs is not one I want to get involved in at all. If it were my choice, I'd leave well alone."

"Well, King Modric seems to know what he's doing."

"Oh, don't take that tone. I know I've pledged twenty of my best to the Feral Queen on his behalf already," the man grumbled. "I just hope it's worth it."

Tannin frowned and rubbed her ears. Surely, she had heard that wrong. The news of her death would have spread by now? And why would the king have his people pledge men to her army if he was simultaneously keeping her prisoner?

Realisation dawned on her as a sick, queasy feeling stirred deep in her belly.

"Dana took my name," she whispered, horrified.

"She's not happy stealing my freedom, my home, my power, she has to steal my fucking name too?!" Tannin yelled to herself and kicked out at the locked door of her chambers.

Malcolm had hauled her back to her rooms as soon as he'd seen the look on her face as she'd realised. It was probably a sensible choice. She was furious.

"Ladies do not eavesdrop. I should have you fitted with a bell like a cat," he had scolded her on the way back, dragging her by the elbow, but Tannin was lost in her own thoughts.

Dana had stolen her name and title. Her legacy. Prince Erlan was going to be within the same walls as her, and she couldn't do a damn thing about it. She still had no way to tell Ava and Flint she was alive.

Tannin's inner fire struggled under the weight of the sealing runes and sputtered burning heat down her spine and into her limbs. It filled her head with a fiery fog. She roared as she swept everything off her writing desk. Candles melted in her hands as she ripped them from their bolted-down holders and threw them against the door.

"I earned that name," she muttered as she did so. "I killed for it. I bled for it."

The room filled with the sounds of tearing silk as she tore apart her pillows while feathers filled the air like snow. She broke everything that she could. She wanted to destroy. She didn't care what they did to her afterwards.

"Ohhh," Tannin laughed. "Oh, I'm really gonna kill her now."

With a last burst of rage, Tannin picked up the chair for her writing desk – the only piece of furniture that wasn't nailed to the floor – and slammed it against the wall. It crumpled and she tore off one of the legs.

"What do you think you are doing!?"

Tannin whirled to see a familiar, iron clad figure staring at the mess. Before she could reply something sarcastic, he had crossed the room in two strides, grabbed the chair leg and ripped it from her grasp. His other hand curled around her throat.

"What do you think you are doing?" he asked again, this time in a deadly whisper.

Tannin clawed at his hand ineffectively. He had previously caught her making herself bleed, trying to scratch at the edges of her bracers and forcibly had her nails trimmed down into useless stumps.

Malcolm wasn't holding her tight enough to cut off her air. Regardless, she couldn't breathe. The pressure around her throat consumed every corner of her brain. A hand. A rope. A jeering crowd. Heat. Her warg-fire whimpered in her chest behind its glass confines.

"Let go of me," she squeaked, trying to ignore her screaming instincts.

He released her with a disgusted snort. She sank to the floor. It was reassuringly solid under her as she rubbed her throat, trying to convince herself there wasn't a rope around it.

"Stop this nonsense," he barked at her as she sat there panting. "Or else."

Long after he left, and the walls had stopped closing in, Tannin scraped herself off the floor and wiped her eyes. Her chambers were in ruin, her blood had cooled and despair was starting to creep in. The fading sunlight on the wreckage cast long shadows across the floor. But a little spark of intrigue kept her from falling apart. She had heard something Malcolm hadn't. When he threw away the broken chair leg, it had hit the balcony door. There had been a tinkling as something metal fell to the floor.

Tannin blinked, the fog clearing from her mind. She crept closer to the balcony door as if the sadly swinging latch might scurry away. The latch that she had tried a hundred times to break open but wasn't anywhere close to strong enough. But Malcolm had been strong enough without even trying. She had wondered if there had been more to making him her keeper than just as a humiliation for him. They needed someone, *something*, strong enough to handle a warg, if need be. Her grandfather's diary had spoken of immensely strong Remnants. Descended from the balors.

Malcom is a balor-blood.

Tannin reached out tentatively and pressed her palm flat to the balcony door. It opened with only a slight groan of protest.

The cool breeze that slipped in was heavenly as it danced across Tannin's skin. She closed her eyes and breathed it in. A smile stretched itself across her face.

Oh, I do believe I feel like a little exploring.

She curled up in her nest of torn bedding for the rest of the evening. It was torture to wait for nightfall, but without the cover of darkness, she wouldn't get away with sneaking out. Plus, Malcolm kept checking in to see that she wasn't wreaking more havoc. He had smugly told her she would be confined to her rooms for the next few days to which she had told him to fuck off. After several hours, she resigned herself to the fact she wasn't getting dinner that night either.

Eventually, Orlaith was sent in to clean up. The maid's face fell in dismay when she saw the mess. Tannin felt a twinge of guilt and embarrassment about adding to the girl's workload by acting like a child throwing a tantrum. She felt even more like a child when Orlaith picked stray feathers from her ruined pillow out of her hair and then left without saying her usual goodnight.

Tannin gave it an hour before she made her move.

She arranged her freshly made bed with pillows under the blanket so that if anyone checked on her in the next hour or so it would hopefully look like she was fast asleep. The replacement bedding was of lesser quality that the set she'd shredded. That was fair, she reasoned.

With fluttering nerves, she coaxed the balcony door open and slid out into the bitter cold. Light glowed from a few windows, and torches were lit in the small courtyard below her window, but otherwise, the night was a cloak shrouding the Falcon's Rest.

The climb down wasn't easy, but she managed with only scraped fingertips to show for it. Getting back up would be another story entirely, but she decided she would just have to worry about that later. She'd already taken the first step and she was determined to get her speaking stone back.

Whatever the cost.

Her feet made no sound as she crept through the fort. She made sure to keep to the shadows and ducked out of sight whenever guards or wandering servants drew too close. It was refreshing to not feel the prickle of being watched on the back of her neck. She stole through the covered walkways and corridors like a shadow.

On the upper floors, close to where the laird's private wing was located, she paused as she saw the main gate through the window where she had entered with her own procession and banners. Swinging torches marked the guards patrolling across the bridge. She could take on one or two of them. Maybe.

Turning away from the gate was nothing short of torturous, but she knew she couldn't escape. Even if she got through the gate, they'd see her. And if they didn't manage to catch her on the bridge, she had no supplies to make the journey and only a vague idea of the way home. They'd hunt her down laughably easily, and with her powers still sealed away, she could do nothing to stop them simply scooping her up and bringing her back.

Every step up to the laird's wing creaked under her weight. Tannin cringed every time, just waiting to be discovered. As she reached the entrance, it occurred to her that all it would take was one locked door and that would be the end of her adventure. Picking locks was Flint's thing. He'd taught her the basics, but she hadn't ever had cause to practise. If the door was anything other than a basic tumbler lock, she would have had to admit defeat and slink back to her rooms empty-handed. Or she could try and cause some mayhem. She entertained the thought briefly. It could be fun and probably the catharsis she was craving, but it would also make trouble she couldn't afford. As if she wasn't in enough trouble already.

Luck was on her side, and she even let herself have a silent victory dance as the door swung open at a single push.

Flecks of dust hung in the gloom as she peered down the lightless corridor. With a thrill of fear, Tannin considered that the laird might actually sleep up here and she could very well accidentally walk right into his bedroom. She stilled and listened for any tell-tale sound of breathing, but all she heard was her own heart.

She found what must've been his war room first. Just like the council chambers back in Dunoak, a table with a map engraved into the wood stood in the centre. Coloured pieces denoting troops littered the surface.

Tannin wrestled with the urge to mess with the pieces.

The laird's wing was larger than she had hoped for. Too many rooms to search in one night. Too many chances to get caught. She had to be smart about it. What would he have done with her things?

The first door she tried was locked and so was the second.

Even though worry niggled in the back of her mind that the Falcon would have had her belongings burned, something told her he was the type to keep trophies.

Trophies.

Tannin did a double-take as she passed by a long hallway. It was decked in tapestries and art. That in itself wasn't unusual. What was unusual, however, was the head mounted on the wall.

She crept forward in disgusted awe. The grey skin was leathery with age, and the eyes had been replaced with shiny, black stones, but the expression of pure rage was creepily lifelike. The redcap's lips were pulled back in a snarl. Tannin half expected it to snap at her as she reached up to wave her hand in front of its face. She shuddered in revulsion, remembering how they had stripped the flesh from the mercenaries' bones whilst they were still alive and screaming.

She didn't let the mounted head out of her sight until she was a safe distance away. More heads lined the corridor. Mounted on burnished plaques, most were skeletal, and all were creatures she could have only dreamt up in her nightmares.

Glass cases held ancient books that looked like one touch would have them crumbling into dust. Tannin recognised a sightlens in another case – this one complete, unbroken, and with additional amber coloured lenses attached to the sides. Something spherical and squishy-looking floated in a glass jar beside it. Tannin elected to not look too closely.

Ava would lose her damn mind here, Tannin mused.

She was so caught up in a display of pearly scales she almost screamed when she turned and came face to face with a towering figure. Clamping a hand over her mouth, Tannin steadied herself against the wall.

It's not real, you fuckin' eejit!

She looked closer.

The carved, wooden mannequin stared back at her from inside its glass case. It was wearing her tunic. Her axe was wired to the mannequin's hand while a crude approximation of her fanged crown sat perched on the wooden head. Below the crown, a grotesque face leered through the glass.

In any other circumstance, she would have been offended, but one thing in the case made her heart glow with hope instead. Her brooch was pinned to the tunic. Ava had been right. No one had seen it for what it really was.

I should have learned by now not to doubt her.

She slid open the glass door, careful not to leave any incriminating smudges on the surface, and unpinned the brooch with trembling fingers.

The chime of a timepiece pricked at her sensitive ears from somewhere on a lower floor. Midnight.

With a heady rush of excitement, Tannin pricked her finger on the brooch's clasp and squished the bead of blood against the speaking stone.

"Please, please, please." Tannin pressed the stone against her lips as she whispered, "Come on you stupid piece of shit. Work!"

Oh, thank the gods you're alive.

"Ava." Tannin sank to her knees in front of the display case and held the brooch to her chest.

I knew she was lying. I knew that wasn't your body. I knew it. Tannin, are you alright?

Tannin slumped further, resting her head on the side of the glass cabinet, letting Ava's voice wash over her. With her eyes closed, she could imagine Ava there beside her. She hadn't realised how much she had missed her voice.

Have you been listening for me every night?

Always. Tannin, where are you?

They left me here. At the Falcon's Rest.

Tannin's throat started to feel tight and she swallowed hard.

Dana and the others. They planned it.

She told us you fell in battle. An ambush.

Aye, it was a fucking ambush. Them all against me. Dana gave me bracers covered in binding runes so I couldn't Change. I didn't know until it was too late. I still can't Change. Tannin sniffled as she filled Ava in on the rest.

Gods, I should have seen this coming.

Tannin could almost see her pacing holes in her rug and pinching the bridge of her nose as she went through it all and all the things she could have missed.

How in the fuck could you have seen this coming?

Tannin could almost hear her rolling her eyes.

It's all about alliances. Gormbrae can't take the Brochlands alone, but with Dana's support, they theoretically could from the East. If she then has Gormbrae and the Brochlands, then Sommer is outnumbered even with her wargs, and Dana could get you out of the way to take the throne for herself and deal with the others later.

You have to admit, it's a very neat and tidy solution. You have to factor in Rill too. They might ally with Dana and the Gormbraens if it came down to it, but they'd never have allied with you after what you did to Erlan, and admit it, you wouldn't have allied with them either even if it made tactical sense.

Oh, and you would have? Tannin shot back sourly. *Also, will you stop admiring her please? And that's nothing new. Get Gormbrae on our side, take the Brochlands as amicably as possible and then take on Sommer. That was always the plan. She didn't have to stab me in the back like this. Fuck it, if she'd asked nicely, she could've had all the power she wanted.*

Calm down. It's—

Don't you dare tell me it's okay. Oh, and it gets worse. I found a massive Triquetra carving here. I think the Falcon's in it. Maybe the head of it.

Silence stretched out between them and Tannin thought for a second the connection had been lost.

Are you safe?

Right this second? Not really, 'cause I've broken out of my rooms and I'm snooping Laird Cormack's private wing. If they find me here, I'm fucked. But in general, aye, I guess so. They're treating me well. He says he wants me to be a Lady in his court. I don't get it. I really don't get why they're keeping me alive.

Because you're still useful. The laird is clearly hedging his bets so that if his alliance with Dana goes wrong, he still has you. And political prisoners are always treated well, especially a queen.

Tannin scoffed.

I'm no real queen and everyone knows it. They let me put on a crown and play a part and make an absolute fool of myself.

Stop that. You're safe for now and we know where you are. We can make a plan to get you out.

No, you need to get away from Dunoak before Dana decides to get rid of you. She doesn't like you, and I can't protect you anymore.

If I go, she will suspect I know something. It could compromise you.

She is going to compromise your head right off your shoulders.

Tannin's head suddenly jerked up.

What did you mean you knew it wasn't my body?

I don't know how they did it but...Tannin, they had your body. They must have altered another corpse. An experienced druid-blood could probably do something like that. It was very realistic.

If everyone saw my body...No one will ever believe I'm still alive.

Tannin's fist clenched around the brooch. If there was no doubt about her death, then no one was coming for her. Dana had planned her betrayal so thoroughly. Even if she got a message out, no one would come.

Anger clouded Tannin's thoughts, and the connection became hazy. Dana. She mused about all the horrible ways she could kill her.

That's hardly helpful.

It's making me feel better.

No, it isn't.

Shut up, Ava.

I know the truth. I'm coming to get you.

How in the hell are you going to do that, huh? Just stroll up and be all "Hi, can we have Tannin back please and thank you?" Dana has zero reason to keep you around, and you're still worth a hell of a lot of coin. Just get Flint and get the fuck out of Dunoak before it's too late.

We can possibly turn this to our advantage. She doesn't know that we can communicate.

No, Ava. No scheming. Just get out of there.

There is an opportunity here. I'm not going to waste it doing anything rash.

When I get out of here, I'm going to kick your—

Tannin's head snapped back in the direction of the door. Footsteps clacked on the stone stairs leading to the Laird's wing.

"Shite."

Tannin raced out of the trophy hall just in time to see the main door start to open. Dropping to the ground, she slid the last few feet until she was safely out of sight underneath the table.

I'm so gonna get caught.

Tannin chewed her lip and scrunched herself into the tightest ball she could as someone dropped into one of the chairs and a set of long legs stretched out towards her.

"I must say, you do have a nice place here, Cormack." Erlan's voice sounded from above her. "I have, however, heard an unfortunate rumour about your newfound taste in exotic pets."

The laird chuckled over the sound of clinking glasses and sloshing liquid as he poured drinks.

Is that who I think it is?

Ava's voice in her head was murderous and Tannin shushed her.

"I take it you are referring to my wargish guest."

"A dangerous guest."

"She will prove useful in time."

"I would urge you to dispose of that creature."

Tannin wished she could flip the table and rip his damn head off. If she still had her wargish abilities, she wouldn't have been able to hold back a growl.

Aren't you glad you didn't marry him?

Exceedingly. Although, it would have given me plenty of opportunities to smother him in his sleep.

Smothering is too good a death for him.

"Your personal history does not interest me, Prince Erlan, nor do your prejudices. I tolerate the unsavoury business of Rill regarding other Remnants because they suit my own purposes, but my plans concerning the young warg are my own. Let us discuss our plans instead, hm?"

A clinking sound came from above as if they'd tapped glasses together.

"Indeed."

They spent some time haggling over contract amendments. Tannin could feel Ava's interest in the back of her mind being piqued. At least this drivel meant something to someone.

"Might I also suggest an additional strengthening of our union?" There was a slurping sound from Erlan's side. "A marriage.

My sister is now of age, and a marriage to your son would boost your standing immensely."

"My boy, are you in a position to make such an offer? The last I heard, you did not represent your house anymore."

"My father will see the logic in such an arrangement."

Tannin could imagine the sneer across Erlan's face as he continued, "The whole affair in Armodan was down to that beast, you know. The one you're now coddling."

"The past is the past," Cormack replied mildly. "I believe in looking to the future. If you can set up a meeting with your father to discuss terms, I believe that would benefit both our futures."

They toasted to the future and their part in it with another clink of their glasses.

Tannin's legs were numb and her back was aching, but she didn't dare move a muscle in case she made a noise. She sent a silent prayer to every god she could remember the name of for them to be done before anyone noticed she wasn't in her room.

Someone must've heard her prayers and cared enough to answer because only another ten minutes or so passed before Erlan broke into a loud yawn and proclaimed that he would take his leave.

Thank fuck.

She waited until long after their footsteps had faded before emerging from under the table. She had planned to leave immediately, but a stack of parchment on the table caught her eye. It was maps with arrows and symbols scrawled all over it.

This make any sense to you?

She didn't even really have to ask. The elated satisfaction that bloomed in her belly told her enough. Ava could use this.

She looked through the papers long enough for Ava to note down the details before she sped back to her own chambers as quickly as she dared and clambered back up to her balcony. The roughness of the stone made the climb easier than she had expected.

Made it.

Thank goodness. Keep your head down, Tannin. I'll think of something to get you out of there, but it will take time.

Tannin nodded before realising Ava couldn't actually see her.

I will. I miss you.

Silence.

Ava?

Tannin looked again at the stone. Her blood across the surface had long since dried and was flaking off. They must have been out of time.

I miss...you...too.

It came as a delayed echo. More of a whisper than anything else, but it was enough.

Tomorrow. Tannin promised the stone silently.

Just as she was about slide back in through the balcony door, Tannin paused. The brooch. She couldn't take the chance of it being found, and there was a very good chance that her rooms were searched regularly. She examined the window from the outside. Maybe there was a loose stone or a wee nook she could hide it in? No such luck. The grooves in the window decoration were too slanted to balance it anywhere, and the stone wall itself was firmly welded together. Same went for the balcony tiles. The floor and railings were solid and gifted her no hiding places. She puffed out an annoyed exhale and then looked up. A stone gutter ran around the edge of the roof several feet above her window. It was her last option. She just had to hope there would be no heavy rain to wash the brooch away. The climb scraped her fingers raw as she dug them into crevices to haul herself up to the gutter. Standing on the delicate masonry at the top of her window, she was able to reach up and tip the brooch into the stone groove.

"Be safe," she whispered to it and then dropped down to the balcony. The landing jarred but otherwise she was unscathed and slipped back into her rooms.

She barely had time to rinse her dirt-covered hands and sneak back into bed before the click of the lock sounded throughout her chambers.

I'm done for. They know.

Tannin shut her eyes and took a breath before forcing herself out of the comfort of her bed. She'd meet her fate standing. Footsteps came closer. They would take her to the dungeon. There was no doubt about it. Cold, dark, underground. Her knees shook. Sunless, trapped, alone. She squared her shoulders and jutted her chin out defiantly as the handle of her bedroom door turned.

"Oh Miss, you're up! Did you sleep well?"

Chapter Fifty-Three

No Time to Delay

Ava

"Wake up, shut up and follow me," Ava said as soon as Flint opened his eyes. It still was the middle of the night but after speaking with Tannin, Ava knew she had to time to delay.

"Whu—?" Flint sat up in bed and rubbed his temples. "Owww, my head. What time is it?"

"Time for you to stop drowning your sorrows."

When he didn't make a move, she hauled him out of the bed herself.

"Ava, ow! What—?"

"Shh!"

"But—"

"Shhhhh!"

She took his hand and towed him out of the room and down into the pantry. Now that she knew she wasn't the only one making use of the keep's unfortunate acoustics, she was extra careful. Cook had been so careful sealing the pantry against mice that she had inadvertently created the most secure place in the building to share secrets.

"Ava, I don't want a snack. What are you doing?" Flint grumbled as she ushered him in and closed the door.

She dropped her voice. "Tannin is alive."

Flint gave her the bleakest look she had ever seen.

"That's not funny."

"I'm not joking. The body was a fake. I spoke to her tonight."

"No, Ava." Flint took her hand and patted it. "Did you have a dream? Remember, we saw her. She's dead. We burned her body."

Ava snatched her hand back.

"Listen to me! Before she left, Tannin and I did a ritual, a blood magic ritual, so that we could communicate. I had a bad feeling, and I was right. Dana betrayed her and left her with the Gormbraens to secure an alliance. They faked a body and that's what we burned. She managed to contact me through our connection. Tannin is alive."

Flint blinked at her.

"I saw her face."

"Gormbrae is the home of the druids. They have powerful Wielders. But, Flint, it wasn't her."

"I..." Flint shook his head. "I can't deal with this."

Ava grasped his face in both hands and made him look at her. "She is alive. But we won't be if Dana finds out we know. We need to leave Dunoak. The sooner, the better."

Flint's eyes were unfocused as he scrabbled for words.

"What...what did she say? Tannin. You said you spoke to her?"

"She's okay. They've got her locked up, and Dana tricked her into wearing binding runes so she can't Change. She told me to get out of Dunoak and..." Ava's voice cracked. "And that she misses me."

Flint studied her face, and for a fleeting moment, Ava feared he was going to tell her it was a dream.

"She's really alive?"

"She is."

"How can we get her back?"

"I don't know, but we need to get out of here. Tannin was protecting us more than you know. Dana won't hesitate if she thinks we pose a threat."

"We're fucked, aren't we?" Flint puffed his cheeks out in a long exhale and then reached up for a tin on the shelf behind Ava's head. "Want a biscuit?"

Ava stared at him, certain that she had misheard. "What?"

"Can't think on an empty stomach," Flint said, fishing a crumbly biscuit from the tin. His voice lacked its usual humour, but he attempted a weak smile. His chapped lips cracked with the motion.

Ava accepted a biscuit from the proffered tin. She hadn't realised she was hungry, but the second the butteriness hit her tongue, she was suddenly ravenous.

"So, what do we do now?"

There was one other person they could tell. One other person who had enough experience to believe a conspiracy when it was presented to her. One person who had pledged to Tannin and not to the Feral Queen. Ava just hoped that Nyesha didn't slit her throat before she could explain herself, that her oath not to do her harm hadn't died with Tannn.

"Nyesha. She's our best chance. We go to her tonight, right now, and tell her what we know. We can't lose any more time."

"We're going against the wargs. You know we're probably going to die."

"Regrettably, yes. But we have to do something." Ava cracked her neck and stood tall. "Bring the biscuits."

Nyesha's one eye glared at them shrewdly as they stood before her, heavy cloaks thrown hastily over their nightclothes. She sat behind her heavy oak desk, a figure of authority and respect. The red-haired young man she referred to as Mackie hovered behind them.

"It's late," Nyesha growled.

"This can't wait," Ava insisted.

"Ye have some nerve comin' tae my hoose. I leave ye be as per my oath, but yer pushin' yer luck."

"Tannin isn't dead," Flint blurted.

Nyesha's eye slid to him. The corners of her mouth pulled back in what could have been a smile.

"Well, now." The woman leaned back in her chair and drummed her fingers on her fancy desk. "That's a big accusation."

There was a satisfied look to her expression.

"You suspected," Ava challenged.

"I suspect everythin'," she snarled back.

Flint caught Ava's hand and gave a squeeze. When she glanced up, he gave her a meaningful look. He should take the lead. Nyesha hated her and wasn't going to be forthcoming if the plea came from her.

Even if I was the one who figured it out.

Ava reluctantly swallowed her pride and nodded.

Flint puffed his chest and straightened his spine.

"We need your help."

"Worked that out by myself, lad, ye bein' here an' all. What is it ye want?"

"We need to get out of Dunoak. Dana sold Tannin out to the Gormbraens and we want to rescue her, but we're in danger here. We need somewhere safe."

"How many of ye?"

"Well..." Flint glanced at Ava. "...Just the two of us?"

Oh damn, I forgot to tell him.

"Catriona and Douglas as well," Ava muttered.

"Wargs?!" he yelped.

"Some are still loyal to Tannin! They don't agree with what Dana did. There may be some of the warg-bloods who will stand against her too."

Nyesha stroked her chin. "Hm...yer askin' a lot."

"If there's anyone who can help, it's you. We need to outwit them and who better than a Skirter legend to do that?"

Ava smiled to herself as Flint ratchetted up his charms. Even someone as experienced and hardened like Nyesha wasn't immune. She gave a wry smile.

"Dinnae overdo it. I pledged for the wee lass, and if she is alive, then I've still got a blood debt to pay."

"Thank you," Ava whispered in relief but Nyesha's glare was back.

"I ain't doin' this for you. And dinnae think for a moment that I've forgotten what ye really are. Wee serpent in the weeds."

If her carpet hadn't been so lush, Ava suspected Nyesha might have spat on the floor to make her point.

"Leave it with me. I've got some ideas." She pushed back her chair to walk them out. "Dinnae do anythin' to attract attention in the meantime. I'll come tae ye when I've got somethin'."

As she ushered them out, she caught Ava by the shoulder. Bringing her lips close to her ear, she hissed low enough for Flint to be oblivious.

"I'm watchin' ye, *princess*. Give me a reason, just one, and I'll skin ye alive."

Chapter Fifty-Four

A Cure for Restlessness

Tannin

Tannin forced herself to act normally, even though her whole body was buzzing with nerves and impatience to speak to Ava again. She was still half-convinced she hadn't actually gotten away with it, so when Malcolm entered her chambers that morning, she assumed the worst.

"Laird Cormack's office. Now," he said without preamble.

"Can I finish my tea?"

"Now."

Tannin slurped the last third out of her mug, dripping a little down her front in her haste. If this was the end, she wasn't going to damn well go with her last cup of tea undrunk, even if she felt like she was going to throw it back up again the whole walk to the laird's office.

Malcolm ushered her in and closed the door.

"Ah, Lady Tannin." Cormack looked up from the parchment he was writing on. "Just one moment."

"I didn't do anything," Tannin blurted.

He chuckled. "No need to be so defensive. Although, you should bow or curtsey in my presence, or have you forgotten your manners already? No mind. Sit. I'll be with you shortly."

Tannin did sit, but she couldn't sit still. She alternated crossing her legs, crossing her arms, picking at a loose thread on the chair's cushion.

Get on with it! She wanted to yell.

Eventually, Cormack stopped writing and sealed the parchment with a dollop of wax. He leaned back in his chair, eyes scouring her face that she tried to make look as innocent as possible.

"So," he began, "Malcolm tells me you've been a little...restless lately."

Tannin chewed her lip. She'd been so focused on her little night-time trip being discovered, she'd completely forgotten she would be in trouble regardless for her tantrum and trashing her room.

"Show me your bracers."

She grimaced at the mention of them but rolled up her sleeves. Her metal coated forearms dropped down on his desk with a thunk.

He inspected the runes, running a fingertip over one or two of the lines. Although she couldn't feel his touch, the notion of his hands on her made her skin crawl.

Tannin swallowed.

"Are your chambers not to your liking?"

"They're fine," Tannin said quickly. There was a threat in there somewhere.

"As I've previously shown you, the Rest offers other accommodations if your current lodgings are not suitable for you."

Ah, there it is.

She clenched her jaw. She wouldn't apologise, which he seemed to realise because he continued, "If there are any more damages, there will be consequences. Do I make myself clear?"

Tannin didn't get a change to reply because at that moment the door swung open and the artisan stepped into the room. Tannin recoiled.

"Tsk, tsk." Cormack waggled his finger at her and indicated that she should place her arms back on the desk. "Those etchings need a little freshening up if you can break all my furniture, don't they?"

Tannin's hands trembled as she did as he asked.

"Try to stay still, my lady," the artisan murmured as he unrolled a set of tools across the desk.

She gave him a filthy look and clenched her hands into fists.

The Falcon watched her over steepled fingers as the man worked, almost daring her to try pulling away. She held his gaze, glaring back unblinking, but she couldn't stifle her gasps. The bands of iron she felt around her chest were constricting more and more as the artisan continued his etching. There was no burning pain this time, but the sharp needle-like tools screeched as they dragged over the metallic surface.

Every so often, he asked Tannin to move so that he could get to every one of the symbols. No line was left untraced, and when he was finally satisfied, he polished the metal with an unpleasant smelling balm.

"I am finished, my laird," he said mutedly, bowing and stepping back from the desk.

Tannin rubbed her chest. She thought she had grown accustomed to the feeling of wrongness it gave her, but whatever boost her bracers had just been given disturbed her deeply.

The smile the Falcon gave her would have been warm, but his eyes were steel.

"There," he said. "That should help you with your restlessness."

He nodded to the artisan and then to Tannin. "You may leave."

Tannin had only managed the stairs down from the laird's office and half a corridor before she needed to take a break. Her energy had been sapped out. She leaned heavily on a window ledge to catch her breath.

"Fucker," she muttered under her breath.

"Do you require assistance?" Malcolm asked smugly, trailing behind her as always.

Tannin gave a hollow, "From you? No. Fuckin' snitch."

"You've had a trying morning. May I suggest a little nap?"

He was most definitely laughing at her from behind his helmet.

"Fuck you." Her head swam but she still managed to glare at him. "What is even your problem?"

"My problem?" he sneered. "My problem is that I am a knight. A fighter. A warrior. My brethren are, at this moment, fighting for their kingdom on the Brochlands front and I am here. Carrying out this honourless, thankless task."

"It's not my fault you've got a shitty job." Tannin closed her eyes. She felt so weak.

In the end, Tannin did retire to her bedchamber even though it was barely midday. Not that she was being permitted to leave her rooms anyway. She slept for hours and only ate a few mouthfuls of the food Orlaith set out for her that evening. Her head was fuzzy and her limbs extraordinarily heavy.

That night, getting the amulet down from the gutter was almost impossible, and as she crawled back inside to sprawl face-down on the rug in exhaustion, Tannin still wasn't sure how she managed it.

You're late. I was worried.

Tannin squeezed the brooch, letting her thoughts flow uncoordinatedly from her mind, hoping that Ava could unravel the jumble.

A re-etching? Oh Tannin, I'm so sorry. You should get used to the new restriction in a few days from what I know of it. Try to rest. Did you really have to do that? Oh, you fool.

Ava might have been calling her names, but she said it softly. Gently. Tannin wanted so much to hear those words spoken aloud. To have her hair stroked or her back rubbed. She squeezed her eyes shut.

Just...distract me. Ava, please? How was my funeral?

Sombre at first. We burnt your fake body. There was some singing. And then everyone got drunk.

Ah. Good. Wouldn't have had it any other way.

That's what Flint said. He said you would have wanted a piss-up, a dance and for him to find a pretty girl by the end of the night.

Tannin laughed as she crawled across the rug to lean against the foot of her bed. It was so much effort.

Have you told him I'm not dead?

Yes, he knows now. Gauging from people's reactions, I think I've managed to work out who would be on our side. We'll gather those who are loyal and then leave. The sooner the better.

Tannin considered it.

Okay, that's actually smart. You and Flint wouldn't last a day on your own.

Ideally, I want to leave in two days' time, as soon as the sun rises.

You are gonna stage a mass desertion in broad fuckin' daylight? Are you insane?

Correct me if I'm wrong, but wargs can see in the dark.

Yes, but—

So, why would we disadvantage ourselves? Personally, I quite like being able to see.

Okay, smart-arse. Seems like a risk, though.

It's riskier to stay. It's only a matter of time before they either realise we know or Dana goes through with her plan to ransom me now that you're not here to fight for me – don't deny it. I know you did. Besides, they won't even know we're gone until it's too late. They'll be too busy.

Busy with what? What are you going to do?

I'll keep you updated, of course, but you know I can't tell you anything. We'll be safe when we get to the caves.

What caves?

Tannin.

I know, I know. You can't tell me. Just be safe. Please.

After she was finally let out of her chambers, Tannin spent her time loitering in the gardens and feeling sorry for herself. She actually felt like she'd missed out, not having been at her own funeral. She wondered what Dana had said in her speech. Had she written it on the journey home after leaving her here, the traitor? She'd make sure Dana never had a funeral, Tannin promised herself as she shredded a leaf she'd picked off one of the hedges as she sat in the garden. She'd die un-mourned.

Tannin reached for another leaf with numb fingers. It was damn cold, and she was bundled up in a thick cloak and furry hat, but she refused to stop going out into the garden every day. She didn't have the energy to walk for any length of time anymore though and had to take regular breaks to gather her strength back. She felt pathetically frail.

Leaves rustled around her, disturbed by the chilly wind. No...not by the wind. Tannin narrowed her eyes in the direction of the sounds, and sure enough, caught a glimpse of a face and a flash of dark hair from behind the bushes.

Her usual watchers were a lot sneakier than that.

"Who's there?" she called, causing whoever it was to startle and rustle the bush.

She heaved herself off the bench and strode to the bushes. By the time she got there, all that was in the space behind them were footprints in the frosty grass.

"What are you doing, little bird?" Malcolm was in a bad mood like he always was when Tannin made him go out in the cold. She told him he was welcome to stay inside and she'd go alone, but he always declined.

"Someone was watching me." Tannin thwacked at the hedge.

"Probably just the gardener," he replied stretching out his stiff legs. "If the gardens are too…overstimulating for you, then maybe you should return to your chambers."

Tannin heard the veiled threat.

"No," she said quickly. "I want to stay outside."

Today was the day Ava and Flint were staging the desertion. If she had to spend today stuck inside, she was going to lose her damn mind with worry.

Distraction. She needed a distraction, and the calm of the neatly tended gardens wasn't providing it.

She cocked her head to the side. She could hear the crack of blunted swords. Guards sparring in the courtyard. That would have to do.

Tannin didn't visit the main courtyard often for the simple reason that there were always people there, but today, that was exactly what she wanted.

She sniffed as she walked out to the top of the staircase that led down to the courtyard. The hidden guards watching her today were the ones she had named Onion and Musty in her head. They all smelled vaguely like sweat, leather and metal, but by now, she could tell one from the other. There was Onion, Musty, Smoky, Fishy, Sawdust and Alehouse. At least two of them were always hidden somewhere nearby. When they weren't on hidden spy duty, she sometimes saw them walking around on other errands or when they were outside her door. With their faces covered and identical uniforms, there was very little to use to tell them apart. But Tannin had her suspicions. She willing to bet they were Remnants. Just like Malcolm. She supposed she should feel honoured that she warranted such special sentries even in her powerless, weakened state.

The guards practicing down in the courtyard, though? Not so much of a threat. Tannin stifled a laugh as one of the young men was knocked on his arse by a blow from a shield.

She wasn't the only spectator either. A gaggle of young serving women stood almost directly beneath where she stood on the stairs. Dotted around the edges were a few of the older nobles looking for a little entertainment. One young man in particular seemed to be attracting a lot of the attention. He wore no helmet, his dark hair slicked back with perspiration, and his bare arms rippled with muscle as he brought his blunted sword down in a brutal overhead swing to smash into his opponent's shield so hard it forced him to the ground.

"Yield!"

The cry came before the dark-haired man could bring the sword down again on his hapless foe. Instead, he offered the fallen guard a hand, and upon pulling him to his feet shoved him away to the side of the square with a jest and a slap on the back. The audience below applauded politely and he bowed to the young ladies.

He must be someone important.

The man joined the other trainee guards at the side and accepted a tankard from one of them. It seemed the sparring was over. Tannin pouted. She had hoped for more of a show. She was going to turn away and maybe head to the library or back to the gardens when there was a whistle and the pounding of hooves.

A cheer rang up from below. Clearly, this next entertainment was what they were waiting for.

The two horses snorted as they trotted into the square. The woman on the back of the leading horse swirled her ribboned spear artistically to the sounds of applause. A knight? Tannin smiled to herself. Maybe a little spiteful fun would help take her mind off her friends being in mortal peril.

She slunk down the stairs to mingle with the serving girls below. She heard her keeper following, slightly more urgently that usual. Malcolm is a suspicious one, she thought with a smile as she took a casual stance at the edge of the square right where the horses would pass by.

If she hadn't been watching for it, she would have missed the shudder that went through the beasts as they caught her scent. With the blinkers fastened to the sides of their heads, they couldn't see her yet, though. And they were trotting ever closer.

Just as the nearest horse turned its head in her direction, she flipped her hair over her shoulder, the motion catching its attention, and locked eyes with the animal.

It froze instantly, jolting the rider in the saddle. Its eyes grew impossibly wide and rolled back as the horse tossed its head and let out a piercing, terrified scream. It bucked and staggered backwards, the knight fighting to control the reins. The terror was infectious, and soon, both knights ended up on the ground as the horses fled.

Tannin covered her mouth to hide her laughter and hoped she looked suitably shocked. A looming presence over her left shoulder ruined the moment.

"You did that on purpose," Malcolm growled, glaring at her through the eye holes of the helmet.

"Did what?" Tannin replied with an angelic smile. "I didn't do anything."

The scent of onions and mouldiness had grown ever so slightly stronger. Tannin wondered if they had their crossbows aimed at her already, or if they gave her more of the benefit of the doubt than Malcolm did.

"Yes. You did."

"Let's agree to disagree."

"They could have been badly hurt. This is not funny."

"As I said, not my fault."

"You are pushing it, little bird."

She gave him a sweet smile. "I've done nothin' and you know it."

In the end, the thick fluffy snowflakes that started to fall forced her back inside before she was quite ready to. Malcolm let her take another book from the library at least before she was locked in her chambers again. She picked at the peeling leather of the spine as she nursed a cup of tea on her window ledge seat and listened to the wind howl outside as the storm picked up. She hadn't managed to muster the enthusiasm to actually read any yet.

Would it be storming over Dunoak too? Was that good or bad for her friends' escape? Had they gotten out yet? Ava had said they would take off first thing in the morning, but who knew?

Pacing would be suspicious, so she forced herself to remain glued to the window ledge as usual. Tannin bit her nails and watched the snow pile up outside. They'd grown a little since Malcolm had made Orlaith trim them, but at the rate she was chewing them, soon she wouldn't have any left.

Even when Orlaith said her usual goodnight and blew all but one candle out, Tannin still stayed at the window, clutching her empty cup.

Chapter Fifty-Five

Escape from Dunoak

Ava

"You are insane. This will never work! They will know!" Flint whispered as they stood in the pantry in the dead of night. It was the only place Ava felt safe enough to talk.

"Thank you for your faith in me," Ava replied drily. "Just drink from your own cup and you'll be fine."

"What did you put in the ale?"

"Nothing." Ava gave him a wicked grin. "I can't be sure everyone will drink the ale."

"You're going to poison all the drinks?" Flint's cheeks were already pale with apprehension, but as she had told him her plan to make sure no wargs followed them in their escape, he had steadily lost more and more colour.

"Of course not. Too risky." Ava reached into her skirts to hold up the vial she had prepared earlier. "I'm going to poison the goblets."

The poison she used wouldn't kill. Slow acting enough that they would suspect bad meat or a stomach flu before anyone said the word "sabotage", Ava had picked the toxin carefully. No one had looked hard enough at her little memorial garden to see the deadly herbs amongst the pretty petals. She poured a generous measure of the liquid into a cloth and wiped it around the rim of every goblet the kitchens had to offer. It was potent enough to put a warg out of action. She grimaced inwards to think of how it would affect any human who drank from the tainted cups.

Still not enough to kill. But it won't be pretty.

By the following evening, Nyesha and her Skirters were already on the road, having left one or two at a time all day to avoid suspicion. Eoghan and Collum had gone with them. Catriona, Douglas, Ava and Flint would follow with a handful of warg-bloods the next morning at sun up. They would meet in a glen to the west and then onwards to a network of smugglers' caves that Nyesha said would be empty. When she'd asked how she could be sure, Nyesha had given Ava a smile full of secrets and said it was better she didn't know the details.

Throughout the dinner, while everyone around them was unwittingly poisoning themselves, Ava tried to distract Flint with card games. At least then his eyes weren't darting around the room. He might have been a cunning conman back in the Skirts of Armodan, but this level of subterfuge was clearly playing on his mind. A thin layer of perspiration beaded his upper lip, and Ava didn't think he'd managed more than two mouthfuls of his stew. To be fair, it was eels again and she never felt like eating it either.

When it was finally a reasonable enough time to excuse themselves, she had to pinch him to stop him from actually running out of the hall.

"Will you calm down!" she hissed at him under her breath when they were out of earshot.

"I can't help it!" he hissed back. "Oh gods, I think I'm going to be sick."

"We have a little time now. Make sure you have everything you need and double-check the horses."

Old Angus, the horsemaster, would be distraught at the loss of his treasured beasts, but they needed them more. If anything went wrong tonight, they needed to get out as fast as possible. Ava hoped he would understand.

She hadn't even attempted sleep, knowing how futile it would be. Her stomach roiled with nerves. Her and her brothers had once taken a boat out on the seas during an official visit to Rill. They'd been caught in a surprise summer storm. She had felt a similar level of sick and terrified then as they were tossed on the waves.

The sky was lightening when she crept out of her room to the stables. Silently, her and Flint packed up the horses with their scant belongings. Catriona and Douglas would leave separately to avoid spooking the animals.

"Ready to go?" Flint whispered, giving his grey dappled mount an affectionate pat on the nose.

"Wait. Not yet." Ava took a deep breath. It had been playing on her mind, and now that it came to it, she couldn't just leave it. "I have one last thing to get."

"What is so important?" he demanded.

Ava set her jaw.

"I can't let her have Tannin's crown."

As Ava approached Dana's room, she was heralded by the sound of heaving. It appeared her plan was very much working and the wargish leader was indisposed. She wouldn't be leaving the latrine any time soon. Ava slipped into her chambers.

The curtains were drawn, casting the room into gloom despite the lone candle that flickered on the bedside table. Dana's room was huge. Easily double the size that Tannin's room in the guest wing had been, Ava realised with a flicker of anger.

Dana always saw herself as the leader, even when proclaiming Tannin queen. She had coveted that crown from the very start.

Speaking of crowns...

On the dressing table, Ava spied the varnished, wooden case that she knew held Tannin's disgusting fang crown. Taking the whole box would be too obvious. Ava had brought a cushioned sack with her to hold the atrocity while they travelled. She could get a proper case for it later.

She knelt to insert a pin into the tiny lock. After Flint had offered to teach her, Ava had practised almost every day. No lock could stand in her way now. The lock clicked satisfyingly. Ava lifted the hideous, bony crown from its velvet resting place in utter silence.

Silence.

The sounds of Dana's misery had stopped.

"What is this?"

The snarl came from directly behind her and Ava spun. Dana stood in the doorway, raven hair plastered to her forehead and a wooden bucket clutched in her arms.

"Uh...."

Words failed her as Dana stalked into the room.

Actions, however, did not. One arm looped through the crown, the fangs scraping the inside of her wrist, Ava seized the box and threw it at the warg as hard as she could.

It missed, but Dana still ducked. And then stumbled. She hit the floor. The poison had left her weak. Ava saw her chance. She ran. The doorway was a hair's breadth away. All she had to do was—

The wooden bucket crashed into the back of her legs, sending her sprawling into the carpeted hallway. The crown flew from her grasp. On her hands and knees, Ava frantically started to crawl after it, but a vice-like grip closed around her ankle. She shrieked as she was dragged backwards. She twisted around in time to see Dana raise up on her knees, arm drawn back and claws extended. Her face was a twisted snarl of fury.

Ava managed to throw up an arm to shield herself and cried out as those blade-like claws bore down on her. She braced herself for pain that never came. Cautiously, she lowered her arm. Dana was panting with exertion. She swayed as she took in the scratches she'd made across the floor, inches from Ava's head. Her eyes were unfocused.

She missed.

Ava seized the momentary respite. Her heart rattled in her ribcage. She was certain that, without her little poison trick, Dana would have been able to cleave her in half in one swipe.

She scrabbled down the front of her dress to the whistle she'd kept there since she realised the wargs' betrayal. It was a bastardised version of the one she'd used to check Tannin's Remnant status all that time ago in an alley in the Skirts. She hadn't had time to test it. All she had was hope. She brought it to her lips just as Dana's teeth started to lengthen.

No sound came from the thin reed whistle. None that Ava could hear. But Dana's eyes grew wide for an instant, and then her face crumpled as she curled in on herself, hands clamped over her ears. An agonised, keening wail ripped from her throat, and blood leaked from between her fingers.

Ava scooted backwards, away from Dana. She scrabbled to her feet and bolted from the room. She had just stooped to retrieve the fallen crown when a small, petrified voice stopped her in her tracks.

"Miss Ava?"

Oh no.

"Alby," Ava gasped, spinning round. "Alby, what are you doing here?"

"I heard..." The boy trailed off as another tortured moan came from the open door to Dana's chambers.

"I have to go Alby. It's not safe for me here anymore." Ava straightened up, tucking the fanged crown safely into the cushioned sack.

"I'm coming too."

"No, Alby. You can't come," Ava said desperately. "You can't come where I have to go."

"I'll follow you."

Ava's argument was cut off by an ear-splitting scraping. Blood-tipped claws grasped the door frame as Dana dragged herself through. Her hair was matted with blood, her eyes wild as they slid from Ava to Alby.

Ava gave the whistle another savage blow, relishing in Dana's pathetic whimper as she once more cowered. But the damage was done. She'd seen them together. She couldn't leave Alby here to face her wrath.

She turned to him breathlessly. It wasn't safe to take him, but it would be worse to leave him behind. His huge eyes were filled with fear, but there was a determination there. He wasn't going to accept being left behind.

"Alright, you win. Ready for an adventure?"

Chapter Fifty-Six

Close calls

The bustling of breakfast being set up in the other room roused a groggy Tannin from her sleep. Even though she'd quickly changed into dry night clothes and buried herself under her blankets the night before, she could feel the beginnings of a vicious cold.

Stretching and rubbing her eyes, she stumbled into the room, trying and failing to straighten her rumpled nightshirt, to find a note delivered to her rooms along with breakfast.

Tannin read it, scoffed and scrunched it into a ball.

Orlaith gave her a questioning look.

"An invite to a yuletide carriage ride in the snow with some other nobles. I bet everyone got one this morning."

"Well, that sounds lovely," she chided as Tannin tossed the balled-up invite in the air and caught it again.

Tannin stared at her until she realised and then turned red.

"Oh."

"Mhm. Still a prisoner here, remember?" She tapped her bracers with a piece of bacon she'd grabbed from the platter. "Horses don't like wargs anyway."

Orlaith visibly flinched at the word warg.

"What's the matter? Did you forget I'm a big, scary monster?"

"I said no such thing."

Tannin quirked an eyebrow. "Warg."

Orlaith flinched again.

"Cutlery is on the table," she said pointedly to change the subject.

Tannin scowled and plucked another piece of bacon from her plate with her fingers.

"So, where do we stand on getting a fire going in here? You have to admit this is way too damn cold to be healthy." Tannin took a gulp of tea. "Orlaith, did you hear me?"

Tannin turned, intending to say something peevish when the maid still didn't answer her, but the words died in her mouth when she saw Orlaith frozen, staring at the broken latch to the balcony doors. As always, Tannin had balanced it carefully so that nothing looked out of the ordinary, but it must have come loose and swung back down sometime during the night. Orlaith glanced at Tannin, face pale.

"Something wrong?" Tannin tried to sound nonchalant, but she knew she looked as guilty as sin.

The maid's eyes darted from Tannin to the door where the usual guards were no doubt stationed right outside.

"Don't—" Tannin warned but Orlaith darted for the door.

Tannin was faster and grabbed her around the waist, both of them toppling to the floor.

"Listen to me!" She slapped a hand over the girl's mouth before she could yell for the guards. "No harm, no foul. I'm still here, aren't I? If they see this, then we're both in trouble, so shut your goddam mouth and pretend you didn't see a thing."

Tannin blabbered it out and the servant's expression turned to one of dismay. Tannin could see her thought process as she weighed up how much trouble she'd be in if she said anything versus how much worse it could be if they found out later that she'd hidden it.

"Sir Malcolm broke the lock and he would get in so much trouble if people knew."

She hoped she had read the girl correctly. With all the glances and blushes and innocent comments about "Sir Malcolm", Tannin was sure Orlaith fancied the hell out of him. The dismay that flickered across her features at Tannin's comment just about confirmed it.

"So, are you going to keep this between us?"

After what seemed like an eternity, Orlaith's head bobbed in agreement and Tannin released her.

"I didn't see anything," she mouthed, eyes still wide and fearful.

Tannin breathed a sigh of relief. "Smart girl."

Orlaith side-eyed Tannin warily as she stood and straightened her skirts. She cleared her throat.

"Will that be all for now, Miss?" she trilled.

"Aye. Thank you, Orlaith."

Oh gods, she'd better keep her mouth shut.

"You need lessons if you are ever going to pass for a lady of the Gormbraen courts," Malcolm said as he escorted her from the library where she'd spent the day.

The storm hadn't relented, and the air was thick with flurries that whipped at the windows and forced freezing draughts through every gap. Malcolm had tried to get her to stay in her rooms, but she'd insisted on visiting the library at least to get a new book and was set on staying when she saw the crackling fire in the grate. She'd given up on the last book completely before the second chapter, and she was determined to find one that didn't make her want to turn it into kindling. If Ava could be so enthusiastic about the damn things, then Tannin should be able to find at least one she liked.

"Excuse me, what?"

"You," Malcom sneered. "Every inch of you just screams common."

"Maybe because I am?"

"Not anymore."

"You have got to be kiddin' me," Tannin said in dismay as she opened the door to her chambers. Instead of her usual evening meal, Orlaith was setting up her small dining table with a white cloth and polished silver utensils.

"It's the laird's wish that you integrate with the courts." Malcolm had followed her into her chambers. "Therefore, you will have to learn all the subtleties of court life to avoid embarrassment."

"I am not having dinner with you," she said flatly.

"You are if you want to eat dinner at all. Sit. It's time you learn how to be a lady."

"Because you're such a lady yourself," Tannin muttered under her breath but took a seat at the table regardless. She usually looked out the window when she ate, watching the birds or the leaves or the clouds or anything that wasn't contained within the walls of her chambers.

Multiple sets of cutlery accompanied a myriad of differently sized plated and wine glasses. As Tannin twirled a tiny spoon in her fingers, Malcolm rounded the table.

"You gonna eat with your helmet on?" Tannin raised an eyebrow. "Seems impractical."

"Put the spoon down."

"Oh, look it's you!" She picked up a solid silver salt cellar with a domed top and made it walk across the table. "My name is Malcolm and I am a shiny tin man," she said deepening her voice. "I have no sense of humour and I—"

Malcolm reached over and slapped it out of her hand.

"Now, now," she chided, "that wasn't very lady-like."

Malcolm refused to indulge her by taking the bait. He sat down opposite her without a word as his gauntleted fingers fiddled under his chin for the clasp of his helmet.

Underneath, his face was flushed either in anger at her or just from being crammed in a metal box all day, and his reddish brown hair was plastered to his head. A hand dragged through it unglued it a little, but it still lay stubbornly flat against his skull. He didn't have all that unpleasant a face, Tannin decided, apart from an ill-advised attempt to grow a moustache.

"Nice to put a face to the name at last."

Chapter Fifty-Seven

Smugglers' Den

Ava

"Why in the damned circles of hell is there a bairn on yer horse?"

After the incident with Dana, there had been no time to pack anything for Alby. He sat behind Ava on the horse, swamped by one of her cloaks to hold off the chill. It made him look even smaller than he was.

"Who are you calling a bairn?" he piped up from behind Ava. She'd explained the wargs' treachery on the way to the glen where they met up with the rest of their deserters, and he had gobbled it up. He had babbled about avenging and righteousness for the last half hour, and it seemed to have emboldened his spirits. He did, however, grip Ava's waist tighter when Nyesha turned her eye on him.

"We had some…complications," Ava offered as she disentangled herself from the kitchen boy and dismounted. She was keen for rest and some food. It wasn't far from Dunoak to their meeting place, but it was far enough that she was already worn out.

"Were ye followed?"

"Not out of the city," Flint replied. "Ava slowed them all down."

Ava shot him a grateful look for the vote of confidence.

"Still, looks like we cannae afford tae lose time." Nyesha turned to the gathered group.

Catriona and Douglas had beaten the horses there. Leaving the animals at a safe distance, Ava approached. With them were two young men Ava recognised as warg-bloods from Tannin's protection escort. At the questioning look Catriona gave her, Ava gave her what she hoped passed for a reassuring smile.

"Did you take care of scouts?" Ava asked her.

When Ava had told her the plan, Catriona had offered to call in a debt to make sure they were not tracked after leaving the city. Adair himself was still in Dunoak, but his rangers were out patrolling and monitoring as always. Ava had hoped that her poison stunt would call them in to help rather than send them chasing after them.

"We've got friends in the woods," Catriona replied with a confident nod. "They'll send word if we're followed.

"Get ready to move yer arses in ten minutes!" Nyesha's growl sailed over the group.

"That's it then," Ava muttered under her breath. "We're really doing this."

"Yep." Flint's face was drawn. "We're really doing this."

Usually, Ava would have followed their route with rapt interest, noting landmarks and plotting maps in her head. Not this time. She was bone-tired from days with little to no sleep and scared out of her mind. Every bird call in the trees had her startling, convinced that an army of slavering beasts was going to descend and kill them all. She knew they had travelled south-west and that was it.

The snow had held off, but bitter winds still nipped at them, especially at night. Under Nyesha's orders, they never stopped for more than a few hours at a time, snatching little more than a nap's worth of sleep at a time. On the first night, Alby had offered to sleep next to Ava. To protect her in case the monsters came, he said. The next night, he hadn't asked but scooted up right beside her anyway. She'd held his freezing cold hand until he drifted off.

The evening of the third day, they arrived at Nyesha's network of smugglers' caves. They left the horses in a sheltered, leafy ravine and continued on foot. A narrow crevice in an otherwise unremarkable jumble of stones led to a narrow tunnel, supported by thick, wooden beams. Brackets for torches stood empty along the walls.

Douglas offered to go first. As a warg, the darkness didn't bother him, and he assured them all that if anything or anyone had made a home in the caves since Nyesha was last there, he was more than willing to evict them. The tunnel was a tight squeeze for his hulking frame.

When he returned, brushing spider webs from his beard, he announced the coast was clear. The party gratefully lit torches and followed him back inside.

Ava hadn't let herself think of what living in a cave would be like in case she lost her nerve. Whatever she could have dreamt up, though, she would never have expected the sight that met her eyes. As the tunnel widened out, the light of the torches barely brushed the cavernous ceiling. The roaring echo of running water nearly deafened her as they continued further until the cavern opened out completely. Ava couldn't stifle her gasp. Glittering water fell in a cascade from what seemed like miles above their heads to crash into a crystal pool. Nyesha ushered them further, to an adjoining cavern that branched off into other tunnels and crevices. Here, the ceiling and walls had, again, been reinforced with wooden beams. Tables and benches – enough to seat two dozen – stood in the centre. Covered in dust but entirely sturdy and useable. In the adjacent "rooms", Ava could see barrels, crates, boxes and shelves full of jars and bottles. If those were full, they could feed their small group for weeks. She shot Nyesha an amazed, incredulous glance.

"Told ye this place was perfect." The older woman smirked. "Fresh water and aboot half those stores will still be good. Lots of escape tunnels."

Ava sat down heavily on a bench, not caring about the dust, as Nyesha barked out orders of where to store the supplies they had managed to bring. Weariness had made her dizzy. She didn't get to rest long.

"Come wi' me."

Nyesha didn't make it sound like a request.

Ava reluctantly followed through a maze of antechambers until Nyesha came to a stop in a shadowy corner. Ava glanced behind her. They were alone.

"Are you going to kill me?" Ava blurted. She was too tired for diplomacy.

Nyesha laughed.

"Now, what would be the point in that?" She folded her arms and regarded her shrewdly. "We're gonna have tae work out some sorta agreement here. My people follow me tae the death, but the rest are lookin' tae you. Gods know why."

"What do you propose?" Ava lifted her chin. She wasn't going to be bullied out of the chance at leadership. Not after she'd risked everything.

"I'll admit, yer no the pampered, wee, lying, jumped-up, royal bitch I thought ye were."

"Thank you?"

"Don't get me wrong. I still dinnae like ye. But ye've earned yer place."

Ava held her hand out. "A partnership, then?"

"Dinnae get ahead of yerself." Nyesha ignored the outstretched hand with a scoff. "This is still my place and mostly my people. Ye can be...now, what was it the wargs called it?...my second."

"And you won't kill me in my sleep?"

Nyesha's smile carried no humour.

"If I come for you, lass, you'll be awake for it. Promise."

That was not at all comforting.

Ava swallowed. "I accept."

Bed rolls were set up all in one room, side by side, and before everything had even been unpacked, Ava had crawled into one. She wasn't even sure it was hers.

She ignored the mutters of disapproval that floated past from Nyesha's thugs. Ava knew she was weaker than the rest, but at that moment, she could not have cared less. They had made it. They had survived. They were safe.

A few of the containers had been cracked open so that they could have a celebratory dinner of salted meat, stale crackers and jam. The smugglers' provisions would keep them fed, but they certainly wouldn't offer any enjoyment, it seemed. Food-wise anyway.

Over the general hum of conversation, the sound of Eoghan's flute lilted into the sleeping chamber. Ava trailed her finger over the cushioned sack beside her. She hadn't let anyone else take responsibility for it, and she hadn't told anyone what it contained. She and Nyesha would present it together with an emotion-filled, motivational speech to their loyal troops, she decided as she nuzzled into the furs.

And then, they would go save their queen.

Chapter Fifty-Eight

Dining with the enemy

Tannin

The occasional etiquette lesson aside, Tannin's days consisted of huddling by the library fire or pacing her sitting room. When a summons to dine with the laird and a "special guest" was delivered, she was elated at the possibility of something to do. Until she saw what it arrived with, of course.

Tannin stood with her arms crossed and glowered at the box that had been delivered with the dinner invitation. Inside was a dress. A dress the Falcon had picked out for her.

"I hate it," was the first thing that spilled out of Tannin's mouth when she saw the gift. "And I'm not going."

"It's not optional."

Tannin narrowed her eyes at her keeper, trying to decide how far to push it.

As if reading her thoughts, Malcolm barked at the servants who had accompanied him, "Get her dressed. I don't care how you do it. Have her ready by six."

He locked the door behind him. Tannin clenched her teeth.

"Stupid fuckin'..." she muttered under her breath and ran her hands through her hair.

Choose your battles, Tannin.

In the end, she let the servants bathe, dress, paint and decorate her in Gormbraen finery, even as her discomfort mounted. She wasn't surprised that the dress chosen for her was red. Of course, Laird Cormack wanted her in Gormbraen colours as she was paraded about like a prize. Marking her as Gormbraen property. Tannin's lip curled back from her teeth in a snarl as she realised it. The servant trying to do her make-up chided her.

The gown was beautiful, though. And it had been clearly made for her or at least heavily tailored. Gold stitching and gems decorated the fabric, and the skirt flowed in velvety waves. It hugged every one of her curves and fell gracefully to the floor where, when she put on the shoes that went with it, it barely brushed the stone.

She swished her skirts and grimaced.

"Alright, I don't hate it."

The only thing she completely balked at was the gorgeous, ruby necklace that came with the rest of the jewellery. Even after all this time, the thought of something around her neck had her blood freezing in her veins and her stomach turning to water. She knew she wouldn't be allowed to refuse it, so when the servants' backs were turned, she broke the clasp and then unconvincingly feigned innocence when asked about it.

At six o'clock sharp, Malcolm returned to collect her and gave an approving grunt when he saw that she was indeed dressed and ready. She followed him mutely to the laird's private dining room.

"Do not forget your lessons and do not embarrass me," he growled in her ear.

"Wouldn't dream of it." She gave him a nasty smile in return.

It wasn't like she had known nothing at all. Ava had taught her well in preparation for the visit to Gormbrae in the first place as well as scolding her for lapses in manners on a daily basis. Lessons with Malcolm had been prickly and frustrating and weren't even mellowed by any decent conversation. Besides dry instructions, they ate in silence. They walked in silence. If Malcolm could have instructed her in small talk in silence, he would have. He seemed to despise her more and more as time went on, and she was thoroughly glad to be rid of him for an evening even if it meant dinner with the laird in her stupid, fancy dress.

The Falcon rose when she entered the room and inclined his head. "Lady Tannin."

"Laird Cormack," Tannin said, ducking into a curtsey that was only barely low enough to be acceptable.

"I see you received my gift."

"I did."

His expression suggested he expected thanks. Tannin hoped hers expressed how much that wasn't going to happen.

"The colour becomes you."

Laird Cormack moved aside so that Tannin could see the other guests. The young man who had inspired so much admiration while sparring with the guards stood from the table. Now that they were in the same room, there was no mistaking the family resemblance between him and the Falcon. Benwald. Laird

Cormack's son. She thought she'd overheard he wasn't supposed to be back from the Brochlands front for weeks.

The lairdling dipped his head in her direction.

"Benwald. A pleasure to make your acquaintance, my lady."

"Hm." He tipped his head to the side to regard Malcolm as he hovered behind Tannin, clearly unsure if he was expected to stay or not. "You've certainly got yourself a ferocious guard dog. Mal, that's you in there is it not? Bit of a step down for you surely?"

His tone was friendly enough, but there was no denying the cutting insult behind it. Tannin clamped her lips together to stop from oohing.

Malcolm dipped his head stiffly, respectful in spite of the resentment that was radiating from him in waves.

"Ben."

"Thank you, Malcolm. That will be all."

If her keeper chafed at the laird's swift dismissal, it didn't show as he marched from the room.

Tannin turned her attention back to the guests. She didn't recognise the other man seated at the table.

"Lady Tannin, I'd like to introduce one of my oldest friends and advisors, Sir Richmund." Laird Cormack clapped the man on the shoulder. "Richmund, meet our latest ward, Lady Tannin."

Tannin startled. Richmund. The father of the young man from the dungeon. The one the Falcon had had beaten to within an inch of his life. If Sir Richmund lamented his son's fate, he certainly hid it well as he stood and took one of her hands in his. He pressed his lips to her knuckles.

Ugh.

"Your Majesty," he inclined his head respectfully as he stood but the layer of mockery behind his words was evident.

Benwald smirked across the table and Tannin froze.

"Ah." Tannin grit her teeth.

"Old Cormack informed me that he had a...special guest." His eyes grazed over her. "I admit I took some convincing, but I suppose the tales do match. The fearsome Feral Queen really is just a pretty little thing after all."

Tannin shot Laird Cormack a glare out of the corner of her eye. He merely pulled out her chair for her and filled her glass with a dark red wine.

"How are you finding life here at the Falcon's Rest, my lady? Is everything to your liking?"

Tannin shrugged. "As much as can be expected."

She tried to curb her common accent and speak like Ava did, but it felt wrong on her tongue. Even straightening her spine, shoulders back, sitting the way Ava showed her that she should felt wrong and uncomfortable.

I feel like an eejit. I bet I look like an eejit too.

Laird Cormack watched her discomfort over steepled fingers. Benwald clicked his fingers for the jug of wine to be refilled, but Richmund wasn't done with her yet.

"You are much different to the stories I've heard, my lady."

"I hear that a lot," Tannin said smoothing her skirts.

"So young."

"I'm older than I look."

"And more trouble than you look, I've heard." He chuckled at his own joke. "Or you were anyway. His lairdship tells me you're on your way to becoming a lady of the courts."

Over my dead body.

"You certainly look the part," he said, scanning her appearance. "Excellent choice, Cormack."

The two men were also finely dressed, with jewels on almost every finger and exquisitely tailored doublets. Benwald had chosen to skip the dress code it seemed and wore a simple linen shirt. Although, Tannin had to admit he was one of those people who probably would have looked good wearing anything.

Laird Cormack's lips twitched into a smile at the compliment.

"Since we are discussing gifts, I have one more to bestow." He beckoned to a tall servant who had been hovering near the door with a heavy-looking, wooden box in his arms. "For you, my son."

Benwald grinned in slight confusion as the box was placed on the table. "What for?"

"You're becoming a man now. You've visited the Brochlands front on behalf of Gormbrae and stood before our men – men who will follow you one day. I want you to have a weapon that shows your strength and the strength of the Falcon name."

Not actually your name, but whatever.

Tannin fidgeted. This seemed like a private moment and she felt downright awkward just sitting there. Why on earth had he picked this moment to give this gift?

Benwald squared his shoulders and opened the box. Tannin stood on her tiptoes to peek inside.

Oh.

Inside were a pair of gleaming axes. Tannin's axes.

"I don't quite understand, father," Benwald said cautiously, as he peered at the simple weapons. "I would've thought your father's sword..."

Laird Cormack tutted. "My father's sword is a relic. A symbol, yes, but these too are a symbol." He slung an arm around his son's shoulders. "The weapon of a fallen foe is a powerful thing."

His eyes flickered to Tannin, and Benwald followed his gaze. Tannin was sure her face was as red as her dress. She didn't trust herself to speak.

Cormack continued, "Let these be a symbol of Gormbraen strength. Druidic strength. Make them your own."

Tannin realised his tactic now. This was just yet another jab, another blow for her to take, another game for her to lose. Well, she wasn't going to bloody play. She forced herself to calm down as Benwald weighed her axes in his hands and flipped one over. He thanked the laird profusely but shot her an almost apologetic look as Cormack then turned to Richmund.

"Now that the formalities are over, shall we dine?"

At a click of his fingers, servants appeared with dish after dish of decadent foods until there was enough on the table to feed a dozen people.

As they dug into the feast, Cormack and Benwald exchanged some small talk on the younger's continuing lessons and plans to re-join the Brochlands front in the spring. Richmund contributed every now and again with anecdotes from his own boyhood education.

"You're very quiet," Sir Richmund remarked, turning to Tannin. "On my travels, I've heard so much of your exploits, and now you sit here silent?"

You'd been hoping for more of a show, you mean.

"Nothing to say." Tannin pushed a carrot around her plate. She had no appetite and no desire to be their plaything. Anger still coursed through her, but she squashed it. It was what they wanted.

"You are speaking to a good friend of mine and a Sir," Cormack said with a chiding edge to his voice.

"I don't care for titles," Tannin said lightly. "I've met kings before."

And done a lot more than dine with other royalty.

The thought threatened to make her smile and she stomped it down.

"Ah yes. King Florian." The name clearly left a bad taste in the Falcon's mouth. "Let's not talk of such things tonight."

"What do you want to talk about?"

"Well, you are by far the most interesting person in this fort. I know I want to hear your stories." Benwald grinned at her as he popped a morsel into his mouth.

"What do you want to know then?" She sighed.

"How about, what will it take to get you to smile for me?"

The two older men chuckled. Tannin fought the urge to mime vomiting. Benwald seemed to have forgotten that he had just been gifted her possessions. Either that or he hadn't realised the significance of it. She had been sure he had given her an apologetic look, but maybe that was some kind of smoulder he was going for. Did he even know they had been hers?

She might have been able to flirt some information out of the lairdling if they were on their own, but under the watchful eye of the laird, she knew she was just going to have to endure being the evening's entertainment.

"If you know who I am, you know I'm not here by choice. I don't have much to smile about."

"Maybe I can change that."

"My imprisonment or my smile?"

Benwald laughed. "Your beautiful smile, of course. And it's not so bad here, is it?" He gestured around the opulent dining room. "In fact, my father is throwing a masked ball to celebrate the yuletide."

"Is this going to be an invitation or a command?"

"Let's call it a non-negotiable invitation." His eyes, as green as his father's, crinkled as he smiled.

"I doubt I'll be allowed to go anyway." Tannin's eyes flickered to Cormack. She half hoped she wasn't allowed.

"Nonsense, of course you will attend. A lady of the courts should always attend a ball given by her laird." He gave her a wink. "Perhaps you'd like to honour my son with a dance?"

As much as I'd like to poke pins in my eyes. Is he trying to set me up with his son? Why the hell would he want that?

She forced herself to smile. "Well, that would be...nice."

She added a belated eyelash flutter.

Gods, I hate myself.

"Try the boar," Cormack said, changing the subject and indicating to a platter with a jab of his fork. "It's from today's hunt."

"You're lucky it didn't gore you to death," Tannin said mildly over the rim of her wine glass.

"That is a risk one takes. Hunting is a dangerous necessity. Accidents happen out there on the hunt." He paused. "That's what happened to your father isn't it?"

Tannin choked on her wine.

He pretended not to notice as she coughed and continued, "Just after you were born, wasn't it? Shame about your mother."

Tannin wiped her lips with the back of her hand.

"Dana has a big mouth," she growled, stabbing into a slice of meat more for something to do with her hands than because she actually wanted to eat it. If he was looking for a sore spot, he wasn't going to find it by taking a jab at her parents' deaths. She'd never known them. Childbirth took her mother, and like Cormack said, her father followed only days later.

"Mm," he said noncommittally. "Raised by your grandparents, I was told. Do you know I actually met your grandfather?"

He stopped, clearly waiting for a response.

"I didn't know that," Tannin said carefully.

"It was years ago. He came here, the ragged old fool, wanting to bargain. Said he had something that could make or break the wargs of the north if I was interested." He chuckled to himself. "Of course, at the time that meant nothing. What would I want with a bunch of recluses from the mountains? They were no threat to me. Now, however, I can't help but wonder what might have happened had I heard him out. Maybe you and I would be sat here together after all. On the same side. And you wouldn't be thinking about stabbing me with your cutlery."

He nodded to the fork clenched in her fist and tutted until she put it down. "Maybe we could have taken the Brochlands already. Who knows. A blood heir to Stonestead. Your grandfather didn't present as much of an ally, but you might have been. You still could be."

"You think I'll help you?" Tannin snorted in disbelief. "Why would I? You are literally keeping me prisoner here."

"This isn't just a whim of King Modric and I to bring you over to our side. It's been on my mind since I heard all about your...adventures in Armodan and connected the dots with old Aldrich. He mentioned he had a granddaughter. Alliance with the Dunoak wargs was the natural progression, and Dana only needed a little push to suggest this arrangement."

"You manipulated her."

"You'll find that the ones who think of themselves as the big players are the easiest to guide. I have players all across the board.

People who, when the time is right, will take action. You could be a part of the winning team."

"I could've won myself if I hadn't been stabbed in the back," Tannin snapped.

Richmund laughed outright. "The wargs are powerful, yes, but in the same way a wild beast is. Unorganised and brutish."

He stabbed himself a slice of boar, pointedly.

Cormack continued, swirling his wine, "Whereas we druids are more patient hunters. Organised. Cautious. And we are everywhere. Even the Armodian royal bloodline is blessed with druid blood."

Tannin fought to control her expression, but he was studying her closely and she failed miserably. She blamed the wine. She hadn't been allowed anything stronger than apple juice during her confinement, even though she had tried to wheedle Orlaith into bringing her some firewater.

"Hm, I did wonder if you knew. That answers that question."

Tannin swallowed.

"Triquetra," she said hoarsely trying to steer the conversation away from Ava.

"Well done."

"Not really. There's a massive fuckin' carving on the wall. Subtlety ain't your strong suit"

"Indeed, indeed." He smiled wryly at her outburst. "Where is she?"

"I don't know what you're talking about."

"My dear, I do not wish her harm," he said exasperatedly, rubbing his forehead. "I want Princess Avalyn on the throne of Armodan. Don't you see? Druid blood in control of the largest kingdom. Under our guidance, we could even unite Gormbrae and the Brochlands. Without bloodshed. We could take the north too. And if you sided with us, I'd even grant you regency over Stonestead if you liked. I'd give you all of Cascairn."

"No, you bloody wouldn't," Tannin scoffed. "Unless I was just your wee puppet."

"I'll let you think it over." He cocked his head at her. "I imagine a messenger to Dunoak will find the Princess Avalyn, won't it?"

Tannin didn't answer.

The Triquetra very much knew where Ava was, considering they'd tried to have her kidnapped. Either that meant those mercenaries weren't working for them or...someone within the Triquetra had gone rogue.

"She should never have been allowed to leave Armodan." He rubbed his eyes. "It complicates things a little. But she will take the throne eventually."

"But Prince Justus is next..." Tannin trailed off at the look he gave her. "You're going to kill him?"

"Oh, don't be so crude. When the time is right, he's just going to have a little accident."

"Just like Florian," Tannin whispered.

"Now you're getting it. There are plans that have been in motion from before you were even born."

"Did you..." Tannin frowned. "Did you plan Ava being a druid-blood?"

His eyebrows twitched at Tannin's use of her nickname. Tannin cursed herself for being so stupid.

"One could say that."

"How?"

"A tale as old as time, my lady," Richmund said and he and Cormack shared an amused look at a shared joke. Benwald looked as lost as she was.

Impatience scraped at her composure until Cormack spoke again.

"I simply sent one of my more charming ambassadors along as an emissary and straight into the queen's bed - her reputation did proceed her after all. A little fertility elixir and there you go. Ready-made, druid blood heir. Our little ace to be kept in hand until we were ready to play."

"She's not yours."

"Oh, but she is. She will play her part in time. As will you."

"What happened to the ambassador?"

"He forgot his duty."

"He's dead, isn't he?" Tannin said flatly.

"We all outlive our usefulness at some point."

"And what do you want from me? When do I outlive my usefulness?"

"Your cooperation is enough for now. We will discuss more when King Modric graces us with his presence in the spring." He was enjoying toying with her far too much. "You can relax until then. Appreciate the life of luxury that has been provided for you."

"But—"

"I think that's enough for one evening, don't you?" Cormack leaned back in his chair and smirked. "It's getting late, and you've been so very tired these days."

Tannin's fists knotted in her skirts.

"Cormack is right," Richmund said gesturing to the door with his wine goblet. "Run along to bed now, my lady."

Embarrassed and indignant as she was about being sent to bed like a child, Tannin couldn't even muster up a murderous daydream of revenge as she returned to her rooms. She was so out of her depth. If Cormack was telling the truth, then there were plans and plots and subplots and schemes running so deep that it would take her an age to try and figure out the slightest piece of the puzzle.

Telling Ava what she'd learned was just as awful as she thought it was going to be. Following her instructions, Tannin let the memory of the dinner play in her mind while holding the stone and let Ava see and hear for herself everything that they had said. Afterwards, she was quiet for such a long time that Tannin thought she was gone.

We have to warn my brother.

How exactly are we going to do that? There's an unknown assassin in your house. We have no idea who it is or when they're coming for you or who you can trust but good luck?

Don't make jokes about this!

I'm sorry. Tannin swallowed hard. *You have to go to Armodan. You have to warn him yourself. We don't know who we can trust.*

I am not leaving you.

You can't get me out of here, so what's the point? Tannin tried to keep the bitterness out of her thoughts. *You have to go. I'll find another way out.*

I'll come back for you, I promise. But in the meantime...
What are you thinking?

The Gormbraen troops are digging in for the winter. The last thing they'll be expecting is an attack...

Tannin's inner warg-flame perked up at the implication and at the raw savageness of Ava's feelings pouring in through the blood connection.

They could fight back.

Chapter Fifty-Nine

Ava's Army

Ava

One week after Tannin had dined with the laird, Ava's patchwork army of wargs, peasants and Skirter thugs prepared to attack the Gormbraen forces.

Ava stood at the table in the main cavern with her hand-drawn map of the camp rolled out in front of them. She'd stolen the parchment and ink from the camp itself.

She had been surprised how easy it had been to just walk in unchallenged. Dirt-streaked villagers combed the camp, begging for coins and scraps. With a torn shawl thrown over her shoulders and her hair crusted in mud, she had become invisible. The camp border was less than a day's walk from the cave's western entrance. She had organised shifts to cover the entire camp and note down their stores, supplies, numbers and weapons, as well as having Catriona or Douglas backtrack and check that Dana hadn't succeeded in tracking them down. In just one week, Ava and her spies had everything they needed to destroy the army from within.

"Group one. Nyesha's team. You have the most crucial job, and you'll have the most work to do. I'm trusting you to get this done. We know they have scouts on the ridge and patrolling in pairs. You work quickly and take them out as soon as darkness falls. Then, you each have your targets inside the main camp."

"We take them out quietly," Nyesha said glaring around at the group with her one good eye.

"Silently," Ava insisted. "If the alarm is raised, we can't hope to survive. Surprise and stealth are our only advantage."

Nyesha met her gaze and gave a solemn nod. As much as the old gang leader had been against a partnership, that was very much what their relationship had become. A grudging respect had brewed between them, and while they weren't about to sit together in the evening and chat, they had the same goal.

"I'll take group two into the camp itself and target their supplies." Ava patted the leather satchel that was slung over her shoulder, heavy with poisons and palm-sized ceramic balls filled with flammable liquids. The group eyed the bag with unease. They had seen her trial runs, launching the little spheres into a nearby clearing, leaving the grass scorched and smoking. No one wanted to get close.

"Group three will go to the village here, four will take the village here. No well or grain silo survives the night. We want this army to starve."

"What about the villagers?" Mackie, Nyesha's apprentice, asked with a frown.

"These villages are mostly empty now because of raider attacks. You've seen what's left of them."

Mostly empty.

Ava ignored the guilt that gnawed at her. Maybe forty villagers to take out a whole army. That was a price she could pay. A price she had to pay.

"Flint and his group five will take care of the horses here, here and here." She pointed out the stables that had been inked on her map. "I want at least ten brought back for us if you can manage it, and I want as many of the rest as possible taken out of the equation. Poison the corpses after. No fresh meat for these bastards."

Even in the dim candlelight of the cave, Ava could see the green tinge of Flint's face. He had volunteered for the task. He knew the beasts best and could give them a quick and painless death, he had said. She knew it would kill him to do it, but he made a good argument. He was, logically, the best choice for it.

He swallowed hard and his mouth was a grim line. As ill as he looked at the thought of it, Ava trusted him to do what he had to.

"We go at midday. I want everyone in position by dusk. Wait one hour for Nyesha's team to clear the way and then do your job. We meet on the ridge at sunrise."

"Do not get taken alive," Nyesha growled. Her eye lingered on Ava's face, clearly wondering if she had the guts to carry out that order.

Ava herself didn't know if she did. Her fingers found the clasp of her satchel. She would have to find that out at the time.

The wait crouched in the rocky outcrop above the camp was one of the longest waits of Ava's life. The minutes dragged on, and every distant shout from the soldiers below had her heart leaping into her mouth.

She placed a hand on the leather satchel at her side. She had everything she needed. She'd checked it thrice but couldn't help the twinge of unpreparedness. This whole operation was rushed. Yes, they technically had a plan, but it was more a rough sketch than anything she would call complete.

As the sun sank below the horizon, her adrenaline spiked. Nyesha's team would be getting to work. Ava checked her time piece and nodded to Collum. He would be coming with her, but she'd sent Eoghan with Flint. It was a little heartless, but she knew the brothers would disobey her instructions if it looked like the other was in trouble, and she needed everyone's focus.

It was time to go.

As they scrambled over the rocks, they found no signs of the lookouts or patrols on the hills. Nyesha's people were brutally efficient. It disturbed her a little how much they seemed to enjoy their work.

Under the cover of darkness and with the patrols taken out, the teams split up and snuck into the campgrounds without incident. Fires glowed from in between off-white tents and cast long shadows across the trampled ground.

Ava wore thick leather gloves in case any of the toxin spilled. Coaxing the stopper from the bottle was trickier than she'd anticipated, but she managed to tease it out and pour it into the first of the wells. The second and third, she poisoned mechanically until Collum's sharp intake of breath startled her. She looked up just as a man in a soldier's uniform staggered past. He unfastened his breeches and with a groan of relief emptied his bladder against a scraggly tree.

Collum had ducked out of sight, but Ava wasn't fast enough as the man turned around.

"Hey," he slurred catching sight of her. His gaze lingered on her chest. "You want coin for the night?"

"Oh, uh," Ava said flustered. "No. Sorry, I'm just leaving."

"Free then. Even better."

His hand curled around her arm, and he yanked her towards him. She lost her footing and stumbled against him. He reeked of ale, and she tried to push him away.

"Let go of me!" she hissed but he was relentlessly dragging her towards the entrance of one of the tents.

She drew her dagger from its sheath and held it up so he could see it. Moonlight glanced off the blade.

"Get your hands off of me," she threatened. "I will use this."

"Oh, feisty." He leered, his other hand grasping for her. "I like it."

Ava slashed with her dagger.

He shoved her away and she stumbled, her foot catching in a rut left by a supply cart. Instead of plunging deep into his belly, her blade scored along the length of his thigh instead.

"You missed," he growled, lunging for her. His hands curled around her throat and squeezed.

"Did I?" she gasped.

His eyes went wide, "What..?"

The burning feeling would have started. The poison she'd coated her dagger with was a much more potent variant of the mixture she had dumped into the water. The toxin was by far the most cruel and vicious she'd ever worked with.

He released her, and his hands scrabbled at the shallow cut in his leg.

"What did you...?" His voice was strained but still too loud.

Ava lashed out with her knee, catching him in the chin. As he thudded to the ground, she climbed on top of him, pressing both hands over his mouth and praying that the poison ate through his insides before he could scream. He thrashed and spasmed, his face contorting and blood vessels in his wild eyes bursting. Foam squeezed out from between her fingers, and Ava shot backwards, ripping her deteriorating gloves from her hands before the acid could burn her bare skin. The soldier was still moving, muscles jerking and fingers clawing at the dirt beneath him. The stench of rotting, burning flesh was so strong she could barely breathe.

Ava scooted backwards, panting, desperately trying to hear anything over the pounding of her heart. Any tell-tale sound of discovery. But it was silent. She murmured a quick, breathless prayer, dragged herself to her hands and knees to a patch of grass.

Oh gods.

If there was anything in her stomach, she would've thrown it up. Wiping her mouth on the back of her hand, she sat back in time to see Collum sneaking past a nearby tent. She waved him down and made an "I'll tell you later" gesture in regard to his horrified look at the dissolving corpse on the ground.

"We're finished?" she mouthed.

He nodded.

That was it. All of the water was now tainted. Poisoning the supply wasn't the same as poisoning some goblets, and she was far more uncertain of her concoction. It would take a few days for the first to fall ill, if she'd gotten the measurements correct. If not...She cast a last, disgusted glance at the fizzing, almost unrecognisable lump of flesh sprawled on the ground. They couldn't even drag the body somewhere without burning themselves. The thing would probably fall apart if they touched it anyway. All they could do was hope no one saw it before the rest of the groups were done.

The pair had just left the last of the tents behind them when a sound had them clinging to each other in terror. Horns.

Ava's mind raced. The alarm sounded too far away for it to have been because of the body they'd left. That she'd left. Someone else had been seen. Or caught. There was no time to dwell or to change plans. Whoever it was, was on their own.

They clambered up onto a high ridge overlooking the camp. Nyesha's group hadn't bothered to hide the corpses they'd made here, and the rocks were wet from slit throats. Ava paused to look out over the camp. More and more lanterns were being lit, figures moved between tents, and voices rose as a jumble to where they stood, breathless and impotent. Ava looked again. Squinting and scanning every part of the landscape that stood before her as if she stood over her own hand-drawn map. She knew where the different groups should be and the most chaos seemed to be coming from...oh no.

The stables. Flint.

"Look!" Collum's voice dragged her out of her panic and she followed where he was pointing.

Horses were thundering through the camp. One group in front and another hot on their heels. She counted quickly. Four in the front group. That was the number of people in Flint's group. She let herself feel a moment of relief. They were alive for now.

"Make for the trees," she muttered under her breath.

As if the wind had carried her command, the group changed direction and hurtled towards the forest. Fast. Too fast. Ava cursed. The horses would falter on the uneven ground and throw them. Flint had to know that. What the hell was he doing?!

Ava could only watch as they were swallowed up by the thick forest.

"The sun will be up soon," Collum said. His mouth was set in a grim line.

"We can't help them now."

Entering the forest while it fills up with soldiers would just get us all killed.

"They will meet us on the ridge as planned." Ava hoped she sounded more confident than she felt. "Let's go."

"Tell me again. Spare no detail," Ava demanded.

Group five hadn't shown up. They'd waited an extra hour already and Ava could tell the rest were getting antsy. Nyesha had already tried to suggest moving on, but Ava had shot her down with a look. They could give them one more hour.

Once again, groups one to four repeated what they had already told her. Nyesha's group had taken out all of the captains she had identified, but the commander still lived. The villages' meagre supplies were in ruins. She in turn told them of the poisoned water. She left out the mishap with the soldier. No one knew what had become of group five other than they seemed to have triggered the alarm but made it to the trees.

One of Nyesha's cutthroats was brave enough to speak. "Maybe we should—"

"No. We wait."

"But—"

"Perhaps you misheard me?" Ava hissed. "I said we wait and so we wait."

"'Cause you miss us?" Flint's voice was like music to her ears.

The returning group were grass-stained and shining with sweat but gloriously alive. Eoghan had taken a glancing blow to the side from a horse's hoof and was being half-carried by one of the warg-bloods, but he managed to give her a weak grin.

Ava pulled Flint into a tight hug but refrained from kissing his cheeks like she wanted to. She had to at least look like she was in control and not terrified out of her mind.

"Summary," she barked, hiding the fact that emotion was threatening to close up her throat.

"We've got no horses. They've got very few horses."

Ava nodded stiffly. "It'll do."

By the time they arrived back at the caves, Eoghan couldn't support his own weight at all, and his breathing was coming in pained gasps.

A small antechamber with natural light filtering in from above had become their healery where Ava dealt with the day-today bumps and bruises. She ordered him taken straight there and raced ahead to collect her kit. Nyesha could do the debrief and breakdown of the mission without her in the main hall.

Alby jumped to his feet when he caught sight of her. He always wanted all of the gory details first-hand, but his smile died as she strode straight past him.

"Eoghan's injured. Get fresh water and meet me in the healing chamber. Now, Alby!"

He saluted and left at a sprint.

By the time Ava had gathered her things and made it to the chamber, Alby was already staggering down the tunnel with an overflowing bucket.

Inside, Eoghan was laid flat on a stone block that served as a table. His eyes were clenched shut as he wheezed. Ava instructed Alby to sponge his forehead with the cool water as she started to unbutton his shirt.

"No!" Eoghan's eyes flew open, and he grasped Ava's wrist. "Don't."

"Your ribs could be broken, Eoghan," Ava murmured. "I need to look."

"No," he moaned again.

"Alby, can you wait outside, please?"

Her apprentice nodded and left. He never liked to be sent away, but he always did as she asked. He would wait just behind the curtain they used as a door in case she needed him.

"Eoghan," Ava began sternly. "I need you to not fight me. I'm trying to help you."

His green eyes were streaming, tears flowing into the curls at his temples, but he nodded.

Once again, Ava's fingers went to his buttons. Underneath the roughspun shirt was another layer of fabric, wound tightly around his chest. Too tightly. The bare skin she could see was already turning purple from the blow he'd taken from the horse's hoof. No doubt, there was considerable swelling.

"This is what you didn't want me to see?"

Eoghan's eyes were closed again. His teeth were clenched, whether with emotion or pain, Ava couldn't tell. She paused for a moment to stroke his hair back from his damp forehead. He groaned.

"Shhh. We can talk later, okay? But you know it has to come off. It's putting too much pressure on your injury."

Eoghan started to protest but she shushed him.

"I am cutting it off and that's the end of it."

He flinched at the cold touch of her blade against his abdomen as she carefully worked it under the fabric and cut through it. At the last snip, it fell away and Eoghan's chest expanded suddenly as he was able to take a full breath. He hissed through his teeth and clenched his fists as his lungs filled.

"Shallow breaths," Ava murmured, tracing her fingers over the contours of his ribcage. She couldn't tell if it was just bruising or if something was broken underneath, but from the amount of pain he seemed to be in, she was leaning towards broken. The skin was intact, though. That was one mercy.

"I'll get you something for the pain."

She dipped the severed fabric into the cold water before laying them back over his chest. They would cool the angry swelling as well as give him a semblance of privacy.

Ava stroked his hair again and murmured some soothing words before popping her head out into the tunnel to ask Alby to go prepare a tea. However, it wasn't Alby she came face to face with. It was Collum.

"He's okay," Ava assured him. "Eoghan will be fine."

Collum swallowed and nodded. Words seemed to stick in his throat.

"Good," he managed finally.

"Could you tell Alby to prepare some tea for the pain? He'll know what to do."

Collum nodded once. A war of emotions played out across his face. Anxiety and fear mostly.

"That's my brother in there."

"I know."

"Do you?" Collum's eyes filled with tears. Not quite as green as Eoghan's. More hazel. One of the only few differences in their features. "He is my little brother. Been just the two o' us for the last few years. Folks back home, they didn't..." He choked a little. "He's had it hard, alright? But he's my brother."

"I understand." Ava took his hand. "He's going to be fine." She dropped her voice. "And no one will hear anything other than his recovery process from me."

Collum nodded again and then cleared his throat. He jerked his thumb over his shoulder, questioningly.

"Yes, please go get Alby."

With Eoghan in a peaceful slumber after drinking several draughts of medicated tea, Ava finally left the healing chamber. She'd held a sack filled with snow against his side for a good half hour. Her fingers were numb with cold, but it had soothed the swelling.

As she trailed back to the main chamber, Ava mused on what Collum had said. The brothers told so many stories, Ava had never realised they had never spoken of their own tale.

Gods. I am getting slow.

She wondered how much more there was to the two of them than met the eye. As she turned into the main hall, dinner was being served. She looked into the faces of each of the people there. Human. Warg. Warg-blood. She hardly knew any of them, and yet she'd risked their lives today. They'd risked their own lives on her words alone. She'd told them she had an informant within the Falcon's Rest, but for all they knew, that was a lie. She certainly didn't receive any letters or messages that they could see. They trusted her implicitly. As she looked from face to face, the question stirred in her mind.

How far am I going to push that trust?

"No losses," Nyesha said from right behind her. Ava hadn't heard her approach. "I'd call that a success. Wouldn't ye?"

"No," Ava replied with grim determination. "I'd call it a start."

Chapter Sixty

Masquerade

Tannin

Tannin was pretty sure she had used up a lifetime of luck with her nightly snooping in the laird's wing, but if it could scrape Ava an inch of an advantage, then she was damn well going to keep doing it.

Her spying was fruitful. She was able to tell Ava where the highest commanders and officers were stationed. Nyesha's assassins gleefully went for the throat, taking them out and displaying their bodies in the most gruesome ways they could think of while the rest of Ava's ragtag army picked at their supply lines and caused havoc wherever they could.

Tannin was burning up with jealousy and impotence as she watched through Ava's eyes every night and moped around the fort every day. Her restrictive bracers sapped what little energy she had, and the lack of sleep at night was picking away at her. Some days, she didn't leave her bed at all.

Yule and the promised masked ball approached faster than she cared for. Once again, she found herself in her sitting room, glaring at a new dress that had been delivered for her.

Red again, with heavy skirts and a white fur shawl to drape around her shoulders to ward off the chill.

And it was sleeveless. Her ugly bracers would be on full display for anyone to see. She wondered if that was the point.

"Am I not supposed to be hiding these?"

Orlaith merely shrugged and fussed over the scarlet flowers she was weaving into Tannin's curled and pinned hair. "It's not my place, Miss."

The last piece of the ensemble was a red mask that was fitted over the top half of her face and tied with a red ribbon. Silver studs and what Tannin suspected were real diamonds decorated the silken surface.

Malcolm escorted her, even giving her his arm like a proper gentleman despite being in full armour. He had forgone the helmet for the evening though, and his ruddy hair was combed neatly. He'd also made the wise decision to shave off his pathetic moustache. Orlaith had all but swooned at the sight of him and delivered a flurry of stuttered compliments. He hadn't even looked at the serving girl.

They walked, as usual, in silence but it didn't seem quite as prickly as usual.

Maybe he's finally stopped being a miserable git.

The illusion was ruined, however, when he snapped at her to stop stroking her furry shawl.

"It's not a pet," he hissed.

Heat warmed her cheeks, and Tannin dropped her hands. She hadn't even realised she was doing it. It was very soft.

She'd been placed at one of the high tables. A seat of honour. Not the top table but close enough to still feel the waves of self-importance coming from it. Laird Cormack was, of course, seated front and centre and surrounded by simpering nobles, who were hanging onto his every word and laughing far too loudly.

From the way some of them were leering at her with a mixture of morbid curiosity, apprehension and a hint of triumph, she was dead certain he had just told them who she was. Boasted about it. Tannin tightened her grip on her goblet and stared at the dancefloor, refusing to let them see she was affected by their stares.

Let them stare. I'll poke their eyes out when I get my claws back.

Tannin smiled into her wine and tried as subtly as possible to kick her shoes off under the table.

The thought of revenge was the only thing these days that made her smile. That, and her precious few minutes every midnight when she could speak to Ava. It was a shame, Tannin thought, Ava would probably love this ball.

I'd only like this if I could be dancing with her.

If she ever managed to get free and get a real title for herself, she decided, she'd throw her own ball.

The guests weren't the only ones watching her. A masked servant across the room had been staring at her and looked away when he realised she had seen him. His face was hidden and he was wearing the uniform of a server, but Tannin would have sworn it was the same face that had been watching her from the garden. What was a gardener doing at a ball?

"Well, hello there. I hoped I'd be seeing you tonight. The red looks lovely on you."

His dark hair was slicked back and his upper face hidden by a sparkling golden mask, but there was no mistaking the lairdling.

Great.

Tannin suppressed an eyeroll and stood to perform the barest suggestion of a curtsey.

"I don't really get the choice of where I go or not," Tannin replied. "What do you want, Benwald?"

"Isn't it obvious? I'd like to honour you with a dance." He gave her a glittering smile as he bowed and extended his hand.

"Oh gods," Tannin groaned. "Is no an option?"

He just gave her an amused look and she grimaced.

"Lemme get my shoes," she muttered. "Maybe I'll get lucky, fall off them and break my neck."

"Nonsense, I'm an excellent dancer and I won't let you fall."

He took her hand with a light touch and led her onto the dancefloor. Every set of eyes on the top table bored holes in her back as they took their place amongst the other couples and the first few bars of a new song lilted through the maze of silk and velvet.

The first chords of the song rang out, and then they stepped in unison into the dance.

"I am surprised that you know this dance."

"Did you want me to stumble and make a tit of myself?"

Benwald looked startled by the coarse expression but played it off smoothly as they coasted across the room.

"Not at all, not at all. But by all accounts, you are...how shall I put it?" He twirled her.

"A filthy commoner with no class?" She cocked an eyebrow behind her mask as he once again caught her in his arms to repeat the steps.

He laughed. "Well, yes."

"Well, it's all true. I just know this one. A friend taught me this one."

"A friend." It was his turn to raise an eyebrow. "I see."

"I'm not going to talk about it, *Ben*, so don't even ask."

"And this?" His fingertips brushed over the gruesome scar on her shoulder where the fine straps of her dress left it visible. "A memento from a past life?"

"Something like that."

He twirled her again. The layers of her skirts billowed, brushing against the pair dancing closest to them.

"It looks like it was painful."

"Getting stabbed tends to be. If it bothers you, stop looking at it." Tannin grumbled. "And stop trying to talk to me. I'm trying to remember the steps."

He chuckled but seemed content enough to pass the rest of the dance without conversation, which Tannin was quietly thankful for. When the musicians stilled, he spun her one last time before dipping into a deep bow. A respectful gesture, but she knew damn well he was just toying with her. They all were.

"Perhaps I'll seek you out for another dance before the night is through."

"Please don't."

To her dismay, Benwald accompanied her to the side of the dance floor.

"You'll want to watch this next part," he said lightly touching her arm and directing her attention across the room to where musicians had taken up new instruments.

A young man with a mop of fair hair nudged his way to join them. He was clothed and masked in a deep blue and slapped Benwald on the back as a greeting as the first notes rang out.

"Caiden! About time." The lairdling was about to make an introduction when the lights dimmed.

The music started low and deep as a side door opened. In swept a group of dancers. They couldn't have looked more different from each other, but one thing they had in common was that they were all truly the most beautiful people Tannin had ever seen in her life. Lithe and fluid, with faces that could have been carved from the finest marble, they captured the attention of everyone in the room without making a sound as they took their places on the vacant dancefloor.

"They're selkie Remnants," Benwald whispered in her ear.

Tannin couldn't help but reply.

"They're stunning," she said under her breath.

"When it was the old Fair Folk selkies, the slightest skin on skin touch can make you fall in love with them."

Benwald's friend smirked. "It's still true. Every time I've had one of your father's courtesans, I could've sworn I was in love for the night."

The selkie-bloods' bodies swayed with the music. Rhythmic and hypnotic. The thin, floaty fabric they wore flowed around them to the beat. Fluttering on the breath of some unseen entity. Tannin was entranced.

The woman at the front of the group was like no one Tannin had ever seen. Her skin was so dark it was almost blue. The golden glitter dusting her limbs made her reminiscent of the night sky itself.

Tannin could've sworn the woman caught her eye on purpose.

After the first of the selkie-bloods' dances, Tannin murmured her excuses and slipped through the gawkers to steal a vacant chair. These days, one dance was enough to exhaust her and she was feeling light-headed. Whatever Benwald had said about dancing with her again, there was no way she could manage another unless it was one of the torturously slow ones where the couples held each other as close as lovers. She would feign illness immediately if it looked like she was going to be asked for one of those dances.

She exhaled long and slow as she plopped herself down, her wide skirts fanning out around her. She hadn't meant to bring attention to herself, but one of the nobles watching turned to look at her. He stumbled a little as he did so, his mask askew.

He opened his mouth to talk to her, his smile more like a sneer, but at that moment, the dancers glided into the audience. They slid from person to person, a hair's breadth away but never touching. Teasing. The woman who had been at the front of the group, who had caught Tannin's eye, swept up behind the man, and with a tinkling laugh, readjusted his mask.

Tannin was thankful for the interruption and tried to escape back to her proper seat, but the beautiful dancer wasn't finished with her fun yet. Before Tannin could chart a course through the heaving crowd, the woman slid onto her lap.

"What are you—?"

The woman trailed her fingers over Tannin's lips and shushed her before dropping her hand to trace over her waist. The dancer flipped her hair and rotated hips to the music. The men watching whooped and jeered as she ground against Tannin.

Tannin flitted between humiliation and anger, but with every rotation of the woman's hips, she slipped further from coherent thoughts and became less aware of there being anyone else in the room at all.

Her fingers trailed from Tannin's hips to her thighs. She pinched her suddenly. The sharp pain snapped her focus to the woman's face. Tannin's mouth opened to say something in outrage, but the deep brown eyes were staring at her intently with something more than a façade of lust dancing behind them. There was an urgency there.

The woman smiled silkily and leaned in to nuzzle the side of her neck.

"They are watching." Her warning was barely a breath against her ear. "We do not have much time. Do not speak. Just listen."

The selkie-blood Remnant let out a tinkling laugh followed by a sensual moan and looked at Tannin pointedly.

When Tannin failed, to react the woman exasperatedly hissed into the crook of her neck. "Get much better at acting or this is going to end badly for us all."

"What is goin' on?"

"I said don't speak," she hissed. Her tone was jarring compared to the smooth motion of her body as she swayed to the music. "Not everyone in Gormbrae follows them. You don't know who we are, but we know you and we have plans. Be patient and do not act. You will not see me again until it is time."

"Time for what?"

"Just wait for the signal and all will be well."

"But—"

"I'd love to stay," the dancer said loud enough for others to hear. "But I can't keep such a lovely thing all to myself now, can I?"

She tapped Tannin once on the tip of her nose and winked as she swept back into the crowd, taking the spectators' attention with her like dogs lusting after a fine steak.

Tannin watched her go, speechless.

"Well, well," Benwald drawled. "I see now why you didn't want to dance with me."

Tannin glared at him, still flushed.

"Maybe I'll send her to your room later as a gift," the lairdling's friend, Caiden, jeered. "You can tell me all the filthy details in a thank you card."

Tannin huffed and left her chair, intrigue now firmly replaced by humiliation. She found her keeper who, of course, was lurking nearby, and demanded to leave.

"It would be rude to leave so early," Malcolm said, a tone of warning clear.

"Then I'll be rude," she retorted.

"You cannot leave yet."

"Oh, would you just—!"

"There's just nothing quite like that sea breeze from the deck of your own ship," a nearby voice drawled to a small group of masked figures. It was a voice she knew.

Tannin's head whipped round so fast her neck clicked.

Rage reared up inside her at the sight of him. It boiled with such violence that she had to stifle a gasp.

Erlan. Of course, he is here.

She'd seen no trace of him at the Falcon's Rest except for that one night in Cormack's private wing. He was dressed in Bayfort blue. As he made an extravagant gesture to the room at large, Tannin saw with a twinge of pride that he now sported a delicately engraved metal hand. Ava had mentioned that the healers had to amputate his lower arm after the damage Tannin had done to it with her claws.

I'll finish the damn job.

With a growl in the back of her throat, Tannin took a step towards him but was stopped as an imposing figure slid in front of her and blocked her line of sight.

"Malcolm, move," she snarled.

"I don't know what you think you're doing, but it would be wise to stop it now."

"Ah, Lady Tannin."

This night just gets better and better.

Tannin forced herself to smile as Laird Cormack approached with open arms. Like his son, he wore a gilded mask. "Allow me to introduce our guest of honour. Prince Erlan of Bayfort."

His eyes locked onto Tannin's, a smile teasing the corners of his mouth. Challenging. Daring. He knew of their history damn well enough to know murder was on her mind, and he loved dangling it in front of her.

Tannin ground her teeth and then wrestled her features into what she hoped passed as a pleasant expression. Erlan's own face began to shed its look of utter terror that it had assumed at the mention of her name to one of wary caution.

I can't kill him right now. Not here. Not now. Gods, I want to though.

"A pleasure to see you again, Prince Erlan," she said as evenly as she could.

"What," he said through clenched teeth, "is *that* doing here?"

So much for being civil.

Tannin hid her balled up fists in the folds of her skirt.

"Prince Erlan." Cormack tutted. "The young lady is my guest."

Erlan's eyes raked down her body in a way that made her want to scrub herself clean and then lingered on her bracers.

"I see." He gave her a filthy look, which she returned as soon as Cormack wasn't watching. "I had hoped that a higher standard would be adhered to for a formal gathering."

If Cormack was insulted by the slight, he didn't show it.

"Come now. Tonight is a night for merriment!" He clapped Erlan on the shoulder. "Any former animosity can be put aside for one night. Let us have more wine!"

He turned, scouring the room for a jug-laden servant to call upon.

"I was leaving anyway," Tannin muttered attempting to back away, but Erlan snagged her wrist.

"You'll pay for what you did to my arm," he hissed, quietly enough that the Falcon, who was occupied with his goblet's emptiness, didn't hear.

"I'm a little short on change right now, sorry."

"You are going to regret—"

"How about I make them match for what you did to Attilo?" she shot back.

"Who's Attilo?" he asked, genuinely bewildered

"He…" Tannin was seething. "The bodyguard. Ava's bodyguard. Your men killed him with that exploding thing."

Comprehension bloomed across his features.

"Ah yes." Then he shrugged. "Bodyguards die, that's what they're there for."

It was truly a show of ultimate self-composure that Tannin did not throttle him then and there.

"He was ten times the man you'll ever be." She filled her voice with as much disgust and derision as she could. "He was a good man. And you are pathetic. Let go of me."

She tried to shake him off, but he didn't budge.

"That's quite a grip you have there," Tannin snarled, even though she couldn't actually feel it through her bracers. "Guess that comes in handy on those lonely nights since I stole your wife."

Half the people within earshot stifled their snorts, the other half outright laughed. Erlan's face purpled.

Regret flitted through her as she remembered he now had a fist made of literal iron and his expression told her he was about to try and shatter her cheekbone with it. She flinched but before Erlan could make a move to strike her, a protective wall of armour was suddenly between them. Malcolm's hand clamped down on Erlan's arm. He squeezed and the prince winced.

"Sir, please release the lady," Malcolm said flatly. "My lady, I will escort you back to your chambers."

"That thing," Erlan said, his lip curling back even as he let go of Tannin's wrist, "belongs in a cage. Or better yet, an unmarked grave."

"Big words, Erlan," Tannin murmured with lethal softness as Malcolm's hand found the small of her back to steer her away. "I look forward to making you swallow them."

Chapter Sixty-One

They know

Tannin

Tannin had tried to thank Malcolm for stepping in and protecting her from Erlan. He had snorted and told her she would have deserved it and he only did it because it was his job to keep her from harm as per the arrangement with Dana. He had then gone on to inform her that he wasn't her servant, her thanks meant nothing to him, and if she insisted on insulting any more of the Falcon's guests, he would personally make her regret it. If anything, since the incident, he was even more sour than usual.

Malcom wasn't the only one. The air at the Falcon's Rest over the next few days was tight with tension and unspoken words. Tannin had kept her nighttime snooping to a minimum to avoid being caught. Even so, she had still found enough absolute gems of information hidden in the laird's study to keep Ava busy. The princess had been using the information with deadly efficiency. Nyesha was in her element as she and her Skirters tore bloody chunks from the Gormbraen army in the dead of night, leaving them reeling.

The next time Tannin saw Laird Cormack in person was the day after Nyesha's assassins had taken out one of his favourite captains.

Of course, he might not even know that yet. Tannin watched the ravens arrive every day. Ava had told her how long it would take them to fly from the army's camp to the Gormbraen border, so she could usually judge when the bad news was going to arrive.

As she watched over the top of yet another dull, dusty book she'd picked up from the library, a servant raced out across the walkway to greet him and sketch a hasty, breathless bow.

The wind had picked up, and its howling through the small nooks of the fort made it difficult for even Tannin's sensitive ears to listen in, but she caught a few key words. The captain was dead.

Tannin expected to see anger on the Falcon's face. Or frustration. But to her horror, he smiled. Her stomach lurched.

Oh, shite. I think I fucked up.

The assembly was called immediately, the bells tolling throughout the entire fort. Everyone's presence was mandatory from the laird himself to the lowest of servants. Dread filled Tannin from her head to her toes as she tried to feign confusion.

The hall was packed with barely enough space to make a path for the Falcon to stride through and take up his place on the dais. He didn't waste any time.

"Someone in this fort is a traitor and a spy, and no one is leaving this hall until I find out who it is."

Fuck.

The room erupted into panicked shouts and accusations. Tannin kept her mouth shut and made herself as small as possible. With this many bodies crammed together, the heat was already rising.

"Anyone with information, come forward now."

Nobles fell over themselves trying to simultaneously accuse their rivals and proclaim their own innocence. Erlan was half on the dais, both trying to plead his own innocence and try and wrangle a place of authority to glare out at the crowd from. It was chaos. Tannin tried to shrink back into the shadows, but between the press of people and Malcolm's breastplate jostling against her back, she was trapped.

"SILENCE," Laird Cormack roared. "I want information. Not excuses."

Tannin felt a prickling down the back of her neck and scanned the room. She was used to being watched, but this felt different. Across the hall, where the servants were gathered, Orlaith was staring at her. Hard.

Oh, she knows. Does she know? I think she knows.

The gears in Orlaith's mind seemed to screech even above the din in the hall. Tannin stared back at her. The latch. The office. The attacks.

She knows. And she knows I know she knows.

Brown eyes bored into grey.

Do not. Tannin willed her. *Do not do it. Don't you even think about—*

"Sir!"

Fuck.

"I...I think I have information."

Tannin bit her thumbnail.

Fuckfuckfuck.

"How could you possibly—" Laird Cormack stopped mid-snap and his eyes slid to Tannin. "Of course."

Erlan, by now having wormed his way to the Falcon's side, followed his gaze. His face twisted into a snarl. Tannin tried. She really did. But nothing on earth could have stopped her from quirking up the corners of her mouth into a smug, evil, little smile.

"You. Girl. Speak." Laird Cormack swept from the podium and bore down on Orlaith.

"She, I mean the Lady Tannin, did not, well, she didn't always keep to her chambers at night." Orlaith flashed her an apologetic look. "And she said some things. I don't...I think she was communicating with someone."

"Is this true?"

All trace of Tannin's smile vanished. "I don't know what she's talkin' about."

She winced. Even she could hear the untruth in her words. Everyone could.

She could do nothing as gauntleted hands clamped down on her upper arms. At a gesture from the laird, the rest of the guards pushed in to surround her.

"As for you," the laird sneered down at Orlaith, who shrank back in terror. "You had information that could have prevented this. And you chose not to speak."

Orlaith stammered through an apology and stumbled over excuses.

"I have no use for disloyalty."

"Oh, for fuck's sake she didn't do anythin'—OW!" Tannin twisted in the grip of several guards, but they were relentless in dragging her from the hall. She couldn't turn enough to see what was happening.

"I'm loyal!" Orlaith protested, her voice shrill with fear. "I swear! I didn't know what she'd done! Please! No! I told you what I knew! I tried to help! I tried! Please!"

"Take this one too."

Tannin swore under her breath as Orlaith's wails filled the shocked hall.

"You eejit!" Tannin hissed as soon as they had been yanked into the corridor. She lashed out at Orlaith with her feet. "You should have kept your mouth shut! You have no proof I even did anythin'!"

The guards responded by jerking her back and twisting her arms behind her. She grunted with pain. Struggling to get free was futile, but she couldn't help but fight their grip.

Orlaith's response was made incoherent by the strength of her sobs.

"I didn't want you to get into trouble," the serving girl wailed. "I care about you, Sir Malcolm!"

Tannin's keeper looked down on her in disgust.

"What?"

"You broke the damn latch. Not me," Tannin said with satisfaction.

"You would get in so much trouble!" Orlaith sniffed. "And with your brother, I—"

Malcolm's palm met her face with sickening force. Orlaith slumped, eyes dazed and mouth slack. Malcolm's gauntlet had slashed open her cheek, and blood splashed down her pristine uniform.

"Do not speak of my family!" he hissed. "You could very well be the reason he is dead!"

"It's not her fault!" Tannin yelled.

"You're right." He turned on her. "It's yours."

Inside his helmet, his eyes were like ice.

Tannin lifted her chin. Daring him. His fingers curled into fists, but he didn't strike. Instead, his mouth curled into an unpleasant smile.

"Take her to interrogation."

I have regrets.

Tannin drummed her fingers on the arm of the sturdy, wooden chair and tried to breathe evenly. Grooves ran under her fingertips where some other wretch had dug their nails in hard enough to score the wood. She eyed the rows and rows of gleaming tools that lined the walls and shuddered. Someone took good care of their toys. Tearing her eyes away, she looked up at the ceiling instead and immediately regretted it. All manner of hooks and chains hung from the stone. She told herself that she did not want to know the purpose of that. Waiting was making her nerves worse. She wanted to pace, to fidget, to scratch her damn nose, but thick leather straps ensured she would do no such thing. She couldn't feel the ones that pinned her hands to the arms of the chair since they were fastened over the unyielding steel of her bracers, but the straps around her ankles and waist were digging in. Malcolm had made sure of that right before he promised her that if he heard one more peep out of her, the next thing to come out of her mouth would be her teeth. He would probably suffer for this too, she realised, since he was supposed to be her keeper.

Fine by me.

She blew a strand of hair out of her face and then shivered.

The room itself wasn't freezing cold. When the guards had searched her, however, they had also unceremoniously stripped her to just her shift, and the air was cool on her sweat damp skin.

Tannin squirmed.

Goddammit, I have to pee.

She expected the ancient door to creak when it did finally open, but it swung smoothly on well-oiled hinges. She'd also expected her first visitors to be more guards or even the laird himself, but it wasn't.

"Professor?" Tannin squinted. "What are you doin' here?"

"Hello again." He smiled. "I wondered how long it would take you to end up down here. Creatures can't change their natures however much they try. Violence is just in your blood, isn't it?"

His apprentice, Finn he had said his name was, lurked in the shadows, notebook at the ready and quill poised above the page. The feather quivered in his hand.

Tannin's attention flickered back to the older man as he extracted himself from his cloak.

A Black Cloak.

Unwanted memories flooded Tannin's mind. Not only were Black Cloaks little more than leeches in her experience – soothing the worries of those close to death and promising salvation for a price – they also had the job of escorting the condemned to the gallows. She'd had enough experience with Black Cloaks for a lifetime. She wondered if Professor Marwick knew how many of his colleagues she had killed that day. She wondered if he was about to avenge them.

He smiled. "Have you been keeping secrets?"

The unruly strand of hair fell back into her eyes, and she puffed at it ineffectively.

"I dunno what you're talkin' about."

"Oh, I doubt that very much," he said, selecting a long, thin knife from the table.

Tannin pressed herself back against the hard chair as he approached.

He reached out with the knife. Tannin leaned as far away from the blade as she could and then stilled as he continued to advance. She stared at it until it came so close it blurred. He paused with the tip of the blade a fraction of an inch from her eye. She was sure if she blinked, her eyelashes would brush steel. He kept the blade there, his hand as steady as stone and unwavering for a few thundering heartbeats, and then, with an unconcerned flick, sliced through the strand of hair that had been tickling Tannin's face. He gave her a warm smile, stepped back and returned the knife to its place on the table as she suppressed a whimper.

"You see, it's more of a you help me I help you situation," he said, his voice light and conversational. "You answer my questions and I can make you more comfortable. Understand?"

"How about you help me now and I'll get back to you?"

He laughed. A deep booming laugh that echoed through the cavernous room and then stopped so suddenly that Tannin flinched.

He strode towards her, and although expecting some kind of attack, Tannin wasn't prepared at all for the old man to suddenly reach out and grasp her chin, pulling her lip back to inspect her teeth. She snapped her jaws, and he jerked back with a chuckle.

"What are you doin'? Get off of me!" She tried to shake him off, but she had no leverage. She could do nothing when he laid his hand on her forehead and pinned her head back so that she was staring at the ceiling. He pried her left eye wide open. The back of the chair pressed hard into her skull.

"Bring the lantern here, Finn. Look here – see that? Would I be correct in saying you can see in the dark?"

"Fuck. Off." Tannin ground out through clenched teeth.

Her eye had started to sting from the lantern light and being held open so long. When he finally let her blink, her eyes watered. He didn't let go of her head, though. She flinched when once again cold fingers touched her skin. This time on her neck just under her jaw. His apprentice timed him as he took her pulse.

"A little fast," he commented, sounding disappointed.

Tannin flinched again as his fingertips traced the scar on her shoulder, visible under the thin sleeves of her shift. He made a clucking sound.

"What are you doing?" A mild voice caused both Tannin and the professor to jump. Finn dropped his quill.

Out of the three of them, no one had heard the man enter.

"I believe that you were to get your specimen *after*."

Specimen? After? After what?

The professor gave a nervous chuckle. "My laird. Can't blame me for my excitement, can you? A few non-invasive tests that's all. Just to keep the old thinker occupied."

He finally removed his hand that had been keeping Tannin staring up at the ceiling. She rolled her cramped neck as she righted herself.

"I know you're very keen to play with your new curiosity, but we all have to share."

The way he looked at her chilled her to the bone. Laird Cormack stood in the doorway with all the glee of a fox spotting a rabbit in a trap.

"Well, well, well."

Tannin swallowed hard. He had murder in his eyes.

"Hiya, Cormack," she said, faking brightness. "Is this how you treat people when you have no evidence they've even done something?"

"We have a witness."

"Who saw what exactly? Nothin', that's what."

Cormack chuckled without humour. "You are so very lucky that King Modric wants you to live."

"Ah," Tannin squirmed. "Pass on my thanks to ol' Mo then, would you?"

Cormack looked momentarily confused and then furious. "Shut that disrespectful mouth."

"Mo." He shook his head. "If she'd done her job, we wouldn't be here in the first place."

It was Tannin's turn to be confused.

Mo? Mo...

Tannin groaned as she realised. How could she have been so stupid? If she could've moved her hands, she would've smacked herself in the forehead.

"The healer. Ava's nursemaid. That's what you meant about having people in Armodan to get Ava on the throne. It was her. She tried to kill me. Wait, did she kill Ava's brother? Is she going to kill her other brother? Justus?"

"Enough. We have business to attend to."

He surveyed the tools laid out on the table. His hand hovered above a particularly nasty-looking instrument, and he hummed before moving on to the next.

Tannin swallowed again. Her mouth was dry as ash while rivers of sweat ran down her back.

"I haven't done anythin'."

"Liar," he said softly. "After all I offered you."

"Nothing you offered me was real," she hissed back. "I got to pretend to be a lady at court? Big fuckin' deal. At the end of the day, I was still betrayed and locked up here against my will. You took my powers, you took my crown and—"

Tannin slammed her mouth shut. She'd said too much. Cormack's smile told her that much.

"So, you thought you'd be a little rat instead?"

He selected one of the tools and twirled it in his long fingers. It looked like the ones they used in the markets of Dunoak to gut eels.

"Hmmm, so many good options."

"You can't harm me," Tannin squeaked in desperation. "That's the agreement with Dana. You want to be an oathbreaker, huh? The wargs will never ally with you if you do. No one will."

He tutted and replaced the tool on the table. "Harm is...relative."

"Oh gods," Tannin groaned and tugged at the straps pinning her hands. There was no way she could twist free unless someone loosened them.

"But," he said, replacing the tool and picking up a second wooden chair instead. He placed it directly in front of her and draped himself across it. "I'd rather not argue semantics with wargs. They seem like the type to hold a grudge, and while I would very much like to carve you up like the thieving, lying, little rat you are, I have a different method in mind."

He took a jewel-stoppered vial from an inner pocket and held it between his forefinger and thumb.

"Do you know what this is?"

"Just do whatever it is you're gonna do to me and get it over with. I don't want to play your games. I'm not tellin' you anythin'."

If he tortures me, I'm gonna crack like a fucking egg. Fucking hell.

"That's right. You play your own games, isn't that right," he sneered. "This is a truth serum."

"Horseshit," Tannin replied. "That's not a real thing. That can't be a real thing."

He uncorked the vial with a sinister smile.

"Wait, no! Don't you dare!" Tannin thrashed in her restraints as Laird Cormack stepped up beside her.

"Don't make this difficult," he murmured. "Drink it."

Like hell I will.

Tannin pressed her lips together and gave him the filthiest look she could muster.

"Have it your way. Guards!" Cormack yelled, making Tannin jump.

No, no, no!

Despair threatened to crush her as the two guards who had been outside stomped in. One of them was Malcolm.

Cormack held out the vial and nodded towards Tannin. No words were needed.

"Malcolm. Malcolm, don't do this."

Tannin struggled, leaning as far as she could away from them, but there was nothing she could do.

"My brother was in one of the camps your little friends attacked. He didn't make it. My father? They don't know if he will live or die," Malcolm whispered as he dug his fingers into her jaw, trying to force her mouth open.

He growled as she continued to fight him. Pinching her nose shut with one hand, he pried open her mouth with the other, letting the other guard tip in the contents of the vial. She tried to spit it out, but he slapped his hand over her mouth as soon as the vial was empty.

"Swallow it," he advised her, pressing harder on her mouth and nose to emphasise he wasn't letting go and she wasn't getting to breathe until she did.

She had no choice. She swallowed and then let out a muffled, panicked scream when he didn't immediately release her.

"That will do. Back to your stations."

He gave her a smirk before letting go. She sucked in a huge breath and then coughed it back out, spluttering and swearing.

"Oh, I'm gonna kill you fuckin' slowly!" she yelled at his retreating back as she spat over the side of the chair.

"There, there," Cormack cooed, taking a silken handkerchief from his pocket and dabbing at her chin. "That wasn't so bad."

"Get off me," Tannin snarled in frustration and tried to wrench herself away so hard that the straps holding her creaked.

"It should take effect in a few minutes."

"It's not real." Tannin shook her head. "It's not real, it's a trick."

"If you truly are innocent as you claim, then a little truth serum shouldn't be so bad," Cormack said.

Tannin gave him another dirty look.

"You are going to tell me everything. Who you've been communicating with, how and where to find them."

"I won't say anythin'."

"It helps to get the flow started with some easy questions," Cormack explained. "Let's start with the basics to ease you in, what is your name?"

Tannin glared in sullen silence. The serum had been unpleasant as it slipped down her throat, and she could swear she felt it pool in her belly. She pulled against her restraints, shuddering with discomfort.

"What is your name?"

She shook her head and clenched her jaw. The rest of her body had started to relax against her will and she couldn't even keep her hands curled into fists.

"That's it. Relax. Tell me your name."

"No." Tannin shook her head again. "It's a trick. I won't."

But even as she said it, she knew she would. She was going to spill her damn guts. She could feel the serum coil around her mind. It was soothing her. Coaxing her. Telling her it was all okay.

"You won't tell me you name? How about your favourite colour then? Just an innocent little question." Cormack was back by her side. A light touch stroked her hair as he spoke. She didn't try and shake him off. "Think of your favourite colour. Tell me what it is. It's that easy."

The image of Ava's blue eyes filled Tannin's vision. The way they sparkled. Sky-like. Clear, cool water. The intensity of them when she was concentrating. The way they filled with mischief when she teased her. The way they filled with desire when she...

I won't give you up, Ava. I won't.

"Come on now, what's your favourite colour?" Cormack repeated.

A single tear slid down Tannin's cheek, and she sniffed as she looked at him. She huffed a hopeless chuckle.

"Blue."

And then, placing her tongue between her teeth, she bit down as hard as she could.

Chapter Sixty-Two

The Truth Hurts

Tannin

The interrogation chamber swam back into view and Tannin blinked. Her head was pounding even more than the last time she'd had that white powder thrown in her face. She raised her head with caution and then groaned as pain blossomed. Her mouth was packed with some kind of gauze. She couldn't even feel her tongue – it was just a big haze of throbbing pain. For a moment, she wondered if she'd actually succeeded in biting it off before she'd been knocked out, but she doubted it. She'd certainly done damage, though.

She hadn't been unconscious for long. The blood that had poured out of her mouth and down her front was still glistening and the tang of it filled the air. But the scent wasn't just blood, and it wasn't just her top half that was wet. A glance confirmed it. She had pissed herself too.

Ugh.

"You little fool."

Tannin peered up through the haze. Professor Marwick stood at the table, cleaning his blood-streaked hands with a damp cloth and wearing an expression of extreme distaste. Cormack sat in front of her, spotless and sneering.

She gave as much of a smug grin as she was able, relishing in the pain.

Try and make me talk now, arsehole.

"Oh." The Falcon's face split into a pitying smile. "You actually think you've done something, don't you?"

Tannin frowned and made a questioning sound in her throat.

He sighed. "This would be amusing if you weren't trying so hard. Sorry to disappoint you, my dear, but truth serums don't make you speak. They make you tell the truth."

She just then noticed the guard standing beside her. It wasn't Malcolm. Over the smell of blood filling her nose, she could make out the cloying scent of his pipe. It was one of her hidden watchers – the one she'd named Smoky.

Laird Cormack brought forth a quill. "You are right-handed, aren't you?"

No. No, no, NO!

He handed it to Smoky.

"Make sure she doesn't stab herself with it, won't you?" he drawled. "She seems to be in a masochistic mood today."

Tannin's frantic gurgles of protest were ignored as the guard untied her right hand and forced the quill between her fingers, wrapping his hand around hers.

Cormack slid a board with a roll of parchment underneath.

Tannin tried to wrestle for control of the quill, howling through her mouthful of bloody gauze, but she was outmatched.

"Now then. Where were we?"

She told them everything.

Her traitorous fingers spelled it all out for them. The speaking stones, the plan, locations, names and numbers. She even drew a map. Ava had been careful with what she let slip, but it was enough, and the laird was knowledgeable enough to fill in the gaps. Tears rolled down her cheeks in an unending stream as the next words appeared on the scroll.

Princess Avalyn

Tannin sobbed and hung her head as she wrote it.

"Well, isn't that interesting. And who is the princess to you?"

He said it with a smile. He knew exactly who they were to each other. He just wanted her to say it. Or write it.

Tannin glared at him with red-rimmed eyes.

The tip of the quill tore through the parchment as she scrawled a single word.

MINE

"Is that so?" Cormack reached out to pat her cheek. "We obviously need her alive, but I'll make sure she gets an extra special greeting just for you."

Tannin jerked her hand out of Smoky's and slashed at the laird with the quill. The strap at her waist limited her lunge, and he leapt back just in time to avoid injury. It was the first time she had seen him look undignified as he stumbled and touched his fingertips to the ink splashed across his cheek. The look he gave the guard was one of pure violence. Tannin could feel him tremble as he strapped her wrist back to the arm of the chair. Undoubtedly, he would pay for that little lapse later.

"As for you," Cormack tapped her left bracer with the tip of a dagger he'd picked up. His brow furrowed as he pondered her fate, scraping the blade along her metal-coated arm.

Tannin gave him a blank look. She didn't care what they did to her. After what she had just told them, she deserved it.

"Drop her in the deepest, darkest hole we have where she can't do any more damage. I never want to hear her name again, understood? I'll write to Dunoak to inform them of the situation. As soon as we have a release from the agreement, the professor can have her in pieces."

He turned back to Tannin with a sneer, using the tip of his dagger to tilt her chin up. "You won't be killed, but you will beg for death before this is over. You have my word."

They weren't joking about a deep, dark hole.

The barest trickle of torch light filtered in from high above her. In addition to a padlocked grate, the pit was covered by a thick, round lid, like the lid of a barrel, sealing her in. Not that it mattered. Tannin could see perfectly well in the dark and knew that there was nothing to see. Rough damp walls, rough damp floor, a drain.

She lay curled up in a foetal position, swamped with self-loathing. Her tongue was still swollen and pulsed with every heartbeat. Her hip throbbed from where she'd hit the ground when the guards threw her into the pit. Her knees were grazed too from being dragged through the dungeons. That was her own fault, though, since she'd point blank refused to walk.

It didn't matter what they did to her. The images in her head were torture enough. She couldn't stop seeing the chaos of Ava's camp in her mind when they spotted the Gormbraens coming for them. They wouldn't be prepared. They didn't have the fighters, the defence or the time to escape. It would be a slaughter. Some might try to run, but they were all doomed...Because of her. Because she'd sold them out. Betrayed them.

Tannin huddled against the wall with a whimper. The shackles on her wrists and ankles clanked as she moved and echoed with her shivers. The noise was already driving her mad.

She ground her fists against her eyes and then hid her face in her hands. Her traitorous hands that had spelled out destruction for her whole army. Between the fear, desolation and serum messing with her mind, she had lost track of time, but it must have been past midnight by now. Ava would be waiting for her, and she wouldn't ever respond. The princess would never know what had happened to her. Well, when the Gormbraens poured down on them, she could probably make a good enough guess. That Tannin had given them up.

Of course, Ava would live – the Triquetra needed her alive. But the rest...They would all die in some godsforsaken cave at the point of Gormbraen swords. Flint would die.

Because of me.

She sat up and slammed her fist into the wall of the pit, again and again until blood oozed from the knuckles of her traitorous right hand. With the chains linking her wrists, she couldn't draw her arm back as much as she wanted to or hit with much force, but it was cathartic enough. Just. She wanted to break it into a thousand pieces. Or rip it off.

By the tenth or maybe twentieth blow, her shoulders were shaking too much with sobs to continue. She dropped her bloodied hands into her lap, threw back her head and screamed in frustration and pain. A thousand ghostly echoes screamed back at her, bouncing off the walls and reverberating through her skull.

She folded her arms over her head as best she could and cowered from them until they faded into cold silence.

When she screamed a second time, she didn't try to cover her ears. She let the howls wash over her.

May as well get used to being haunted.

Chapter Sixty-Three

The War is Coming

Ava

Tannin had been caught. It was the only explanation for the deafening silence from the speaking stone and the sudden increase in patrols. Not only had she been caught, but they'd managed to get something out of her. The patrols knew they were looking for caves. Caverns near the camp were swarming with armed soldiers.

Ava fervently hoped that Tannin had just let it slip and that it hadn't been forced out of her. Back home in Armodan, she had listened in from within the walls and at closed doorways to know a hundred different ways to loosen a reluctant tongue. A hundred ways to beat, burn and rip out secrets.

She'd had to tell everyone that she suspected her informant was compromised. Nyesha and Flint were the only ones who truly knew what that meant. While the rest advocated for moving camp or one last bloody attack before the Gormbraens found them, Ava could read the thoughts of rescue blazing through the other two's heads from across the room.

She was saved from crushing their hopes by Catriona's arrival. She had been on the latest shift, monitoring the army's movements. The fact that she had returned hours earlier than expected did not bode well. Neither did the shine of sweat on her face and her heavy panting that suggested she had run the distance back.

"I need to talk to you," the warg gasped looking from Ava to Nyesha. "Both of you. Right now."

"Speak." Nyesha was never one to waste words, and she barked the order as soon as the three of them were alone.

"Across the far ridge. We went around to see if we could get a better view. So many tents. So many men."

"The Gormbraens sent reinforcements," Ava said with dismay.

They were already hopelessly outnumbered if it came to a fair fight. They had already been pushing their chances by nipping at the heels of the original group. Additional troops would crush them.

"No," Catriona shook her head. "Not Gormbraens. These troops came from the north, and their banners are purple."

Ava's gut sank to her boots.

"Brochlands' colours."

Catriona nodded.

"So, they'll fight the Gormbraens for us," Nyesha grouched. "I dinnae see a problem wi' that."

"You don't see a problem with a battlefield on our doorstep?" Ava snapped. "If the Gormbraens don't know the Brochlanders are there, then they're at a disadvantage, but that means double the number of scouts at least. They'll be looking to cut off the Gormbraens' retreat to the east too to force them back south."

She chewed her lip and paced.

"I wouldn't be surprised if the vanguard isn't already circling around."

"And we're right in the middle," Catriona finished for her.

"We have to know their eastern position."

"Douglas is already on it. I came straight here, and he took the eastern road."

"Good initiative."

"Dig in or leg it. Those are our options," Nyesha mused. "How much do ye know about Brochlander strategy?"

"They'll try and make the enemy retreat rather than engage directly. They'll edge them out. They have the numbers."

"That'll take time." Nyesha exhaled. "We cannae survive a long stand-off. We dinnae have the resources or the structure here."

"It makes no sense that they would do this in the middle of winter!" Ava pinched the bridge of her nose. "No sense at all!"

"Unless..."

Ava looked at Nyesha questioningly. "Unless what?"

"Unless we've got a mole." Her expression had turned dark. "The time it would take tae get the manpower organised and mobile...they've been informin' on us from the very start. What I dinnae know is why."

Ava swore under her breath.

"I know damn well why. I should have seen this coming. Of course they're here. They're everywhere."

"Who?"

"What do you know of the Triquetra?"

After assuring her that she still had energy left to make the trip, Catriona had left to catch up with Douglas. Ava told her to use everything she had to make it as quick as possible.

"You mean...?" Catriona's eyes lit up.

"Yes, use your other form. Time isn't on our side."

Ava frowned. She knew from Tannin that the wargs only used their other form in times of great need to respect the spirit. From the many times she'd seen Tannin flex her claws just for fun, she hadn't considered that the other wargs took that rule very seriously.

Ava watched from the cave entrance as Catriona stripped off her boots and tossed them aside. Her excitement made Ava wonder just how long it had been since she'd had a good enough reason to fully transform.

Although she had seen Tannin and also Douglas and Dana transform, Ava still couldn't suppress a shudder at the contortions and snapping of bone. It was not a graceful process.

In her warg form, Catriona was stunning. Deep brown fur with darker markings around her wolfish face where her tattoos would have been. The musculature under the thick pelt stood out and radiated strength. Even if, from this close up, Ava could tell she was significantly smaller than Tannin in her warg form, the sight still took her breath away. Black-rimmed, grey eyes gazed into her own as Catriona gave one last nod, turned and loped off into the trees. Frost shook from the leaves in her wake.

Ava wished she was going too. Wished she had a task that would take her mind off what had happened to Tannin. What was going to happen to her. To all the people relying on her in those caves. Reluctantly, Ava returned inside.

In the few minutes she'd been gone, Nyesha had been busy. The caves were a hive of frantic activity.

"What's going on?" she hissed as she found the old gang leader.

"We cannae just sit around for news, lass. We've got tae be prepared," Nyesha snapped as she ducked under a crate that two warg-bloods were carrying. "We've got three entrances that I want guarded round the hour in case those bastards find us. There's at least two more exits, but they're more of a last resort squeeze and one of 'ems caved in anyway."

"We fortify everything," Ava said in agreement.

"Aye. And if we do have time tae run, we need everythin' packed and ready. Everyone on alert."

"Do you have somewhere in mind to run to?" Ava asked out of the corner of her mouth as people rushed by them in their haste to grab supplies.

"Let's focus on the here and now, aye?"

That means no.

Ava swore again under her breath.

"Everyone tae me!" Nyesha bellowed.

The activity halted immediately as people huddled into a vague circle around where she stood.

"We may no be in the battle, but we're in the fuckin' war whether we like it or not. From now on, everyone carries a weapon, and everyone takes their shift on watch. No exceptions. Each watch has a horn. If ye hear the horn, ye haul yer arse out of here. You grab what ye can and ye run."

She glared at each individual face.

"Ye don't go back for yer friends. Understood? We'll be trapped like rats in here if folk start trying tae move back through the tunnels and block the rest of us. Like any other blockage in our path, ye'll be removed. UNDERSTOOD!?"

The final yell was so loud, Ava was terrified that the stalactites dripping from the roof were about to shake free and impale them all.

"Hopefully, it won't come to that," she added. "We should be able to make an organised evacuation in plenty of time.

Even if they managed to run, any one of her people could still end up caught in some gods-forsaken scrap of battlefield, an axe in the gut, a spear through the throat, broken limbs. The Skirters hid it the best, but everyone was thinking the same. Everyone was scared. Ava was scared.

She seized a horn. She had to lead by example. She had to stand strong. And she had to find that damned mole.

"I'll take the first watch. Who's with me?"

Chapter Sixty-Four

Opportunity Calls

Tannin

Tannin was thudding her head against the wall when a new sound filtered through the gloom. She often heard muted voices from the cells above. Sometimes screams. But this was different. There was banging, running footsteps and then a yell that was abruptly cut off.

She sat up straighter and cocked her head to listen.

"I'm looking for a girl." The feminine voice from above carried a hushed urgency. It was vaguely familiar.

"Might want to try a tavern for that, sweetheart," a deeper voice that was more of a sneer replied.

"She would have been brought here a few days ago."

"What's in it for us?"

Schiiick, thunk. A howl of pain. And then a different voice, slightly panicked.

"Alright, lady! Point made! Wee, fair-haired lass? Dunno where she ended up. Looked a right mess. All bloody. Don't even know if the wee thing was alive."

It was true that when they took her from the interrogation chamber she hadn't even tried to walk. She'd just flopped limply and let them drag her through the dungeons until they'd dropped her into this pit.

The first voice swore. "Where did they take her?"

Another thunk and a cry.

"I don't know! No, wait! Don't—!"

Tannin waited with bated breath to hear more, but the talking had stopped. There were, however, footsteps. She squinted. Two sets at least. She strained to hear, but they were walking further away and it was getting more difficult to keep track. By the sound of things, they had just killed at least one person, and she wasn't sure whether she wanted them to find her not.

She didn't want to die, but a quick death at the hands of unknown assassins might actually be her best option. She kept reflecting on Cormack's promise to let his professor have her. She did not like the sound of that at all. And she didn't want to die in this pit either.

Fuck it.

"Hey." She tried to shout but it came out as a weak croak.

She cleared her throat and tried to summon some moisture into her mouth.

"HEY!"

Only a chorus of echoes answered her, and then, silence.

Tannin was just about to resume smacking her head against the wall when she heard the footsteps again, faster this time. The sound became louder too as they found the staircase.

"Is anyone down here?" Now that the voice was almost directly above her, Tannin could identify it. The last time she'd heard that voice, its owner had been sitting on her lap.

Tannin gave a low chuckle. What was it the selkie-blood dancer had said? Be patient, don't act, wait for a signal. Well, so much for that.

"Lookin' for me?" Tannin croaked.

The scraping sound of the wooden cover being dragged off the grate sent shivers down her spine and she shuddered.

A lantern was dangled over the grate, and a silhouetted face appeared through the bars. Tannin shaded her eyes against the sudden light.

"Oh my..."

"Is it her?"

"Unfortunately."

The selkie-dancer called down. "What part of wait for the signal was unclear?"

"Who the hell are you?" Tannin retorted.

"The person who is here to save you."

I don't deserve to be saved.

Metallic clicks and scratching came from above. Someone was picking the padlock on the grate.

"What do you want?" Tannin peered up at her, chains rattling as her eyes became accustomed to the light and she let her hands fall into her lap.

"To rescue you. Obviously."

"Why?" Nothing came without a price. "What do you get out of it?"

The lock gave a final click. The grate above her clanged open, and a rope ladder was thrown down.

"How about we get you out of there first, and then we can talk?"

Tannin wasn't going to argue with that. The shackles on her ankles, however, made even scrambling to her feet difficult.

"I can't climb!"

A groan sounded from above. "Fine. We'll pull you up."

Tannin eyed the rope. "Who's we?"

The dancer gave her an annoyed huff. "Grab the damned ladder. We do not have time for this!"

Tannin grabbed it. Her right hand hurt like hell as she closed her fist around the rope, and the movement pulled at her raw knuckles. She slightly regretted trying to break it now. But only slightly. She deserved the pain.

She hung on, cramped muscles protesting until her head popped up over the ledge and she squinted in the light of the lantern.

The dancer looked just as beautiful as she had at the masquerade ball, but that was the only similarity in her appearance to that night. Tannin's mouth fell open, and she almost let go of the rope and toppled back into the pit. Instead of a flowing dress and ribbons, she wore studded leather armour. Flowers and gems were replaced by throwing knives strapped to almost every part of her body. Her glittering make-up was gone and replaced by a grave look of determination.

The other set of footsteps Tannin had heard belonged to a burly boy in simple, roughspun clothing. Tannin recognised him too. He was the face in the gardens.

The dancer grabbed her hand and pulled her the rest of the way up, wrinkling her nose as she did and then stepping away. She clearly did not want to stand anywhere close to her, and honestly, Tannin didn't blame her as she suddenly remembered that she was covered in dirt, blood and piss. She probably smelled wonderful. Tannin could feel the heat of embarrassment warm her face.

Tannin dropped her gaze in shame and accidentally locked eyes with the gardener. "I know you. You were watchin' me in the gardens."

The dancer gave him such a fierce glare he actually cowered. "So much for subtle."

"Do you have water?" Tannin hated how pathetic she sounded.

"Here." The selkie-blood tossed her a water skin.

The water was lukewarm and stale, but to Tannin, it was the most wonderful thing in the world as it flowed over her still swollen tongue and down her parched throat. She glugged at it almost frantically until she'd drained the whole thing.

"Food?" she asked hopefully but the woman shook her head.

"We need to get moving."

Tannin stood her ground. "What's the catch? Why are you helpin' me?"

"It's simple," the selkie-blood countered, something playful lingering in her voice. "For revenge. Don't you want some of your own?"

Something primal fizzed in Tannin's belly at the word. Oh yes. Yes, she very much did.

"On who?"

"On everyone."

"Sounds good to me," Tannin let a savage grin play over her features. "You still know me, though, and I don't know you."

"My name is Bronwyn. This is Fraser. We can talk more later, but right now, we need to get out of here before they start the coup."

A coup?

Before Tannin could ask more, Bronwyn strode off at a speed Tannin couldn't hope to match. The chains on her ankles limited her to an awkward shuffle.

"Hey!" she hissed and the other girl reluctantly slowed to let her catch up.

"This won't work."

"You think? Get these damn things off me," Tannin said holding out her shackled wrists.

Bronwyn nodded to her companion. "He can pick the lock, but we should get somewhere more hidden first. We don't want to get caught here. Fraser, put the cover back over. With luck, they won't even know you're gone. Come on. We'll find somewhere where he can work."

"How? I can barely walk!"

"Fraser." Bronwyn nodded her head at Tannin.

"What? Oh no, don't!" Tannin cringed as the boy swept her up in his arms. She couldn't really argue against it, though. She was completely useless without help and she would have slowed them down to a snail's pace.

Despite Tannin's filthiness, Fraser was gallant enough to not let it show on his face. He followed Bronwyn as she palmed a pair of fighting knives and strode off down the corridor.

They managed to navigate their way around the dungeons without incident but also without a shred of success. The buzz of escape had worn off, and Tannin was back to being tired, hungry and so thirsty that her throat may as well have been made of sandpaper. Her stomach rumbled and Bronwyn gave her a disparaging look.

"Like I can help it! Next time you rescue someone from a dungeon, bring some damn food. I haven't eaten in days."

Fraser apologised without looking her in the eyes. Bronwyn reluctantly agreed that it was an oversight.

"We will get you something just as soon as we—ooft!" She had been looking over her shoulder as she rounded the next corner and smacked straight into a person coming in the opposite direction.

A stack of heavy books clattered to the ground, and the skinny boy who'd been carrying them looked at them in dismay. Finn's expression was one of indignant anger as he puffed himself up to yell at whoever had been so clumsy as to knock them out of his arms. It melted when he saw Tannin.

"Oh gods," he breathed, staggering back a step.

"Oh! Oh!" Tannin wriggled in Frasers arms and pointed. "Professor's apprentice! Get him!"

Finn opened his mouth to scream, but Bronwyn moved like lightning to punch him in the gut before he could make a sound. Fraser let Tannin slide to the floor, then folded the apprentice into a headlock with ease.

A door a little way down the corridor was still slowly creaking closed. Finn must've come from there. Wordlessly, they made for it, Fraser dragging the apprentice with him.

Inside the room was a lair of horrors. The interior bore a vague resemblance to Ava's workroom with shelves stuffed full of books and jars with dried herbs hanging from the ceiling, but that was where the resemblance stopped. The rest of the room was nothing short of a torture chamber. Similar to the one Tannin had been interrogated in, but this one was far worse for wear. The tools and blades hanging from the walls and littering the countertops were most definitely used on a regular basis. Every groove was crusted with gore. The gaps between the stones of the floor were discoloured by the brownish red of old blood. A metal table stood in the centre of the room with straps hanging off the sides.

It stank of death and misery.

The four of them stopped just in the doorway, taking in the horror before them. One row of jars was crammed full of what Tannin would have sworn were human body parts. One, at least, definitely had fingers in it.

Finn scrabbling at the headlock Fraser had him in brought them all back to the present. The burly gardener lifted the smaller boy and slammed him onto the table and Bronwyn buckled a couple of the straps over him, pinning his arms to his sides. A rag grabbed from one of the dusty shelves shoved in his mouth stopped him from yelling for help.

"Get on with it," Bronwyn snapped at Fraser as she pressed her eye to the door to keep a look out.

He flinched a little, and then motioned for Tannin to sit in one of the rickety chairs at the desk, which she did.

"So," Tannin said conversationally as Fraser started fiddling with the shackles to free her legs. "Who the hell are you and what do you want with me?"

The selkie-blood answered without looking away from the door. "We are working with Sir Richmund to lead a rebellion against the Falcon and then against King Modric himself."

"That actually makes sense. I saw what they did to his son."

"Mm. He died from his injuries two days after they found him."

Tannin exhaled and tried not to think about the terrified young man's face as the whip had been raised again and again, and how by the end, he didn't even have the energy to scream.

"Try to stay still," Fraser murmured.

"Sorry."

"This plan was already in motion, but the death of his son has pushed him to act. And also you. He wants to get to you before the Falcon gets his claws into you and convinces you to join him."

"Oh, that ship has most definitely sailed." Tannin said. "Sailed and sunk."

"Clearly."

"So, he wants me to join his rebellion?"

"Everyone is racing to get wargs on their side. The Golden Queen is too far north to be of any use to us, and the Feral Queen – sorry, the pretend Feral Queen," Bronwyn made sure to correct herself at the look Tannin gave her, "has already aligned with Modric. That leaves you. The last queen with no firm alliances."

"You must be so pleased with your options," Tannin said sourly.

"Beggars can't be choosers. Besides, you do have a considerable following still, especially if the other Feral Queen can be exposed as a fraud."

At that moment, Fraser made a satisfied sound and Tannin found her feet free.

"I'm impressed," she said offering him her wrists so he could unlock them next. "My friend can pick locks but not nearly that fast."

Fraser grunted in acknowledgement of the compliment but didn't look up from his task. His ears had turned bright red.

"You'll want those bracers off too," Bronwyn said slyly from the doorway.

Tannin's eyes went wide as her heart leapt in hope.

"You can get them off?"

The dancer nodded. "But we need something from you first."

"Of course, you do. What's the catch? What do you want?"

"I can tell you what Sir Richmund wants, which is for you to pledge to his rebellion. He knows you still have loyalists out there, and he wanted them to aid his takeover from Laird Cormack. Or I can tell you my plan."

"Oh gods, more schemes?" Tannin let her head tip back. "I'm so tired. I can't keep up. What is this one then? In small words, please."

"An opportunity. I don't want to go from working for one tyrant to another. Richmund's rebellion is doomed to failure. I want my freedom too, so what do you say to fucking them all and getting the hell out of here?"

"Well, that sounds like my kinda plan. Why do you hate him so much if you're on his side?"

"He's been using us. He's lied to us every step of the way. We were supposed to be doing some reconnaissance for two weeks here in the Falcon's Rest, acting as courtesans."

"Let me guess, one more week followed by one more week."

"It's been over a year," she said venomously and Tannin cringed. "He goes on and on about how useful we are. How we should be happy to help and use our unique skills."

"Who are you really?" Tannin demanded.

Bronwyn smiled. "I'm whatever I need to be. I'm a dancer. A courtesan. A seductress. Someone to keep you company. Someone to spill your secrets to."

"A spy?"

"Sometimes." Bronwyn's expression darkened. "They think that we won't fight back. That we'll just meekly do as were told because we're not the oh-so-clever druids or the strong warriors. I want to show them how wrong they are."

"What do you want from me, though?"

"Free the rest of my people."

"They're prisoners?"

"Possessions," Bronwyn replied grimly.

"Done."

"Kill Sir Richmund and the Falcon."

"With pleasure."

"Get us all out of here. Alive."

"And then?"

"Then you pay me a nice little sum for helping you out, and I go live my life far away from all this."

"Done," Fraser said, satisfied as the manacles around Tannin's wrists loosened.

She shivered with relief as she shucked off the chains. A groan left her lips as she stretched and rolled her shoulders.

"Better?"

"Mhm. Much." She nodded her thanks to Fraser and got to her feet, dusting off her filthy shift. "So, what about me? After we get out of here."

"Do whatever the fuck you want. I don't care. I care about myself and my people upstairs."

"It seems a big risk to get me out of here just to help you. You couldn't do this by yourselves?"

The dancer shrugged. "It was part of Richmund's plan, so it was already set up. I'm just making the most of an opportunity. Plus, I was banking on you being as fed up with kings and lairds as I am. So, are you with me or not?"

Tannin only needed a second to consider it. "If you can get these fucking bracers off me, then I'm in."

"Give me your arm," Bronwyn ordered holding out her hand.

With a nervous twinge in her gut, Tannin held it out. Bronwyn took a thin tool identical to the one the artisan had used to seal the bracers and pressed it against one of the symbols. With razor sharp focus, she began to alter one of the engraved symbols. It was only a few lines, but her brow was so furrowed up into deep canyons of concentration that Tannin didn't dare make a sound.

The minutes stretched on until Bronwyn was satisfied and moved on to the other arm. Tannin ached to shift her weight onto her other foot, to stretch out her spine, to scratch the back of her neck, but she forced herself to stay still. Just like she'd practised all those months ago with Theo. The precise work needed a steady hand, and the last thing she needed was to lose the chance to get the damn things off once and for all.

"Okay, that's done." Bronwyn exhaled. "Fraser, give me your arm now."

He looked utterly bewildered but held it out anyway. Tannin was under the impression that if Bronwyn told him to leap out of a window, he would probably do that too without question. He didn't even withdraw his arm when she pressed one of her knives to his vein.

Bronwyn had positioned Tannin so that the blood that dripped from the cut fell onto the altered symbols on Tannin's bracers. It ran down the length of Tannin's arms and then dripped onto the floor.

The three of them stood listening to the steady dripping.

Tannin's throat grew tighter with every second that passed. It hadn't worked. The bracers still held her in their inescapable grip. She crumpled against the wall. Her warg-fire reached for her from behind that glass pane as desperately as she reached for it. She sucked in a ragged breath. The disappointment was crushing.

"I don't understand," Bronwyn said, looking from her blade to the symbols. "It's all correct. The symbols, the druid blood..."

"Oh...Uhm." Fraser blinked at her in a mixture of sheepishness and apprehension.

She narrowed her eyes at him. "What 'uhm'?"

"I'm not a druid-blood."

"What?" She rounded on him, knife still in hand. "You said you were!"

He stammered, "No, you asked me if my father was. He is! He's a druid-blood artisan."

"Your father did this to me!" Tannin hissed.

Bronwyn's expression was like thunder, and she stared him down until he dropped his gaze and whispered.

"I'm adopted."

"Ugh! You're useless." She barged past him. "We need druid blood. That's the only reason you're here!"

"I just wanted to help."

Tannin watched the two of them bicker, taking slow, measured breaths to calm herself.

There was still a chance.

"We just need a druid blood?" she asked, a spark of hope surfacing. "This place is full of them. We just need to..."

Tannin stopped talking and sniffed and then sniffed again. Behind the stench of whatever potions and poisons they were cooking up was something else. Something that smelled good. She snooped around until she found it and moaned with delight when she unwrapped the cloth to find a small bundle of cold chicken legs. She tore into them eagerly.

"Enjoying my lunch?" the apprentice sneered. He'd managed to spit out the rag and was glaring at them.

"Shut up," Bronywn warned him.

"Mm," Tannin grunted with her mouth full and then swallowed. "It's a little dry."

She sucked the grease from her fingers as she perused the documents on the desk.

"What the fuck is this?"

She took one glance at the sketches and the familiar measurements beside them before nausea bloomed in her stomach. She wished she hadn't eaten the chicken so quickly. Letting the last bone fall to the floor, she rifled through the rest of the papers.

"Is this meant to be me?" she asked in horror, pointing at the contorted figure in the drawing. "Is this what you were planning to do to me? Seeing what it would take to break my bones? To poison me? To burn me?"

Finn didn't answer and stared at the ceiling, jaw clenched.

"Answer me!"

"It's research," he snapped. "No one has had a warg specimen in centuries! These are fundamentals."

"I am not a specimen," Tannin snarled and then stopped utterly horrified. "Have you...done this to others? Other Remnants?"

He answered her with a sick smile.

Before Tannin had a chance to learn more, yells erupted from the hallway outside followed by the pounding of feet.

"They know I've escaped," she said but Bronwyn waved away her panic with the fluttering of a hand.

"No, Richmund has started the coup upstairs. Bastard didn't give me nearly enough time. We have to speed this up."

She beckoned Tannin over.

"You're a druid-blood?" she asked the apprentice.

"Of course," Finn answered primly.

"Good." She grabbed a jagged blade from the table, yanked the apprentice's head back and slashed it across his throat.

The hot, salty blood splattered over Tannin's face, chest and arms. She shrieked and then spluttered as some of the blood got in her mouth.

"What the hell?!"

"You're welcome," Bronwyn said, throwing the blade back on the desk as the apprentice gurgled out his last ragged breath and pointed at the fresh symbols carved into the metal of Tannin's bracers.

She watched wide-eyed as the blood ran in rivets through the scratches marked on her bracers. Ran faster than simple gravity should have allowed. Ran around, up, down, until the metal was covered in a writhing, red mass. Tannin gasped as the red turned to glowing yellow and hissed and sputtered like flame, sinking into the metal. By the time it touched her skin underneath, it was black and smoking and she was screaming. Molten iron dripped down her wrists to the tips of her fingers and onto the flagstones, revealing skin that was scorched and raw. Clean, smooth skin leeched from the bloody flesh and slid over her arms as it patched itself together.

Tannin gawked at what had become of her arms. Bare and visible for the first time in weeks – scarred and mottled but bare. She felt so much lighter. Like she'd been choking and could finally breathe.

Her warg fire burned strong in her chest, and when she reached for it, it reached back. But it was a different creature than she remembered. This was a beast that had been caged. The restlessness of the flame raced through her veins until she felt like she might explode. She was alight with pure power. She opened her eyes. Both Bronwyn and Fraser were staring at her in a mixture of apprehension and hope. She could see the blood pumping under their fragile skin. She could hear the rapid beat of their hearts.

Prey.

No!

PREY.

She growled around her expanding teeth as she fought to gasp one word of warning before she lost control.

"Run."

Chapter Sixty-Five

The Beast of Falcon's Rest

Tannin

Tannin swirled blood around in her mouth before spitting it onto the floor and straightening up to survey the damage.

She'd swept through the lower levels of the fort like a rage-filled hurricane. Her bloodlust had finally been sated enough for her to Change back into herself after she'd finished with this last room. It must've once been the guards' dining hall or their break room or something. Now it was a bloodbath.

The screams had finally stopped, and it was delightfully still and quiet. Silent even, apart from the crackling of the fire in the hearth. Tannin held out her hands to feel the warmth. The guards' bodies had been warm when she tore them open. It was a different warmth, though. This was a nice warmth. Cosy even. She splayed her fingers and watched the shadows flicker and dance. She could have stayed there watching them play forever if her stomach hadn't started rumbling and pulled her out of her trance.

Food. There has to be food here somewhere.

She'd surprised the guards whilst they were eating what was to be their last meal. They didn't even get to digest it. She clicked her tongue at the thought of that wasted food. If she'd gotten there ten minutes earlier, there would have been more for her now. She licked clean any bowls of stew that weren't smashed to pieces or contaminated with body parts until she found a stash of bread rolls and then washed them down with the last of the ale. It wasn't even remotely satisfying, but it at least quietened her wailing belly.

She wandered back through the halls, chewing on some tough dried meat she'd found in the back of a cupboard. She whistled a tune as she walked. Her memory was a little hazy, but she had definitely come this way. The scored floors and streaks of blood and gore were enough evidence of that. Every now and again, she came across a body – or the remains of one – but thankfully, so far none of them had been her rescuers.

She wasn't entire sure where she was or where she was going when she heard the cries. She cocked her head. She knew that voice. Tannin followed the wails of anguish until she came to a heavy, iron-banded door. She pressed her ear against it.

"I'm so sorry!" Orlaith's voice was distorted, but it was definitely her.

"Did you think I would ever even look at someone like you? Did you?!"

Tannin knew that sneer well. Malcolm was in there taunting the poor girl.

"Look at you now." His voice dripped with derision and was followed by a thud and a pained grunt.

Tannin cracked the door open, horrified, claws already lengthening. Orlaith was sprawled on the straw-littered ground with the guard looming over her. He was so much bigger, so much stronger. He was a goddamn balor-blood, for crying out loud, and armoured head to toe. Orlaith's simple dress offered her no protection from his anger. He was going to kill her. Even as Tannin watched, Orlaith spat blood onto the straw and Malcolm raised his boot again.

My turn.

She threw open the door with her widest smile plastered across her face.

"Ohhh, Maaaalcooooooolm!"

Tannin grunted as she heaved against the glass case and whooped as it shattered. She didn't give a damn about sneaking any more. Let them come.

The distant clamouring of a fight spiked Tannin's pulse, but she ignored it. She had other things to do first. She'd left Orlaith in her cell with Malcolm's shredded body. It was better that she was out of the way for what came next. Plus, Tannin was still mad at her.

Tannin picked through the glass to retrieve her warg-wool clothing. As much as wearing the blood of her enemies was badass and poetic, she was actually quite chilly. Plus, they were *hers*. The material was just as soft as she remembered. She held it to her face. It still smelled like Dunoak. Like wet wood, smoke and slightly mouldy. She held it to her face a second longer, breathing it in.

Her brooch would be long gone. Destroyed, most likely. Her axes were missing too, of course, but that was fine. Tannin lengthened her claws and flexed. It was deliciously satisfying to be able to release them at will. She felt whole again.

I don't need weapons.

Tannin almost skipped as she made her way through the corridors of the fort that had been her prison for so long. She was so light on her feet she felt like she might even fly. Quite a few guards had tried to intercept her as she made her way down from Laird Cormack's office. It had been laughably easy to kill them. And she did laugh. Her laughter bounced ahead of her down the corridor.

She assumed that by now all the hell that had broken loose during Sir Richmund's coup was well contained. Bronwyn certainly hadn't been enthusiastic about their chances. If that were the case, Tannin reasoned, then the Falcon would probably gather people either in the courtyard or in the throne room to boast his victory. The patter of raindrops told her that the throne room was the better bet.

She wondered if he knew she was out yet as she hummed a jaunty tune and teased a stringy bit of flesh from between her teeth.

Well, he will soon.

Tannin crouched next to the carved stone railing of the balcony, invisible to those below, and listened. Bronwyn had been right. The coup had been squashed with embarrassing ease by just a handful of the Falcon's household guard. Richmund himself had been brought in along with a handful of his loyal rebels and forced to his knees in front of Laird Cormack's chair.

"I expected a coup, but, my dear Richmund," Cormack tutted. "I expected better."

Richmund didn't react. He simply knelt staring at the floor.

Movement at the back of the hall dragged Cormack's attention from his former friend as the door slammed open and a guard raced in. The dishevelled man whispered something to the Falcon, whose look of fury at being interrupted faded and he went very, very still.

"This game is far from over," cackled Richmund, his carefully blank expression morphing into a leer.

"Where is she?" Cormack asked. His calm demeanour was betrayed by a quiver of rage.

Richmund responded only with laughter.

The door banged open again, and Tannin allowed herself a frown as she saw that the guards who entered were dragging Bronwyn and Fraser with them.

Oh good, I didn't kill them.

Bronwyn had been disarmed, though, and both looked like they had been roughed up. Fraser's nose was bleeding.

"Where is she?!" Cormack bellowed.

"She's gone," Bronwyn said, breathless but with eyes like fire.

Richmund's eyes widened. "Where...?"

"Gone."

The disgraced sir launched himself to his feet.

"What have you done, you useless whore? How dare—"

Richmund's tirade was silenced, half because the Falcon had abruptly stood and held up his hand for quiet and half because Bronwyn had ducked around her captors and punched him in the throat.

I like her.

Tannin wanted to whistle in appreciation, but she kept it to herself. She wanted to make a dramatic entrance, and it would ruin it if they knew she was there too soon.

"Enough! On their knees," Cormack roared, drawing his sword. The blade still looked mostly decorative and the gesture was lacklustre.

Still spluttering and clutching at his throat, Richmund was forced back to the ground. Fraser sunk down of his own volition. Bronwyn, however, refused to go without a fight. The guard nearest her quickly found himself weaponless, and she twirled to face off with the rest of them, sword poised and expression set to kill.

If Bronwyn was at all perturbed by being outnumbered ten to one, it didn't show on her face. She tightened her grip and set her stance. Tannin would have bet money that she would take down at least two of them before they could disarm her. Maybe more. Cormack knew it too.

"Archers!"

His cry was met by a heavy silence.

Tannin snickered from the balcony where she was crouched, watching the events below unfold with glee.

"Archers! Where are my archers!?"

My time to shine.

Tannin reached behind her to grasp a broken bow that she'd relieved one of the archers of. They had arrived before everyone else, and she had been waiting for them. She tossed the bow over the railing and stifled her laugh as gasps of horror sounded from below.

She glanced behind her and grinned.

Why not?

She tossed the archer's severed arm down too. This time, she let herself laugh to the tune of the screams.

Well, in for a copper in for a crown.

She heaved the mangled corpse off the balcony like she'd done with the arm and giggled again at the utterly horrified shrieks it resulted in.

"Enough! ENOUGH! Show yourself!"

Tannin popped her grinning, blood-streaked face above the balcony wall. "Well, hello there. Did you miss me?"

"Lady Tannin," Cormack growled, scraping together some composure. "How nice of you to join us."

"I thought you never wanted to hear my name again?" she crowed back.

"I freed you!" Richmund hollered from the floor, "I freed you! You owe me! I command you to—!"

A guard's armoured fist to the side of the head silenced him.

"Kiss my arse." Tannin bared her teeth in a bloody grin.

"Who do you think you are?!" Richmund clutched at his head and snarled.

Tannin smiled a terrible smile.

"Who do I think I am?" A deep chuckle rumbled in Tannin's throat. "I am the Feral Queen. I am the Beast of Armodan. I am the blood heir to Stonestead. True blood warg. I am Tannin Hill. And I am fucking FURIOUS!"

The people below quaked and cowered as her voice boomed to every corner of the hall.

"That's right. You should all be shitting yourselves right about now, but you should also be takin' a good look at your laird. He did this. I was invited here under false pretences. He pissed on the ancient rules of hospitality." As she spoke, she let a hand trail over the stone banister, out of the shadows, to scrape along the carved decoration with her wickedly sharp claws, sprinkling the nobles below in a fine dust. "Usually, that would mean a curse on your bloodline for generations, a blight on your land, blah, blah, blah, but honestly, I'd settle for killin' you really, really horribly."

"Evacuate," Cormack hissed under his breath. "Evacuate now!"

"She's disabled the drawbridge, Sir!"

He cursed.

Tannin's eyebrows shot up, impressed. Bronwyn must've done that, but she'd gladly take the credit. It was a good idea. They were all sitting ducks.

"Come down, you coward!" Cormack yelled, losing his patience at last.

"I'm not a coward, I'm just havin' fun," Tannin called back. "But have it your way."

She vaulted the railing and dropped the fifteen feet or so to the ground. She hit the floor gracelessly, heavy-footed and stumbling.

"I can never stick the landing," she grumbled and brushed dirt off her palms.

She gave an exaggerated, mocking curtsey and then gestured with her bloodied hands. Benwald, standing beside his father, gave her a disgusted look that only barely masked his utter terror.

"Didn't you always say that red looked good on me?"

The throne room doors banged open for a third time, and Tannin groaned in annoyance.

Why can I not have my moment?

"BEAST!"

Tannin narrowed her eyes as Erlan shoved his way to the front, with his personal guard trailing close behind.

"I should have killed you when I had the chance."

"Mhm. I imagine Laird Cormack is thinkin' that right now too." Tannin paused. "And Sommer. And King Florian. Maybe Dana too when she hears about this. You lot should form a support group."

A gesture from Erlan had his guard spreading out to surround her, weapons raised and expressions grim.

"Five against one?" Tannin cocked an eyebrow. "That hardly seems fair. A gentleman would at least give me a sword."

Her eyes fell on the lairdling. "Actually, never mind the sword."

She crossed the platform in a few strides, coming face to face with Benwald. He looked at her with a mix of fear and bewilderment.

"Relax, I'm not going to hurt you. But those," she said stopping mere inches from him, "are my axes."

The lairdling's fingers trembled as he freed her weapons from his belt, but he at least managed to look her in the eye.

"You wanted to know me better." She yanked her axes from him. "How do you like what you see?"

She whirled and threw the axe at Erlan's nearest guard, splitting his skull like a log.

"What? Were you waiting for a fucking invitation?" She grinned. "COME ON THEN!"

The next guard drew his blade as Tannin stalked towards him. She didn't slow her pace, not even when he brandished the sword. She smacked it aside with her axe and punched him in the face as hard as she could. The crack of his jaw breaking was as satisfying as she'd hoped.

She ducked the next sword that came for her head and shoved the guard with the broken jaw into his path.

From the corner of her eye, she caught the third guard lift his sword for a vicious downward cut that would have cleaved her in two.

If she were human, that is.

She darted in close before he could bring the sword down, too close for him to defend. She dropped her axe in favour of grabbing his head and yanking it to the side. She grinned as his eyes went wide and he realised what she was going to do. His last words were lost in a pained gurgle as she sank her sharpened teeth deep into his throat.

She relieved the corpse of its weapon before she let it fall to the ground and spun neatly to meet the blade that was about to plunge into her back. She was stronger, so much stronger, and her parry sent the guard stumbling. His head left his shoulders before he regained his balance.

The guard with the broken jaw was still on the ground. He tried to scurry backwards, away from her. But no one was getting away from her. Not today. Two long strides had her towering above him. She struck before he could plead for her not to, skewering him to the floor with his friend's sword.

She straightened up and flicked her hair over her shoulder. Erlan was backing away, glancing over his shoulder with eyes like saucers, searching for an escape.

She licked her bloody lips and gave him her sweetest smile. "And then there was one."

"Wait!"

She did not.

Her claws sunk into the flesh of his belly and up under his ribcage. He fell against her as claw scraped bone.

"This is for Attilo," she hissed in his ear as he garbled and burbled.

Her clawed fist closed around her prize. Ripping her arm from his chest, Tannin dropped his lifeless corpse to the ground and held up the bleeding glob of flesh and muscle for the terrified nobles to see.

She let it fall from her hand. Blood dripped like gems as she brought her foot up to meet it and pelt it across the hall. It slapped against the throne wetly, then fell to the ground with a sad splat.

Godsdammit. If the Falcon hadn't moved at the last minute, Erlan's heart would've smacked him in the face. That would have been glorious.

"So." Her lip curled in distain as she nudged Erlan's crumpled body with her toe. "Who's next?"

Chapter Sixty-Six

Burn It All Down

Tannin

Tannin huffed in exertion as she dropped the last corpse off the ledge, put her hands on her hips and smiled in grim satisfaction as the vicious spikes below caught it and it oozed down the pike.

Her gruesome additions decorated every part of the fort where she could possibly mount a spike. As well as lining the path to the front door, of course. She'd let any of the servants leave to brave the snow if they wanted to. If they stayed, then they worked for her and took an oath sealed in blood. She accepted nothing less. Everyone else, though… She looked out over the Falcon's Rest. The nobles' fine clothing that fluttered in the wind from atop their respective pikes brought a splash of colour to the otherwise white walls of the fortress. Of course, she'd burned all the Gormbraen banners and had hastily dyed black sheets hung up in their stead. It was a poor substitute for her beautiful, black banners, but there was no doubting who this fort belonged to now.

A monster.

A corbie let out baleful croak at her from the ramparts as it eyed her latest offering. It was waiting for her to leave before it began its feast. They would be well-fed this winter.

Tannin rubbed her eyes with her sleeve. She was bone-tired, but sleep didn't come easily. If not for the treacherous snows, she would have left there and then on the night of her escape. She had possessed just enough of her wits to know she couldn't make that kind of journey in the dead of winter. Now, though, she was stuck in a kind of purgatory – just as trapped as she had always been. It didn't help that it had taken over a day to fix whatever Bronwyn had done to the drawbridge.

Even though she barricaded herself into one of the finer rooms when she needed to rest, she didn't trust a single soul in this fort, and every tiny noise had her jolting awake. One of the servants who had laid down arms and pledged to her had already attempted to catch her unawares with a poisoned dagger. She'd taken that personally, since she'd already given them the opportunity to leave, and strung him up from the main gate as a warning to anyone else who was thinking about it.

She stalked back to the room she'd picked for herself, washed up and changed into clothes that didn't stink of death. She'd found years' worth of memoirs and journals in the old laird's private wing to pick through.

For all his previous boasting and little breadcrumbs of information over the last few months, the Falcon was being infuriatingly silent now. However much she had longed to tear him into teeny, tiny pieces, Tannin knew his worth. If the Gormbraens did decide to risk it and come for her now – unlikely given the weather and the strength of the fort's position – a hostage or two was a sensible choice.

"You should kill him," Bronwyn said as she entered the office just as she had suggested every time they spoke.

"Not yet."

"He needs to die."

Tannin gave her a stony look. "I want peace and quiet for the next few hours. Go do something useful."

"What?"

"Anything that's not here," Tannin snapped. "Oh, and Bronwyn? Don't touch Cormack. That's an order."

She scowled but inclined her head anyway. "As you wish."

The selkie-bloods had reluctantly agreed to her rule until they could go their separate ways. They mostly kept to themselves, although Bronwyn made sure to remind Tannin of her promise to kill the Falcon at every opportunity. She had hoped that letting the mysterious selkie-spy have her own revenge on Sir Richmund would have been enough to sate her, but it hadn't lasted long. Bronwyn wanted Cormack's head and wasn't going to give Tannin any peace until she had it. She wanted the lairdling dead too. Tannin hadn't had the stomach to kill him when he had sunk to his knees in surrender. Two hostages were doubly useful, she had told herself. She'd knocked him unconscious just like the laird, before slaughtering the rest of the guards and any nobles who were stupid enough to stand in her way.

"Should I leave too?" Orlaith's whisper was barely louder than a breath.

Despite Tannin coming to her aid and later ordering her release from the dungeons, the former serving girl was utterly terrified of her. Her face was a mess. Bruised, swollen with bloodshot eyes. The gash on her cheek from Malcom's gauntlet would leave a gruesome scar.

Despite her fear, she had pledged her loyalty to Tannin. Her oath was accompanied by a tearful monologue of unrequited love and a thousand breathless apologies. Tannin had decided that the poor girl had suffered enough.

"You can leave." Tannin exhaled and turned the page. "I want an estimate on the weather again before sundown. The second that storm is over, we're out of here."

Orlaith nodded and Tannin watched her limp to the door before slamming the book closed and dragging her fingers through her hair. She was too anxious to focus. She hadn't found her speaking stone. She had no idea if the Gormbraens had found Ava's hideout or not. If Ava had made for Armodan to warn her brother or had stayed put. She didn't even know if she was still alive. Not knowing was torturous.

The raven-keeper had fled with most of the servants, and the tower was a mess. Tannin had, of course, cut off access to the ravens that sent messages from the Falcon's Rest to stop any traitors calling for aid. She also intercepted all incoming correspondence. However, the troops Cormack had sent after Ava had sent no word. If he had even sent the troops yet. She couldn't be sure. Asking him didn't help.

She'd had a cage brought up from the dungeon to the throne room. She'd told Bronwyn that she wanted him to see her on his throne. In reality, though, she just didn't want to ever have to go back into the dungeon. Not that he was being particularly forthcoming anyway. Mostly, he called her names, made threats and tried to goad her. He only gave her what she wanted when she threatened to bring him pieces of his son. Still, he never gave her full answers or elaborated on any of them, and since he technically did answer her, she couldn't justify retribution. He knew she was bluffing.

Snow still dusted the trees and the edge of the loch was still frozen, but the roads were clear enough to travel. Tannin wanted to get as far away from the fort as possible before the Gormbraen troops got there – and they would be coming. Letters had gone unanswered for too long to not be suspicious. It wouldn't take a lot to work out that something was very wrong at the Falcon's Rest.

Important matters, however, still had to be taken care of.

Benwald had been imprisoned in Tannin's old chambers – with the balcony doors now barred, of course. Tannin twirled the key in her fingers as she paused outside what had once been her prison. She hadn't entrusted it to anyone else. Even if they had pledged to her, she didn't trust that they wouldn't help the lairdling slip away. Food was occasionally sent up via the pulley system, but no one had been allowed into his chambers. She had listened occasionally just to check he was still alive.

He had been so docile when she'd had him locked up that she wasn't expecting any resistance as she unlocked the door and strode inside. He had coped better with incarceration than she had. The room was still in decent enough condition, although the lairdling himself looked a little haggard. His hair was uncombed and a whisper of facial hair graced chin, but he still stood tall as she entered.

"Evenin'," she said amiably.

"Your Majesty," he said without a trace of sarcasm and dipped into a bow.

"You're takin' this surprisingly well."

"It's not ideal, but I don't have much to worry about." He relaxed and sprawled onto the uncomfortable sofa.

"What do you mean?"

"You don't have much here. You'll be needing men and weapons...coin. I imagine you'll be organising a deal with King Modric for my father and I in exchange. You'll be able to boost the deal for the release of the rest of the court."

The rest of the court are currently decorating the walls.

"It is awfully dull in here, though," he remarked, his eyes roaming the walls as they had no doubt done a hundred times since she'd locked him in.

"I am familiar."

"Ah, yes." He spread his arms wide. "What can I do for you, my queen?"

"Your father is shite company. I'm hoping I'll get more information I need from you."

He leaned forward in interest, a smile playing on his lips. He truly believed he was too valuable to be in danger. "And what is it to be if I refuse? Threats of torture?"

Tannin brought out the bottle of firewater that she had been hiding behind her back. "I actually prefer bribery."

"An excellent choice."

She poured them both a generous measure and settled into the chair the Falcon had occupied when he had first come to visit her. It seemed like a lifetime ago.

"To bribery then?"

They clinked glasses and drank. Tannin poured him another.

"You've been to the front. I want to know numbers and strategies."

He squinted at her at he sipped his second drink. "Are you to support the Brochlands, then? Are you aware of the bounty on you there?"

"You're not really in a position to be askin' the questions."

He held his hands up in mock surrender. "I apologise. And I'm afraid I can't help you. I was only at the front for a few days, and I am unaware of my father's larger scale plans."

When her gaze turned as cold as the gale battering the windows, he hurriedly added, "I can tell you that the section I was with had been told to stop the advance. To wait. It seemed to me that something had not gone to plan somewhere else along the line. That's why I returned home. There was no point in me sitting in a snow drift all winter."

Tannin had a good idea of what had gone awry. Whoever the mole was in the capital had had to admit that Ava had gone missing. Their key to legitimate rule of the Brochlands.

Tannin brought out the map she'd tucked into her belt.

"Show me where the bulk of the troops are."

He showed her the general direction. She quizzed him on their strategies, but he wasn't much help, especially as she kept topping up his glass.

"Realistically, if you want my opinion," Benwald said slumping into the pillows. "Your best bet is to play the game. You'll make the deals with Modric to surrender the fort – you can't hope to keep it once spring comes – and then what? You have to make another deal. And another. 'Cause you don't have any power. You've got one fort. So, ally with Gormbrae just like my father planned. Fight your enemies and ours. Get your own kingdom back far in the north and then everyone wins. That's how you play the game."

Am I going too far?

But he had a point – not the one he wanted to make, she was sure, but a point nonetheless. She was alone. A handful of household staff and the selkie-blood courtesans against Gormbrae, Sommer, Dana and everyone else who wanted her dead. She could probably add the entirety of Bayfort after what she'd done to Erlan.

She couldn't afford mercy. When she had so little and still had so much to fight for, was anything really far enough?

"And what if I kill your father instead?" Tannin replied, unblinking.

Benwald struggled to sit up straight. "In cold blood? You have proved that you are more than I ever thought, but you are still a young woman underneath all that. It would be a senseless slaughter."

"I can't let him live."

"Wait, wait." Benwald was starting to panic. "No one else has to die. Yes, you killed a lot of guards and the Rill prince but—"

"I killed a lot more than that."

He swallowed hard. "Who?"

"All of them," Tannin said lightly, refilling his glass again. "They are all dead."

"...all?"

The lairdling grabbed the glass, drained it and shook his head like he was trying to clear it.

"R-Really?"

Tannin gave a slow nod as Benwald paled.

"My father," he choked finally. "If you must kill him, then let me say goodbye."

"It's too late for that."

"You've killed him already," Benwald lamented, lifting a hand to his brow.

"What if I've killed you first?"

"What..." Benwald stared at the glass in his hands in horror. "But you drank it too."

"Not nearly as much as you did." Tannin lifted the glass from him and refilled it.

"Why?"

"Because I've taken your home. Sabotaged your army. I've killed your friends and I am gonna kill your father. I can't let you live to take revenge."

A tear slid down his cheek. "I wouldn't have taken revenge."

"It would be too a great risk."

He nodded slowly.

"Well then." He drained his glass and drew a ragged breath. "I guess there are worse ways to go."

His last request had been to not die alone. She could grant him that and stayed until his eyes closed. When he started to snore, she gave him a booted kick in the shin.

Startled, his eyes flew open.

"This was a test, by the way. There was no poison in there. Well, no more than usual." She grinned at his confusion. "Congratulations, you get to live. Enjoy the hangover."

Everything was packed and ready to go as Tannin walked to the throne room one last time. The Falcon's Rest had been ruthlessly plundered until nothing but the bare bones were left. The stores they had chosen not to take with them had been piled around the hall with their straw filling spilling out.

Tannin's warg clothing hugged her comfortingly under her thick cloak as her boots clacked on the unswept floors. Bronwyn followed closely. Tannin didn't want her to miss what she had been waiting all this time for.

"You'll be happy to hear that we're leaving."

Cormack was slumped in his cramped cage as always. He gave Tannin a filthy look and spat on the floor.

"You think you can take on Gormbrae with a few courtesans with illusions of grandeur and a grudge? You're a fool."

"I'd say "watch me" but I'm afraid you won't be around to see it."

She took a sip from a bottle she'd plucked from one of the crates and tipped the rest onto the floor.

Tannin took a step closer and struck a match from her tinderbox. The laird's eyes widened as he took in the crates of firewater and straw covering the floor. Even Bronwyn looked at her in alarm.

Tannin watched the tiny flame dance. Doubt flickered in the back of her mind. But only for a moment.

She'd set multiple fires all throughout the fort. Smoke billowed through every crevice, and the occasional lick of bright orange flame escaped through shattered windows.

The stone would blacken and her corpse decorations would char. Ghosts would haunt this place for centuries, and she'd make sure the whole Five Kingdoms would remember who was responsible.

But she had one more message still to send. To the King of Gormbrae.

Benwald was quaking as Tannin's group stood, stamping their feet against the cold, at the end of the bridge to the Falcon's Rest as it smoked behind them.

"Bring him a horse and supplies for, oh I don't know, two days? You can fend for yourself for the rest of the time."

"Where is my father?" The lairdling's voice was almost lost to the wind.

"He made surprisingly good kindling."

He looked back at the burning fort, aghast.

"If it helps, he was already dead."

Even after all she had done, in the end, she couldn't bring herself to burn a man alive. She had driven a spear into his heart as the flames took hold.

"You're a monster," he whispered.

"Yes. Yes, I am." Tannin leered. "Remember that when you tell the king what happened here."

She caught the front of Benwald's cloak and yanked him down so that they were eye to eye. "I spared your life. You owe me. Take the message to the king and then disappear. If you come for me, I won't hesitate."

She released him.

She'd considered writing King Modric a gloating letter, but she wasn't sure it was a sensible thing to provoke him further. Then again, killing his people and burning his fortress to the ground was pretty provocative in itself, so the damage was already done. If she could have thought of something witty to write, she probably would have done.

She did, however, send a letter to Dunoak. She'd penned a simple message in her neatest handwriting on parchment that she'd sprinkled with Laird Cormack's blood.

Regards, Tannin.

"We go northwest," Tannin announced to her huddled group. They were a sad-looking bunch, but they were all she had.

"What's your plan?" Bronwyn was swathed in furs, and Tannin didn't even want to guess how many blades she had hidden under it.

"Get far away from here. Save a prince. Conquer some kingdoms maybe. Don't die in the process." Tannin bared her teeth in a grim smile. "But first, I'm going to go get my princess back."

Chapter Sixty-Seven

Last Resorts

Ava

Ava had hoped that now the worst was over and that things would get better. She was wrong.

She gazed out over the rocky outcrop at the approaching riders and let out a stream of curses that Tannin would have been proud of.

Flint arched an eyebrow. "What?"

"Those are my brother's men."

"Why's that a problem?" Flint asked, shading his eyes and squinting at the fluttering, purple banners. "I thought we were going to your brother eventually anyway."

That had been their plan as a last resort. The vanguard coming in from the east had trapped them in their caves before they could run, and their stores were getting dangerously low. Foraging and hunting were risky, and more often than not, fruitless. They couldn't hold out much longer. Nyesha had broached the subject of contacting the Brochlands' army directly. They were Ava's people, after all. If she went to them to plead for their safety, they might survive.

"Yes. But on our terms. If I try and tell him we wanted to warn him of a threat now, it will merely seem like another desperate attempt to save our own skins. *Damn it.*" Ava slammed her hand against the stone and took a breath. "We're out of time."

A lone rider was sent to the entrance of their hideout. He waited respectfully, his horse puffing clouds of white and stamping its hooves, until Ava sent out her own representative. A request to talk. Ava agreed. If Prince Justus wanted to storm their hideout, he very well could anyway regardless of her permission.

How did they find us?

Ava waited just within the entrance where traces of warmth still lingered. She wondered if her brother would even recognise her now that her luxurious gowns and furs had been replaced with crudely stitched animal hides and a dagger at her hip.

"Avalyn," Justus' shoulders sagged a little when he saw her.

"Hello brother."

She guided him and his escort to what passed as a war room. They had pinned up a list of their high profile kills on the wall while Ava's hand-drawn maps littered the table.

Prince Justus was the only thing polished and neat in the room. The picture of a prince. His hair was just long enough to start curling at the nape of his neck, where a gold chain disappeared inside his collar. His fur cloak trailed on the dusty floor.

"Leave us," he commanded to his men, and to her annoyance, her people too.

Everyone filtered from the room, leaving the two siblings facing each other across the table. Neither seemed to know how to start. They had never been close, not like she and Florian had been.

"How have you been?" Ava asked awkwardly and then wished she hadn't said anything at all as Justus' face twisted.

"How have I been? We have an army on our doorstep, my sister is cavorting around with my enemies, there's a warg queen setting up in our capital and demanding all kinds of things for her assistance, father had taken ill with the stress of it all and I have had to play king!" he exploded. "How do you think I have been!?"

"Father is ill?" Ava blurted. "How long has he been ill?"

Her mind sprang to poison.

"You are coming home with me," Justus said. "Enough of all this...this ridiculousness!"

"Ridiculousness? It's thanks to us, thanks to me, that the Gormbraen forces are on the brink of collapse," Ava retorted. "I suppose a thank you was a little too much to expect."

"A thank you? Avalyn, you humiliated our family, Armodan, the whole damn Brochlands when you sided with that beast against us. You made us look weak. Do you even care?"

"She was never against you."

"Oh really? So, the Feral Queen has not allied with Gormbrae and is not gathering an army to attack us at this very moment? My, my, I must have been getting some bad information in that case."

"That's not her. Another warg stole her title. Tannin is—"

"Enough, Avayln," he said, his voice softening to the point of patronising. "She wasn't who you thought she was. I know your heart is broken, but it's time to give this up and come home."

"My heart is fine! And this isn't about that. You don't understand. I'm actually helping here!"

Ava hated how young she sounded.

"I might have a suggestion." A voice came from the doorway.

"I thought I said leave us," Justus snarled and then abruptly recoiled when he saw who had spoken. Nyesha tended to have that effect on people with her gruesome scars and medley of weapons strapped to her torso.

The older woman raised her hands placatingly from where she leaned. "Just hear what I have tae say."

"What are you doing?" Ava hissed but Nyesha ignored her.

"Ye have tae admit we're a benefit here. We're smoke in the night. We can get in where yer shiny soldiers cannae. How about we keep doin' that for ye?"

"Avalyn is coming home with me," Justus said, drawing himself up to his full height.

Nyesha shrugged. "Take her."

Ava's mouth fell open. "What?"

"Ye did good, lass, but we dinnae need ye to keep goin'. I can take over just fine."

"How dare you—" Ava began but Nyesha talked over her.

"Ye can have the princess back, and then we can talk aboot us continuin' our work here, and of course the compensation we can expect for oor labour. Supplies and the such like."

"You cannot—!"

Both Justus and Nyesha held up a hand to stop her tirade. They studied each other.

"I accept your offer," Justus said finally. "Come along Avalyn."

"I will not!" Ava exclaimed in outrage, balling her hands into fists.

"Now, Avalyn."

Ava glared and didn't move.

"I can package her up for ye if ye like," Nyesha smirked. "With a pretty wee bow."

"That won't be necessary. Come."

"You'll regret this," Ava snarled. She knew she was in no position to make threats, however, as Justus took her by the elbow.

"Ye forgot I don't owe my allegiance tae ye. I owe it tae my queen, and ye ain't her," Nyesha waved as Justus steered Ava out of the hall. "Until we meet again, Yer Highness."

Ava sat alone in the carriage as it jostled over the uneven pathways. Justus was somewhere ahead leading the group on horseback, but she knew sooner or later he would come back to share the carriage with her. For all of his soldier bravado, he was still a pampered prince at heart.

She was playing the part of a rescued princess. Although, considering they had taken away her daggers and all but locked her in the carriage, she may as well have been a prisoner. Justus had denied giving her a horse in case she tried – in his words – to desert her duty again.

But Ava had no plans to run.

Nyesha had played her part perfectly, better than expected, especially since they had barely enough time to hash out the details. She would keep harrying the Gormbraen troops for Justus but keep her ear to the ground for information Ava could use to get Tannin back and garner support for the true Feral Queen. There had already been whispers on the wind that the Falcon was dead. She just hoped Tannin had had the pleasure.

And that she was safe.

Oh gods, I hope she's safe.

Ava's fingers traced the coiling scar on the inside of her arm. It had been weeks since she had heard even a whisper about Tannin. As far as she knew, the true Feral Queen was still a captive at the Falcon's Rest. She would have to work with that until she had more information.

And as for Ava...she was going home. Home to the nest of snakes that were more venomous than she had ever realised. But, Ava thought, remembering how the soldier had dissolved from the inside out from her poison, she could be just as venomous.

Even so, there was a vast difference between a heat of the moment slash with a poison-coated blade and a stone-hearted, carefully thought-out assassination.

Ava peered out of the carriage window as a rider passed by. It wouldn't be long until they were back in Armodan.

Back within striking distance of the woman who had arranged Florian's death. The woman who had tricked Tannin into poisoning herself. Who was most likely responsible for her father's timely illness. Who was lying in wait to kill Justus.

Could she do it? Could she kill the woman who had raised her more than her own mother in cold blood?

Ava looked down at her hands. Her nails were caked in grime and her palms were calloused, but they didn't tremble. Not even a little.

Yes. Yes, I could.

The End

Glossary and Pronounciations

Balor	A giant from Irish mythology
Bairn	Baby or small child
Brae	Hill
Ceilidh	Scottish traditional dancing
Clipe	Tattle-tale, snitch
Corbie	Crow
Dram	A measure of whisky
Dunt	Nudge forefully
Eoghan	Pronounced oh-wen
Foosty	Mouldy, old, off
Glen	Valley
Kelpie	Shapeshifting waterhorses from Scottish mythology
Orlaith	Pronounced or-lah
Outwith	The opposite of within
Redcap	Goblins
Selkie	Seal. In myth these are shape-shifters, but in parts of Scotland, seals are still called selkies
Torc	A solid C-shaped necklace that denotes stature

REMNANTS

OF

POWER

H.F. Cunningham